Praise for *A Royal Pain*

An NPR Best Book of 2012

"This book is a romantic, fantastic, enchanting treat. If you ever had the dream of marrying a British nobleman, don't miss *A Royal Pain*!"

—Eloisa James, *New York Times* bestselling author of *The Ugly Duchess*

"Megan Mulry's vivacious Bronte is every Englishwoman's nightmare—the straight-talking, hot-blooded all-American girl who bags the Duke! Now, if only all English aristos could be as delicious as Max…"

—Hester Browne, *New York Times* bestselling author of *Swept Off Her Feet*

"If you liked *Sex and the City*, you're going to love *A Royal Pain*… Filled with urban, rich, and royal characters, *A Royal Pain* is a wonderful debut that shouldn't be missed. I anticipate spectacular things from this author."

—Catherine Bybee, *New York Times* bestselling author of *Wife By Wednesday*

"With fashion and flare, Mulry mingles American ambition and English aristocracy… a dazzlingly stylish and dreamily satisfying read."

—Katharine Ashe, author of *How to Be a Proper Lady*

"A whole new twist on trans-Atlantic romance—sexy, fresh, and delightfully different."

—Susanna Kearsley, *New York Times* bestselling author of *The Firebird*

"A light and breezy read... Filled with clever characters, witty banter, and steamy sex, readers won't be able to put it down."

—*RT Book Reviews*, 4½ stars

"Though the premise may be that of a fairy tale, the very human characters keep the plot fresh, funny, and engaging, with Mulry's lavish descriptions of fashion an added bonus."

—*Booklist*

"This delectable story... is all about second chances and every girl's secret fantasy of marrying the perfect guy... A charming book worth reading again and again."

—*Publishers Weekly*, starred review

"Great characters, and their troubles are explored in a natural, entertaining way."

—*Long and Short Reviews*

"A fun, steamy, and entertaining read."

—*Minding Spot*

"A little bit *Bridget Jones* mixed with a little bit *Pride and Prejudice* with a side of steamy interludes! I can't recommend this book enough. You'll cheer for Max and Bronte!"

—*Anglotopia*

If the Shoe Fits

MEGAN MULRY

sourcebooks
landmark

Published by Sourcebooks Landmark, an imprint of Sourcebooks, Inc.
P.O. Box 4410, Naperville, Illinois 60567-4410
(630) 961-3900
Fax: (630) 961-2168
www.sourcebooks.com

Library of Congress Cataloging-in-Publication Data

Mulry, Megan.
  If the Shoe Fits / Megan Mulry.
     pages cm
  (trade paper : alk. paper) 1. Young women–Fiction. 2. Aristocracy (Social class)–Fiction. 3. Love stories. I. Title.
PS3613.U4556E27 2013
813'.6–dc23
                              2012049874

Printed and bound in the United States of America
VP 10 9 8 7 6 5 4 3 2 1

Chapter 1

DEVON HEYWORTH CRACKED ONE eye open into the shrouded, artificial darkness of the hotel room. One of several bodies passed out in the huge suite groaned from somewhere to his left. He let the palm of his hand reach across the smooth surface of his large bed's empty sheets and stretched. Waking up in Vegas was always entertaining.

"Shit." A flat American voice broke the silence as a woman sat up quickly from one of the four white leather sofas. "My shift starts at seven. I have to hustle."

"Seven what? It's still morning, isn't it?" Devon asked with a lazy scratch of his fingers through his two-day growth of beard.

"What? It's six thirty at night." She laughed as she flipped on a lamp on the side table across the room. Devon watched with detached interest as she pulled on her tight tank top and then bent over to get a better look around for her pants.

"Not possible," Devon answered easily, stretching out on the huge bed. "I have a wake-up call scheduled for two. I have a flight to London at four forty this afternoon and I never miss a flight."

"Are you for real?" The woman—Devon thought her name was Clarity or Chastity or something equally unlikely—was laughing at him. She had great dark-and-stormy eyes that were even better with that smudge of tarty mascara. A good-time girl. And from the look on his friend Archie's face, passed out behind her on the couch, the two of them had had a good time.

She stood up and pulled the curtains wide, the blistering glare destroying Devon's mirage of his control on life. She pointed her finger at the lowering sun. "That is the west. That is the setting sun. I may be a cocktail waitress, but I grew up on a farm and I know how to tell time. You might be an earl—"

He rolled his eyes. "I am not really an earl—"

"Whatever! All your friends call you The Earl—"

"It started as a joke—"

"Oh, never mind!" She was losing patience.

He liked women like this. She'd had her fun and she was ready to carry on. Good.

"Okay." He peered at the clock and then picked up the phone next to his bed. "Hi, this is Devon Heyworth. Is it six thirty in the morning or the afternoon?"

Calamity shimmied into her tight black pants. She put both of her hands on her hips and shook her head in Devon's direction. "Fucking Brits. Incredible." She leaned over the couch after picking up her purse, and kissed Archie lightly on his forehead. He patted her behind and off she went.

"It was fun, Earl," she said as she passed near where he was sitting at the edge of his bed, now in shock. "Have a good trip back to London."

"Thanks. Yeah, it was a lot of fun. Bye… Verity!" She smiled when they both realized he'd just recalled her name, then she laughed and pulled the door shut behind her.

He was in such deep shit. If he missed his brother's wedding because he was partying in Vegas with a bunch of layabout ponces and cocktail waitresses, he was going to be flayed. Devon picked up his cell phone and called the concierge people at American Express. A female voice introduced herself as Diane.

Talking while he threw everything into his leather duffle, he pulled on a pair of jeans and a wrinkled black T-shirt.

"Hey, Diane, this is Devon Heyworth. I think I just missed my

Virgin Atlantic flight from Vegas to London. Yeah…" He went into the bathroom, brushed his teeth, then used his forearm to rake his toiletries into his bag. He pulled on his trainers and took one last look around the hotel room.

"Hold on one second—" Devon put the phone against his chest and yelled across the hotel suite, "Hey, you scallies! I have to get back to London for the rehearsal dinner. You'd better be there by Saturday for Max's wedding." Three heads lifted slowly from couches and beds, nodded, then flopped back asleep.

Devon headed out the door to the elevator and resumed his conversation. "Yeah, I might lose you when I get in the elevator. Okay, here's the deal, whatever it takes… I have to be in London by tomorrow afternoon."

"Yes, absolutely, sir." He listened to the click of a computer keyboard on the other end of the line and tried to ignore his reflection in the brass elevator doors that had just closed in front of him. He pulled a pair of mirrored sunglasses out of the side pocket of his bag, double-checked that he had his passport and wallet, then raked his fingers through his hair. The sandy blondish-brown mass was practically touching his shoulders, and his mother would give him shit for looking like a shaggy rock star in all the wedding photos in *Hello!* But at least he would be in attendance.

"We don't have any private jets available until… oh, wait… okay! Here we go—" Diane was on it.

Devon was striding across the lobby of the Wynn hotel, smiling briefly at the concierge he vaguely remembered from last night. He'd been generous with a tip and she looked like she had appreciated it. While he half listened to his cell phone, Devon veered over to his new best friend behind the concierge counter and whispered, "I need a car to the airport right now. Can you get that for me, love?"

She smiled and nodded and clicked a few taps on her keyboard. "Out front now, Mr. Heyworth," the Wynn concierge whispered.

From his phone, Diane was explaining, "There is a flight to Dusseldorf that leaves Las Vegas at eight forty-five. If you can get to the airport *right now*, I think you're good. You only have a carry-on as usual, right?"

He nodded his thanks to the hotel lady and continued out to the front of the hotel. "Yeah. Just the carry-on. So I change planes in Dusseldorf—"

"You will make a connecting flight that gets you into Gatwick at 7:30 p.m. It will be very close, but Dunlear Castle is close, yes?"

"Perfect. And a car to pick me up there?"

"Of course."

"Great… and thanks, Diane."

"Always a pleasure, Lord Heyworth."

He disconnected the call and smiled at the thought of the reliable Dianes of the world. He loved all the anonymous voices at American Express. Their sole purpose for the ten minutes he was in their orbit was to do whatever he wanted. And then he never thought about them again. He never understood why people opted for an office and a secretary and employees. What a bore. All those pesky attachments.

One of the Wynn courtesy limos pulled up in front of the sweltering chrome-and-glass exterior of the hotel and a large body-builder-type chauffeur jumped out. "Mr. Heyworth? Any luggage?"

Devon lifted his shoulder to indicate his carry-on. "This is it, thanks. Let's go."

Staring out the window at the passing mayhem that was the constant building and rebuilding of Las Vegas, Devon marveled at the nature of the American psyche. Bigger. Faster. Improved. So much immediate gratification. He looked forward to many years of enjoying the blessed freedom of being a single man in the twenty-first century with the ways and means to enjoy it for as long as he possibly could. Maybe forever.

He made the flight to Dusseldorf without a problem, slept most of the way, and made the connection to Gatwick easily. The car and driver met him as planned to take him to Dunlear Castle. After slipping in the back door, taking a thorough shower, and changing into a maroon velvet smoking jacket and proper trousers, he was ready to attend his brother's rehearsal dinner.

The fact that he had missed the actual rehearsal in its entirety would just have to be chalked up to Devon being Devon.

"Could you two cut it out with all the swooning, please?" Devon grumbled at his older brother fawning over his fiancée, coming up behind them in the crowded living room.

Max Heyworth, the nineteenth Duke of Northrop, laughed as he swung around, keeping his arm around the slim waist of his fiancée, Bronte Talbott. "You're late. Even Abby got here before you." They were all still having drinks in the drawing room, the dinner gong set to ring in a few minutes, at nine. "And don't tell us to cut it out... you're just jealous." Max tried to scowl.

"I hate to break it to you," Devon said, grabbing a passing flute of champagne, "but I am so far from jealous—no offense, Bron."

"None taken," she said with a mischievous smile. "What kept you?" She widened her eyes at his just-showered, devilishly sexy appearance.

"Airport trouble in Vegas."

Max snorted a quick laugh. "Is that what they're calling it these days?" They'd all been in Las Vegas the previous weekend for Max's bachelor party, and Devon and several of their friends had stayed on. Devon had managed to throw in a little business trip to rationalize extending his stay. "I'd call it man-whoring," Max said.

Bronte nearly spit out her champagne. Max hardly ever spoke in anything but his crisp, Etonian British, both in terms of his vocabulary and his accent, so when he said things like *man-whoring*, Bronte always found it ten times funnier than if some guttersnipe like herself had said it. "Max!" She elbowed him.

"Look." Devon shrugged, as if his *man-whoring* were simply a fact of life. "I'm twenty-eight and blessedly *single*, so there's not very much that I'm holding back on. You two are just the typical about-to-be-married couple with this line of cock-and-bull about how great it is to be young and in love and all that. Spare me."

His sister-in-law-to-be gave him a shrewd look, then smiled. "I couldn't agree with you more, Dev. Enjoy your freedom while you've got it because someone's going to come along and then you're going to be just as idiotic and hog-tied as we are. I tried to put it off as long as possible." Bronte turned to her fiancée and stared lovingly into his eyes. "But some things just can't be helped."

"Quit looking at him like that," Devon chided. "It's upsetting. I need to mingle. I don't want any of that star-crossed nonsense to rub off on me. You two are distressing."

They weren't that distressing, Devon thought with an unfamiliar twinge of envy as he looked around the crowded reception room. Bronte Talbott was that rare bird who didn't need a big, stinking three-ring circus to let the world know she was getting hitched. In fact, she'd been ready to do it at City Hall in New York, but his brother Max was traditional in his way. They were keeping it relatively small, but Devon of all people knew about relativity.

In this case, "small" meant that the rehearsal dinner was at the groom's home, Dunlear Castle, a family pile that was a Grade I listed architecturally significant piece of British history. Mother-in-law-to-be was the formidable Dowager Duchess of Northrop (who was at that very moment sporting the full diamond parure that offset her angry gray eyes as she tried to stare Devon right out of the room for his tardiness). The flower girls were royal princesses. Max and Bronte were saying their vows not at Westminster Abbey or St. Paul's Cathedral, but at their own Fitzwilliam Chapel, dating back to 1380. Yes, "relatively small."

Devon scanned the room, noting the middle-aged couples and boring aunts and uncles looking just as they had on the previous seventeen social occasions at which he'd seen them in the past three months.

"Just point me in the direction of any single American dolls that might want a little *Four Weddings* action and I'll take it from here." He winked at the loving couple.

"I think the seating arrangement might take care of that," Bronte said with an answering wink.

The sound of the light dinner gong trilled into the room from the front hall.

Devon gave Bronte a quick peck on the cheek. "You look gorgeous as usual, Bron. And always looking out for me. Thanks."

"You're my fellow outlaw, Dev. You scratch my back, I'll scratch yours. Just get me on your mother's good side and I'll throw a few treats your way."

———

A few minutes later, Devon was admiring his treat. Apparently, she was a department store heiress from Chicago who dabbled in the shoe business, but Devon was far more preoccupied with her generous cleavage and the revealing scoop neck of her dress that was barely concealing it, fringed in a devilish bit of mink.

She was talking animatedly to Devon's cousin, James Mowbray, about his pending store opening in New York. Their conversation offered Devon plenty of time to look at the creamy white skin of her neck and the full turn of her shoulder that kept peeking out from the useless woven shawl that refused to stay put on her delectable upper arm. Before he could look away, he was caught in the act, as it were, staring longingly at her beautiful proportions. She was looking down at him somehow, even though they were both seated. He was taller by far, so how, he wondered, did she manage to look down at him?

"And you must be the brother of the groom? A bit difficult to rehearse without a best man, you know." She took a sip of her champagne and set it down carefully in the sea of glasses and china and silverware that crowded the large round table. The delicate clatter and ping of the caterers and sommeliers and light conversation of everyone who had come to celebrate Max and Bronte's wedding wafted around them.

Devon had been unconscionably late. He knew that Max and Bronte didn't give a fig, as long as he showed up on the day with the rings intact. But clearly this was the type of woman who appreciated a splendid apology. He was happy to oblige.

"I am indeed. The very tardy, penitent, *younger* brother of the groom. Devon Heyworth, best man, at your service." He dipped his head in his best courtly manner. "And you are?"

"Sarah James. The very prompt, accusatory, *younger* friend of the bride. Maiden of honor. Pleased to meet you." She smiled, but it was a bit thinner than he'd hoped. She reached out her hand to shake his and he brought it to his lips in an absurdly romantic gesture, trying to catch her eyes with his, from his lower position.

She burst out laughing with such a surprising bark that conversation came to an abrupt halt at the rest of their table. His mother shot Devon a sharp, questioning glance, then raised one aristocratic eyebrow before resuming her conversation. Bronte tore her attention from Max and widened her eyes in silent question toward Sarah. Seeing that Sarah was perfectly capable of handling the perfectly rakish Devon, Bronte returned her attention to her fiancée as he continued the story about his recent trip to Budapest.

Sarah wiped small tears of mirth from the corners of her eyes. "Oh, Lord Heyworth—"

"Devon. Please call me Devon."

"Oh, all right, Devon then." She tried to tamp down the laughter that still bubbled out of her. "Not Earl?"

He tried to look chastened but she seemed to see right through him. "Look, that's all a bunch of nonsense that the American press whipped up. Dukes and earls and all that. You all"—he gestured at her as if she embodied all things American—"always get all of that mixed up. You think if my brother is a duke, then I must be an earl." He smiled and continued, "And then I thought, who am I to turn down a courtesy title?"

"The Earl of Naught?"

"What can I say? I was drunk. And it sounded funny at the time. Like the Fresh Prince or King of Pop or something. How did I know that the reporter was going to coin it into some kind of K-Pazz nonsense."

"K-Pazz?" Sarah could barely contain her laughter.

"R-Patz? Brangelina? I don't know. It's your country, not mine."

He tossed one of his long, elegant hands in front of his face to dismiss the whole idea of "her country," and Sarah was taken aback by the strong confidence of those hands. Her body was responding to him in some strange, disconcerting way she hadn't felt in… in forever.

"You are really fabulous," she blurted.

He was now sitting with his hands lightly clasped and resting at the edge of the table, a small pout forming on his full lips. "I suspect that is not a legitimate compliment."

"Well, it's legitimate in that it's not false. Whether or not you *believe* yourself to be astonishing is something else altogether."

He shook his head with a reluctant half smile.

Sarah continued blithely, "But I suspect you're more of a secondary definition type… and think of *fabulous* as wonderful or marvelous." She took a sip of her champagne and closed her eyes for a second at the pleasure, then opened them with a quick blink and pinned him with the full force of her sapphire gaze. "I avoid secondary definitions whenever possible."

"It is quite possible that you are insulting me horribly right now, but I can't bring myself to care one way or the other, what with that *fabulous* shoulder of yours and its failed attempt to remain covered by that wispy rag of a thing you have tossed over it."

In her effort to prevent the champagne in her mouth from spraying across the table at the very erect Duchess of Northrop, Sarah was forced to let half of it up her nose, causing a painful combination of watery eyes and burning nostrils.

Finally collecting herself, she said, "I'll have you know this wispy rag was hand-sewn by nuns in the south of Spain and is considered a work of art by many experts in the industry."

"And what industry would that be? The Iberian Virgins' Lace Industry?"

Sarah could do nothing but stare. Then, "Are you flirting with me?"

"Well, nothing like the direct question, then. Max warned me that you American ladies like to hear it straight. So yes, I am most certainly flirting with you, and while we're at it…" Devon took a quick look to his right, and then left, across Sarah's place, to make sure the people sitting near them were fully engaged in their own conversations, then he lowered his voice and continued, "While we're at it, I have cleared my schedule for the weekend, so we don't need to stop at flirting. We might as well skip right to shagging."

She was unable to prevent the mischievous, receptive spark in her eyes.

On he went. "You are probably staying here at Dunlear, right? So just let me know which room Bronte has put you in and I'll meet you at midnight and all that. You Americans love that kind of thing, right? Trysts… rendezvous… rakish lords?"

"You've freed up the entire weekend, have you? And enough with the waggling eyebrows. Let me think for a minute." Sarah looked across at Max and Bronte, then down one length of the obscenely grand, medieval dining hall, with its mellow wood paneling and priceless old masters hanging placidly along the walls, then briefly up to the intricately molded coffered ceilings, all the while twisting the stem of her champagne flute methodically, as if she were contemplating a stone-cold business deal. "All right, but here are my terms."

In that moment, Sarah had the calculating realization that if she was going to rid herself of her virginity once and for all, here was a golden opportunity. Another country. Isolated incident. There was no chance this arrogant (okay, incredibly sexy didn't hurt either) man was going to go all saucer-eyed over her. No chance of bumping into him at some bar in Chicago or New York, where she now split most of her time. And when the construction on the London store got underway, he could be a casual, port-of-call boy. He could be a perfectly contained episode. Tidy.

"A businesswoman. Excellent. Terms. Do go on," he prompted.

And he appeared to have a devilish sense of humor. She decided to have a little fun with him. And if it led to a casual weekend something-or-other, great. And if not, no harm done.

"First of all, I am not staying here at the *castle*. My parents decided to make a family outing of it—well, technically my step-mother pretty much invited herself—but anyway, we're having a short holiday while we're here, staying over at Amberley Castle Hotel, about fifteen minutes from Dunlear."

He nodded to let her know he knew the place, but clearly the idea of a family vacation had put a damper on his plans. "Family?"

"I have my own room, not to worry." She tried to play it cool, slanting him an encouraging smile. "Anyway, here's the deal," she said quietly. "I don't have time for some complicated emotional mess, so let's just keep it to a fun weekend, okay? Deal?"

He stared at her as if she'd just offered him the Holy Grail, nodding his agreement in stunned silence. "Deal."

She pressed on in a low, confidential voice. "Why don't you plan on taking me back to Amberley after the party tonight so we can dispense with this unwieldy seduction and enjoy the rest of our meal?" Sarah went so far as to give him a pat-pat on his strong hands, feeling downright accomplished at this flirting thing. She went for the final turn of the screw. "Not to worry. I'm a sure thing. For the weekend, at least."

And with that, she turned from Devon's stunned (gorgeous) face to resume her conversation with James Mowbray, who was just finishing a discussion with the Duchess of Northrop about the regrettable dearth of cellists in the new schedule at Wigmore Hall. After the Duchess finished her complaint, she smiled briefly at Sarah then turned to her left. The whole merry-go-round of socially prescribed conversational partners had been thrown off with Devon's interruption. Sarah leapt right back into the conversation she and Mowbray had been having before Devon had introduced himself and taken her attention away.

"So, James, back to your idea about not spreading further into the U.S. market... what makes you think New York sales alone will be enough to justify the substantial financial commitment you're making to build the store? If it's not revealing any trade secrets, I'm particularly concerned with spreading myself too thin at this stage—I spent this week scouting for a possible London location—but you are already totally established in terms of your..."

Devon stared at the blond bombshell's back and let the sound of her sexy, no-nonsense talk about exit strategies, net present values, and P and Ls wash right over him. None of that resonated in the least. Two other words did: Sure. Thing.

All right then. The caterer removed Devon's appetizer plate and he turned to his Aunt Claudia to hear the latest news on the renovations of her country house in Cornwall.

"Bear with me, Devon, dear. I know I'm not a young and risible American woman, but I think you can spare me a few minutes of witty repartee during the main course."

He smiled and enjoyed the comfort of his aunt's familiar, if acerbic, company. "I'm sure you had your share of risible Americans, Aunt Claudia; no need to go all judgmental on me. It doesn't suit you."

"Right you are, Devon. But none of them ever drooled on me like you were about to do to that lovely innocent."

Innocent my ass, thought Devon with a quick look at Sarah's cascading blond hair and overgenerous chest, and then he gave his reluctant attention to his viciously fashionable aunt. She was wearing something diaphanous and purple that offset her eyes and her diamonds. She even smelled expensive.

"When are you going to step up, Devon?"

"I beg your pardon?"

"No, you don't. You don't beg anything of anyone." Claudia was his mother's sister, best friend, and mortal enemy. They had been born ten months apart and had competed for everything in the six decades ever since… including dukes and earls.

"Very well," Devon conceded. "I don't beg your pardon at all. I have nothing to step up for. Max has found a suitable wife—"

Claudia's tiny bite of poached salmon could not have caused the slight choking sound that followed that statement, but Devon gave her a little smile and let it pass. "Well—" Devon leaned in to his aunt—"he's found a wife who suits *him* perfectly. And she's not marrying my mother, after all!"

Lifting her champagne flute, Claudia toasted Devon. "Ah, my dear. You must know you are in danger of being bagged. Your mother has done her duty by marrying off Claire to the—"

"Don't say it, Aunt Claudia—"

"Very well. She married Claire off to that horrible Marquess of Wick—"

Behind closed doors, everyone referred to him as The Prick of Wick.

They both looked across the table and, even from the distance of the large formal table for twelve, Claire's discomfort and strain were evident. She was pristine in her appearance, as always, but her tender formality was in grave danger of evolving into plain old bitterness. Her husband was absent, as usual. Not that anyone minded, especially Claire, but it still smarted that the Marquess of Wick couldn't make the effort to show up for his brother-in-law's wedding.

"Off spending her money, I suspect." Claudia was as close to sympathetic as she'd ever been, having burned through her share of cruel and careless husbands until she finally met the right man in her current husband.

"Well, Claire made her bed… and all that." Devon took another sip of champagne.

Claudia narrowed her shrewd gaze and shook her head slightly. "I never knew if she really did… you were just a little ring bearer then, weren't you?" Claudia kept her gaze on the pale blond woman sitting across the table. "I think your parents may have made that bed…"

"Oh, please. *Poor Claire*. Yada yada. It's such a hard life being a marchioness in a huge castle in Scotland. Cry me a river." Devon waved a hand across his face as if swatting away a fly. "Don't get me started."

"Very well. Anyone else at the table we can dissect while we're at it? Your mother can't focus her attention on Max any longer… he will provide an heir, probably already has if you ask me—"

Devon almost spit his champagne at that. "Claudia!" His voice was raspy and choked and the beautiful Sarah James turned quickly to make sure he was okay. She let her hand rest briefly on the oxblood-red velvet of his forearm. Then, seeing he was fine, she smiled at him and Claudia, then released him just as quickly and returned—again, damn it—to James Mowbray.

"So that leaves you." Claudia took another sip of champagne and set her glass down.

"And Abigail," Devon lobbed.

Lady Claudia rolled her eyes. "Don't get me started on that one. Have you ever seen a lovelier creature? Just look at her…"

They both let their gazes settle across the table on the wild black curls and sparkling gray eyes of Lady Abigail Heyworth, fourth (and final! his mother was always quick to point out) of the Heyworth children. Devon and Abby had been partners in crime for as long as any of them could remember. They were both what was delicately known as hard-to-pin-down.

"Very well, you are quite right," Devon finally agreed. "Abigail will never bend to Mother's will."

"And you? She parades you around like one of her prized parures." Claudia's pinched expression was a perfect mix of disgust and envy.

"She can parade me all she likes, but Mother knows that when it comes to getting me to heel, she'll never succeed."

Claudia leaned forward to get a better look at Sarah James. She was smiling and talking in animated conversation with both his cousin James and the aforementioned Mother.

"I wouldn't be so sure." Claudia took the final sip of her champagne and raised a finger to signal for the waiter to refill her glass. "Looks to me as though your mother is already locking and loading on your weekend foray."

Devon shook his head. There was no point in being surprised that Claudia had probably heard his entire sordid conversation with Sarah. Why give the older woman the satisfaction of knowing she was, as usual, quite right?

Before the dessert was served and the toasts began, Bronte gave Sarah a quick wink-and-a-nod and the two got up and went into the ladies' powder room together. Bronte shut the door, double-checked that no one else was in the adjacent water closet, then came out squealing.

"Is Devon hitting on you?"

"Well—"

"Oh, Sarah! You are too much. You are such a vixen I can't stand it! I know you are so saucy and the Sarah James It Girl—I mean, I created the whole concept—but—"

"Bron—"

"Are you going to fool around with him tonight?" Then lowering her voice while still somehow squeaking, she said, "Are you going to sleep with him?!"

"Bronte! Stop!" Sarah was five years younger than her dear friend, but they often joked that they were both emotional twelve-year-olds when it came to guys. Bronte had nearly botched her whole engagement to Max through a string of mistakes and misunderstandings. Sarah, truth be told, had never really had the opportunity to botch anything. But it was better to play up the whole It-Girl thing than to confess a life devoid of romance. "He is such a parody of himself," Sarah said, "with all that rakish *fake earl* foolishness. I mean, he's not even an earl. It's just ridiculous. He's just ridiculous." She applied more lipstick, then continued, "But he's so hot. I guess I'm sort of playing with him. I finally just told him I was a sure thing so he could quit it with the smarmy seduction and we could get on with some interesting dinner conversation."

Sarah had turned to the mirror to double-check her mascara and lipstick and caught Bronte's openmouthed gape in the reflection.

"What?" Sarah asked, her lipstick poised in midair as she was about to put the top back on.

"You did not!" Bronte covered her mouth and started to laugh. "Oh, Sarah, you are priceless. He is so fawned over around here, you have no idea. His mother ignores everyone in the family except Devon, his sisters act like he is the best thing since sliced fucking bread."

"Bron, I thought you were trying to cut back on the swearing... you know, becoming a duchess and all that."

"Don't remind me. I'm already shitting bullets about walking down the aisle in that vintage Valentino dress… I keep picturing all those yards of priceless lace getting caught on the edge of one of the goddamned pews and my very nervous self tripping flat on my fucking face."

Sarah grabbed Bronte's hands in hers and gave her a warm smile. "You are going to be a star, Bron. Don't give it a second thought. The dress is divine. The chapel looked beautiful tonight at the rehearsal, and it will all be perfect."

"Thank you so much for coming. All these Etonian-Oxonian-Cantabrigian mates are a bit overwhelming. I will be relieved when the rest of the Yanks arrive tomorrow. My mom is not helping."

Sarah gave her an encouraging hug and then the two women headed back out into the surreal world of Dunlear Castle: ancestral home to the nineteenth Duke of Northrop and his ne'er-do-well younger brother. If Sarah was going to lose her virginity, she might as well do it in style.

Chapter 2

WHETHER IT WAS A curse or a blessing—Sarah still hadn't decided—she was able to drink vast amounts without getting drunk as long as she stuck to champagne. Devon, on the other hand, seemed to be showing the signs of one too many glasses. His goofy smile was plastered on his face as they fell into the back of the courtesy limousine that had arrived from Sarah's hotel. The car headed out the Dunlear Castle gravel drive and onto the small country lane that would take them to the Amberley Castle Hotel. It was times like this she wished that she actually *did* feel the effects of alcohol.

Sarah was reminded of all those idiotic parties in her early teens in Lake Forest when she had tried, almost desperately, to get tipsy, buzzed, or even flat-out drunk—anything to take the edge off the overarching awkwardness that plagued her. Her mother and father had always babied her and told her how pretty and kind and lovely she was, but Sarah knew better. Her skin was nearly blue, it was so pale. Her fleshy middle and thighs were impervious to jogging and sit-ups.

And then the boobs.

Well, suffice to say, her chest was ample.

When Elizabeth James died soon after Sarah's twelfth birthday, Sarah said good-bye to her mother and, unwittingly, to her childhood. In the midst of her mourning and depression and isolation and futile attempts to love her father out of his own misery, Sarah took no notice of her body's transformation from pudgy preteen to voluptuous Lolita. By the time she was fourteen, her father was still bringing home old-fashioned smocked dresses when her body was better suited to a *Maxim* cover shoot. Just like everything else in her life, as far as Sarah was concerned, her body had been *all wrong*.

Somehow sex just never made it to the top of her to-do list. And now that she was a successful twenty-five-year-old business-woman, it would have seemed patently absurd to tell anyone that she was still a virgin. Bronte Talbott, of all people, who had single-handedly crafted the advertising and PR campaign that depicted Sarah James as the quintessential voluptuary, would never have believed her.

But something about the way Devon touched her made her feel like her too-big, too-soft body might be quite fine as far as he was concerned. Maybe even better than fine. A permanently smiling Devon Heyworth draping his hand over her shoulder and tracing his index finger along the arch of her left breast made her feel like the whole world was better than fine.

"You do realize you are touching my breast, right?" Sarah blurted.

Devon looked at her, continued to smile, continued to touch. "Are you going to narrate the entire evening?"

Sarah blushed. Not just rosy cheeks, but hot, ferocious waves of heat up her chest and neck. Luckily, the back of the car was dimly lit.

"Are you blushing?" Devon looked at her closely, his hot, boozy breath against her cheek, then looked out the car window, still touching her breast absently. "Hmm. I was under the impression that American women no longer blushed. I will have to report back to the Royal International Seduction Society at their quarterly meeting next month."

She smiled, mostly relieved that her narration faux pas hadn't given her away. In that split second of contemplation at the dinner table, after which she had nonchalantly informed Devon that she was a sure thing, Sarah was all of a sudden 100 percent committed to getting rid of her virginity once and for all. It was just hanging out there in the ether. Undone. And she wanted it done.

But she didn't want to go through some long, tedious relationship that would require doting phone calls, feigned intimacy, and the dreaded nicknames and baby talk. Devon was undoubtedly the man for the job. *Just look at him*, her alter ego cried. Could he have been any better looking? Sarah thought not. And she had been around her share of photo shoots with hot Italian male models. Not to mention that he arrived prevetted, being the younger brother of her best friend's ducal husband-to-be. Devon Heyworth was royal and witty and… fondling her breast… and…

Sarah shook herself slightly to clear her head.

It also helped that he was buzzed enough that he wouldn't even know it was her first time. As long as she kept her mouth shut. Because she had to confess she *did* tend to err on the side of narration, especially when she was a little nervous. One more reason she probably excelled in business, because instead of cowering in the face of questions or criticism from potential buyers and investors, she simply launched into lengthy downloads of information that she had committed to memory for just such occasions.

What did one talk about while kissing? Well, nothing if lips and tongue were otherwise engaged, of course. But the whole rest of the time… silence? Idle chat? Sarah looked down at her lap and smiled to herself. She was more worried about topics of conversation than the actual doing of the deed.

"What are you smiling about?"

"Nothing. Just thinking about how much or how little to talk, and if so, about what—"

And then there was no more talking.

Devon's right hand, which had been idly resting against the cold glass of the car window, reached across to Sarah's mouth. He dragged his thumb across her lower lip, his skin transferring an exhilarating chill. He moved it back and forth. Maniacally slow. And that other hand was still making those lazy tracks along her left breast.

His thumb went tentatively into her mouth, tugging on the soft inside of her lower lip as he slowly pulled it out. "Your lips are insanely gorgeous, you know. I kept trying to decide where to look at you tonight. So many excellent parts…"

She closed her eyes and gave mental thanks to all that was holy that she would not have to come up with a single topic of discussion for many hours to come. If this was how it was going to go, he could just talk and talk. Her body responded to his voice like it responded to his touch, with deep, warm waves of pleasure.

When his full lips touched her for the first time, it was right at the base of her neck. "Like this part," he whispered with that delectable British accent, husky and prim somehow. "It is just a simple" (kiss) "meeting of neck and shoulder" (kiss) "but there's something utterly delightful" (sucking kiss) "about the way it all fits together."

The kissing on the neck, the finger in the mouth, the hand along the breast.

Sarah started to laugh.

Devon stopped everything. "What is so funny?"

"Please don't stop," she whispered, putting her hand at the back of his neck, the crisp fold of his shirt collar catching into the strong neck, then the silky fine hair, then her hands were wandering on their own.

"Are you laughing at me?" he pressed.

"No, I was laughing at me. Why would I be laughing at you? You are making me feel better than I've—well, better than I've felt in a very long time."

He didn't seem satisfied; clearly, the Royal International Seduction Society did not take kindly to real or perceived slights.

Or mockery.

"If you must know"—Sarah let her hand drop from behind his

neck and folded both of her hands into a prim clasp in her lap—"I was enumerating... pleasures... thumb in mouth... lips on neck... hand near breast... I suppose I was *narrating*."

Devon shook his disobedient light brown hair out of his face with an efficient jerk and moved to look out the window again as the limo turned into the entrance of Sarah's hotel, then he shifted back to meet her questioning look. "I like you." The way he said it hinted at a strange combination of gratitude and reluctance. How was she to know he hadn't actually *liked* someone in a very long time?

He gave her a perfunctory kiss on the lips that would have passed the ratings board in any G movie and hopped out of the car as it rolled to a stop in front of the extensive forecourt of the Relais & Châteaux country castle hotel. Before Sarah got her bearings, Devon had spoken quickly with the chauffeur and was standing at attention next to Sarah's open car door. "My lady," he said, proffering one gloved hand to help her out.

"My lord," she replied, then smiled up at him as she exited the car and unconsciously licked her upper lip, which had gone inexplicably dry.

He pulled her into an embrace, gripping his arms firmly around her waist and nuzzling into her hair. He whispered into her ear, "If you are prone to narration, I had better keep this lively," and with that, he grabbed her bottom in both hands and gave her a delicious squeeze, then swept his lips down to hers for a very thorough kiss. *Right here in the driveway*, she thought vaguely, *and very non-G-rated.*

⁓⁓⁓

By the time they got up to Sarah's hotel room, the brisk night air and long flight of steps seemed to have rid Devon of any residual inebriation. He felt particularly focused. He stood with the door closed behind him, watching Sarah James move tentatively into the unfamiliar room. His weekend plans just got a whole lot better.

He moved slowly, the moonlight coming through the windows enough to allow him to avoid tripping over the furniture and to appreciate the silhouette of her gorgeous full figure as she bent over to take off one perfect shoe.

"Let me do that," he said lightly as he came up behind her. With his hand barely touching her lower back, he guided her over to the window seat, where the waxing autumn moon created a cool, romantic glow. He put his hands on her shoulders and sat her down on the firm cushion that covered the built-in frame and doubled as a cover for the radiator. The gentle warmth from the heater started to come through the bouclé knit and silk lining of her cocktail dress. The brisk autumn air seeping through the antique windowpanes grazed her upper shoulders in a lovely counterpoint.

Devon dropped down on one knee, then wrapped both hands around her right calf. The smooth silk of her stockings evoked a tantalizing friction against his palms. He moved both hands slowly up her leg, passing the turn of her knee, letting one finger loiter at the sensitive back of the bend, and then continued with relentless care. When he reached the lacy elastic edge of the stocking, immediately followed by the butter-smooth skin of her inner thigh, Devon's eyes closed in momentary pleasure, for the moment itself and for all it promised in the very near future.

"Thank you to the genius who invented the garterless stocking," he whispered with a grateful sigh.

Sarah was also sighing in response, her head dropping forward, her hand reaching out mindlessly to run through his thick, light brown hair. It was a little bit longer than she had realized; earlier in the evening, it had been slicked back, and now it was falling in loose waves into his eyes. His cheekbones were hard by comparison.

He moved his hands to the other thigh, her dress riding up her legs, one of his fingers tracing maddeningly close to the elastic of her lacy thong. She made some sort of inarticulate groan as his hand moved away and back down the left leg.

He smiled like a devil and said, "I think we might leave the stockings on for a little while."

Then his deft fingers reached for the tiny clasp of her four-inch heels, which she had hand-trimmed herself with black Russian sable around the ankle strap. The effect was one of wicked, sensational proportions: Anna Karenina's welcome manacles. The scooped neckline of her dress was similarly trimmed in the luxurious black texture. He paused before actually undoing the shoes.

"These shoes are very, *very* naughty, Miss James." He ran his middle finger between the fur and her skin. "What were you thinking?"

She hummed a sweet, nonverbal reply of approval. Devon smiled and brought his lips to her ankle, kissing the sensitive skin just above the bone through the thin membrane of her stocking. She inhaled with renewed pleasure.

"I think the shoes will stay on for a little while also," Devon declared as he set her foot back down.

Sarah practically whined with frustration. "If everything is staying on—"

"Those are the only items that are staying on." He pushed her dress up her thighs and removed her useless underwear in one quick pull down her legs, tossing them carelessly across the room. He pushed her dress farther up over her hips, letting it bunch around her waist.

The effect was devastating.

From the waist up, she was completely clothed: she could have been sitting at her desk or across the dining table at Dunlear Castle and she would have looked totally appropriate.

Perfectly normal.

And her stockinged legs and perfectly shod feet were still in pristine condition. The simple removal of one tiny thong and she was entirely exposed to this veritable stranger. It was intoxicating. Then terrifying.

Her legs tensed momentarily against his firm hands. "Are you cold?" he whispered as he breathed a warm stream of air between her legs. Her legs relaxed completely into his steady hold. "That's better," he said.

He readjusted his position so he was between her legs, on both knees. She had been lulled into some sort of passive state of pleasure, but when his lips touched her *there*, she nearly leapt off the seat, banging the back of her head against the medieval lead windowpanes behind her skull. She rubbed the back of her head with one hand and tried to repress her nervous laughter.

Devon's hands rested on her knees and he retreated somewhat, sitting back on his heels.

"What was that about?"

"I just… it was unexpected, I guess… I wasn't prepared…"

Devon tilted his head to one side, trying to discern if this woman was once again making fun of him or if she was for real. "Unexpected?"

She smiled again, her eyes glittering with amusement and residual pleasure.

"If I'm not mistaken," Devon proceeded carefully, "you invited me here. I think we need to be pretty clear on your, er, expectations." He paused again. "On your *terms*. Because even though we are from two countries separated by a common language, as they say, I think the phrase *sure thing* has a universally accepted meaning." His hands were massaging her thighs again, his thumbs kneading her soft skin, smoothing away her startled moment of a few minutes before. "So…"

Chapter 3

"I'm a little skittish, I guess. It's been a while…" She let her voice trail off with uncertainty.

He perked up with a jaunty smile. "Like how long is *a while*? Are you one of those revirgins?"

"What?!"

"You know, someone who hasn't had sex in so long, it's like being a virgin again… a *re*virgin." Devon held Sarah's eyes.

She smiled cryptically then answered with a broad smile and a slow nod. "It's *exactly* like that. How have I never heard of that phrase?"

"I think I heard some bloke on the tube using it a couple months ago. I am so pleased to be the one who gets to repop your cherry, then!" He reached his hands around her backside and rather forcefully moved her hips to the edge of the seat, nearly growling as his lips made their way up her inner thigh.

She had to balance herself with one hand, the other grasping his thick hair as he resumed his task with avid purpose, his hands holding her very firmly in place and gleefully ignoring all future jumps and starts from his very willing, if restless, accomplice.

She was so responsive and ready for him, in fact, that he almost took her right there on the window seat, but since it had been such a long while since her last toss, he decided to be chivalrous and get her properly and well taken care of before moving to the bed. He let his tongue tease her mercilessly, first with long, leisurely strokes, then with deep, penetrating thrusts, then narrowing to her tender, swollen center. He felt her nearly cresting several times and cruelly returned to the long, slow pass. She was becoming desperate.

He was about to bust out of his pants.

He finally gave her exactly what she wanted and what she was, by this time, quite boldly begging for. With a thrust of his tongue that caught the edge of her entrance, then a harsh little sucking tug, he cast her into wave after wave of shrieking bliss. He tried to go in for one more lick, or even a quick kiss, but she pushed his head away with almost primitive ferocity.

"Too much…" she forced out, her voice raspy from her hot, dry breathing. "Holy… oh… my…"

He rose back up on his knees, quite pleased with himself really.

"Come on, love," he murmured softly. "Let's get your quivering, delicious body over to the bed."

He helped her up. She pulled her dress back down over her hips, and then Devon turned her around toward the enormous tester bed with its turned mahogany posts.

"Lean here, lovely."

He guided her hands to the smooth wooden post so her back was toward him. Then he ran his fingers down her neck, the curls of her disheveled blond hair coming loose in delectable disarray. He wrapped one curl around his finger and brought it to his lips, then he let it drop and continued toward his original goal of removing her dress. He unzipped the long side zipper then raised the surprisingly light woven fabric over her head. He turned and put it down gently on the window seat, then turned back and paused in astonished appreciation.

Sarah was standing there, arms extended languidly against the bedpost, head resting against her upper arm: a wilted, satisfied, wanton woman, slowly stretching out her back, in nothing but bra, stockings, and the most erotic black fur, ankle-cuffed shoes he had ever come across.

The moon was limning every curve.

"Where are you?" she whispered into the darkness.

"Right here, goddess."

"I am so *not*... a goddess..."

Her voice trailed off weakly as the waves of pleasure were starting to dissipate and the cool air from the centuries-old windows started to chill her skin. She stretched her back and started to look over her shoulder, her confidence waning.

"Stay!" he barked, before he realized what he was saying.

She stopped in the exact spot, her head partially turned, her hands tightening their grip on the hard post, her hips tilted by the unnatural angle of her four-inch heels.

"What do you have in mind?" she asked, no longer minding the cool gooseflesh that was creeping up the undersides of her arms. His voice had a demanding, predatory timbre that warmed her from the inside out.

"I could think of a few things."

She could hear the sound of his clothes unbuttoning, unzipping, and flying in various directions across the room. She closed her eyes in anticipatory delight.

His warm, strong hands took her by the waist, slowly coming up under her breasts, then back around again, unhooking her bra and taking the shoulder straps slowly down her arms. She let her hands fall away from the bedpost, and her head fell back gently into his chest. He reached around to her stomach, and she had a moment of feeling like Ingres's *The Source*, all loose flesh and unmuscled torso, a Botticelli long after that shape was considered beautiful. And then she felt the deep thrum of his voice as he cooed in her ear and the strength of his pleasure against her back as he stroked her skin and pushed himself against her. The pure pleasure. No social mores. No visual prerequisites. His simple—their simple—mutual gratification. This was heaven. At long last, for the first time in her life, her body was a trusting friend, rather than an insecure enemy.

Before she knew what had happened, the two of them were a tangle of limbs, hair, tongues, fingers, and desperate caresses tossing around on the oceanic, faux-medieval, king-size bed. Perhaps the champagne had gone to her head after all, because, looking back, the rest of the night turned into a jump-cut viewfinder of some highly charged emotional snapshots interspersed with strangely beautiful, abstracted colors and shapes: the pleats and patterns of the maroon canopy-bed fabric above her in a flash; Devon perched in readiness, resting on his elbows, glaring at her silently the moment before he was inside her; the hourglass shape of the carafe of water with the matching glass resting upside down over the opening on the antique bedside table: a Vermeer still life captured in that split second when she turned her head away from the intensity of his gaze and felt him thrust into her in one clean, smooth stroke.

It was all happening.

It wasn't happening too fast, she thought; it was just (finally) happening.

—⁓—

Sarah rolled over the following morning fully expecting an empty bed. She had known last night that Devon would have to leave early to make his way back to Dunlear to spend the day with his soon-to-be-married only brother. So when the knock on the door woke her from her delicious half-dream, half-reenactment of the night's antics, she assumed it was room service with the breakfast she had ordered the day before. She rolled out of bed and made her way across the room, stopping at the closet to pull on one of the complimentary robes. "Coming," she added.

Just as Sarah unlocked the door, Nelson James bounded into his daughter's room, barely waiting for her to fully open it. His conservative steel-gray hair was combed to precision. His cashmere green turtleneck sweater and gray trousers were immaculate. He was in full captain-of-industry-on-British-holiday mode. Jane had probably organized his packing, individually wrapping each ensemble with a little note that read "Country Outing" or "Dinner in London." He and his overeager wife were apparently ready to tour the local countryside, and he didn't want Sarah wasting time lying around.

"It is well past 9:00," he boomed. Sarah looked dazedly at her bedside table and saw it was 9:04. "And we agreed to meet downstairs in the hotel lobby at that hour."

She was so disoriented, she couldn't even think of anything to say. Enough was enough, his impatient silence seemed to suggest.

"Sarah! Wake up! What in the world are you doing just standing there…" His voice faded out from a bellow to a mere whisper as he looked around the expansive hotel room and noted a veritable spin cycle of clothes flung in every direction. "Uh… your mother, uh, stepmother, and I will…"

Sarah suddenly realized that it wasn't just her clothes that were littering the floor. "Oh my God! Dad! What are you doing in here?! I thought you were room service! Don't you knock?!"

"Of course I knocked!" He was making his way backward, comically, out of the room, when the previously immobile lump of sheets and blankets piled on the bed began to shift and groan.

"Dad! Get out!" She reached to quickly open the door before Devon revealed himself. For some lucky reason, he had burrowed under the whole pile of linens. Then Sarah remembered the reason Devon was cocooned under all the bedding and flushed anew, right up to her hair follicles. "Go! Now!"

"I'm going, I'm going!" Her father was out the door in seconds, muttering inanities about British weddings having the strangest effect on young people.

Sarah shut the door behind him and moaned with embarrassment.

Devon started rustling around and Sarah walked back to the bed, sitting at the edge as she waited for him to emerge. He pulled her back into his arms and slowly undid the belt of the robe. He smiled and said nothing as he reached his arms behind her and hugged her to him, ultimately settling his lips on her neck, then making his way lower still. She made a futile attempt to swat him away.

"Do you have no shame?" she scolded.

"Of course I have shame, but thanks to your fierce protection of my anonymity, I don't have any shame as far as your *father* is concerned." His voice was a muffled caricature of itself. His kisses resumed along the ridge of her breast, then lower toward her navel.

"Cut that out!" Sarah half laughed, half reprimanded. "You are relentless."

"Isn't that the idea?"

She turned and sat upright, pushing some pillows behind her and tucking the robe firmly back across her chest. He lifted his head on one elbow and looked up at her expectantly, his face boyishly framed under the bedding.

"Devon…"

"Sarah…" he said, mocking her serious-Sarah voice.

"Well, I mean, I'd rather not get embroiled in some family con-flagration with my father and my stepmother and you all having some meet-and-greet in the lobby. Let's just call it a night, or a day, or whatever, shall we?"

"It's a bit early to call it a day… it's just starting."

"Don't you have to be somewhere?" Sarah sounded like she was talking to a stray dog.

He looked almost crestfallen, then smiled.

"I get it. Over and out. Roger that. Pizza and a six-pack and all that. I'm not complaining!" Before she knew what he was doing, he was up and out of the bed, strolling stark naked around the chamber, looking through the shotgun spray of clothes and undergarments that littered the floor and furniture.

When he came upon her microscopic white lace underwear, he held them up with his curved pinky and asked, "Are these yours or mine?"

Sarah pulled the sheets up over her head and squirmed. "I am *so* mortified!" she squeaked from under the covers, then peeked one eye out to see him.

"I suspect they are yours." He rubbed the fabric between his fingers, as if assessing the quality, then nodded his approval and tossed them onto the bed. He continued his naked parade around the room looking for his own kit, Sarah's gaze following him with what could only be described as raw lust. His body was insane, the hard planes of his stomach, the sinewy pull of his shoulders. Every muscle screamed, "I'm alive!" His arms. His back. His legs. Sarah sighed and let herself enjoy the view.

"Enjoying the show, are you?"

"Mm-hmm," she answered.

After a few minutes, he was more or less dressed and came to the edge of the bed to say good-bye. She loved the pressure and warmth of his body as he sat on the mattress next to her. All of a sudden, he tugged the sheet down until he had a full view of her flushed, beatific face, rather than that single roving eye. Her hair was a wild mass of mussed gold, honey, and barely brown loose curls, framing her cheekbones and jawline. Her eyes were... going to be the death of him. Cornflower. Aquamarine. Rimmed in a dark, mischievous cobalt. Devon let the back of his fingers trail down her cheek and neck, then came in for a farewell kiss.

"My breath!" Sarah squawked, pulling the sheet up to her nose.

Devon laughed, yanking the sheet down to her waist and pulling open her robe. Her hands flew up to her breasts.

"Didn't you know lovers never have morning breath?" he whispered as he let his right hand rest warmly on her rapidly fluttering lower belly, his mouth taking hers for a deep, passionate kiss that felt more like the beginning of another seduction, rather than the good-bye it was clearly meant to be. Sarah went limp with renewed pleasure and he chuckled and pulled away.

"This is *not* over. By the way." He got up from the bed and walked over to the window seat to put his shoes and socks on.

Sarah pulled the sheets back up to cover herself and he smiled and shook his head. His dress shirt was open at the collar and his tie was shoved halfway into the side pocket of his dinner jacket.

He looked delicious and he seemed to be enjoying Sarah's endless gawking, a small half-smile playing across his lips. The shadow of his morning beard, the mussed hair falling into his face as he bent to tie his other shoe, the sparkle in his gray-blue eyes when he stood up.

Sarah sighed again.

"So, I'll see you at the altar, then," he crowed with a wicked smile and headed out the door, taking a moment to look right and left out into the hallway before he departed. "The coast is clear!" he called in a loud stage whisper, one hand forming the metaphorical megaphone on the side of his mouth. Then he blew her a kiss and whispered a soft, endearing, "Bye, lovely."

And then he was gone.

Sarah was not usually one for kicking and screaming, but she couldn't resist the urge to turn her face into the huge down pillow and squeal with adolescent delight. She pounded her legs and arms in a little horizontal victory dance. She had done it. It was done! She was officially *not* a virgin anymore.

The world seemed a lighter place, somehow.

Her father's punctual arrogance aside, it was well after nine and she *had* ordered her breakfast to be delivered to her room at eight thirty. She reached over to the hotel phone on the far bedside table, getting a wonderful whiff of Devon as she made her way past his side of the huge bed. After being patched through to the kitchen via the main switchboard, the housekeeping staff apologized for the delay and said her breakfast would be up in about fifteen minutes. She didn't want to antagonize her father endlessly so she called his room next to see if he wanted to go ahead without her.

"Hi, Dad, it's Sarah."

"Hello, Sarah."

"Hi, Dad. Probably best if we begin the day anew, don't you think?"

He grunted his reluctant agreement.

"So… *Hi, Dad!* The breakfast order I placed last night went astray so I'll be ready and down in the lobby around ten. If you and Jane want to head into the little town now, I can catch up with you a bit later on…"

They went through the motions of a perfectly courteous conversation and Sarah almost laughed at how hard it was for her father to refrain from making some comment or inquiry about her… overnight visitor.

"All right, then. Sounds great," she continued in her best deadpan business voice. "I'll see you two in the lobby in half an hour."

With that done, she slid down off the high bed and walked into the bathroom to shower and get ready for a few hours of sightseeing and antiquing with her stepmother and father before she headed over to Dunlear to be with Bronte before the ceremony. Sarah noticed several used condom wrappers in the bathroom trash bin and thanked her stars that one of them had been the responsible adult last night (and in the middle of the night and earlier this morning), and she chided herself for being so flighty.

Now that she was a promiscuous adult, she needed to get with the program.

She felt tender everywhere when she stepped into the scalding shower. She cleaned herself from head to toe with meticulous care, realizing that her skin was still responding with a heightened sense of tactile awareness: the water was particularly silky as it sluiced down her back; the washcloth was thick and rough as she dragged it across her stomach and under her breasts; the muscles of her inner thighs and backside were sore in a way that somehow served as a wonderful reminder of their unaccustomed use.

Sarah felt her insides start to ramp up, her nipples were taut, and a slight throbbing tension was beginning to build between her legs. Her eyes began to close and then she shook herself briskly.

"Get ahold of yourself," she said aloud, with the disciplinary tone of an impatient schoolteacher.

She turned the shower temperature as low as it would go and realized she had always been under the sexist misapprehension that only men used cold showers to stifle those tawdry urges. She turned off the water, toweled herself with brutal efficiency, brushed her hair as if it needed punishing, and whipped on her clothes as quickly as possible. The housekeeper knocked a few seconds later and came in with a steaming, glittering, sterling silver breakfast tray.

Sarah fought the impulse to treat every sip of coffee as if it were the most delicious sip of coffee she had ever tasted, nor would she allow herself to dwell on the fact that the croissant was, quite certainly, the best, flakiest, buttery-est croissant in the history of pastries. She forced herself to shove the food into her mouth as matter-of-factly as possible, then wiped at her mouth with the soft, linen napkin. She gave in to the harmless desire to rub the edge of the napkin across her lower lip, just once or twice.

Or so.

So what if it vaguely reminded her of someone's cool thumb trailing across her lips? And so what if her jeans were starting to feel a little warm in the crotch?

For God's sake! she scolded herself impatiently, and threw the napkin (now a crumpled ball) on top of the decimated breakfast tray. She grabbed her purse, put on her long camel hair coat, tied a deliciously soft, hand-knit rabbit fur scarf around her neck (*Ugh!*), and tried to get on with her day without finding sexual overtones in every object she happened upon.

That proved impossible.

After an hour of sightseeing—a country antique barn where the wide-plank wall boards were worn yet coarse as she let her fingertips trail along and the autumn air was brisk, moist, and alive in her nostrils and then a local artisanal wool factory where the pervasive, bittersweet odor of lanolin conjured up the sensory memory of Devon's Barbour waxed-cotton coat... he had been wearing it on the way to the hotel last night... where was it?—Sarah finally admitted defeat.

More or less disgusted with herself, Sarah begged off lunch and headed back to her hotel room to rest. The car and driver her father had hired brought her back to Amberley with instructions to return in two hours' time to fetch Nelson and Jane from the charming town nearby. Sarah was completely exhausted and didn't think Bronte would appreciate a wobbling maid of honor, teetering and worn out (from sleeplessness and naughtiness) by her side at the altar. She stopped by the front desk to schedule a wake-up call for two that afternoon, and made her way with heavy, methodical steps up the luxurious, red-carpeted, medieval stone staircase.

She opened her hotel room and was assaulted by a wave of ethereal spring scents—peonies, roses, lilac, gardenia, sweet pea, and ranunculus. An enormous bouquet of outrageously expensive flowers sat regally atop the round drum table under the bay window at the far end of the room. Sarah walked slowly toward the arrangement, bending down to unzip her short boots and remove them on the way. Her stomach began to patter... she had skipped lunch, she reminded herself, trying to remain rational.

The heavy-stock ivory Smythson envelope tucked into the decadent arrangement simply read, "Miss James," penned in a heavy, blue fountain ink. She reached for the card and refused to give in to the insane yearning to smell the envelope before opening it. She slid her index finger under the crisp edge where he had licked it and slowly opened the stiff flap. She pulled out the rigid card and smiled at the simple message.

"Sincerely hope primary definition of 'weekend' includes Friday, Saturday, <u>and</u> Sunday. Yrs, DH"

Or she thought it said *DH*; it was more like a few rapid circles of ink with a quick slash right across the middle of the whole mess. She put the note on the table, letting the corner release from her finger with a firm snap onto the mahogany surface. She stood there for a while just staring at the blooms, each one looking as though it had been chosen specifically to provoke: languorous, lush, bursting. Then she thought, unbidden and sarcastically, that Devon Heyworth was probably one of the most beloved customers known to British florists.

She pulled one flopping peony the size of a large grapefruit from the arrangement and brought it to her bedside table. Pouring a small amount of water out of the carafe and into the delicate drinking glass, she trimmed the stem of the peony with her thumbnail so the entire fragrant bloom rested easily on the rim of the small glass. Sarah stared at the pale pinks and delicate whites of the flower and thought of her mother. What would it be like to have a mother on a day like this? Someone to maybe smile and hug and confide in.

After her mother died, Sarah spent years getting straight As and doing everything in her power to impress her father with her youthful, ambitious summer internships at the Simpson-James department store. She worked in the corporate offices and followed her father's assistant, Wendy Walton, around with slavish devotion. On her sixteenth birthday, Sarah realized that no amount of "best behavior" was going to wrest her father out of his widower's desolation. So, on a rebellious morning in June, one of those spectacular, breathtakingly clear, early summer days on Lake Michigan, Sarah packed a large backpack and informed her father that she was flying to France to stay with her grandmother.

"I'm going to live with Letitia," Sarah stated with mock self-assurance, referring to her mother's mother. The older woman had always demanded Sarah call her by her first name—Letitia proclaimed that she was "simply too young to be a grandmother."

At the time, Nelson James sat behind his enormous mahogany desk, the desk he had used as a barrier to the rest of the world for the past four years. The nine-foot tall windows in the mansion's library refracted the pure morning light of the lake over his shoulder and into Sarah's eyes. Nelson found it nigh on impossible to look at his blond, willful, gorgeous daughter. The curve of her hair over her left ear, the sweep of her stubborn, honeyed eyebrows, her cornflower eyes that darkened to near-black sapphire at the edges: they were Elizabeth's eyes and Elizabeth's obstinate mouth and Elizabeth's golden, thick, wavy hair.

"You should," he agreed simply. "That's a good idea. Just leave the details with Wendy so I know where to reach you." Then he returned to the spreadsheet he was ostensibly working on and held his pencil aloft as if to begin again where he'd left off before the interruption.

Sarah wasn't angling for a fight necessarily, but she certainly didn't think her father would let his sixteen-year-old daughter walk out the door unaccompanied without a *discussion* at the very least. She felt the unfought fight drain out of her, double-checked that she had her well-thumbed paperback, *The Razor's Edge*, in her messenger bag, turned on her heel, and left. Unbeknownst to her, it was the last time she would live in that house.

Leaving that day ten years ago felt a lot like starting her own business. Come to that, it also felt a lot like meeting Devon Heyworth. Promising. Terrifying. Liberating.

—⁓—

Devon never thought he would be grateful for the to-do list of tedious, filial obligations that kept him busy from the moment he returned to Dunlear until the moment he was standing at the head of the aisle of Fitzwilliam Chapel, having successfully ushered his mother to her seat in the front row.

So far, so good.

He patted his pocket for the fourteen thousandth time to make sure the ceremonial rings were still there, and walked slowly across the apse to stand at the right side of the altar, next to his fidgeting brother. The rustle of fabric and papers and shoes against the hard stone floor came to an abrupt halt as the single trumpet began Jeremiah Clarke's *Voluntary*.

Everyone in the chapel rose and Devon watched as his brother's attention was drawn to the entrance of the nave. The large mahogany doors were drawn back and held open by two royal guards in full court dress.

Bronte looked lovely in, well, enough lace to cover a polo field, her train trailing endlessly behind her.

Since her father had passed away many years before, she had opted to walk down the aisle on her own. Getting Bronte to do the whole church business had been a sticking point at one stage of their courtship, then she had done a complete about-face and was now willing to do the whole church, reception, white dress extravaganza.

Devon's eyes wandered beyond Bronte's shoulder and his heart started to slam in a hard, throbbing rhythm.

Sarah James was leaning over the last edge of Bronte's train, attempting to put the massive yardage in proper order before Bronte continued up the aisle. The first glimpse he had was of the top of Sarah's head, where masses of loose golden curls were invisibly held together in a colossal, complicated pile. Devon had to quickly repress the desire to run the length of the church and catch her hair before it all fell down. Then Sarah looked up and winked to let Bronte know all was well with the train, and Bronte began to walk down the aisle. Sarah adjusted one stray blond curl, moving it out of her own line of vision with the very tip of a single finger encased in full-length white gloves.

Devon tore his gaze away, quickly realizing that if he looked at Sarah for even a moment longer, he would be standing in front of three hundred people in a house of God with the evidence of his lust in full view. It took all his willpower to keep his eyes on the vicar and his ears alert for the cue: somewhere in that sea of monotonous syllables, he was going to be depended upon to produce those rings. Bronte arrived at the altar. She leaned forward slightly and caught Devon's gaze.

Then winked.

What a saucy wench, Devon thought happily. Apparently, girls will kiss and tell, even to their friend on her wedding day. He kept his eyes on the enormous stained-glass window over the vicar's head and tried even harder to concentrate. They had come to some order of events in the ceremony where the endless kneeling and standing and kneeling and standing portion of the program was upon them. Bronte turned to Sarah and handed her the bridal bouquet so she could join Max at the prie-dieu. Devon heard the two women whisper with what sounded like conspiratorial tones, then Devon saw Bronte exhale very slowly through her thin lips and kneel next to her future husband, in the eyes of God.

He doubted the rest of the wedding guests could see her barely concealed tremor of nerves.

Figuring all eyes would be on the bride and groom, Devon thought a quick glance in Sarah's direction wouldn't go amiss. The two of them were no more than five feet apart, standing to the side and slightly behind the kneeling couple.

He tried one of those aimless glances that suggests you are looking in a vague direction for no particular reason, then your gaze just happens to fall on something that also happens to be in that general vicinity. He started near the floor, acting as if he were engrossed in the backs of the bride and groom's bent heads, when he caught the tip of Sarah's suede shoe peeking out from the hem of her full-length, chocolate-brown velvet gown. He thought he was being quite blasé about the whole thing when he realized she was moving the very pointy tip of the very sexy stiletto in a quick right-left motion, then coughed to clear her throat. He looked up then, and her spectacular, twinkling blue eyes nailed him for the guilty perv he was. Her lips went up a fraction on the right side only, the tiniest mocking, yet complicit, hint of a smile.

She refocused her gaze toward the vicar and Devon noticed a tiny sprig of lily of the valley tucked behind her right ear. She must have known he was trapped there, staring, since she chose that very moment to adjust the flower with one of those demonically prim gloves, then let her fingertip trail near her nose so she could gently inhale the scent. She let her graceful hand fall, perfectly innocent, of course, across the satin skin of her chest, the warm brown velvet of her bodice, and back onto the wrapped stems of Bronte's arrangement.

His mouth was utterly dry. The entire church seemed ominously quiet. He looked at his brother, Max, standing in front him, then had the delayed realization that he must have missed the part when his brother stood up from the kneeling position and asked him to produce the rings.

"Dev? You have them, right?" his meticulous elder brother whispered.

"Of course. Right here."

The rest of the ceremony was a happy celebration from there on out, including the endless recitations of all the pending joys and unavoidable trials that awaited the jubilant couple.

Devon did not let his eye wander again.

Chapter 4

BACH'S BRANDENBURG CONCERTO NO. 2 in F Major sprang to life, trilled merrily from the twelve-piece ensemble that Devon's mother had brought out from London for the ceremony and reception. The French horn and strings soared through the chapel as Max and Bronte turned, arm in arm, and made their way down the aisle, smiling widely at all of the guests on both sides of the chapel as they passed.

Devon turned to Sarah and offered his bent arm. She leaned aside momentarily to grab hold of the full skirt of her dress, then lifted the heavy velvet slightly so as not to trip over it on her way down the four short steps from the altar to the aisle. When the clarinet and flute were battling joyously in the upper registers, she looked up and smiled into Devon's eyes with blatant intimacy. The marching rhythm of the following stanza shook Devon awake and he escorted Sarah formally down the aisle, his arm held at a stiff, military right angle, his posture rigid, his eyes straight ahead.

The heat and pressure from her kid glove was brutally distracting by the time they swept out of the main part of the chapel and into the vestibule where the photographer was already beginning to take a few shots of Max and Bronte. Instead of turning left toward the bride and groom, Devon quickly veered to the right into a small antechamber. The room smelled of old incense, candles, laundry starch, and a faint citrusy wood polish. The early evening light was watery gray as it came through the mottled, lead-pane windows and shone upon two old wooden chairs, one on either side of the arched door frame.

Sarah began to remove her hand from Devon's arm after he had shut the door behind them, but he pulled her into a rough embrace before her glove had left his sleeve. She dropped the tightly packed bouquet of dozens of pale pink rosebuds that she had been clutching, along with the thick fabric of her skirt.

"You were killing me out there," Devon growled into her neck as he kissed his way down to the edge of the chocolaty brown fabric above her breast. He dipped one finger into the bodice and felt her nipple respond. Her low, throaty moan encouraged him to continue, but the fitted bustier was not giving him enough room to release her. He snarled with pent-up frustration and reached one hand around her back for a zipper, only to discover a battalion of miniature covered buttons running the full length of Sarah's back. "You've got to be kidding me!" he rasped.

Then he looked down at Sarah's face: her eyes shut in pleasure, lips moist and slightly parted, her hair in that delectable state of perpetually imminent disarray, the rosy flush of desire running up her neck and cheeks. He watched as her front teeth came down on her lower lip and bit a small piece of that moist, raspberry inner skin.

He might have to rip the damned dress off after all.

She began to speak with her eyes closed, her head starting to tilt back. "I have spent the entire day feeling your hands on my body, your tongue against my skin, the fabric of your shirt against my fingers, your gaze on my back… even my ears have been in a heightened state of awareness… what is a girl to do?"

Devon's heart ground to a halt, then began to pound with near-terrifying force, slamming into his ribs. Sarah was touching him everywhere. He was going mad. Her light caress trailed down his neck, the soft kidskin glove like a velvet firebrand. Then she massaged his upper arms through his evening jacket, then in and under the jacket and around to his lower back, reaching her hands momentarily under the waistband of his trousers and over his ass, then back out again and along his hips, then—uh, wrong direction—back up to his chest, pushing into the crisp white folds of his formal pleated shirt, then, thank God, down toward the placket of the button closure of his pants.

She stopped at the top button, the very tips of her gloved fingers dipping behind his waistband, snug between the black worsted fabric of his dress pants and the warm, white cotton of his shirt, and her two thumbs slowly rubbing the fabric in front of her fingers.

"Good God, woman, what are you waiting for?" he demanded.

She opened her eyes then and smiled like the devil.

"What do you think I'm waiting for? Your brother just married my closest friend and three hundred people are filing out of your *ancestral* chapel not eight feet beyond that door. Did you think I was going to get down on my knees and give you a blow job?"

"Well…"

Sarah burst out laughing and pulled her hands out from the edge of his pants to cover her cheeks.

"You did!" she gasped between peals of unstoppable laughter.

His hands dropped from her waist and he slowly smoothed the front of his jacket, paying particular care to the immaculate black satin of his shawl collar, meticulously removing a tiny, invisible speck. "Please let me know when your amusement abates…" he tried, in his best approximation of bored lord of the manor.

Sarah's laughter reignited with greater force. "Men are hilarious…" she sputtered between waning coughs of glee.

She reached down to the floor to retrieve her forgotten bouquet and shook out the slightly crushed fabric of her dress. "I'll tell you what," she resumed in a matter-of-fact tone, "why don't we try to behave like rational adults for a few hours and then we can pick up where we left off? Later tonight? Back at the ranch, as they say." She started to turn toward the door.

"You are one stone-cold—"

She turned back quickly, a startled, almost offended look in her eyes, and put a single gloved fingertip against his lips to quiet him.

"I am not stone cold," she whispered into his ear, her hot breath brushing against the soft skin there. She kissed him lightly on his neck, just below and behind his ear, and reveled in his answering moan. Sarah slowly pulled her face away and smiled. "Just practical," she added.

She took a deep, halting breath, stood up a bit straighter as if to fortify herself, then walked out of the little room. The volume of celebratory voices in the adjacent vestibule rose and fell as she opened and then closed the door behind her.

Devon realized he hadn't taken a breath for quite some time and inhaled deeply.

During the subsequent cocktail reception, sit-down dinner, and dancing, Sarah was caught up in a constant stream of photos, brief conversations, occasional dances with handsome strangers, sips of champagne, and the repetitive need to tamp down the waves of desire that seemed to wash over her at inexplicable moments.

It wasn't just Devon, either.

It seemed that every man there had some attribute that Sarah found particularly appealing: James Mowbray's jaw was hard and chiseled to perfection, and she felt a slight jolt of awareness at the texture of his cheek against hers when he crossed the ballroom to greet her and gave her a brief kiss on the cheek hello; Bronte's friend from her Chicago office had gorgeous, thick chestnut hair; some distant cousin of the Heyworth family held her hand firmly in one of his and put pressure on her lower back with the other in a wonderfully powerful way when they danced; even Devon's elderly Uncle Bertrand seemed to have some intellectual magnetism when they spoke about his time in the early days of the Inchbald School.

On the other hand, it was all Devon. Because the cheek and the hair and the pressure on the lower back and the magnetism—when she blinked, it was always Devon's face she saw behind her eyelids and his touch she felt against her skin.

Bronte reached her a few hours later, having finally torn herself away from her husband's side.

"Sarah, I am the bride and I am the one who is supposed to be beaming! But you are on fire!" Bronte smiled and gave her a warm hug. "You are always gorgeous, of course, but there is something about you tonight that is really quite"—Bronte paused to consider the right word—"quite smashing. I think every man in the room has his eye on you."

Sarah gave her a conspiratorial look and then nodded. "It is fun. I've never really gone in for flirting. I mean, I don't know if that's what I'm doing, but I just feel so *open* to everything… is that wrong?"

"Oh, Sarah! You are too much." Bronte held her friend's hands in hers. "It is absolutely not wrong. You should be the princess at the ball for the next ten years at least. Let every single one of them fawn all over you. You are luscious. Let them look."

Bronte paused to look around, caught Max's eye, smiled widely, then turned back to Sarah with a more serious look in her eye. "But watch out for Devon, Sarah. I mean, I know you'll have your fun, but he is a total player. I feel like a mean sister already, because I love him, and I love you, but just… what?"

"What does it mean if someone refers to a pizza and a six-pack after… you know…"

Bronte's face turned stormy with anger. "Did Devon say that to you? It's when you finish—you know!—and you wish the other person would miraculously turn into… pizza and a six-pack…" She started to look around, probably for a blunt weapon to hit Devon with. "I will—"

"Bron! Stop. He..." Sarah smiled and looked embarrassed. "I think he thought *he* was the one... you know... that I wanted *him* to turn into a pizza and a six-pack..."

Bronte burst out laughing with such a loud cry that a few people nearby turned to make sure a small farm animal hadn't somehow slipped into the grand ballroom. The guests smiled wanly and turned away when they realized it was only the crass American duchess being crass and American again.

"Oh, Sarah. You are divine. You have your fun and I'll talk to you in a few weeks when we get back from our honeymoon. I won't worry about you! Clearly, you are much better at fending off the Heyworth charms than I ever was."

Bronte started looking for Max again, gave Sarah another swift hug when she spotted him, and headed back across the ballroom to be with him.

Sarah was finally beginning to feel the waning of the adrenaline rush that had been fueling her for the past couple of days. She made her way into a quiet corner of the ballroom, where a few small tables had been set up for the older crowd who might not want to stand for hours at a stretch.

She was starting to wilt.

Despite Devon's royal sexiness, she might have to call it a night. She couldn't imagine how her exhausted body could possibly rebound for another episode of—

"You are not fading on me, are you?" His voice was right behind her. He had somehow slipped between the large potted palms that had been brought in to soften the perimeter of the ballroom. The trees also created an exotic play of shadows when the chandeliers shone through the barely swaying fronds.

She closed her eyes at the warm, liquid pleasure of his voice.

"I am a bit tired," she admitted as he sat down next to her and took one of her gloved hands in his.

"Well, I wouldn't want to"—he looked down for a moment while his fingers worked the four tiny buttons at the wrist of her pristine white gloves—"exhaust you." He smiled wickedly when he freed the fourth button and let his index finger enter the small opening and caress her sensitive skin. That single finger was doing devilish things to her insides. "Maybe you just need a little pick-me-up." His finger reached as far into the slit of fine leather as it could go, straining across the baby-soft skin of her inner forearm.

"What are you doing to me?" she whispered.

"Seducing you," he replied with no hint of irony.

"Why?"

"Because you want me to."

"Do I?"

"Very much."

"And after the seduction?"

"There is no after."

"There is always an after…" Her eyes were closed in feline pleasure as his finger continued to send shocks through her body with that one tiny touch.

"I will always seduce you."

"Always?"

"Anytime you want me to…"

"What if you're busy?"

"I will make the time. Besides, I'm not busy right now, and just like you and secondary definitions, I try to steer clear of hypothetical conversations." His voice turned matter-of-fact and he began buttoning up the small opening of her glove.

She pouted, feeling a bit dismissed. "Are you punishing me?"

"I will if you want me to." His smile was pure mischief. "That bed at the inn is quite the thing… sturdy and all that… I would have thought after your, well, time in the wilderness, you might have preferred a more gradual reintroduction, but I am always game—"

Sarah felt herself go pale with embarrassment. "I meant… I liked what you were doing with my glove… and then you stopped… and turned sort of businesslike… and…" She thought crawling under the small table and its protective table skirt might be *quite the thing*.

Devon just stared. "Are you for real?"

"What do you mean?"

"I mean"—he pulled at his stiff, formal collar to loosen its irritating hold on his neck—"one minute, you are the god-damned sexiest thing I have ever laid eyes on, lips parted, eyes closed, practically humming like an engine for Christ's sake, your kicked-up heartbeat visible through that fantastic skin. Shoes like mink manacles for Christ's sake. And then the next minute, you are, well, a bloody innocent. It's a bit off-putting." And that was putting it mildly.

Sarah wasn't sure if he was trying to chastise her for being a tease or just venting a little sexual frustration. She felt like she might be slipping a bit out of her depth. "Like how off-putting?" she asked with just a hint of sarcasm, trying to protect her fragile, give-me-a-break-I-was-a-virgin-yesterday ego. "Like all that seduction talk was 'just talk' off-putting? Or like 'minor hiccup' off-putting?"

"Luckily, I am not easily put off." His smile made it entirely clear that he had been momentarily frustrated by his own desire, rather than accusing her of taunting him.

She smiled with genuine relief. "Well, that *is* a boon."

"See, like right there! Your whole face, your whole being just beams this message of invitation… I am not saying you are a tease—"

Her face must have shown that that was exactly what she'd thought he was saying.

"Oh! Charming! You must take me for quite the gentleman." He raked one hand impatiently through his hair to get it out of his eyes. "It's not that. At. All. It's just, you are so *right there* for the taking. And then, swoosh, it's like Game Over."

Sarah looked down at the floor, then tried to be honest without sounding like an idiotic teenager spilling her guts. "I tend to compartmentalize. Let's just leave it at that. I don't really get the whole goo-goo ga-ga schmoopsie-pooh thing. Like Bronte is kind of freaking me out right now, but it's her wedding day, so I am trying to make allowances."

"Damn!" Devon made a low, barely audible whistle. "You are every man's dream come true: all of the attraction with none of the fatality!"

She smiled again. And blushed.

"And the blushing! I thought so in the car last night, but it was so dark, I couldn't be sure. You are to die for. Please, let's get out of here." He hauled her up and, with one of her hands firmly in his, headed toward the bride and groom. "Max! Enough is enough. Don't you need to consummate this marriage?" Max and Bronte looked up from—what else—gazing at one another, and turned in unison toward Devon and Sarah.

"Somewhere you need to be, Dev?" Max grinned.

"It's not just me. All these old, crusty windbags need to get home to their Viagra. Give old Bertrand a break."

"Well, if it's Bertrand we're talking about, then…" Max's eyes swung over to Sarah. "Hi, Sarah. Are you having a good time?"

Sarah had met Max several times and always thought he erred on the side of serious. Now, not so much.

"Why, yes, Max. I'm having quite a good time. Dunlear is very hospitable."

"Dunlear, is it?" He raised one eyebrow and smiled again at Sarah, then let his face return to mock-seriousness when he met his younger brother's look. "Devon, please go tell Mother that we will be leaving the reception now and would like to have a few words with her before we go."

The final half hour of the wedding was a complete blur of hugs and more photographs and hip-hip-hoorays. And then a drowsy fifteen minutes, eyes closed and head on Devon's shoulder, in the back of the hotel limo until, before she knew it, Sarah found herself collapsing in her hotel room's enormous bed, the crinoline and velvet of her dress forming a vast cloud around her. She could hear—feel, really—Devon prowling around the room, adjusting the lights, checking the fire in the fireplace, taking off his cufflinks and studs, and dropping them with a little clink into a small decorative dish on the mantle.

Sarah was so tired, so physically exhausted, that she thought she might really just fall asleep. All of his seduction talk notwithstanding. She started to hum with the imminent pleasure of simple, sweet sleep.

"You don't want to sleep in this gown, do you?" His voice was so close that she could feel his breath against her skin, maybe even his lips.

"Mmm-nnng…" She was drifting away.

He turned her onto her stomach, gently kissing her neck, and started working his way down her back. Forty-two buttons later, he was rewarded with the sight of the full length of the perfect alabaster skin of her back. She stretched like a cat, enjoying the final freedom from the garment that had been confining her for the past eight hours. She hadn't worn a bra because the dress was completely structured from the inside out, with stiff stays, a built-in cantilevered brassiere, and attendant hardware. It was as though she had been encased in a formfitting cage the entire time she'd been wearing it.

Devon pulled the warm velvet fabric gently down over her shoulders and her arms. Then, turning her onto her back, he pulled it the rest of the way off her torso. The crinoline underskirt was a separate piece altogether. He unsnapped the tiny hook-and-eye closures at the side of the underskirt and pulled that slowly off as well.

And there she was. In all her splendor.

Her eyes were glazed when they fluttered open and she realized she was splayed out atop the bed in nothing but her transparent lace underwear and thigh-high brown suede boots. In some vague approximation of modesty, she murmured something that sounded like gratitude, let one tired arm drape across her breasts, then smiled and let her eyes close again.

Devon decided he was going to take his time with these Sarah James boots. What kind of mind even thought up such things? A very compartmentalized mind, apparently.

The boots had some sort of elastic in the suede, so the material was like a second skin against Sarah's creamy thigh. He ran a pinkie between the high edge of the boot and her skin, testing the elasticity and letting it snap. Sarah gave a little moan of approval. He let his finger go deeper into the sheath, then pushed one whole, flat hand in, snug against her luscious skin. She started to squirm a little. He retrieved his hand and tried to think.

"I don't even know where to begin." He was sitting back on his haunches, naked, looking down at her incredible body. She was intoxicatingly beautiful, and sexy, but as he had told her earlier, there was something utterly pure and untouched about her. She wasn't shameless, exactly; she was more like Eve before the fall… as if there was nothing to be ashamed of in the first place… the way her body moved and stretched to find the most comfortable position, her large breasts arching up. The whole movement was perfectly natural and then, suddenly, totally erotic.

He leaned down and began kissing and licking and taunting her body until she was whimpering in confusion.

"What is happening to me?" she murmured, distracted.

"I don't know. Describe it to me," he said between provocative kisses in the most inappropriate places.

He could see her hand beginning to stray toward her unattended breast. "Do you want to touch it?" he asked.

"Mm-hmm."

"Why don't you?"

He pulled his mouth away and blew cool air on the wet peak and watched her head roll back in bittersweet pleasure.

"Here, let me help you," he said.

He released his hand from her waist and used it to guide her free hand toward her right breast.

She hesitated, as if she were unwilling to actually touch herself. Devon wondered momentarily if it was possible that she had never touched herself in front of a man, then dismissed it as an impossibility.

"Show me how you like it, Sarah."

His other hand was massaging her left breast. "Do you like that?"

She was nodding, and then her head flew back again when he gave it a firm pinch. "I thought you might like that too. I want to see you do it."

Her own hand fluttered over her other breast, then tentatively rested at its side. Devon began tweaking the left one again, almost absentmindedly letting all of his fingers touch the very tip, back and forth, back and forth, then he brought his mouth down to it again and she arched her back and cried out an inarticulate plea. He sucked and taunted and watched her hand on her right breast, inches from his eyes, then he sucked harder and guided her hand, taking her fingers under his until she was touching herself there.

Her head started to shift from right to left, disoriented. He moved her fingers in the same rhythm as his mouth, mimicking the pressure and cadence. His teeth grazed; her other hand pinched. His tongue circled; her flat palm circled across the other peak. It was a duet of her own pleasure.

He reached his hand down toward her waist, then lower, and she practically bucked to meet his palm. She was so ready for him. He wondered how close she might be; he reached just inside the edge of her panties, then farther until he felt how swollen she was, and all the while, he kept sucking mercilessly on the same breast.

He gave her a nearly cruel bite on that hard, taut nipple just as his hand gripped her warm center and he felt wave after wave after wave course through her. Her other hand clenched and unclenched protectively, provocatively, over her breast.

He finally pulled his mouth away from her chest, ripped her underwear off, tore a condom packet open, and had himself sheathed in a matter of seconds. He had never wanted to be inside a woman with the intensity he felt at that moment. He moved between her legs, pushed the brown suede boots akimbo, and lifted her perfect, generous hips up to meet him. He looked at her face—flushed, far away, a dream—and thrust into her with such complete abandon, he wasn't quite sure where he was, or who he was; all he could think was "Sarah."

She was still in the throes of her own release when she felt the fulfilling, all-encompassing joy of his body joining hers. It felt even better than it had yesterday, if that was possible. Her eyes were floating open and closed of their own accord, and she kept hearing her name on his lips. It was a soft breeze of desire when he said it, a small poem.

He leaned down and whispered hoarsely into her ear, "Sarah… come again."

"I couldn't possibly," she croaked.

"I bet you can," he taunted.

"You would know better than I would," she murmured.

He looked at her with a quizzical tilt of his head, shook his hair aside, then pulled her arms above her head, lacing each of her hands into each of his, then firming his grip.

"I would, would I?" He began a slow, easy rhythm.

She was happy to go along for the ride. Let him have his turn.

He was watching with a small, amused grin when he began to go deeper, to take her from the passive, spent woman of a few minutes ago to see bewilderment cross her face as the deep pull of desire began to build inside her again. The undeniable craving welled up. For a split second, he wondered again how she could be so unaccustomed to the joys of her own body. And then he was so close to his own release, and she to hers, that the thought—and the subsequent memory of it—splintered into an infinite fractal cascade of shared ecstasy. She was half breathing, half moaning when he finally pulled away from her satiated body. He lay there for a few minutes, lost in a place of bliss… thoughtless yet meaningful bliss.

She had curled up next to him and was already dozing off.

Out.

He slipped off the bed and went into the bathroom for a few minutes. When he returned to her, he tenderly removed the mile-high suede boots and set them on the floor. Then he pulled the sheets back and tucked Sarah and then himself into the huge hotel bed. Sarah, already asleep, turned away from the warmth of Devon's body, then shimmied back to rub the length of her back and derriere against his stomach and pelvis in a slinky, selfish, catlike gesture.

For the second time that day, Devon realized he had stopped breathing. He made the requisite effort to get oxygen into and out of his malfunctioning lungs, overly conscious of the basic act of inhaling. As he drifted off to sleep, he pondered whether or not oxygen was, in fact, necessary when you had to choose between that or sex with Sarah James as the alternative.

Chapter 5

SARAH WOKE THE NEXT morning surprisingly rested. She turned to look over her shoulder and saw Devon asleep in a position of sheer abandon: one arm thrown over his head, the other flung across her hip; his hair a tousled, sexy mess of light honey-brown strands falling across one eye; his lips, almost smiling even in sleep, full and slightly parted. She wallowed for a moment in the surreal fantasy that waking up next to him was a totally common, natural turn of events. He would make the coffee, pick up the newspaper off the front porch; she would make breakfast and set the table; they would spend the day on the couch swapping sections of the *New York Times*.

Then Sarah shook her head and laughed quietly at the absurdity. She didn't even know how to boil water… and where exactly was this breakfast table one spoke of… and an actual newspaper, made of paper? She had never had a newspaper delivered anywhere, much less a paper one on a porch. Her iPad was a streaming newsreel 24/7… why would she need more news on Sunday? What was the point?

Well, now she was starting to imagine what the point was… kind of a sweet, romantic point. She almost reached out to touch the strong line of Devon's cheekbone, then thought better of it. This train was leaving the station and there was no point dragging out the inevitable departure. She slid out of the bed as gently as possible, so as not to disturb him, and quietly closed the door behind her as she went into the bathroom.

Twenty minutes later, she was showered and dressed.

Twenty minutes after that, she was totally packed, sitting on top of one of her grandmother's vintage Louis Vuitton steamer trunks and ready to dry her hair. She hesitated, worrying that the high-pitched squeal of the blow-dryer would wake him.

Oh well, he had to wake up at some point. And she had to skedaddle. She gave her hair the full treatment, making it razor straight, and put on a light foundation, a few quick strokes of mascara, and lip gloss.

She needn't have worried overmuch about the noise, since apparently Devon slept through earthquakes. According to Heyworth family lore, on a trip to San Francisco, he had, quite literally, slept through seismic activity. She called the bellman from the phone in the bathroom and asked for assistance with her luggage, shoving it out into the hall so he wouldn't have to come in and see her *lover* (ugh!) sprawled out on her bed. She was starting to feel like a harlot.

Peeking out into the hallway, she saw the bellman making his way down the hall. She smiled and put her finger to her lips with a little "shhh." The formal man gave a small smile of understanding and started hauling away the first of three enormous pieces of luggage.

That taken care of, Sarah made another pass around the room, peeking under the bed and the couch, and back into the closet, and through the bathroom drawers and under the sink, and then went to stand by the side of the bed, looking down at Devon. She rested her hands on her hips and tried to commit every line of his face to memory. She was particularly fond of that corded muscle that ran the length of his neck. And that jawbone. She finally worked up the courage to touch him, giving him a gentle prod on his strong, bare shoulder.

He grunted.

Sarah smiled and gave him another jab on the upper arm.

Nothing.

She looked down at the bedside table and saw the enormous, flopping peony sitting there, picked it up, dried off the dripping wet stem with the edge of the sheet, then proceeded to trail it provocatively along that muscle on his neck, then along the firm line of his jaw, then across his brow. He was starting to smile, a very happy grin indeed. She was going to be traveling all day and she didn't want to mess up her hair and makeup, but she couldn't resist one final kiss. She put the flower back down on the table and turned back to see Devon just coming awake.

"What are you doing?" He looked disoriented and a little concerned, worried even.

"I am… I was about to kiss you good-bye."

"Where are you going?" His hand was reaching up to pet her cheek, and his voice had an alluring roughness.

"I'm flying back to Chicago. I split my time between there and New York, usually two to three weeks in each place, then back again. I have meetings at my headquarters in Chicago the rest of this week. I've already been here a week, looking at properties in London, and I have a board meeting the week after next—"

"I mean, when am I going to see you again?"

Sarah's eyes held his. "Don't do that." She started to turn away from the bed, but he grabbed her wrist.

"I mean it." He was starting to come fully awake now and his grip was rather strong against her skin.

"So do I," said Sarah, pulling her hand away impatiently as she turned toward the window. "Please don't pretend this was anything more than a fling…" She turned back to face him, her arms crossed over her chest, and gave a small smile. "An utterly delightful, fabulously sexy, wonderful fling."

Sarah girded herself. She was in full battle regalia: long, blond hair no-nonsense straight; pristine ivory Akris jacket with high collar; perfectly tailored wool trousers; big gold hoop earrings paired with her mother's chunky gold charm bracelet; and her favorite Sarah James caramel suede ankle boots. She was armed.

"Let's just let it stay that way. Okay?"

Devon tried to entertain the very unfamiliar notion that he was not getting his own way. He was speechless.

"All right then," she said, taking his silence for tacit agreement and letting her hands drop to her sides. Her palms began to pat the sides of her legs in an impatient gesture. He thought for a split second that she might reach out to shake his hand, then he started laughing so hard, he couldn't stop.

She looked at him, then toward the door.

"Were you about to shake my hand?" he wheezed, then rolled back onto the bed, facedown, and let his laughter be absorbed by the deep, down pillow. He came up for air and she was all business again, arms crossed, toe tapping. "Priceless!" His face fell into the pillow again, his laughter vibrating through the mattress.

He finally composed himself and turned back to face her, mirth still sparkling in his eyes, resting on his elbows. Sarah tried to look away; it wasn't really fair of him to flex his back muscles like that, with all that turning and stretching.

"You are stupendous," he said, shaking his head in amazement. Then his voice switched to a fairly good imitation of an American drawl. "All righty then! I'll see ya when I see ya!" He gave her a little wave, like you would give a small child who had come down from the nursery and disturbed a grown-up dinner party. "Off you go!" He was about to burst out laughing again but was somehow able to hold it in.

She came toward the bed, leaned down, and kissed him on the cheek, then pulled away slowly, trying to get one more inhale of the delicious sleepy smell of him. "You are really something, Lord Devon Heyworth. Take care," she added with a curious smile, then left the room still shaking her head in tiny left-right motions.

Devon flipped onto his back and spread out in the big warm bed with a huge smile across his face. "If that was just a fling, then I'm off my chump," he muttered and then fell promptly back to sleep.

———

A few minutes later, Sarah spotted Jane and Nelson in the conservatory downstairs having their breakfast. She made her way over to their table and sat down at one of the two empty seats.

"Did you all have a pleasant evening?" she asked.

Jane put down her coffee cup and widened her eyes in anticipation. "We did. We had a delightful dinner here at the hotel. But how was the wedding? Any star sightings?"

"There were a few royal types, of course, but I didn't really get too close. James Mowbray was there, so I got to talk to him about his business plan for their store opening in the States, and other—"

"But were there any handsome *rakes*? Any dashing viscounts or *earls*?" Jane smiled. Nelson frowned and went back to reading his paper. Clearly, he had not shared with Jane his unintended intrusion into Sarah's love life yesterday morning. The only silver lining of that debacle would have been Jane's relief that, perhaps, Sarah was not destined to be a shriveled old maid after all.

"Um, yes, there were quite a few. I danced the night away." Sarah smiled at the waiter as he finished pouring her coffee; she added cream, then continued talking to her stepmother. "But, alas, back to my labors for this Cinderella."

"Oh, dear. You have so much ambition. You are so *committed*." Jane meant well, or at least she did her best to appear to mean well, but Sarah couldn't help feeling that her stepmother would have preferred a different sort of stepdaughter. Maybe one who spent long days at the spa. And even more hours than that at the gym. Neither of those things were ever going to happen.

The one time that Sarah had attempted a "spa" vacation with

Jane, it turned out to be a starvation and military boot camp falsely advertised as a wholesome, serene retreat in the mountains of central California. Instead of massages and mojitos, the menu included hot yoga and high colonics. Sarah ended up sneaking off the property for wine and chocolate to supplement the sprouts and leaves that were supposed to pass for food. She also brazenly slept through two of the "recommended" morning hikes, which Sarah referred to as forced marches. Not surprisingly, Jane did not find Sarah's attempt at exercise humor in the least amusing. Exercise was not a laughing matter.

"I do love my job." Sarah smiled back, choosing to ignore the implied double meaning of *committed*. Obviously, Jane James would consider it psychotic to work sixteen hours a day when the proverbial coffers were already full to bursting. In that way (only), she was quite like Sarah's grandmother, Letitia.

Unfortunately, Jane was feeling particularly generous with her opinions this morning. "I know you love it, Sarah, but maybe you should take a little break. You are such a lovely girl, and with just a tiny bit of exercise and—"

Nelson shook his newspaper; it could have been to straighten a page, or it could have been a precursor to saying something.

Jane hesitated before continuing. "Well, maybe, I just thought if you ever want to meet with my trainer in Chicago or let me introduce you to some of the handsome young men—"

Nelson cleared his throat: again, could have been food, could have been a warning salvo.

Jane paused again, then patted Sarah's hand for good measure. "You are a lovely girl."

And what was she supposed to say to that? Yes, you're right, I am lovely!? What she wanted to say was: *There is a smoking hot, totally satisfied, blindingly handsome young man up there in my hotel room, you emaciated Second Wife, you! My extra inches didn't seem to bother him in the slightest!*

But.

That would have been petty.

"Thank you, Jane. And I'd love to meet any handsome young men you might have in mind in Chicago. I think I might stay for a couple of weeks this time, so just let me know and I'll give them a call—"

"Oh, dear, of course you wouldn't have to initiate such a thing. I will call Tina Ballard and Monica Schuller and you will have a string of dates lined up before we land."

"Well, I don't need a string, Jane. One or two would be nice while I'm in town. Just the cream of the crop." Sarah tried to give that last a hint of conspiratorial fervor, some approximation of a colluding mother-daughter grin. Maybe if she got Jane on the man hunt, she'd get off the Sarah-makeover bandwagon.

Nelson James folded his newspaper with precise finality and looked across the table at his wife and his daughter. And all he could think was: night and day.

"All righty then!"

Sarah almost spit her coffee out of her mouth—her father's American accent sounded identical to Devon's parody of a few minutes before.

"What's so funny?"

"Oh, nothing. Something about that expression just reminds me of a funny story. Someone at the party last night… never mind. The Brits have such a dry sense of humor, don't you think?"

Nelson looked at Sarah and narrowed his gaze as if to say: I do not want to know. "Shall we get going?" Nelson was up and out of his chair before he finished the sentence, not expecting a response.

Their luggage had been sent ahead in one of the hotel Range Rovers, and the unlikely trio left the country house hotel amid a flurry of good-byes and thank-yous to the very kind staff. Sarah surreptitiously palmed an overgenerous tip into the hand of the bellman who had been saddled with moving her steamer trunks, his returning glance confirming her unspoken implication that it was really hush money about the guest who remained in her room.

Sarah tried to see her odd little family through the bellman's eyes, the three of them as different from one another as possible. Nelson James had gone totally gray after the death of his first wife. It had aged him considerably at the time, but now that he was in his late sixties, he looked remarkably young. He had always adhered to a well-tailored, if nondescript, fashion sense: blue blazers, khakis, and Belgian loafers on weekends; single vent suits (navy or gray, no stripe), white Oxford shirt, and wingtips during the week.

Jane was a very tidy fifty-five. She kept her hair in a jet-black Coco Chanel cut (she traveled with a pair of professional haircutting scissors to trim the rare, unruly wisp) and always wore clothes that were one shade too bright. She had once commented to Sarah that having such dark hair allowed her to wear such a wonderful array of colors. Sarah wanted to let her know that just because she was allowed to did not mean she should.

Today she had on a blinding, lemon-yellow leather jacket that was, not pleasantly, reminiscent of Claude Montana circa 1985. It was probably vintage and fabulously expensive, but it looked a bit too young on Jane. She paired it with a black leather miniskirt, opaque black tights, and black suede pumps. She looked like a tiny, well-kept bumblebee.

Sarah always felt too large around her. Even if she were to lose the supposed twenty pounds that would make her *fabulous* in Jane's eyes, Sarah was certain her very bones were simply too big for Jane's taste. Jane was a bird; Sarah was, well, a mammal, at least.

The trio traveled in the hired limousine to the private airfield where Nelson James's G6 private jet was fueled and ready for takeoff. Sarah thought the driver looked familiar, but she tried not to make eye contact, fearing he'd start up a conversation regarding late-night, nonsolitary transportation from one local landmark to another. She took out her iPad and scrolled through the news, answered a couple of emails, and put it back in her slim bag. She looked up when she realized her father was looking at her across the rear-facing seat of the limo.

"What?" she asked.

"Nothing. Just another generation, I suppose. Always distracted by the latest thing. Willing to spend $2,000 for a pair of shoes." He shrugged and looked out the window.

Sarah took a deep breath and tried not to care.

"But," Nelson said, turning back to face her, "I guess if you are the one selling them and not buying them, I shouldn't be too concerned by your folly."

Refusing to be drawn into the same argument that had boiled between them for years—that high-end shoes were at best absurd and at worst obscene—Sarah refrained from pointing out that his wife Jane was in possession of *many* pairs of $2,000 shoes that Nelson had, in effect, purchased. Instead, she shook her head and looked out at the passing scenery, realizing that the large pile on the distant rise was Dunlear Castle. Bronte and Max were actually married. Maybe Sarah would visit them the next time she was back in London.

Maybe she'd see Devon.

Her cheeks went inexplicably red at the thought and Jane, ever observant, asked if she was having a relapse of the rosacea incident that had plagued her when she'd returned to Chicago from France.

"No, I'm fine, thanks. It's probably just the wool in this jacket. I should be more careful." Sarah tugged at the high collar, as if it were the culprit, and wondered if the so-called free ride on her father's private plane was worth eight hours of intense observation and parental scrutiny.

She thought not.

Nor did she have the heart to tell her stepmother that the rosacea of three years ago was brought on by the fact that her father had somehow forgotten to mention that he'd married Jane while his only daughter was living in Paris with her grandmother. So, when she returned to Chicago, ready to take the city by storm with her avant-garde shoe designs and shrewd business plan—and to shake the need for (or obtain) her father's approval once and for all—Sarah was momentarily overwhelmed by the unforeseen existence of Dear Jane. Once the reality of said stepmother was acknowledged, contemplated, and digested, said rosacea was no longer in evidence and never returned.

While the whole "rosacea incident" had been a nightmare at the time, it had also taught Sarah the valuable lesson that her body was not, as she had so often treated it, a separate entity from (nor mere vessel for) her constantly clicking mind. After her frisky weekend in England, she was worried the pendulum might have swung in the opposite direction altogether: she was starting to suspect that her brain might be taking a backseat to the demands of her treacherous, awakening body. She shook off the thought just as the Range Rover arrived on the tarmac and spent the rest of the trip in deep preparations for her upcoming board meeting and expansion plans.

——⁓⁓⁓——

Devon slept for a while longer, surrounded by the pleasant scents of Sarah's perfume happily interwoven with the mingling aroma of the large floral arrangement he'd sent over the day before. He finally got out of bed around ten, foregoing the shower since he'd have to get back into his day-old clothes anyway. He called down to the front desk to see if there might be a car available, momentarily cursing Sarah's foolishness about not wanting his car parked in the hotel parking lot. He knew he was going to be the brunt of Max's jokes when he returned to Dunlear in the Amberley Castle Hotel limousine. Luckily, the more rugged Range Rover was the first car to hand, and Devon was able to make his drive of shame in relative peace with the local gamekeeper from the Castle Hotel's falconry school as his chauffeur.

Unfortunately, he didn't make it up the back stairs fast enough, and Max and Bronte called him into the morning room when they caught sight of his retreating form silhouetted in the far door frame.

"Trying to sneak past us, are you?"

He turned reluctantly back. "Aren't you two supposed to be on your honeymoon or something?" Devon walked into the room with trepidation; he looked well used.

His sister Abby was sitting at the other end of the table, and she smiled at his ridiculous appearance when she looked up from the newspaper. She raised her coffee cup and gave Devon a wink.

"Our flight leaves from Heathrow at two o'clock. We didn't want to have to rush out at some ungodly hour of the morning." Max looked him up and down. "Have you been out for a morning stroll?"

Devon could do nothing but smirk his silent reply since he was wearing his formal jacket and trousers from the night before, with his pleated white dress shirt wrinkled and untucked, and his hair looking like he had combed it with a nearby fire iron. "Very funny."

"You might as well join us." Max gestured for Devon to take a seat.

He reluctantly complied, dreading his older brother's inquisition and his younger sister's ridicule.

Max launched at him first. "We don't have that much time before we go and we'd love to hear how you enjoyed the… wedding. What was the holdup with the rings, by the way?" Max had been spreading orange marmalade on his scone while he was talking and proceeded to put a piece in his mouth as he waited for Devon's reply.

"Yeah, Dev," Abby ribbed him, "what was the *holdup*?"

"No holdup." Devon had taken a seat a few places down from his brother and stretched his arm out casually across the back of the empty chair next to him that separated him from Abby. It was like a goddamned interrogation. "I was just distracted. I mean, I'm sure all that religious toing and froing was meaningful, but I just sort of spaced out, I guess, and then you were standing there and, well, it wasn't *egregious*, was it?"

Bronte had been unaccountably quiet, sitting far too close to her *husband* (she loved saying it over and over) and letting her left hand rest on his thigh. She was like an adoring concubine, for goodness' sake.

"Did you and Sarah hit it off?" Bronte asked idly, managing to tear herself away from lusting after her *husband* long enough to procure a little gossip on behalf of her friend.

Both men looked at her as if she had two heads.

"Why are you looking at me like that?" she asked, all innocence.

Max just shook his head and smiled. "What can I say, Dev? She's direct. So, did you and Miss James *hit it*?"

"'Hit it *off*,' you fool. Not 'hit it!'" Bronte grabbed Max's thigh harder under the table and he gave her a quick smile in return.

Devon saw his exit. "If you two are going to coo all over each other and grope under the table—"

"It is rather disgusting to see them being such a couple all the time," Abby said from behind her newspaper.

Devon tried to turn the tables. "Speaking of couples, where's Tully, anyway?"

Abby lowered the newspaper enough to see Devon across the top. "She left early this morning. Something about another oil spill in Russia."

Devon rolled his eyes.

Abby shook the paper. "You know, I should really defend her, but I have to confess I'm growing a bit tired of all her saving-the-world." Abby shrugged. "But what am I supposed to do? Baby. Bathwater. And all that. I'm on my way back up to Findhorn to meet up with her in a couple of days. Mother wants me to come to London for some reason, so I thought I'd try to be *obedient*." Abby gave Devon a look that said, in other words, she was going to try to be more of a kiss-ass like he was.

"Shit. Is she still here?" Devon rose off his seat slightly and looked around into the hall, fearing that his mother was about to make an entrance.

Bronte laughed. "She's just now finished punishing the caterers and informing the party planners where they fell short and has headed back into town. I had the pleasure of her company for a full thirty minutes. Apparently, the ways of packing are mysterious and riddled with pitfalls. I had to be schooled. You can thank me later for throwing her off your scent."

"Thanks, Bron. I don't think I could have handled her just now."

Putting the newspaper all the way down, Abby looked at Devon and shook her head. "What does Mother have on you, anyway? You are such a patsy."

"Oh, cut it out, Abs. I just like to keep the peace and you like to stir the shit. That's how it's always been. That's how it'll always be."

Max and Bronte watched the exchange like a tennis match, popping bits of scone and sips of coffee into their mouths between volleys.

Abby tried to stare Devon down, then, finding it impossible, finally conceded. "Oh. Fine. You keep keeping the peace and I'll keep stirring the shit."

"Are you two finished bickering?" Max asked.

"Are you two finished groping?" Devon sniped.

Bronte let her hands fly up, as if she were in a holdup, and said, "Look! No groping. So quit stalling and let me know what you think of Sarah."

Devon shook the flop of hair out of his eyes and looked out the window for a few seconds. "I think quite a lot of her, but she doesn't seem to think much of me. I don't think I've been so summarily dismissed since, well, since ever. But this entire conversation is ungentlemanly in the extreme and I will not—"

Abby gave a low hoot. "Someone has dared to dismiss The Earl?!"

The other three started laughing and Devon pursed his lips.

"What?!" Abby ribbed him. "You started it." She went back to reading the paper and muttered, "Mr. I'm-not-an-earl-earl. What an idiot."

"Devon!" Bronte cried, wanting more gossip. "Ignore her! It's me, Bronte… hello?! Are you kidding me? I've seen you hit on every woman from chef to chauffeur—chauffeuse?" She turned to Max with a questioning look. "And now you're going to pretend you're feeling high-minded about giving me the goods on Sarah—"

"It was just a fling. Don't push it, Bron." Devon tried to keep his tone light, but the edge of something sharper came through. "No big deal," he said, softer.

Abby looked at Bronte across the long table and raised an eyebrow.

"Oh, okay. Okay," Bronte said. "No need to get prickly. We're all grown-ups. Well, I'm not, but apparently you are suddenly keen to try it. No fun." She pouted and went back to staring at her *husband* again.

Devon rose to take his leave.

"I'll leave you two newlyweds to your… whatever it is you see in each other." He gave Bronte a friendly wink and made for the door back to the kitchen. "Have fun in London, Abs. Call if you want to meet up for a restorative drink after Mother rakes you over the coals."

Abby hummed her agreement and kept reading.

"Hold up a minute, Dev." Max had been saying something quietly to Bronte before calling out to his brother across the room.

"What is it?" Devon turned, one hand resting on the doorknob, and girded himself for more sibling razzing.

"We wanted you two to be the first to know that Bronte is expecting."

Devon stared, in shock. The dumb, gaping look made his face appear exactly as it had when he was eight years old and lost the fishing lure (again) and had to get Max to set up a new line, a new hook, and a new worm. Max never seemed to mind. He was patient about things like that.

"Wow. Since last night? That was fast," Abby said with a mischievous gleam in her eye.

"Not quite so fast." Bronte looked at her with a hint of a guilty grin.

Devon was striding back to congratulate them, giving his brother a firm shake with one hand and half hug with the other, then lifting Bron up out of her chair and spinning her around in his arms. "Well done, you. I'm going to be an uncle!"

"You're already an uncle," Max pointed out dryly.

"Oh, Lydia doesn't count!" He waved his hand to dismiss his sister Claire's eighteen-year-old pain-in-the-ass daughter.

"Not just an uncle… a godfather, we hope?" Bronte looked wide-eyed and particularly fetching in her creamy white travel suit—did all these American women have to be so spotlessly put together?—and Devon had a momentary flashback of Sarah standing by the bed earlier that morning.

"Of course, godfather at the ready." He gave a mock salute and hugged her a second time. "Congratulations again. I guess since I am the first to know, you won't be spreading the happy news just yet?"

Bronte looked at Max for guidance.

Abby started to laugh. "Are you actually deferring to Max? This is hilarious! One day of marriage and you're already the little lady! Classic!"

Bronte smiled at herself, then at Devon and Abby. "You know what they say: love's a bitch."

"I wouldn't know!" Devon said, with far more conviction in his voice than he felt, then bid them all good-bye and rushed off to clean up before the newlyweds left for good.

"Congratulations, Bron." Abby had come down the length of the table and hugged her sister-in-law and brother. "I'm so happy for you."

"Can't say it was really all my doing." Bronte smiled.

Abby waved her off. "I don't need any gory details. But when are you due?"

The two women were sitting back down at the end of the table, while Max stayed standing. "Bron, I'm going to run upstairs and make sure I've got everything in the bag. You want to hang with Ab?"

She looked up at her glorious *husband* and nodded yes. "Do you mind?"

"I think I'll survive without you for the next twenty minutes." He reached out to touch her cheek. "Barely." He leaned down and kissed her quickly on the lips.

Abby looked down at her lap.

"Bye, Abs. Thanks again for being here."

"Of course." She looked up at her older brother. So precise. So happy. "I wouldn't have missed it for anything."

"Not even an oil spill?" he joked.

"Not funny. Go already."

He smiled and headed out of the small dining room.

Bronte's face turned from misty-eyed to brass tacks in a flash. "What the hell is going on with you and Tully?"

Damn it, thought Abby. She had thought she was going to make a clean getaway. "We're fine."

"No you're not," Bronte said plainly. "You looked totally annoyed with her last night, and this morning, you barely got up from the table to say good-bye."

"I put the paper down," Abby said with a guilty pick at her cuticle.

"Abby. Look at me, honey. What's going on?"

Over the past few months, Abby and Bronte had bonded quick

and close. Their shared outlaw status in the eyes of the dowager duchess threw them into one another's highest estimation.

"I don't know, Bron." Abby looked up and tried not to cry. "I just don't…" She looked away, unable to hold Bronte's look. "You and Max just look so effing happy. It's not realistic for the rest of us, you know what I mean."

Bronte grabbed her friend's hands in hers. "Abigail Heyworth. It is totally realistic. If things have cooled with you and Tully, that's just the way of it. I was so devastated when I broke up with the guy before I met Max. We can't always get it right the first time around. Tully didn't look like she was having the best time either, you know. Maybe one of you just needs to start the conversation…"

"Why does it have to be me?" Abby whined.

Bronte laughed. "Oh. Now that's a really good reason to stay in a relationship. Too lazy to break up."

Abby smiled at least.

"You'll figure it out. But you're so fabulous—"

Max's sister snorted.

"What?" Bronte barked. "You are! It's ridiculous how you play right into your mother's hand that you can't be hip and smart and gay or not or whatever you want to be. Just don't wallow, okay? It doesn't suit you."

Abby nodded. "Thanks, Bron. I'll try. But I just can't see myself telling Tully…what? *You're just not enough…* that sounds so horrible."

Bronte shrugged. "She's not enough for you. There. I said it. You need some dynamic woman who's going to make you shine like the fucking sun."

Abby laughed. "Thanks for the vote of confidence, Bron. But I don't know about that. Sounds like someone ends up burned."

Max poked his head in the small room. "You two still solving all the problems of the world?"

"I wish," Abby said. "If I have to read one more story about those women in Afghanistan, I'm going to throw up."

"Charming," Max said.

The two women stood up and Abby gave Bronte a strong hug. "Congratulations about the baby, Bron."

"Thanks, Ab." Bronte held Abby a bit away from her. "Take care of yourself, okay? You deserve every good thing."

"Car's waiting," Max prodded.

"Okay! Okay!" Bronte gave Abby one last hug and then turned to Max, and the three of them went out into the courtyard to load up the car that was taking the newlyweds to the airport.

Devon had gone up to his room to shower and change and pack. He'd left his car at Dunlear the week before, while he was in Vegas, so he could drive himself back into town. He finished collecting his things, threw his bag into the trunk of his Aston Martin, and was back in front in plenty of time to bid the happy couple farewell on their way to the airport.

There were still tons of workers breaking down all the wedding paraphernalia, hauling out rented tables, sound equipment, banquet chairs, and potted palms. Devon and Abby stood amidst the controlled chaos and watched their brother and sister-in-law—the duke and duchess, they amended—being driven down the long gravel lane.

He turned to Abby, both of them quickly ducking to avoid an eight-foot metal pole perched carelessly on a mover's shoulder.

"Party over," he said to his younger sister.

"What happened with blondie, Dev? She take a little piece of your stone-cold heart?" Abby joked as they walked across the black-and-white marble floor of the vast entry hall.

Devon became peevish. "Why does everyone keep implying I'm heartless?!"

"Whoa." Abby stopped them both at the bottom of the

red-carpeted stairs. "I never said you were heartless. It was a joke. You okay?"

He shook the flop of hair off his forehead and shoved his hands into the pockets of his beige moleskin jeans. "Yeah. I'm fine. I guess she got under my skin a bit. I'm not used to it."

"Ha!" Abby laughed. "This is going to be good." She slapped his upper arm. "I'll see you in town later this week. I have some stuff I need to do before I go." With that, she turned up the stairs and went to pack her bags.

The motorways were not crowded since it was still early in the day on Sunday, and Devon was back in town well before supper. He thought of calling round to one of his mates, but decided to pick up a curry and stay in. His flat was on the south bank of the Thames River in one of architect Daniel Russell's most famous large-scale, mixed-use, commercial-residential projects: Quayside. The open plan, ultra-modern, minimalist apartment suited Devon Heyworth perfectly. He might have been perceived as the foppish faux-earl when he was playing that part (smiling gamely for the photographers from *Hello!* or attending the infrequent royal wedding), but his real interests were far more serious, and almost entirely unknown to everyone.

Except Max.

Devon had, from a very early age, been quite adept at puzzles, codes, games of chance, and tests of logic. And while he thoroughly enjoyed playing chess or batting around financial equations with Max, he never did so with anyone else. His mother's not infrequent references to him as "the spare" had led to his deep-seated belief that any show of confidence, proficiency, or intellectual expertise on his part would lead to her version of runner-up ducal training. He had given very little thought to what he *did* want out of life, though he was quite certain about what he did *not* want: deputy duke instructions from the dowager duchess topped the list.

A woman of his mother's cunning was no fool. One did not rise to the rank of the Dowager Duchess of Northrop through sheer happenstance. Devon had to pay particular care to his tone of voice, speech, and topics whenever they spoke. She was too shrewd to overlook the slightest deception and would have picked up on the merest hint of irony. So, for as far back as Devon could recall, if his mother happened to be home from London and came upon Max and Devon discussing something esoteric, Devon would immediately leap to greet her, hoping his effusion would bar any interest she may have had in what they were talking about. His hopes were realized. A combination of her ego and his eagerness led to the unanticipated, happy coincidence that the duchess misinterpreted his very particular concealment for a very particular attention to her. As a result, she adored him unequivocally.

Claire was her first child, on whom she had lavished years of "only child" attention, imprinting her with what Devon saw as an unhealthy mix of arrogant female entitlement and piquancy. Next came Max, who was the duke. Period. Devon was her Dearest Devon. In her mind, he admired and honored her, whereas the rest of her children simply misunderstood the extent of her responsibilities. As for Abigail, well, to the Duchess of Northrop's mind, there was no accounting for Abby and her eccentricities. When asked about her wayward fourth and final child, the duchess simply smiled blandly and half-joked that she probably should have stopped at Devon.

Chapter 6

By the time he got to university, Devon had spent so much time hiding behind his false front of average intelligence at Eton that he had fooled nearly everyone. Ironically, he had inadvertently created the very role he sought to escape: he was always a very strong second.

Then, after three months at the London School of Economics (his feigned mediocrity extended to his refusal to apply to either Oxford or Cambridge, bolstered by his desire to misspend his wild youth in the heart of the capital), he slipped up. While more or less dozing through yet another mathematics lecture, he heard the professor ask a particularly easy question and, in a daze, Devon raised his hand, answered the question, and went back to doodling random calculations for the radius of a circumsphere.

The room went completely quiet.

He looked up at the professor and stopped doodling. He hated drawing attention to himself, to his academic self, and was worried he had done so. The professor put down the stylus he had been using to write on his tablet computer, which was projected on the screen in the front of the lecture hall.

"Mr…"

"Heyworth," Devon offered tentatively.

"Mr. Heyworth. Please elaborate."

"I'm sorry?"

"Very well. If you are unable to admit you just grabbed that number out of a hat, I might get on with the lecture that, some students at least, have come to hear. If you, on the other hand, would be less bored elsewhere, perhaps you should consider transferring into a more *challenging* course."

The silence was almost physically painful in Devon's ears. No one was going to step in for him. Where was Max?

He was embarrassed to admit that that was always the first thing that popped into his supposedly postadolescent mind when he felt the claustrophobia of his intelligence. The terror of discovery. Max knew how to deflect anyone.

On the other hand, Devon was not an infant, and this was a maths lecture after all. He didn't need to play the *utter* fool.

"Well, I… could you repeat the question please?" He was only stalling, of course, and it seemed this teacher was not the droning idiot Devon mistook him for.

"I think not. Explain your answer, please, Mr. Heyworth."

"Very well. For the regular tetrahedron, the formula for a solid angle at a vertex suspended by a face will, in my experience, produce steradians identical to those in the apex angles in excess of one radian. Hence, my answer was 4.735."

The rest of the students in the class looked as though they had accidentally stepped into advanced Finno-Ugric when they had, in fact, signed up for basic Spanish.

Professor Millhaus picked up his stylus, seemingly unimpressed, and returned to his podium to continue his lesson.

Devon thought he had sounded acceptably fair to middling.

"Please see me in my office after class, Mr. Heyworth. Now, back to regular tetrahedrons…"

Millhaus continued in his dull monotone, hoping against hope that this Heyworth boy might actually have a brain. Perry Millhaus had spent the past fourteen years teaching first-year mathematics to the entering marketing students who needed to fulfill their requirements before moving on to the more advanced courses. There had been bright rays of intellectual promise along the way, but most went on to acquire business degrees, and—while Perry was the last one to criticize a healthy interest in the acquisition of a tidy income—those students were not genuine mathematicians.

Those interested in pure mathematics were rare in his classroom. Millhaus had somehow spent a decade and a half of his prime years prattling on about the same bland concepts. All he had craved was a tenured position at a respected university, and that was all he got. A childhood of financial uncertainty had made him blindly committed to an adulthood of financial security. Nothing risky. Nothing daring. Just secure. And, if abject boredom was the price he had to pay, then so be it. But maybe, just maybe, the young Heyworth was more than the lazy peacock he appeared to be.

After class, Millhaus pestered Devon so mercilessly that he was finally able to crack the student's absurd attachment to feigned mediocrity. Devon and Perry hammered out a deal of sorts that gave them both a much-needed intellectual outlet. Perry was able to discuss ideas and concepts that he had no interest in broaching with his professional colleagues (faculty camaraderie was anathema to him), and Devon was able to enjoy the freedom of his own intellectual pursuits without anyone knowing. For his part, Perry promised to give Devon no grades above solid high seconds. Since neither of them had a particular care for financial gain (Perry was perfectly secure; Devon was astoundingly rich), they decided to publish all of their joint work directly and anonymously onto open source mathematical discussion boards. Ten years on, Devon and Perry still met on a monthly basis to discuss the latest mathematical conundrum, architectural puzzle, or financial observation.

After an enjoyable university career spent under the radar at LSE—not only under the radar, but usually underground at dance clubs and late-night bars—Devon met with Max to talk about what he should do next. Max had recently decided to embark upon a monstrously ambitious PhD program at the University of Chicago and voiced his wish that Devon should join him.

The laughter that constituted Devon's reply could be heard across the pub and out into the crowded mews off of Berkeley Square. Devon had absolutely no intention of entering an educational institution ever again, having just barely escaped the confines of the classroom and thus fulfilled what he understood and accepted to be his filial debt to his parents. He wanted to do something nominally sexy. He wanted to drive an obnoxiously fast car, live in an aggressively modern apartment that was *not* child-friendly, stock his wine rack with big Barolos, and shag. In reverse order.

Architecture seemed the thing.

Max smiled at his brother over the frothy top of his pint of beer. "Architecture is great. Did you think you might use your degree? Computer-aided design and all that?"

"For some reason, the ladies like architects. That was my main factor when narrowing down the field, of course—that, and what I might be able to do with the least possible effort. I just looked up sexy professions, you know, the guy most likely and all that, and the top five were athlete, fireman, doctor, architect, or model."

Max's smile encouraged Devon to elaborate.

"I'm too lazy to be a professional athlete... snooker maybe, but the hours, you know, or Formula One driving, but then there's all the expense, danger, and travel bother. Fireman... such a mess, and again, unplanned interruptions, late-night calls, going into burning buildings, and all that... I could always do a bit of volunteer fireman stuff if my magnetism starts to wane."

Max was smiling and shaking his head as he listened to his younger brother go on without a hint of irony.

"Doctor? Ridiculous... who has the time to sit through another five years of boring lectures? And again, angry sick people calling at all hours. No thanks. Model?"

Max burst out laughing and almost spit his beer across the bar.

Devon half stood up from his barstool to get a better look at himself in the angled mirror above the shelf of spirits behind the bar. "What? I'm not half bad."

"Oh, Devon." Max tried to contain his laughter. "You are a prize. Of course, you could work the runways... show me your walk!"

Devon smiled and situated himself back into his seat. "So that left architect. And, not like I am looking for a life of the mind or anything, but I thought I could do *some* mathematical or computer-related something or other without the nuisance of graduate study. Honestly, I don't know what you think you will find in Chicago, of all places. Five years of discussing *anything*, much less statistical linear and nonlinear regression analyses, sounds like a recipe for heartbreak." Devon turned to face his older brother full-on, grabbed his upper arms firmly, widened his eyes, and proclaimed theatrically, "Don't do it! Stay with me! I can't bear it!"

Two twentysomething women were walking past just then and smiled warmly at the two brothers: Max had come straight from the office and his suit jacket was slung over the back of his chair, his blue-and-white striped shirt open at the collar, dark wavy hair disheveled, gray eyes gleaming; Devon had on his perpetual uniform of a T-shirt with something ridiculous written on it (preferably provocative or meaningless or both), a perfectly worn-in pair of old blue jeans, and an alluring mop of light brown hair that always looked like it was two weeks past needing a trim and fell seductively across one eye.

Devon released his hold on his brother's upper arms, picked up his pint of lager, and raised it to the two women in mock salute. "Well, hello, ladies."

Devon glanced briefly at Max, then back at the charming little redhead who had apparently decided to stay. "My brother was just leaving, weren't you, Max?" Devon asked, without turning to look at Max. "He's moving to America to blaze his own trail, make his way in the world." Devon made a vague, broad circular gesture with his free hand. "He's a thinker."

Max took the last swig of his beer, stood up, threw his coat over one shoulder, and grabbed his briefcase from where it had been lodged between his stool and the wainscoting at the foot of the bar. "Please take my seat, Miss…?"

"Tina! I'm Tina; nice to meet you." She looked at Max for a split second then let her attention return to Devon.

"Off you go then, Max. And try to loosen up a bit, old man."

Tina climbed up onto the barstool that was still warm from where Max had been sitting, and within seconds, she and Devon were leaning toward one another and sharing humorous, probably scandalous, bon mots. Max just shook his head in wonderment and headed home to his mews house in Fulham.

Devon ended up applying for an entry-level position in the Specifications Department at the architectural firm of Russell + Partners. His grades didn't open any doors, so he had to wait a few months and call in a few favors until he was finally able to ingratiate himself with the friendly female members of the Human Resources Department. By Christmas of that year, he was gainfully employed.

Typically, the Duchess of Northrop thought the entire idea of a job that required daily attendance to the same tasks was preposterous. And it interfered with their spontaneous luncheons in town. She adored meeting her handsome son for lunch at Cipriani or Bar Boulud, then meandering around Mayfair or Chelsea arm in arm, shopping or not. Devon was attentive without being overly precise like his older brother, Max. Sylvia was finding it harder and harder to tolerate Max's inflexibility and pointed retorts. (It was obvious to Devon that Max was exerting a touch of independence, nothing more, but he knew better than to gainsay his mother.)

Now, after six years at Russell + Partners, Devon was exactly where he wanted to be professionally.

Coasting.

No one on any of the design teams ever questioned his curious working habits. He was frequently gone from the office for long stretches of time, strolling in at odd hours of the night, treating the entire office as his lower-ground-floor recreation room. When he decided to buy a flat in the same building as his office, one friend had voiced her concern that he wouldn't ever get any time away.

"All I have is time away," he replied with typical honesty (though he often purposely implied mere humor). The truth of the matter was that Devon could do the complex calculations for suspension bridges, flying buttresses, and undulating titanium fascia in very little time, and from a computer sitting in his lap, wherever that might be.

So, when he showed up, buffed and polished, at 8:00 a.m. on the Monday morning after his weekend with Sarah—*Max and Bronte's wedding weekend*, he corrected himself silently—he received the types of looks usually reserved for workers who sported yesterday's clothes, a two-day growth of beard, and mumbled a request for a spare toothbrush. When he sat down at his carrel, took out his laptop, and fired up his computer, his colleague Narinda Channar couldn't help giving a little verbal poke. "Pull an all-nighter, then, eh? Decided to come straight into the office?"

Devon looked at the attractive Indian woman and gave her as good as he got. "You were here before I was… were you shagging Russell again under the conference table?"

She smiled and went back to her own project.

The architects in the firm were divided into seven design teams, but the Specifications Department worked for all of them. At any given time, Narinda might be working on the local government regulations for the suspension bridge they were building outside of Athens or the labor negotiations for the stadium under construction in Reykjavik. She somehow managed to bend all those bureaucrats to her will. She had a sharp retention of the germane structural details of each project and was able to convey the big picture.

Devon, on the other hand, was happily entrenched in the details. The big picture was sometimes so far removed from what he was doing that he forgot about it altogether.

At work at least, he no longer gave much thought to his youthful paranoia about revealing his abilities to others. After about a year at Russell + Partners, Devon had been tapped by one of the lead architects. Michael Ryman had been commissioned to design a small museum to house an entire private collection of abstract sculptures, large-scale paintings, and a research library for all the provenance. Ryman decided to set up a small competition within the firm to see if anyone could create a structural casing that would be lightweight, reflective, and have zero variability in 120-degree heat or a 10-degree freeze.

The email announcing the contest was accidentally sent company-wide, and Devon started working on it as a game. Four days later, he had a clear idea of the chemical equations necessary, but he did not have access to a lab. He called Perry Millhaus and got the name of a scientist at the University of London, made a few calls, explained his idea, met with the professor, ran extensive tests over the following weekend, and arrived with a prototype that Monday morning.

Michael Ryman rarely stepped foot in the Specifications Department—it was seen as a necessary, but hardly creative, back office function of the business—so he was unacquainted with Devon.

"Excuse me, may I come in?" Devon asked with an attempt at respect, standing in the doorway of the senior architect's office. He thought that most of the lead architects were arrogant pricks, but if they were getting laid as much as those statistics suggested, maybe they were confident for good reason.

Ryman looked up from the paperwork he was scanning and waved Devon into his office. "Sorry, I don't remember your name."

"No worries. My name is Devon Heyworth, from the Specifications Department. Nice to meet you." Devon reached across the cluttered black desk to shake the small, bald man's hand. Ryman took it but did not invite him to sit.

"So… Devon… what brings you here?"

"Well, I saw the email about the Fullerton museum project in west Texas and I had been working on some temperature-resistant polymer alloy ideas—on my own time, I mean, well, in any case…" Devon stopped. He paused for a second, annoyed with himself for actually caring what this pompous, impolite little man thought of him.

The silence rested around them.

Then, Ryman asked Devon to close the door and take a seat.

The silence resumed. Ryman had to lift himself a few inches off his own chair to peer across his desk and down into Devon's lap to see the piece of shiny metal in his hands.

Ryman finally conceded. "Are you going to show it to me or make me beg?"

Devon smiled and handed it across the desk.

Since then, Ryman had offered Devon every possible inducement to leave the Spec Department and work full-time on his design team, but Devon always shrugged him off. He did not want to be beholden to Ryman or anyone else for that matter. Having other projects always pending was a practical and efficient way of fending off any long-term commitment to any one particular project or designer.

Narinda's voice penetrated his concentration. "Do you want me to pick up an extra sandwich for you?"

Apparently four hours had passed while he was working out the details of a plastic-infused concrete block that was being tested in Shanghai. "Sure. That'd be great. Oh, Narinda, by the way, have you ever heard of Sarah James shoes?"

Narinda smiled.

Devon noted that it wasn't even a provocative smile; it was perfectly matter-of-fact and even more seductive for being so. They'd fooled around a couple of times after the Christmas party a few years ago, but both happily agreed that office romance was for the foolish.

Narinda was no fool.

"You planning a little cross-dressing weekend out at one of your fancy house parties, then? Looking for a little stiletto to go with your strapless dress?" she taunted.

She always enjoyed ribbing him about his swanky social life, and he gave her a wink.

"Something like that," he said.

"Come on, tell me why a rake like you is interested in Sarah James? I haven't seen any in London yet, but I got my first pair when I was in L.A. a few months ago. *Très chic*. They're a bit much for the office, but I'll wear them for you some other time if you like." She winked and gave him a little curtsy. "Seriously, what about the sandwich?" She was turning back toward her desk to get her handbag, the light banter finished. He liked that about her. Fun. Then over.

"Sure, I'd love one." He handed her a fiver and returned his attention to the screen.

A few hours later, the half-eaten sandwich was sitting next to his computer and he found himself Googling Sarah James.

Narinda again. "What the hell are you doing?" she asked over his shoulder.

"I think Frank Lloyd Wright was an ass for coming up with that open-plan office scheme for SC Johnson. Mind your own business."

With one hand on Devon's shoulder, Narinda was leaning over his desk and looking at the banner of images that came up with the search. A mix of studio shots of individual shoes—including a picture of brown, suede, thigh-high boots that gave Devon an unexpected wave of pleasure—and a few headshots of a very glamorous Ms. Sarah James.

"Oooh, baby!" Narinda gave a little whistle.

"I know, right?"

"I think the boots are my favorite, maybe the fetish-y patent-leather stilettos, but if I had to choose, under duress, it would be the suede boots. Yum."

Obviously, Devon had been admiring Sarah James the Person, while Narinda had been admiring Sarah James the Product. Win-win.

"All good," Devon murmured.

Narinda wandered back to her desk and answered a call from São Paulo.

Devon clicked away from the Internet and logged into his company's high-security in-house website. He clicked on current projects, then clicked on North America, then clicked on Illinois, and then scrolled through the list of four projects that were underway there, trying to figure out a way to make his presence at one of the sites a necessity. The restoration of a midcentury glass house a few hours west of Chicago might work. They'd come upon drainage issues he could probably work on, but November in the sticks looked about as romantic as dishwater.

The next project was perfect. It was a Ryman design that had run into trouble because the rivets Michael had insisted on using were causing degradation of the original sheathing. The building was right in downtown Chicago and—if they corrected the mistake quickly and quietly—they might be able to stay on schedule and avoid the negative press that always hovered over expensive publicly funded schemes. Devon would be a prince.

"I think I have to go to Chicago."

Narinda had finished her call from Brazil and swiveled her chair to look at Devon. "Really?" she asked suspiciously. "I don't recall you ever *having* to go anywhere. Is it the Ryman rivet fiasco? You just want to go rub his face in it, I presume."

"Well, you can't blame me for trying. I told him they weren't right but he had his little vision."

Narinda could never get enough of Devon the pedantic genius. The way he said "little vision" made it sound like Ryman was a small child who had built a mediocre mud pie and not the award-winning, internationally renowned architect he was. She wished she and Devon had been able to make a go of it when they'd hooked up a few years ago, but the basic truth was that they were just too much alike: hard core realists.

"Devon, you are priceless. What else is in Chicago? I can't imagine you *inconveniencing* yourself for the very real, but small, pleasure of smacking Ryman's nose with a rolled-up newspaper. Fess up."

Devon had clicked onto the full plans for the project and was already making mental calculations for the new, nonferrous, precision-turned screws that should have been used in the first place. Narinda knew better than to try to continue the conversation. Once Devon was running analytical comparisons, he could be mentally AWOL for hours.

———

The private plane began to make its descent into Chicago. Sarah looked through the small oval window and felt the familiar kick of excitement when she saw the Sears Tower and John Hancock rise like the Tetons at the edge of Lake Michigan. It was late afternoon and the early winter sun cast a magical golden glow across the city skyline. It felt like home.

When she had first decided to put her flagship store in Chicago, Sarah had never imagined that it would end up in her mother's nineteenth-century town house. Some of Sarah's fondest childhood memories were the mother-daughter weekends the two of them would spend Christmas shopping or going to the theater and then enjoying high tea at the Drake. After, they would spend those nights in the elegant, precious jewel box on Oak Street. Other than those occasional holiday visits, however, the building had really been more of a museum than a home, especially in the years following Elizabeth's death.

After looking at every possible space from modern to historic while she was scouting for a location for her first store, Sarah finally realized she was living right on top of the best option. Just before her father had married Jane, he had transferred all of Elizabeth James's former assets into a trust for Sarah, including the town house on Oak Street that had been a wedding present to Elizabeth from her eccentric mother, Letitia.

Even then, Sarah's grandmother, Letitia Vorstadt Pennington Fournier, had been… formidable. The town house was clearly designed for a single woman, a fact that Letitia never denied. It was not a wedding present that celebrated marriage, but rather, one that offered a wife refuge from matrimony. Spindly, feminine French antiques. Impractical silk wallpaper. Over-the-top chandeliers and satin curtains. A narrow double bed. The message was loud and clear: this is *Elizabeth's* wedding present, *not* Nelson and Elizabeth's wedding present. Letitia had never disapproved of Nelson exactly—he was too upstanding to be disapproved of in any case—it was just that Letitia painted life in bold, independent strokes and she regretted that her daughter had chosen such a conservative, predictable man.

A few years after Elizabeth married Nelson, the recently widowed Letitia sallied off and married a Frenchman she'd met a month before on a beach near Cannes. Sarah was still very young at the time, but she had a vivid memory of sitting on her mother's enormous bed (especially vast and mysterious to her little girl eyes), listening to her very practical mother argue with her very *impractical* grandmother. In Sarah's squirmy four-year-old mind—the sweet pale scent of her mother's sheets, the cool feel of her mother's hand trailing absently along her small child's back while she talked on the phone, Sarah playing with the big, chunky gold charm bracelet that always signaled Elizabeth James's arrival into any room—these morsels of remembrance were just as lasting as the words that were being barked across the Atlantic cable. Words from daughter to mother instead of the other way around, words like *infantile*, *immature*, and *foolish*, and phrases like *midlife crisis* and *fortune hunter*.

Elizabeth Pennington James had never understood that her idea of immaturity—frivolity—was her mother Letitia's idea of blessed social liberty.

Jacques Fournier may or may not have been a fortune hunter, but it didn't seem to matter, seeing as Letitia had many, *many* fortunes, more than enough to satisfy even the most avid hunter. More to the point, none of the said millions seemed to hold Jacques's interest nearly as much as the particular angle of Letitia's neck or the color of her hair when the sun set over their villa in Cap Ferrat. He was an artist, a bohemian, and a fantastic cook. Letitia used to infuriate Elizabeth by joking that she would give Jacques at least one of her fortunes for his *salade Niçoise* alone.

That summer when she had been trying to escape her father— and the memory of her mother, if she was being honest—Sarah spent three months in the south of France in Letitia and Jacques's enchanting company. After many weeks lounging under their shady veranda humming mashed-up Joni Mitchell lyrics about red dirt roads and people reading *Rolling Stone* and *Vogue*, the sixteen-year-old Sarah decided she had no desire to return to Lake Forest to finish up high school. In fact, she decided firmly, she had no desire to finish up high school anywhere. But on that point, at least, her father took a tangential stand and informed Letitia that some sort of American school, tutor, or correspondence class was required.

Sarah and her grandmother returned to the Fourniers'—well, the Vorstadts' really, since Letitia's father had won it in a card game on the *Lusitania*'s maiden voyage in 1907—glamorous, palatial apartment on the Île Saint-Louis in Paris. With a few brisk phone calls in Letitia's hilarious French (she probably knew almost every word in the Gallic language yet persisted in pronouncing it like the Boston Brahmin she was... *manger* came out like MAN-jay), her grandmother succeeded in securing Sarah a place at an international baccalaureate school in Paris.

Much later in life, Sarah came to the conclusion that the disastrous accent was Letitia's personal act of daily defiance. If all these French women could speak English *wiss zee* sexy *leetle* accent, then she was going to speak French in a way that let them know she was a sensational, independent American woman of a certain age.

Letitia winked at Sarah as she agreed with easy assurances to Nelson James's vague demands on behalf of his only daughter's high school graduation requirements.

"Fine, Nelson. She will be returned to you in June of next year with a *diplôme* and a smile."

"Letitia. Please, try to listen to me. She has two years of high school yet." Sarah could hear her father's voice booming through the receiver from where she sat next to Letitia.

"Surely not. She's a grown woman, Nelson. Open your eyes."

Sarah gave her grandmother a grateful smile and thought, *Good luck getting him to look at me anytime soon.*

"I do not make the educational requirements for the State of Illinois, *Letitia*," he continued pedantically. "She has two years to go."

"And I will not adhere to arbitrary miscellany, *Nelson*. She will be properly educated, she will receive her *diplôme*, and she will make her debut here in Paris. Seventeen is more than old enough to be finished with all of that academic foolishness. I met Elizabeth's father when I was seventeen, come to think of it. Granted, we didn't get married for several—"

"All right, all right. In the meantime, I'll try to come over at Christmas, but it's been pretty busy..."

Letitia let the poor man rattle on about how busy he was and gave her beautiful, sad, lonely granddaughter a conspiratorial eye roll as she pulled the telephone receiver away from her ear and mouthed a silent pantomime of blah-blah-blah to Sarah.

"Sounds lovely, Nelson. Please do come at Christmas. That would be divine. I think we are going to Fiesole, but I'll let you know." She paused to let him interject something urgent of no particular consequence that would excuse him from further conversation, then Letitia interrupted him with a brisk, "Of course, of course. Good-bye, Nelson."

She put the phone back in its cradle and looked across the Louis XV living room. The afternoon light from the Seine shed that inimitable iridescent Parisian glow across the grand, fresco-paneled ceiling. Letitia never failed to take an extra moment to appreciate that.

"Look at the light off the river, Sarah," Letitia ordered. "I don't want you to become spoiled, so always take a moment to be grateful for things like that."

Sarah was sitting casually in a priceless armchair that was upholstered in a priceless tapestry, one careless adolescent leg slung across the frail armrest. Lounging around in T-shirts and shorts in the south of France was one thing, but now that they had returned to Paris, Letitia realized, a shopping spree was the first item of business.

"Take your leg off the arm of the *Louis Quinze* chair, Sarah. *Maintenant.*" She snapped her fingers twice.

For the past three months, her grandmother had not made a single demand of Sarah. She had slept as late as she wanted; had eaten, or not eaten, as much as she wanted; had listened to her music with her headphones and spaced out and stared at the Mediterranean for as long as she wanted; and she'd read and read and read as many books as she wanted.

"Vacation is over!" Letitia proclaimed.

And that, as they say, was the end of that. Sarah moved into a *chambre de bonne*—one of the former maid's quarters—above her grandmother's apartment. It was a tiny two-room unit that over-looked the rooftops of the island in the middle of the river, in the middle of the city, in the middle of the world. It was almost pain-fully charming. The church bells chimed on cue. The angry building concierge snarled at her husband each morning while she swept the courtyard with brisk, efficient strokes of the broom.

Sarah began each day having breakfast with her grandmother and Jacques, then walked the two miles to school, reveling in her new wardrobe, her new shoes, her new *self*. It turned out that her grandmother's version of a shopping spree had been utterly unlike the tortured journeys of the same name she had taken with her father.

Letitia Vorstadt Pennington Fournier knew how to *shop*.

"For better or for worse, you have inherited your figure from your father's side of the family. Generations of Midwestern Gibson Girls. We'll have to proceed accordingly."

Sarah looked down at her flabby body with dismay.

"Why are you pouting? Women pay top dollar for what you have in abundance for free. You just need to learn how to carry it. Come with me."

All of this painfully private conversation was taking place, *alto voce*, in the middle of the main floor of Galeries Lafayette. Sarah tried to "carry it" in some new way, then followed in lockstep behind her very motivated grandmother. Letitia moved through the store with military force, having to forego some of her own favorite design-ers (lanky, tubular classics like Mary McFadden, Halston, and Bob Mackey) in deference to the reality of Sarah's zaftig figure.

To be sure, Letitia was throwing around the credit card (actually leaving it and walking away several times, easily distracted by some shiny, new thing, only to have the breathless attendant trailing after her to return it), but it wasn't just the massive cash infusion that motivated the salesladies. These people seemed genuinely delighted with transforming Sarah's appearance.

Her French was still pretty weak since she had—she now realized—squandered her time on the Cote d'Azur doing nothing more than sitting by the pool listening to American music and reading American books, but she could pick up enough to know that perhaps *skeleton* was not the only option when it came to feminine beauty. The clothes were beautifully made, perfectly tailored—and Sarah was no stranger to beautiful clothes after all the years she'd spent in her father's department store. But for some reason, some very obvious reasons, her father had never gone in for *haute couture*. Sarah was his little girl. End of story.

This was something else entirely. Sarah thought she was in love. The silky tops against her skin, the warm cashmeres around her neck, the fine drape of a light wool peacoat. And lots of miraculous jeans that somehow managed to firm up—or at least contain—her unavoidably round posterior. The textures, the colors, the weight and sheen of all the different fabrics left Sarah feeling sensually excited. Not aroused, just hyperaware of all the luxurious and sultry pleasures that one could derive from beautiful clothes.

And then she saw the shoes.

It was one of those peculiar moments that fizzled and popped, then stopped altogether. Then—after that cosmic pause—everything rushed back into the fast-paced, blood-speeding present. Of course she'd passed through the shoe department at Simpson-James forever. Practical pumps. Ladies' loafers with little bows or buckles on them. Accommodating salesmen with tools to measure and fit a comfortable pair of well-made necessities.

This was something from another realm.

The shoe department at Galeries Lafayette was more like the Temple Mount: a holy crossroads, a multicultural shrine to one of humanity's great foibles. Namely, women's shoes. It was not only vast, at a mind-boggling thirty-four thousand square feet, but it was also laid out—centrally, majestically—beneath the famous landmark Art Deco dome soaring overhead. These people had their priorities straight.

She might have had a brief fling with those bits of silk and cashmere against the tender skin of her neck, but when she slipped into her first pair of four-inch Christian Louboutins, Sarah was madly, butterflies-in-her-stomach, passionately in love. Letitia finally had to rein her in at her fourth pair.

Much to Letitia's consternation, it didn't continue as a healthy acquisitional pastime. Sarah's burgeoning obsession with cobblery quickly escalated to the level of an astute collector. A connoisseur. She became like a glutton who needed to know everything there was to know about the history, design, color, heels, insteps, shanks, buckles, and soles of the lowly shoe. She spent all of her after-school hours feeding her imagination in the archives of *Les Arts Decoratifs*, a division of the Louvre that housed an entire collection about the history of fashion and design. Ultimately, Sarah applied for and won a coveted internship at Christian Louboutin's atelier.

"It sounds as though you are *employed* and that is just *too* much," Letitia despaired one afternoon in February over her glass of Marie Brizard anisette. "You don't need the money... and... and you should be studying."

"Nice try, Letty. You have no interest in my studies—nor do I, for that matter—and, God forbid, yes, I may want to *work*." Her enthusiasm sped up her words.

Letitia cringed at the word and pursed her lips. "*Work*. Just the sound of it." She shivered.

"It's so satisfying. I mean, don't you ever want to dump everything you have into a project and put it out there for the whole world to try—whether they love it or hate it or ignore it—it doesn't even matter? Just the fact that you just have to *do* it?"

"Sounds ghastly. I would much rather have an enormous party on a stupendous yacht and make sure everyone has the best time they've ever had. All this talk of products, it just sounds so *prosaic*. But, as we used to tell your mother, she married into trade. You must have inherited that from your father."

"I know you mean that in the nicest possible way."

"Of course, dear. I suppose I was never inclined to inconvenience myself in that way. But, if that is how you choose to spend your time, then very well."

Sarah smiled and started to leave the cozy library where she had been talking with Letitia and Jacques after dinner.

"But Sarah, what about boys?"

Sarah turned back, amused at her grandmother's disjointed, but predictable, train of thought. "What about them?"

"You do *like* them, don't you?"

How difficult did she want to make this for the poor woman? She answered slowly, as if speaking to a foreigner. "Yes. Letitia. I. Like. Boys. But..." Then continuing at a rapid clip: "I am not going to wait around for some fast-talking smoothie to sweep me off my feet. I am the last person who needs rescuing. But thanks for asking."

That Christmas, Letitia got her wish and planned the best party of the season. Nelson James was able to make the trip to Europe after all, and he was there to dance with Sarah at her debutante ball. The cotillion was a crush of strangers from the European demimonde of deposed monarchs and generations of their offspring. Sarah was escorted by the painfully shy Christophe de Villiers, a perfectly nice nephew of one of her grandmother's perfectly nice friends. She danced the dance, made her bow, had a few glasses of champagne, and then counted the hours until she could get back to her drafting table at Louboutin's studio. After she got her diploma at the age of seventeen, Sarah was promoted to a full-time position and worked in each of the departments at Louboutin, from corporate to distribution and creative. She had found her passion.

On the rare occasions when she wondered about her lack of

age-appropriate lust, she merely rationalized that she was a late bloomer. She tried kissing a couple of times—one particularly adept middle-aged Frenchman came pleasantly to mind. But anything beyond that—anything resembling *pawing*—always felt rather robotic. Disjointed. *The right man would come along*, she told herself. Plenty of other things to keep one busy. Et cetera. Et cetera.

So her summer in France had somehow turned into five years of intense experience. At the age of twenty-one, she was back in Chicago opening her tiny boutique on Oak Street. Then she met Bronte, who helped her launch the second store in New York two years later.

In the midst of all that, men just weren't on her radar.

Sarah looked up and realized her father's chauffeur was pulling up in front of the Oak Street town house. Nelson and Jane had taken another car back to their home in Lake Forest after they'd landed at the private airfield near O'Hare.

"Thanks, Gus." Sarah let herself out of the back of the car and apologized to the driver for her obscenely large steamer trunks.

She opened the door to the shop and let them both in. The ground floor was the store, with a small manager's office, tiny kitchen, and large inventory storage on the east side of the building; the second floor was a private atelier and workspace for Sarah, a desk for her Chicago assistant, Stephanie Newman, and another office for her executive vice president, Carrie Schmidt.

The third and fourth floors were her elegant, out-of-this-world haven. The French antiques that she adored from her early childhood memories with her mother were scattered around the room; the walls were papered in a custom de Gournay chinoiserie. The place was hideously over-the-top and she rarely had anyone over, but it was a connection to her mother and she treasured it for that reason above everything else.

She listened guiltily as the chauffeur lugged the three enormous steamer trunks up all three flights. At some point, she was going to have to join the modern age and purchase a wheelie bag, but it just sounded so grim. Even the words: wheelie bag. No romance. No shipboard entanglements. No style. One day, she might be willing to give up that fantasy. Until then, she would cling to her impractical vintage trunks and think of her mother.

It was nearing dusk on Sunday and the place was dead quiet. Stopping in the airy white marble kitchen that overlooked the back of the town house, Sarah made a mental note to thank her assistant for stacking her mail neatly on the counter and leaving a fresh bouquet of simple flowers for her return. She picked up the pile of correspondence and began rifling through the papers. She looked up and thanked her dad's chauffeur as he poked his head in to say good-bye.

"Sorry, Gus."

He tipped his hat. "My pleasure, Sarah."

"I don't know about that"—she smiled and he smiled back—"but thanks just the same."

He nodded again. "Good night, then."

"Good night. I'll see you soon. Say hi to Maggie for me." She followed him down to the street level and gave him a quick hug good-bye before bolting the door and returning to the top floor to collapse into her bed.

The single bedroom was not very large, but like everything else Letitia designed, it was intimate and exquisite. The double bed was the perfect size for one good-sized person to sprawl out on without feeling like a ship adrift, as Sarah so often did when alone in a king-sized bed while traveling.

The closet-cum-dressing room (hidden behind wallpapered invisible doors that opened on either side of the bed) was designed with a woman's wardrobe, jewelry, shoes, luggage, and linens in mind. It was a beautiful thing to behold. Sarah went in and enjoyed the silly thrill of all those shoes lined up with obedient precision, then toed off her suede half-boots and passed through the bathroom and into her favorite room in the home, what her grandmother fondly dubbed the *boudoir*.

The tiny room was about ten feet by twelve feet and—back in the day—Letitia had hired a designer to recreate an eighteenth-century French room: wood paneling, small fireplace, antique daybed piled with deliciously plump down pillows. Sarah had updated it with a flat-panel television above the fireplace, making it the perfect refuge. The idea that Letitia had basically created a solitary, private hideaway as a wedding present spoke volumes.

When Sarah had questioned her about it, Letitia had stared at her granddaughter and declared, "Just because you marry does not mean you are meant to forfeit your privacy! They are husbands, Sarah, not roommates!"

Chapter 7

SARAH TURNED TO LOOK out onto Oak Street. It was early evening. The flight in her father's plane had been ridiculously luxurious, and she felt like a spoiled pet for even implying that suffering through eight hours of Jane's veiled insults made it a trial.

Picking up her cell phone, she checked for messages. Nothing.

Sarah usually came to Chicago for at least two weeks per month, with an additional weekend thrown in to catch up and simply enjoy being in her own place. New York was exciting and exhilarating and inspiring, but it was also enervating. Her apartment there was a white box that she'd never taken the time to make her own. Chicago always gave her a chance to recharge. She decided to go for a long, leisurely walk in the brisk October night air along the lake, and then she spent the rest of the evening curled up in front of the TV, half dozing on the daybed in the boudoir.

Trying—and failing—to forget Devon Heyworth.

Monday and Tuesday were filled with meetings from eight in the morning until ten at night. Despite being exhausted at the end of each day, Sarah kept waking up at four thirty in the morning with plenty of physical energy and a logy mind. By Thursday morning she was wide-awake again.

She supposed she could go for another walk, but she didn't want to turn into some crazy exercise nut or anything. Walking once or twice was one thing. Daily exercise sounded like a routine. She tried to snuggle deeper into her bed.

The problem was she could not stay in her bed for more than a few minutes after she woke up without being overcome with the desire to have strong, male hands on her body.

On Monday morning, she'd thought she could shake the residual desire of her vague, seductive Devon-dreams without having to actually get out of bed and brave the cold, dark morning outside. That had lasted about five minutes. She'd grabbed her iPad and tried to read the early AP feed, only to realize that her other hand was trailing down her abdomen. Her eyes started to close at the thought of Devon's hands… it was always *his* hands on her… and his lips were good too… and the way that muscle on his upper arm curved? That occasionally came to mind… and his jaw…

Enough!

She'd finally forced herself out of bed, thrown on some approximation of a workout outfit, and walked along Lake Michigan. Now, for the fourth time in as many days, with her iPod blasting away her thoughts, she was trudging along the lakefront trying to pound the desire from her body. At night, she'd fall into bed, her body finally whipped into exhausted submission. Her dreams, on the other hand, were out of her control. Or entirely controlled by lust, more like.

She never remembered any of the details when she first woke up, but throughout the day, little snippets of a dreamy erotic still life would flash unbidden into her mind's eye. During a particularly boring conference call with both Carrie and her assistant in the room, and the two head buyers from Bergdorf Goodman on the other end of the speaker phone double-checking their spring order, Sarah glanced out her office window and a vivid image of Devon's mischievous face, with a devastatingly lascivious smile, materialized… rising up from between her own legs. She swung her attention back to the top of her desk a bit too quickly and tried to stare meaningfully at the innocent telephone.

After the call ended, Stephanie went back out to her desk, but

Carrie hovered a bit. Sarah forced herself to erase the lewd image and stay on task.

"What's up, Car?" Sarah asked without looking up.

If Carrie Schmidt had ever wondered about her boss's sex life, it wasn't something she would ever lob into day-to-day conversations. She and Sarah had always kept their relationship completely professional.

Carrie asked, "May I close the door?"

"Sure." Sarah looked up and smiled. "Should I be worried? You're not quitting, are you?" Sarah's voice went an octave higher with each rapidly fired question.

"Of course I am not quitting, Sarah!" Carrie sat back down in the chair she had been using for the conference call, straightened her pad on her lap, and looked up at Sarah. "It's just, you seem a little... distracted... since you got back from the London trip."

Great. Distracted. You have no idea, thought Sarah. "Well," she continued carefully, "I... it was a lot to do in a short amount of time and I think I'm having a hard time shaking the jet lag."

"Jet lag, hmm?"

Sarah wasn't inclined to confide much of anything to anyone, and she certainly wasn't going to reveal her newfound (and seemingly boundless) lust to her executive vice president. Carrie Schmidt was everything that Sarah was not. She had gone to all the right Ivy League schools and had worked at three of the top luxury shoe companies in the world. When Sarah was headhunting for a seasoned MBA to run the business with her, she was almost too intimidated to hire her. Carrie was thirty-two and had confidence beyond anything Sarah could ever hope to muster. It wasn't arrogance exactly, but Carrie didn't take shit from anyone.

Even now, three years into their working relationship and with Sarah's obvious seniority—she signed her paychecks, after all—the two of them still had a somewhat stilted relationship. Sarah was far more comfortable with her executive director in New York and chalked up her awkwardness with Carrie to the older woman's blistering intelligence. Sarah didn't need to be her confidante; she needed to be her boss.

"It's just exhaustion, I think," Sarah said. "I'm eager to get back to New York and start in on next year's fall designs. I feel like I can't get any really creative work done here." She hoped that didn't sound like the complete fabrication it was.

Carrie stared at her a second longer, then shrugged and stood up. "Okay then. Let me know if there's anything you need from me."

"Everything looks great for the board meeting. I think we're all set. Thanks for doing all that." Sarah went back to double-check the orders that she'd just confirmed from Bergdorf's as Carrie headed back to her own office. The past year had been her highest in terms of gross income, but her net was slipping. She stared at the spreadsheet and continued making more speculative calculations far into the night.

Later that night, she was thinking maybe she should return to New York for the weekend, just to shake whatever it was that was dogging her. She spent hours at her drafting table and couldn't think of a single new design. She stared at spreadsheets for hours and ended up seeing a swimming sea of numbers and no solution as to why certain cost centers refused to turn a profit. She tried to convince herself that the lush comforts of home were causing her to relive her steamy weekend of hot sex with the best man (ugh! she was such a cliché!), and if she just got back to the grit and pace of Manhattan, she'd be back to her normal, competent self.

There was really nothing for it; she started masturbating. Of course, she had done it before, a few times now and again, but it had never felt like this sort of necessary remedy to something... pressing. And a person could only take so many brisk walks along Lake Michigan (especially a person as non-brisk as herself).

Friday morning at seven, her cell phone rang and woke her from a convoluted (needless to say erotic) dream.

"Hello," she croaked.

"Sarah James, please."

Male. British. Official.

"Speaking." She forced herself awake and got into a sitting position against the padded headboard; her heart started to hammer.

"I know we haven't seen each other in quite some time, almost an entire sennight, but I was hoping you might recall a weekend we spent together a while back? My name is Devon Heyworth, in case it may have slipped your mind."

Sarah couldn't talk, her speech having been robbed by the warring demons of lust and shame. She wanted him so terribly, she kind of hated him for it. She took a deep breath and tried to sound nonchalant. "I think I vaguely remember meeting you. At a wedding, maybe? But I just woke up and I'm all… disheveled… and would you mind telling me a little bit more about yourself?" She could almost feel his smile through the phone line.

"I'm more interested in this *dishevelment* you speak of."

Sarah's body was shrieking: *Enough of your feeble attempts to satisfy me! Call in the professional! Do it now!*

"Is this phone sex?" she blurted.

"Oh my, you really are the archetype of subtlety, Sarah." A crackling loudspeaker announcement came through the phone, almost drowning him out when he said her name.

"Where are you? There's some sort of interference."

"I'm at Heathrow. I have to be in Chicago on business for a few days. Are you already back in New York?"

Her heart, which had slowed to a steady, animated trot, leapt back to a full gallop. "Uh, no, I am still in Chicago. What brings you to Chicago? I am ashamed to confess I don't even know what you do for a living. I had just assumed you were a dilettante… or a part-time race car driver."

"Both, actually. But when not being dilettantish or popping

bottles of champagne after a win at Le Mans, I work for an architectural firm here in London." There was a brief silence in which Devon had a very fleeting and very unpleasant desire to be legitimate.

"An architect… really. How curious," Sarah said in that throaty, sleepy voice that was making him crazy.

"I'm not an architect, so don't get your hopes up. I just work in the back office, tracking projects, bureaucratic ducks in a row, that sort of thing. Very unglamorous." Since when did he downplay his own glamour, especially when trying way too hard to seduce a woman?

He could practically hear her smile through her words. "It is difficult in the extreme for me to imagine you as unglamorous—"

"Do you imagine me?"

She caught her breath. "I was saying, it's hard to imagine someone as anything but glamorous when the only two times you've seen him, he's been wearing a velvet dinner jacket one night and a bespoke tuxedo the next. I look forward to meeting this unglamorous Devon Heyworth."

"Would you look forward to meeting him for dinner tonight?"

She paused again, not wanting to let him hear the near-panting enthusiasm that accompanied her internal response. "Yes."

The loudspeaker at Heathrow started blasting again. He waited until it was finished, then continued, "So, do I need to pretend to check into a hotel?"

She looked at her chintz duvet cover, then up and around her almost painfully elegant bedroom with new eyes and was inexplicably terrified. Not inexplicable, on second thought. No man had ever been in this bedroom, much less a strapping, larger-than-life British one who bent her over bedposts. "Uh…"

"Enough said," he interrupted cheerfully. "I will check into the Four Seasons. My plane lands around five this afternoon, local time, maybe an hour to get into town, you think?"

"Uh… that sounds about right."

"Okay. Give me an hour to shower and change and I'll pick you up at, say, half past seven tonight?"

"So… sure… that sounds great. Shall I make a dinner reservation or anything?"

"No, let's just play it by ear. That's the final call for my flight. See you tonight, love."

Click.

That little "love" at the end of that sentence. That little throw-away bit. That was the thing.

Sarah turned her phone off and put it back on her bedside table. She tried to stay composed and then just threw her face into one of the large square down pillows and simply screamed with joy. She pounded her feet up and down into the mattress like a toddler, then fisted her hands and pounded them too. Her body started to tingle with desire and she happily dismissed the demanding pull and jumped from bed. *Someone* else *will soon take care of* that, she thought with anticipatory glee. She went into the bathroom and turned on the sound system that ran through the house from her iPhone app. She cranked "Beautiful Day" then turned on the shower. A few minutes later, Bono was screaming and so was Sarah.

She scrubbed her body with masochistic fervor. She wanted to force her tingling skin to calm down, but quickly realized that Bono's sexy voice and the hot, soapy water were doing nothing to reduce her physical awareness.

Quite the opposite.

She rinsed off with freezing water, dried off matter-of-factly, and tried to think of some unsexy music. She tied a towel firmly around her chest, trying to bind her desire, then put another towel up into a tight turban on her head and switched the music to a Bach harpsichord invention that could have been played in a convent. Much better. As long as it wasn't some throaty Celt going on about touching her and showing her the way.

The rest of the day passed in a blur of happy, busy work. By Friday afternoon, Carrie and Stephanie had put everything together for Monday's board meeting and Sarah even reined in her prurient imagination long enough to make a few tentative sketches for next year's fall line.

Around four that afternoon, her office phone rang and a few seconds later, Stephanie poked her head in to let Sarah know her stepmother Jane was on the line. Sarah walked over to her desk, but remained standing when she picked up the phone, hoping the conversation would not go on for too long.

"Hi, Jane. How are you?"

"Fine thanks. Great news! I got you a date tonight with the most eligible bachelor—"

Make that the second *most eligible bachelor,* Sarah thought with a happy grin, but said, "Jane, I already have plans tonight." Big. Plans.

"What do you mean you have plans tonight? You told me that I could set you up. Your exact words were 'cream of the crop' if I recall correctly. And this young man is certainly the cream of the crop, Sarah. He's only in town for a few days visiting his parents and I won't—"

"Jane, I absolutely cannot change my plans."

"Well. You've put me in quite an awkward position."

"I don't mean to be ungrateful, but you might have called to check with me a little bit sooner."

"You made it sound like you were going to be holed up in your *store* all week getting ready for the board meeting, so I didn't think I needed to *check* with you. Oh, this is all so unpleasant. I try to do something nice and it always turns into something… else."

"Please. Don't let it turn into anything else. I am really glad you went to the trouble, but it just cannot be helped. I have a friend who called me just this morning and will be in town unexpectedly. We are meeting tonight at seven thirty."

"All right, then. Fair enough. Perhaps it would have seemed a bit *grasping* if you were available on such short notice in any case. I will reschedule for tomorrow night. Do you want to go to Charlie Trotter's or Spiaggia? We were thinking the later seating, say nine o'clock. Meet for drinks at eight. Does that work for you?"

"Wait. Are you and Dad coming?"

"Well, we had planned on it. Eliot's parents are business friends of your father's and I've never met them, and we thought it might be fun if we all got together. That way it wouldn't feel so forced."

Right. Not forced. "Um, Jane. I don't know if I'll be free tomorrow night either. My friend is probably going to be here for the weekend and I'd really like to clear my schedule just in case."

"Who is this friend, anyway?!"

Sarah started to answer, trying to figure how much longer she could refer to said friend without having to refer to said friend's gender.

"No! Forget I asked. I don't want to pry."

Of course you do, Sarah thought.

Jane pressed on. "Look, this clearly has not turned out the way I'd intended. Casual, fun, family friends. You have turned it into something more akin to an annoyance and I think I will just let the Cranbrooks know it is not going to work out."

"Eliot Cranbrook?" Sarah had started to glance down at some drawings she'd tossed on her desk and her attention flew back to the phone.

"Why? Do you know him?"

"Yes. Not really. I mean, I have *heard* of him."

"Really, Sarah. You are usually so levelheaded, but lately you seem a bit distracted."

"You are the second person in as many days to point that out." Sarah tried to contain a sigh—was she really so transparent? But Eliot Cranbrook was not to be dismissed lightly. He was a powerful, transformative leader at one of the top luxury conglomerates in

Europe. Devon had to understand if she didn't have *every* minute of the whole weekend spread out before her like the Gobi Desert. Maybe a preexisting lunch or dinner date with someone else might even spice things up a bit with a British rake.

"Oh, well. Now you'll just think I am being mercenary, Jane, but I would really love to meet Eliot Cranbrook. I have admired what Danieli-Fauchard has done with Moratelli, the Italian leather company they acquired last year—"

"Sarah! This is not a business dinner! If you have any inclination *whatsoever* to grill the poor man about mergers and that sort of thing, I will *definitely* retract the invitation. He is here visiting his parents unexpectedly. You will not—"

"Fine." Sarah laughed at herself. She hated to admit that Jane was right. "Okay, you win. I was sort of thinking along those lines, but I would still really like to meet him. Do you think you can finagle the kitchen table at Charlie Trotter's for tomorrow night? I know you are a magician with things like that." A compliment that also happened to be true. Sarah could picture Jane preening on the other end of the line.

"Well, I'll see what I can do, but you are going to have to be flexible. You have to *promise* me that you will be available for either the six o'clock *or* the nine o'clock seating."

"Of course."

"Don't say 'of course' just like that. I mean it: no last-minute business emergencies, no friends in town. I don't know the Cranbrooks yet and I am not going to stick my neck out—"

"Jane!" Sarah laughed again. "I promise! I will be utterly and completely at your disposal for dinner tomorrow night."

"Okay, then. Sorry to have been churlish before." Jane prattled on about a few more details and Sarah thought how her stepmother was good about things like that. She didn't allow little grudges to fester, and she always tried to clear things up right away. It was a relief that she was able to recover her dignity (and allow others to recover theirs), but Sarah wondered about why the woman always seemed to be in need of mending fences in the first place.

It was almost five. Sarah tried to pretend that it was the same as the approach of every other five o'clock, every other day of the week. No big deal. Apparently, the occasional transatlantic plane touched down at five. Whatever.

Sarah held out until ten after. She left her office and asked Stephanie if there were any items outstanding before the board meeting Monday morning.

"The printouts are already done; I've called and emailed all the board members to reconfirm the time and location. I spoke to the Drake and we are all set with the conference room." Stephanie was standing in front of her desk holding a flip-pad and ticking off her item list with the tip of a pen. She looked up at Sarah and smiled. "Do you want to touch base over the weekend or Monday morning, or shall we meet at the hotel Monday at ten?"

"You are perfectly on top of everything as usual, so let's meet at the hotel at ten. We can make sure everything is in order before everyone else gets there at eleven. Thanks again, Steph. Have a great weekend."

"Thanks. You too." Stephanie smiled again, and Sarah wondered if there was a bit of mischief in it. Stephanie was a no-nonsense workaholic who was getting her MBA in the evening program at DePaul. She rarely cracked a smile, much less a suggestive one.

"See you Monday, then." Sarah was glad the workweek was over and she didn't have to worry about her goofy looks undermining her professionalism for another minute.

Sarah poked her head into Carrie's office to tell her about the dinner with Eliot Cranbrook. Carrie silently waved her in and finished the call she was on.

"Terrific. We will speak about the particulars next week. Bye." Then to Sarah, "What's up?"

"I just got a call from my stepmother, and she's put together a little dinner party tomorrow night."

"Lucky you." Carrie smirked.

"Turns out it actually is lucky for once! It's a table for six with my parents, a business associate of my father's and his wife, and their son… drumroll please… Eliot Cranbrook."

Carrie widened her eyes in atypical enthusiasm. "Not *the* Eliot Cranbrook? He's like the wizard of the luxury goods market. How have you never met him before if he's a friend of the family and all?"

"You know the drill. My family is not exactly the close-knit variety. I know about as much as the man on the street about the corporate climate at Simpson-James. You know how hard I've tried to stay as far away from my father's business as possible." Sarah shrugged.

It had been a point of dispute between them ever since they'd started working together. Carrie had argued that Sarah's connections to the department store world of her father did not need to reek of nepotism. Sarah, despite being totally intimidated by Carrie's forceful nature, refused to budge on that particular point. She refused to allow even a whiff of the misconception that her father had played some silent partner role in Sarah James Shoes.

Carrie narrowed her gaze and pinned Sarah with that same penetrating look from yesterday. "I must say, and don't take this the wrong way—"

"I hate that expression because I can't help but think, okay, here it comes!"

They both laughed, but it felt a little forced.

Carrie continued, "No, it's a compliment. I was going to say, from a business standpoint, your timing is ideal, because you are looking particularly, I don't even know how to describe it, but you are somehow more accessible. If Cranbrook has any intention of making overtures to acquire the company, he's going to act on it when he sees you in your new and improved *receptive* state."

Sarah tried to stare her down, but Carrie was not having one bit of it.

"You go ahead and stick to your compact little view of yourself, Sar, but something snapped over there in London and it's all for the better. Just speaking as your business adviser, of course. It's a nice change. You are just a tiny bit softer around the edges."

"Just what I need." Sarah tried to make light of it as she turned for the door. "More soft, round edges! Have a great weekend, Carrie, and we'll see you Monday morning at the Drake at ten."

"Bye, Sarah. You too. Have a *great* weekend!"

Sarah heard her colleague's low chuckle as she made her way toward the stairs that led to her private domain on the upper floors of the town house.

She spent the next two hours primping and panicking. She started by drawing the hottest bath she could bear and looking at her face in the cruelly double-magnified mirror that swung out from the wall over the sink while the tub filled. She plucked a few hairs around her eyebrows and thought everything else looked remarkably fine. She brushed her teeth with the electronic toothbrush for two minutes exactly, then flossed with precision. She slid into the tub with a grateful breath for the intense heat that prevented her from thinking too much about anything but the physical sensation of it. She had a Jo Malone candle burning and the entire effect was completely transporting.

Once the water started to cool, she set about shaving her legs, scrubbing her body, lathering her hair, combing through the conditioner, and then rinsing her whole body from top to bottom with the handheld shower attachment. It was after six thirty by the time she got out.

Sarah started in on her hair, not sure if she wanted to make it formal and straight and silky, or let it go wavy and unruly and... well, that was a no-brainer. She squeezed some mousse into the palm of one hand, set down the dispenser on the white marble vanity counter, and rubbed her hands together, then flipped her head over and squished the creamy white foam throughout her hair. She stayed upside down and blew it dry while grasping large clumps into disorderly curls. After about ten minutes, it was a Botticellian masterpiece. Jane could say what she wanted about that extra twenty pounds, but Sarah's hair was the stuff of poetry.

She applied a bit of mascara and lip gloss, then moved into her dressing room to survey her choices.

When it came to giving a girl an idea about what to wear on a date, "play it by ear" was tantamount to heresy. She opted for her favorite French blue jeans, slimming, boot cut, comfortable, and paired them with a fitted white cashmere ribbed turtleneck that was sexy in some hard-to-reach way. She topped the simple basics with a glamorous, brocade Favourbrook knee-length jacket. She had purchased it on her recent trip to London, overcome by the sheer, irrational luxury of the entire piece: oversized cuffs and collar of a warm, chocolate mink, attached to a Regency-era men's jacket that hugged her body to perfection, the pinched waist almost made to measure. The brocade leaf-green silk fabric was hand embroidered with gold thread that shimmered subtly, without being too flashy. She wore a pair of Christian Louboutin corset-lace-up, pointy gray suede-leather mini boots that gave the whole outfit a naughty, Victorian touch.

Sarah transferred a couple of credit cards, her license, some cash, and a mini lip gloss into a slim gray clutch, then took stock of the whole outfit in the full-length, floor-to-ceiling mirrors. She wasn't vain, necessarily, but she knew her appearance was also a part of her business and she always tried to be as put together as possible when she went out, especially in Chicago, where she felt a bit more recognized than she did in New York. Manhattan, for better or worse, made her feel like she was one of innumerable successful people trying to spin straw into gold.

She turned off all the lights on her bedroom floor, except the overhead on the hall landing, then went down to her living room. She wasn't sure she wanted to invite Devon up for a drink before dinner—everything seemed so fragile, herself included—so she decided to go with one of her favorite decision-making parameters: if you don't know, you know: no.

She turned off the lights in the living room and left one light on in the kitchen for when she came home, then locked her front door at the top of the stairs that led to the public floors. Sarah walked down the stairs that went toward her office and the shop, rather than the other set of stairs that led directly out to the street. She passed through the dimly lit office, and the motion-sensor lights sputtered then blinked on with fluorescent authority; she double-checked that everything was locked, then continued down to the shop.

She adored sneaking into her own store at odd hours of the night. She felt like a sexy cat burglar when she prowled through the quiet boutique. The floors were polished every week to best complement the imported parquet flooring. The shoes were displayed in recessed bookcases of a deceptively simple design. Shoes seemed to float on glass shelves that were practically invisible. The lighting was hidden behind tiny inlaid design elements, illuminating each shoe from every direction. Sarah had researched jewelers and other luxury goods display techniques at length before hiring a local art installer to set up the lighting.

While adjusting a satin red stiletto that she knew was going to be sold out before Thanksgiving, Sarah heard a quick, firm double-tap on the plate-glass window next to the front door.

She tried to keep her chest from heaving, but there didn't seem to be anything for it. The best she could do was finish with the sexy red shoe and then make sure she didn't trip as she walked across the room to unlock the front door. She didn't have time to worry about any residual awkwardness from last weekend (had it only been one week? it had been a very long one) because Devon grabbed her in a rush of joy, one of his hands around her waist, pulling her flush up against him, and the other tangled into her wild hair. He used his grip to tilt her head back and sweep in for a pounding kiss.

Her body sang with relief. At last. Simple relief.

Chapter 8

SHE DID NOT EVEN reach around his neck or body; she just leaned back—her arms hanging useless at her sides, her back arched slightly—and felt the wave of his desire (and her own) wash over them.

He was kissing her fiercely at first, then his lips moved away from her mouth and he kissed her cheek and her neck, then near her ear, and started whispering all sorts of nonsense about how she looked like a Russian princess and how he was going to get those naughty boots off (*how had he already noticed those?* she wondered), all the while gripping her hair in a possessive, thrilling tug.

Then Devon stopped all of a sudden and put both of his hands on her cheeks. Sarah almost fell away from him, not realizing how much she had been leaning into his strong hand at her lower back.

She righted herself a bit drunkenly, then opened her eyes. He was really quite something to look at. Especially at this distance. Four inches looked very good on Devon Heyworth. She licked her lips and smiled from the pure pleasure of staring at his full lips and that inch-too-long hair and those piercing gray eyes that saw right into her fluttering, needy heart.

"Are you happy to see me?" he whispered.

She knew there were some rules about not showing your hand or not coming on too strong or some such foolishness, but all of that had flown out the door with that kiss. "Oh, Devon, you have no idea." She bit her lower lip and closed her eyes, then nearly hummed, "I have been craving you."

She felt him respond against her abdomen, and she pushed herself more firmly against him there and ducked her face into his neck. She wanted to eat him. She licked a tiny bit of skin just visible above the upturned collar of his winter coat.

He groaned, then laughed. "Shall we stay here in the doorway?" he asked, as if that might be a perfectly viable option.

She looked around and blinked and realized they were standing in the half-opened door of Sarah James Shoes. She made a valiant effort at coherence. "Food?" was all she could manage.

"Yes."

"What kind?"

"Any kind."

"What do you like? I don't even know what food you like."

"I love food. I adore food. Any food. I have no discretion what-soever. I like wine too. And beer."

She shuffled to move them both out onto the sidewalk, then turned to lock the front door of the store when Devon let his hands drop slowly away from her cheeks. She came back around and linked her arms around his waist and leaned her back against the door. "If you won't tell me what kind of food, then what kind of atmosphere? What are you wearing?" She reached her hands into the opening of his navy-blue cashmere full-length coat (she heard his breath stop) and felt the crisp, soft cotton of an ironed Oxford shirt, then let her hands trail around his waist and felt a pair of jeans.

"Jeans and a collared shirt. Nice. All right. I have an idea. I'm thinking something spicy—"

He smiled at the pun.

"Very funny," she added. "How about sushi?"

He was nodding mutely.

"Do you want a loud, funky scene or a more laid-back place? Both are excellent."

He kissed her again, just to taste her and reassure himself that he was really here, standing on this ludicrously freezing, blustering American street, in her arms. "I am going to want my hands on you the whole time, so wherever that will cause the least trouble, that's where I want to go."

He was kissing her neck again and she wondered why he was staying at a hotel after all. It seemed so silly now that he was actually standing here in her doorway. "Let's go to Wakamono, then. It's loud and delicious, and we can grope each other all we want."

They stood there for a few more minutes—necking, Sarah supposed was the word for it—then dove into a taxi and continued necking in the backseat until they arrived in the Lakeview neighborhood where the hip Japanese restaurant was located. The booming of the DJ's bass beat was audible all the way out onto the street and through the closed window of the taxi. Sarah tried to get Devon's attention and asked if he thought it was going to be too loud in there.

"I don't care. Let's just eat and get back to bed." He kissed her again, then hopped out of the taxi, paying the driver through the passenger side window.

She was a bit slower getting out of the taxi, seeing as how her jeans were feeling a little warm and confining and her lungs were not taking in as much oxygen as her blood demanded. Sarah tried to take a few calming breaths, then moved carefully out onto the street. Her boots were despicably high on a good day, but given her present *tumult*, she almost toppled over when she stood up on the sidewalk.

"Easy there, tiger." Devon had grabbed her, quickly and firmly, around her waist, and held her until he was sure she had regained her balance. He somehow made her feel much lighter than she normally did. That extra twenty pounds (The Jane Twenty) did not seem to present the slightest impediment to his interest. How was that possible?

Sarah leaned in to take all the steady comfort she could get. "You feel good," she murmured gratefully into his ear. "I feel drunk and I haven't had anything to drink in days."

They stood there as the taxi drove away, the two of them reveling in the mere pleasure of one another. "I suppose we should go in out of the cold, love," he whispered, his hot breath coming through her jumbled hair and tickling her ear.

She squirmed against his shoulder, then pulled away and grabbed his hand, leading the way into the crowded restaurant.

It was only eight o'clock on a Friday night, but the place was already packed: the after-work crowd was still three thick at the bar; the hip college crowd was lounging along the banquette that ran halfway down the exposed brick east wall; the sushi bar was buzzing with customers in low-backed barstools facing busy chefs sporting white coats and efficient expressions, interspersed with bottles of sake, little bowls of soy sauce, wasabi, and ginger, and a hum of jovial conversation. Waiters and waitresses were cutting their way through the thick crowd with trays of drinks and what looked like an endless supply of perfectly presented sushi. And above and around and through it all cranked the aforementioned techno-jazz bass beat, giving the whole room a throbbing vitality.

Two seats opened up at the sushi bar at the far end of the room. Devon gestured in that direction and Sarah followed single file because of the crush of people. Since they were no longer standing next to each other, Sarah started to let her hand fall out of Devon's grasp, but he kept his hand behind his back, loosely but possessively holding hers, unwilling to let go of her even for the short walk to the end of the sushi bar.

"This is going to be fun," Sarah thought, then realized she had said it aloud. Devon must have heard her, because he turned his profile over one shoulder and gave her a ruinous wink.

When they finally got to the two free barstools, Sarah realized that Devon was waiting to help her with her coat. She started to undo the fur tie at the collar, then slowly undid the beautiful, hand-embroidered buttons that were tight as they passed through the hand-sewn buttonholes.

"You and buttons," Devon complained.

"Oh, admit it, you love it."

He looked up and away from her fingers, where he had been enjoying every movement of her hands as she worked the well-made fastenings through the fabric, skimming her fingertips mindlessly across her breasts. He held her look for a moment too long, he supposed, but he couldn't help himself.

"I admit it." He spoke so quietly that she thought she must have misheard, the din of the music making even a shout hard to process.

Sarah turned her back to allow him access to remove the tightly tailored coat. He managed to slide off the jacket while grazing his fingertips along the length of her arms. As if on cue, a helpful waitress came by and offered to take their two coats to the coat check upstairs. Devon handed them over, then gave Sarah a full head-to-toe perusal before offering his hand to assist her on the small climb up onto the barstool. She figured he was going to get into his own chair immediately, but instead he remained standing behind her chair, lifted up her hair with one hand, pulled down the fold of her turtleneck with the other, then kissed her bared neck with a long, slow, patient caress of his tongue along the tender skin near her nape.

She felt her legs begin to tense and worried she might explode right there at the sushi bar. "Please stop, Devon. Seriously," she whispered.

"Only because you said *please*." He released her hair and the fold of cashmere, but let his right hand rest where his lips had just been, his fingers blatantly reenacting what he had been doing with his tongue. After a few endless seconds, Devon let his hand come away from her neck, and he slid into his own chair. He shifted the barstool as close to Sarah's as he could without sitting on her, his right hand coming to rest lightly across her shoulder.

The manager came over and smiled warmly at Sarah. "Sarah! What a pleasure to see you. It's been a few months, no?"

"Hi, Steve!" She smiled. "This is Devon Heyworth. He's visiting from London."

Devon smiled and said hello to the trendy, thirtysomething Japanese man who sported the obligatory black mock turtleneck that served as the unspoken uniform of stylish restaurateurs the world over.

"I have a wonderful hot sake I just got in. Would you both like to try some?"

"That sounds perfect. Thank you." Sarah gave the man another broad, open smile that made her eyes sparkle and Devon was fleetingly miffed.

That was *his* smile. For *him*.

He had no interest in pursuing *that* line of thinking, so he forced himself to unwrap his chopsticks, making a tidy, little architectural tent out of the paper on which to rest the sticks, then put his napkin on his lap and started to look at the menu.

"Would you rather I didn't speak to anyone but you?" she whispered hotly into his ear, letting her left hand settle with delicate pressure on his right thigh.

He smiled but did not look up from the menu. He drew his eyebrows together in mock consternation and set his jaw with a fairly good approximation of a disgruntled child. "Yes. I would. *Rather*. And while you're not speaking to anyone, you'd best not look at anyone either. Or wave. Or smile. Or really acknowledge anyone but me." He kept his eyes on the menu, smiling, as if this were a perfectly natural conversation, akin to telling her about his flight or the delay in customs or the paperback he'd read on the plane. As usual, he thought his blatant honesty would be misconstrued for humor, so he looked up expecting Sarah to join in on the joke.

Instead, she reached her right hand up to his face and slowly traced the smile away from his beautiful mouth with the pad of her thumb. "Okay," she said, so only he could hear. "Ask and you shall receive."

He put his mouth next to her ear, so his words could be heard over the reverberating sound system. "I don't like to ask for things," he said, but what he really meant was that he'd never had to.

She smiled as he spoke, both of them enjoying the easy excuse of the loud music, which forced them to more or less kiss one another's ears every time they spoke. She put her lips near his ear next and replied, "But if you don't tell me what you like, how else will I know…"—she paused for bravery—"how to please you?" She pulled away enough for him to see the mischief in her eyes, but also the truth of it. She wanted to please him. Without guile or manipulation, she simply trembled at the pleasure it would be to send him into raptures as he had done to (for? with?) her.

Devon's thigh tightened under her hand for a moment, and the muscle in his jaw tensed in response to her words. His eyes clouded with something so much more than desire. Sarah might have been frightened if she weren't so thrilled by the prospect of peeling it all away: the clothes, the veneer of jollity. He was a beast. She wanted to see his raw insides. She was going to hammer and scrape at that facade of jovial, superficial levity. She wanted him to attack her. She wanted to taunt him.

Sarah let her hand wander a few inches up his thigh, and he slammed his own hand over hers, preventing her from feeling the hard proof that he was already quite well pleased.

Devon had spent much of his adult life controlling the world around him—how he wanted to be perceived in society, how he wanted to succeed (or not) in business, how he would fit into his family, how he would pleasure a woman—yet this woman next to him (around him) was impervious. She wasn't seeing what he wanted her to see or hearing what he wanted her to hear. She pierced his perimeter.

Years (a lifetime) of building walls and moats around himself were nothing to her. She wasn't laughing at him exactly, but she *was* laughing at his delusional idea that she couldn't see right through him to the barely contained lust and carnality. Fine. Let her see that. It wasn't much of a revelation after all. What man would not be brought to his knees by her?

She was mouthing along the words to a French rap song that had started pulsing out of the sound system. Her lips were even more full and petulant when she wrapped them around that language. He was going to make her speak French to him later. He was going to make her do all sorts of things.

He gave up trying to decipher the menu, which might as well have been written in hieroglyphics, for all he could give it his attention. He put the stiff, laminated card back into its little stand in front of him, then leaned into Sarah's hair and said, "You choose. Whatever you want to order. I'm too distracted."

She smiled and gave her head a little shake of pleasure. Then turned back to his ear. "I like you distracted. I want to see you really, *really* distracted. Agitated, even." She nipped at his earlobe and he told her he might have to forego dinner altogether if she kept it up, and that wasn't a good idea because he needed fuel. He swatted her away with an affectionate, firm hand.

The über-cool Steve arrived just then with a beautiful, narrow raku pottery vase filled with hot sake. He poured the fragrant liquid into two small cups of a similar pattern and handed one to Sarah. She nodded professionally to Steve, then smiled at Devon… for Devon… and took a sip of the steaming, sweet wine and looked as though she might swoon. She turned back to Steve, all business, and told him to bring whatever was freshest from the sushi bar and to keep the sake coming. He nodded his understanding to Sarah, gave Devon a brief look that might have been envy, and then snaked his way back through the crowd.

O-Zone, Freak Power, and the Crystal Method started pounding even louder in the background through the rest of their dinner.

Devon was thankful for the contrived distance the music afforded, having given up on talking in her ear or letting her nip at his, lest he throw her on the floor and take her right there on the gritty, polished concrete. He liked the idea of it, that infuriating, pristine white cashmere turtleneck ruined, her jeans pulled down in haste, maybe to her knees, preventing her legs from coming up around his waist, and just lifting her hips and entering her and having her laughing up at him with abandon as waiters and students and commodities traders and busboys and lawyers were somehow, as in a dream, all around them and oblivious.

Steve appeared again, asking if they wanted anything else, and Sarah gave Devon a provocative wide-eyed look. Deferential. He had a momentary flash of Bronte and Max at breakfast at Dunlear—had that only been a week ago?—and his ridicule of Bronte's doe-eyed gazing. He wanted that. He wanted that from Sarah.

And she saw it all. Was she toying with him? He couldn't bring himself to worry too much about that, with the meal finally finished and the promise of the two of them in bed looming in the very near future. Devon could even spare a smile for the solicitous restaurant manager as he handed him his credit card and told him they were ready for the bill.

They flagged down a taxi on North Broadway and Sarah gave the driver her home address. She turned to face Devon as the car pulled into traffic. "I think we can dispense with the charade that you are going to be spending any time in that hotel room, don't you?"

His broad smile was his answer as he wrapped one arm around her shoulder and pulled her close. After all that surging, techno-hip-hop foreplay, the backseat of the taxi taking them to her place was terrifyingly silent. He wanted her in so many ways, he was afraid to begin here on a cracked and worn, blue vinyl bench seat. She was holding his hand, hard. He looked down at their joined fingers and then brought the clasped pair to his lips, kissing her fingers and his own where they twined together. Devon was reminded of that childhood game where you grip your own fingers together and twist them in a contorted, backward fashion and then lose the ability to tell right from left, index finger from pinkie. He felt the same now, unable to differentiate where he ended and she began.

"You had better not do that," she whispered into the dark silence.

"Why?" he teased, kissing her fingers again, her eyes blinking slowly.

"Because... I can't... I won't be able to stop myself."

Good, he thought. At least she wasn't as all-knowing and in control as he had feared. If he was going to fall to pieces, best to do so in good company. He rested their joined hands in his lap and then pushed the back of her hand into his straining jeans. She groaned and he forced himself to look out the taxi window at the glittering city whipping by in cool, detached splendor.

———

The rest of the night had seemed diamond-bright, with each consecutive moment a precise jewel of exquisite discovery (when she bit him there, when he sucked at her flesh... just... there, the moments of gentleness and force, ferocity and farce, the byplay), and by the next morning, it was all flashing through her mind in shards of unreality. They had fallen into bed right away, but they hadn't fallen asleep until the sky was just starting to turn a morose, pale gray. Devon's firm hand held her, even in sleep, at the top of her thighs.

She started to wake up hours later, her hand still flung above her head at an unnatural angle, the weight of his palm still resting between her legs. She woke up wanting. Her sleep had been an interval, nothing more. They were right where they had left off.

He was such a heavy sleeper... might she just wriggle around under that perfect hand? Have a little something for herself, just to tide her over, then drift back into another interval of satiated rest.

Was it masturbatory? Necrophilic? She didn't need to ponder the depth of her depravations for more than a few seconds because, despite his ability to sleep through a demolition, apparently the slightest indication of her desire was enough to rouse him.

He gripped her tighter and she breathed with a strained relief. How was he able to do that? Before this, before him, in her ignorance, she had assumed one sexual completion (alone or with someone else) was fairly interchangeable with the next. The buildup, the peak, the after effect. Et cetera. Et cetera.

What an idiot.

It was like thinking Froot Loops were interchangeable with foie gras. Just food.

But the thing that Devon was doing with his index finger right then, for example, taunting her, leading her on, was maddening and brutal and cruel. Delectable.

"You are such a tease… you think you can just lead me on—" she ground out through clenched teeth, then gasped when his finger became more demanding.

"I *am* feeling a bit bossy, now that you mention it. Would you let me… I mean, may I have my way with you for a while, just be a little controlling on a Saturday morning, as it were?"

His wicked grin suggested far more than a *little* anything. She wanted so much, but she was also a little afraid of her ignorance.

"How bossy is bossy?" she asked, out of breath, not even trying to hide how much she wanted to find out.

"Really, downright bossy. Like, you don't do anything without my permission, no gasping, no arching"—which drew attention to the fact that she was doing both right then, so she froze. "Okay, maybe a little gasping," he said with a grin, then he did something taunting with his fingers and she clutched at his flexed upper arms and gasped in anticipation.

He stilled.

"Especially no climax unless I say so… when I say so… when I give it to you…"

"I couldn't help that…" she pleaded. "I want to be good… I'll be good…" She wanted to laugh at the game, but it was so all-encompassing, there didn't seem to be any room left to distance herself even momentarily enough to acknowledge her nonsense. She was already far past laughter. She wanted to feel the extent of how far he could take her, how attenuated, how protracted, before he broke her or released her.

Raised her.

"You had better not be imagining anything naughty." His voice gave him away. He was totally on fire, hardly the controlling master he hoped to be.

She opened her eyes slowly, then dragged her tongue across her upper lip. "May I speak?"

He had mistakenly believed that a little dominant play might give him a sense of authority, a modicum of control over this… situation.

Stupid.

Even pinned beneath him and asking his permission to utter a word, she had him in her thrall. That little bit of tongue.

"Don't do that with your tongue." His voice was a tad harsh. Her eyes flashed with a hint of fear and then… God protect him… power. She knew.

She knew everything.

—⁓—

Sarah's heart stopped when he barked that command. Then raced with fever. She knew nothing. She didn't even know her own body. But Devon knew. He knew exactly what to do.

She spent the next hour in a heretofore unknown world of carnal enchantment. He brought her to peak after peak of near-satisfaction only to pull away at the last possible moment. She took great satisfaction in both his grimace of restraint and her ability to endure the knife edge of pleasure upon which he kept her balanced.

When her release finally tore through her, she must have screamed or roared, because the residual silence crackled and sizzled through the room. The popping fireplace noises were magnified against her sensitive ears, interwoven with the sound and feel of Devon's thick, satisfied, hot breath in the crook of her neck.

At the last possible moment, he had released his hold on her wrists and her fingertips were gloriously free: feeling his hair and skittering across his back and marveling at the new growth of beard along his jaw (that he had used earlier to such devastating effect against her inner thigh). The very tips of her fingers were both starved and gluttonously full.

"You are a tyrant," he ground out, as his breath still worked to find a more natural pace.

She laughed so hard at that. She threw her arms around his back and nipped at his ear. "You know," she began whispering in a happy rush, "only you could perceive an inexperienced woman who just spent the last... what? hour?"—she lifted her head to look at the gold French clock on the mantle over the fireplace, then let it drop with a thud back onto the pillow—"pinned beneath you—forfeiting speech, obeying *you*, subjecting herself to you—as tyrannical. Still beneath you, come to think of it."

"Oh Lord." He looked down the length of her body with something like contrition, then slid his weight off her. Her eyes were already drifting closed and she grinned and hummed like a little child about to nap when she felt the sheet and then the down comforter come floating down upon her skin, then tucking lightly around her. He must have gone to the bathroom for a few minutes, because her last memory before the delicious sleep finally overtook her was the abstract weight and warmth of his body as he removed the pillow in her embrace and replaced it with himself.

Chapter 9

WHEN SARAH WOKE UP hours later, Devon was returning from the kitchen with some cold green apples, a package of cheddar cheese, and a pitcher of ice water, two wineglasses held with casual confidence in one hand. He had showered and put on his jeans, but his bare feet and bare torso looked glorious. And then he caught her out in her appraising perusal and she pulled the sheet up over her head in guilty embarrassment, then pulled the linen back down just to stare.

"Hungry, love?"

She nodded.

She hadn't thought much about love.

She loved this or that. (This: the bent control of the two, sure fingers into the rims of those wineglasses. Or that: the perfect skill with which he was now slicing the bitter skin away from the apple; his deft touch.) Or when he tagged the very word to the end of a sentence, like a little peck, it gave her heart a pleasant skip. But she hadn't thought about being *in love*. Wasn't that what a girl was supposed to do? To think about it? To pine?

She thought not. Not with Devon at least. He wouldn't want that from her… he was all loose and free and careless. His whole life was one big ride. Not that he (or she) could stop her feelings if they were fully realized, but like a seedling, inhospitable surroundings could prevent any deep emotions from taking root.

From everything she had read and heard and eavesdropped about love with a capital *L*, it was a gory mess. She thought of her classmates in high school, the young women at the International School in Paris. What better place than Paris to explore your youthful passions, right?

Wrong.

They all seemed miserable. Well, perhaps not *all*, but most. Sarah might have been aloof or alone most of the time she was finishing up high school in Paris, but at least she wasn't suffering any of those emotional bouts of misery. Bronte was practically unable to function after she and Max split up the first time. Sarah conceded that had turned out well enough.

Nor did it seem to get any better once people got older. Sarah's father still missed her mother twelve years on. Jane loved Nelson more than he would ever love her. It just seemed like those deeper emotions were a dragging weight on what was an otherwise delightful enterprise.

As for the physical side of it all, Sarah had always felt young for her age. She *had been* young. During those years of working like a machine at Louboutin, she had always been an outsider. Too young to be hanging out with her more experienced colleagues. Too old to be hanging out in bars all night with her high school friends who were now in university. Too inexperienced to be having affairs. She didn't feel like she was the right age for anything.

But now?

Devon made her feel like she was exactly the right age to be getting on with all of this *getting on*. He started to come toward the bed with the small round tray of food he had just prepared.

"Let's go in the other room," Sarah said, sitting up and letting her legs dangle off the side of the mattress. "I've been in this bed too long."

"Never say *that*," he scolded.

She smiled, slid off the bed, stood in front of him (so naked!), and kissed him on the cheek. She felt the warmth of his gaze on her back as he followed her into her closet, where she grabbed an ivory silk bathrobe that was hanging on a hook, then continued through the dressing area to the bathroom. "Go on into the little front room." Sarah pointed toward the open door on the other side of the shower stall. "My grandmother insists on calling it my boudoir, but it's really just a little den. Let's eat in there. There's a fireplace too, if you want." She gave him another chaste kiss on the cheek, then closed the door behind him.

A few minutes later, teeth brushed, hair brushed (as much as that was possible with all that toing and froing against the pillows), face washed, Sarah found herself standing in the doorway, leaning against the jamb, arms crossed over her chest, marveling at the phenomenal Devon Heyworth.

He had made himself completely at home in her world. He was sprawled out on the daybed, having left a nest of pillows to one side for when she got there. The television was on, and he had the remote control in one hand and a half-eaten slice of apple in the other. He had put the tray of food on the tiny round table near the bay window and set it within arm's reach, in front of where he sat.

He was flipping through channels, pausing for five seconds here (basketball) or three seconds there (Nigella Lawson) or five seconds there again (the history of catapults). Obviously, he had mastered the electronics system, a feat that had taken Sarah weeks and still gave her the occasional headache. She hardly ever even used the surround sound system since it required a whole other level of technological confidence that she did not possess; he had handily figured it out in the time it took her to brush her teeth.

Devon had paused most recently on a French channel that Sarah had added to her cable package last year, thrilled to have the language wafting through her house, if only the rapid voice of a car salesman or the news on the latest taxi strikes in Paris. Best of all, on Saturdays, it showed classic French films and today was *The Umbrellas of Cherbourg*.

"Do you want to watch this?" he asked.

She had started watching it, standing there in the doorway, not realizing that he had been watching her. She crawled up onto the daybed, fitting right into the little snug area he had made for her. He was already getting drawn into the story and absently fed her the remaining half a slice of apple that had been poised, forgotten, between his long fingers. Even though he was watching the television, it was as though he knew the location of her mouth regardless of wherever he happened to be looking at the time. The apple tasted like a symphony had exploded on her tongue, and she must have groaned with the tart, sweet, crisp pleasure of it because Devon (eyes still on the movie) said, "Particularly good apple, eh?"

"Mm-hmm." She rested her head on his shoulder and he snaked his arms around her back.

They spent the rest of the afternoon just like that, with the fire sputtering and hissing, the French lovers singing and crying, and the two of them resting loosely around one another.

As the credits rolled after Catherine Deneuve's desperate triumph, Sarah figured it was as good a time as any to break the bad news of her dinner plans. "So…"

"Is this the bad news?"

"Very funny. No. Well, yes. I have plans tonight that I couldn't break."

"Oh, I figured you would."

"Really?"

"Yes. Really."

"Oh. Well. I do. Unfortunately."

"Yes, it is unfortunate." He gave her a firm squeeze around her shoulder.

"So. How much longer will you be in town? What's the project you're working on?"

"Nothing much. Widgets."

"Widgets?" She wasn't annoyed exactly, but his blasé attitude toward his own interests might wear on her over time. She liked to joke and have a laugh as much as the next person, but when certain topics always elicited a quip, she began to wonder.

"Nothing exciting."

"So bore me."

He started to reach for the remote control and she stilled his hand, holding his wrist gently in her smooth, warm fingers. She picked up the remote control and turned the television off. "Talk to me a little bit about what you do. It's not fair that I am this open book professionally. I mean, you can Google me." His guilty smile told her he already had. "And yet I know next to nothing about your real life."

He wanted to blurt out that he was rapidly coming to the terrifying conclusion that she might very well *be* his real life, but he stuffed that back down. Hard.

"I'm not really comfortable talking about myself… professionally. I hate when guys are all on about what they do…"

"But I'm asking. Nicely."

He looked at her, then out the window at the cityscape. It was almost dark again, even though it was barely the end of afternoon. The October days were short. He was stalling.

She continued, "Look, I'm not going to be a shrew about it. If you don't care much about what you do during the day, nine to five and all that, I guess, whatever, but I just don't see that. You have such an intensity—" She blushed.

He laughed and kissed her cheek.

She tried again. "It just seems curious to me that you're not fully engaged, since you seem to live your life—what little I've seen, granted—with a kind of purpose. Even your repartee has a kind of design to it."

"Interesting choice of words."

"Which?"

"Design. I guess I am a designer of sorts. I've always enjoyed patterns and puzzles, codes... designs. But there were extenuating circumstances. I refused to be an academic."

"I can relate to that!" she chimed in.

And she was so open and honest and wanting him to just be whoever he was, that it all sort of fell away and he told her all the bizarre, convoluted machinations—the designs—that had constituted his so-called secret life. The inventions, the mathematical equations, the inability to be anything but the faux-earl younger brother when he was out in society. He thought she must think him mad or immature or egomaniacal: hiding what must be, ultimately, an overinflated sense of his own importance.

"You are so perverted!" she squealed with glee, clapping her hands together. "You're a closet genius! I *love* that! Anonymously spreading your bits of brilliance around, like little crumbs across the Internet, across the world. Tell me more about the project you're working on here. Specifically. Did you invent the widget? Tell me!"

He looked at her in amazement. He didn't know what he had expected, but this sparkle of delight was not it. He told her about the arrogant architect who had let his own flawed design ("a gimmick," Devon added with disdain) overrule Devon's commonsense engineering. And all the details that he thought (that he *knew*) to be boring, she found hilarious or provocative or wonderful. She got up to check her cell phone, then came back into the boudoir, still smiling at him.

"You are a secret *lover*! It's so fantastic. Most people, I mean, take me for example—I am a veritable exhibitionist, whoring my shoes around the world. I don't want any personal glory—okay, maybe just a tiny bit—but really, deep down, I want to see a woman walking down the street in a pair of shoes I designed and to see that look in her eye: that she is power or she is lust or she is anger, whatever she might be at that moment, and I think, I am a part of that. I did that!"

He continued to stare at her. Her robe had loosened; her hair was wild; she held her cell phone in one hand and the door frame in the other. She was transitioning away from him. Getting ready to gear up for her dinner plans.

"What?" she asked all of a sudden, then, looking down at herself: "Oh, I am a fright."

"You are many things, but you are certainly not a fright." He started to get up from the daybed. "Let me get out of your way. I'll head back to the hotel—"

"No!" she barked. "I mean—" softer now—"You should really stay. Why be holed up in one measly hotel room? I am just going out to dinner with my parents and some friends of theirs, so I should only be gone a couple of hours. I mean, if you want," she added shyly. "After about a halfsecond of seeing you through the plate-glass window of the storefront last night, I realized it was the height of absurdity that you even got a hotel room in the first place. But..." He certainly wasn't making this very easy for her. "Well, you do what you like."

He settled back into the comfortable cushions, put his feet up where she had been sitting, clicked on the television, skipped back to the history-of-war-machines channel, and continued to look at the screen when he said, "I shall be right here when you get home from supper."

She walked over to where he was reclining and gave him a brief, tender kiss on the lips. "I'm glad."

An hour later, she came through the door from the bathroom. He had spent the entire time half-watching an interesting documentary about a new lightweight metal alloy and listening to the charming sounds of Sarah in preparation mode: drawers opening and closing; hangers sliding across the closet rod (no... no... no...

yes); the shower turning on, the hinges of the glass door as she must have been stepping in; her light humming of the refrain from *The Umbrellas of Cherbourg* floating out and over the steam; the shower off; the sink on and off; the blow-dryer; the jars and wands and sprays of makeup and perfume clicking open and closed.

And there she was. Transformed.

From the wild, wanton *tyrant* to the perfectly turned-out daughter.

"How do I look?"

"Is that a trick question?"

"No. I fret more about my appearance when I have dinner with my stepmother than I do before the hottest date. Not that there have been many hot dates, but still."

"Well, you look… immaculate. I want to rip you to shreds. At least I am no longer jealous. There's no way you would be dressed like that for a man."

Sarah felt a zing of feminine pride: he had been jealous? Then she looked down at herself through his eyes. Her hair was as straight as she could make it, the black pencil skirt was a serviceable wool Armani, her top was a vintage Yves Saint Laurent black and white, silky chiffon blouse of her mother's that tied at the neck, off to one side. She had on opaque black tights and a pair of her own Sarah James black patent-leather platform pumps that made her feel invincible.

"Much worse than any man… my stepmother." Sarah's shoulders shifted to defeat, almost imperceptibly. "I am a bit of a disappointment to her."

"In what way?" Devon had stood up to say good-bye and was dangerously close now, circling her like a hungry animal. He used one finger to move the straight fall of her hair to one side, then kissed her at the nape of her neck. "You are hardly disappointing here," he purred in her ear, then his hands made lazy circles on her behind. "Nor here."

"Oh, Devon. You are sadly mistaken. My bottom is utterly disappointing. My chest is too large—my stepmother even offered to give me the name of a doctor who specializes in breast reductions."

"That would have been a tragedy of Euripidean proportions." He was behind her and tracing his hands around her breasts, not wanting to wrinkle the fabric (well, wanting to very much, but refraining).

She leaned back into him and gave herself up to one more moment of his utter lack of disappointment. Her nipples were starting to ache. "Please, stop," she whispered.

His hands fell away and she had to catch her breath for how much she wanted them back. She took a very deep, slow breath. "I will think about how you like me there when Jane shakes her head in dismay at the dessert trolley. Because I am going to order dessert, and I am going to eat every bite… and think of you on my lips." She kissed him again, then went through the door to the hall landing and started down the stairs. "Wait, do you want a key or the security codes in case you want to go out?"

"Sure. Probably should. I was going to have someone from the hotel bring my stuff over, but I might as well go for a little walk and retrieve it myself." He was leaning over the banister, shirtless, and she was looking up at him.

She reached into her purse, pulled out the single key, and reached up to hand it to him. "And I'll turn off the security system when I leave. Wait up for me." She winked and continued downstairs.

Her coat closet was on the same floor as the kitchen and living room. With the unseasonably cold October wind in mind, she chose a long, raccoon cape that Letitia had given her when she left Paris (telling her pragmatically that Chicago and Moscow were probably the only two places left on earth that one could wear such a thing without fear of tomato soup being hurled).

It took her longer than she thought to hail a taxi, so she was the last to arrive, even though it was still a few minutes before the reservation. Jane had left a phone message confirming that she had, *luckily*, been able to get the kitchen table at Charlie Trotter's for the nine o'clock seating, that the Cranbrooks were not able to meet for drinks beforehand, and to be *prompt*. Sarah was always prompt, so she didn't understand why Jane always made a point of saying so. Probably because Jane and Nelson were always early. Her father and stepmother were standing by the maître d's podium, having already checked their coats, but the other three, Eliot and his parents, were standing there in the crowded front area of the busy restaurant, still in their coats and bumping up against one another.

Jane took one look at Sarah in that enormous, ratty old cape and nearly shuddered. Eliot Cranbrook saved the day.

"You must be Sarah." He was obviously American, with his square jaw and easy smile and thick, sandy hair with all those sun-kissed golden highlights, but the years of living and working in Geneva had given his voice a European cadence. The only word Sarah could think of was *debonair*. She was fidgeting with the braided clasps sewn deep within the fur panels of the cape and then looked up to see him waiting attendance upon her, to remove the fur from her shoulders when she was finished.

"Vintage Fendi, is it?" he asked.

Jane blinked back her confusion, then smiled approvingly at Sarah. *So that was all it took?* Sarah marveled. *The attention of a desirable male?* All this time, she had thought that Jane was voicing her own strongly held and well-thought-out opinions, when in actual fact, she was merely scanning about for someone else to approve or disapprove of Sarah and to follow suit accordingly. Since Nelson James had never shown the least inclination to approve or disapprove of his only child, Jane had erred on the side of mild disapproval. It wasn't even disapproval, Sarah had to concede; it was more that Jane took the view that Sarah was *improvable*.

Sarah made a mental note to thank Eliot for that kindness; by legitimating the beloved Fendi raccoon cape, Eliot had somehow made Jane like her a little bit. Sarah thought he might have trailed his hand along her shoulder when he took it off, then she thought she was probably just in a state of heightened *everything* from all those hours of being Devon's plaything. Her face flushed at the memory and Eliot caught it and smiled. He *had* grazed her on purpose after all, and now he thought she bloomed like that from his slight touch.

How professional I must seem, Sarah thought ruefully.

She shook herself free of any Devon daydreams and turned to reintroduce herself to Mr. and Mrs. Cranbrook, with whom she had apparently had dinner when she was eight.

"Penny and Will, please. Do *not* make us feel so old and call us Mr. and Mrs. Cranbrook." It was Penny talking, which seemed to be the way of it. Will gazed lovingly at his wife of forty years and she just talked and talked.

Sarah excused herself so she could properly greet her father, giving him a brief kiss on one cheek, then leaned down to touch her cheek against Jane's.

"Don't you look lovely, Sarah. Doesn't she look lovely, Nelson?"

But Nelson, despite decades—generations, really—as a successful retailer of women's clothes, could never really give Sarah the time it took to appraise her appearance. "Quite nice," he offered, rather effusively for him, thought Sarah. She would never know that the sight of Sarah at that moment reminded him so profoundly of his first wife that Nelson James had to look away for fear of embracing her in an emotional crush.

After an hour at the kitchen table of Charlie Trotter's restaurant, only a truly depressed person could resist the mellow joy and bursts of excitement that punctuated the whole experience. The busy staff was in a blurry state of perpetual motion, whisking, frying, snapping paper orders, tossing aside copper saucepans. And, in the midst of it all, six lucky people were fawned over and regaled with plate after plate of gastronomical bliss. Jane had directed the seating, which must have caused her endless hours of etiquette trauma, since there was no possibility of seating Sarah next to Eliot (the whole purpose of the exercise) *and* separating husbands and wives *and* adhering to the boy-girl-boy-girl dictum.

Jane must have finally decided to forfeit the boy-girl portion of the equation, announcing with politically incorrect levity that they were going to be doing Taliban seating: the women on one side of the table, the men on the other. Sarah had Penny to her right and Eliot to her left, then her father on Eliot's other side, Will Cranbrook next to her father, then Jane between Will and Penny.

Nelson asked Eliot to choose the wine, "Since you are the only one of us living near Burgundy these days," and the rest was a whirl of the restaurant's choosing.

The food came in waves and the conversation bubbled along. Eliot spoke to Sarah's father with an open admiration that never slipped into fawning. He spoke to Sarah with an obvious knowledge of her business success and respect for what she had accomplished in such a short time, and a provocative hint of something more—or that he might wish for something more—unprofessional.

Talk about feast or famine. Would she have even acknowledged the low simmer of Eliot's gaze two weeks ago? Was it all Devon's doing, this ratcheted-up version of herself? Or, more likely, had this Sarah always been there, lying in wait? Whatever the chronology, and as much as she hated to be a traitor to the good, warm man who waited on Oak Street at that very moment for her to return, she couldn't help seeing Eliot for what he was: a strong, intelligent, successful grown-up.

Magnetic.

The white Burgundy was cool and tart against her tongue. She let it rest in her mouth when she took the first sip. She thought that Eliot had been talking to her father, but he must have turned his attention to her when she was enjoying that sip (enjoying it too much) because he was looking at her with appreciative, conspiratorial humor in his eyes as she opened hers.

"A particularly good white Burgundy, no?"

"Yes," she said quietly, after her throat made an involuntary gulping sound. *And I had a particularly good green apple earlier today*, she thought to herself as she smiled with a little guilty grin at Eliot. It seemed men (if not stepmothers) enjoyed seeing a woman enjoy her food and drink.

About halfway through supper, Penny indicated that she was going to venture out in search of the ladies' room and gave Sarah a nod of invitation. Sarah excused herself from the conversation she had been having with Eliot about Moratelli, the Italian leather manufacturer he'd just acquired. (Jane was in her element fawning over Will Cranbrook and didn't have the time or inclination to censor Sarah's lapse into professional conversation… *and Eliot had started it*, she thought peevishly.)

When Sarah and Penny were getting ready to leave the washroom, Sarah pinching her cheeks and giving her hair a quick brush in the mirror, Penny turned to look, a curious expression on her face.

"You are so much like your mother, Sarah. Your father must remark on it all the time."

"I'm sorry?" She was flummoxed.

"You must know you take after her? Your hair, your eyes, your very…" The chatterbox was unable to grasp the right word. "… essence! I only met her a few times, but she had the same love of every little thing that you seem to have. She was easily cheered."

Sarah stared at this woman. "It's… I… my father never tells me anything about my mother."

"Oh dear, have I upset you?"

"No. Well, in a good way, I guess. I can't very well go around asking for lengthy recitations of my mother's goodness with Jane standing dutifully by. It doesn't seem fair… to any of us."

Penny smiled, encouraging her to continue.

Sarah went on. "Well, it's been fourteen years since my mom died, and it's just such a long time. I have these wonderful memories, but they're starting to fade from real, tangible, tactile memories—her smell, the sound of her charm bracelet coming down the hall—to my version of the recounting of the memory. Does that make sense?"

"Of course it makes sense. Let's have lunch the next time we are both in town and we can talk all about her. Here is my card." Penny Cranbrook handed Sarah a small white calling card with her name and telephone number on it in raised navy-blue engraved script. "It's my cell phone, so feel free to call anytime."

"I love how you have taken your modern cell phone ways and woven them into your refined Emily Post world."

Penny smiled and linked her arm through Sarah's. "See? Easily cheered. Now let's go back to the table and enjoy the spectacle of my son falling in love with you."

Sarah nearly tripped over her own feet, then laughed it off with a merry, if nervous, chuckle.

By eleven thirty, the kitchen was starting to wind down. The happy group of parents and adult children were rosy and riding the wave of epicurean pleasure. Jane was particularly pleased that the evening had turned out even better than she could have hoped.

The Cranbrooks and Sarah's parents were a few paces ahead of them, on their way out of the kitchen into the main part of the restaurant, when Eliot put his hand, tentatively—just his fingertips, really—at the small of Sarah's back.

She stopped midstride and he almost continued walking right into her, then she turned to look at him over her left shoulder and asked, "Are you touching me?"

Clearly the wine had gone to her head because she felt like she could do anything, go anywhere, and be anyone she wanted. She could turn to this strong, tall, successful man and call him out. Challenge him.

"I was thinking about it." He raised an expectant eyebrow, defiantly leaving his hand where it was, rubbing the silk between greedy fingers.

She was still looking over her shoulder. She liked the look of his upper arms and the span of his shoulders, his muscles pulling and straining at the fine wool of his jacket. She looked up at his face. "Well, I... I'm not sure that's such a good idea." She was an evil, cruel, hateful cur. Devon was in her house. Right now. And she was flirting... with an Adonis.

He gestured with his chin toward the front of the restaurant, where the two sets of parents were making lengthy work of retrieving their coats, sorting them out, and putting them on, to allow Eliot and Sarah a bit more time. "How about lunch tomorrow, then? I'm only in town until tomorrow night."

"Sorry, I can't tomorrow." *Because I am a harlot with a lover at home.*

"Well. I tried. Perhaps if you are ever in Geneva... or Milan?" he asked hopefully.

"I am. I mean, I'll be in Milan in a couple of weeks, to renegotiate that contract I told you about with my own leather supplier there." They were walking through the quiet main room of the restaurant.

"Great. I'll meet you there," he answered easily. Of course he could meet her in Milan if he felt like it. He was Eliot Cranbrook and he really could do whatever he pleased, not just fantasize about it after one too many glasses of white Burgundy.

Nelson was grumbling about the lateness of the hour and Jane was beaming, probably congratulating herself on her newfound matchmaking talents. Nelson and Jane had a car and driver taking them back to Lake Forest, and offered to drop Sarah off at her town house, "even though it is out of the way," Nelson added.

"We are staying at the Drake," Penny interjected. "It would be our pleasure to drop Sarah home. We insist." The two limousines were warm and the exhaust curled into the cold night air.

Nelson said thank you for the favor, shook Will Cranbrook's hand and then Eliot's, with genuine regard, then gave Penny and Sarah brief air kisses before opening the door to the limousine for his chirping wife.

Eliot opened their car door and helped his mother in, then his father got in, then he winked at Sarah and gestured broadly with his free hand.

"After you, Miss Sarah James."

"Why thank you, Mister Eliot Cranbrook." She nearly squeaked as she felt his hand on her backside when she bent over to get into the low-slung vehicle, then looked up to see Mr. and Mrs. Cranbrook—Penny and Will—reaching out to assist her.

"Sarah, dear, are you all right?" Penny asked.

Sarah hunched a bit, righted herself, then sat in the rear-facing seat behind the driver. "These shoes are some of my favorites, but they are as high as Everest and are not designed for getting in and out of cars!"

Eliot had slipped in right behind her and was in the other rear-facing seat, smiling at her attempt to cover up his overture. Sarah looked across her lap as Penny leaned her head into her husband's waiting shoulder, and she had an image of her head resting on Devon's shoulder that very afternoon while they watched the movie together. She leaned back into her seat, her face hidden from Eliot by the tinkling bar of glasses that rose up between them.

It was fun to be admired, but she was ready to get home.

To get home to Devon if she wanted to be honest with herself.

Chapter 10

SOON AFTER SARAH SET off, Devon had returned to the Four Seasons to gather his things, settle his bill, and return to the warm haven of Sarah's lair. He didn't want to invade her privacy, but after making himself an omelet for supper and finishing the adventure novel he had started at Heathrow, he found himself wandering through her living room, getting a feel for it, for her, picking up small objects. He examined a piece of antique ivory in the shape of a lemon with an intricately carved village scene perfectly rendered in its tiny interior. He contemplated the heft of and possible uses for a heavy silver letter opener or knife that looked to be of North African or Arabian origin.

Devon spent a long time holding an old but lovingly polished sterling silver frame that showed a black-and-white photograph from another generation. A lovely debutante was being presented between two young blades in white tie, her light eyes twinkling with the expectation of many unknown but longed-for pleasures to come, and her lovely fall of blond hair in a youthful, fetching style with one piece partially pinned up and away from her forehead. It was obviously Sarah's mother. Devon knew there was a stepmother, but he had never asked if her parents had divorced or if her mother had died.

He was standing there in the bay window of Sarah's living room, overlooking Oak Street, when a stretch limousine pulled up and another handsome blade from his generation stepped out with alacrity and whipped around the rear of the vehicle to open the door for Sarah and then help her out.

Devon thought he looked far too young to be Sarah's father or one of Sarah's father's work colleagues, and by the way he was gripping her upper arms through that thick pile of fur, Devon contemplated taking the heavy Baccarat paperweight that he'd been moving from one hand to another and hurling it at the guy's head. Devon had excellent aim and could probably knock him out if he took a moment to calculate the angle and distance accurately.

The ass was leaning in for a kiss, but Sarah turned her head at the last possible moment, so all he got was a cool cheek instead of those tender lips. Devon stopped moving the paperweight from hand to hand and felt his grip tighten around the poor piece of expensive crystal that happened to be in his fist. The car pulled away from the curb a minute later and Devon heard Sarah's footfalls on the stairs from the street a few seconds after that.

Why had he been looking out the window in the first place? Was he hovering like a child waiting for her return? *What a jerk*, he thought. And too late to trot upstairs and pretend he had been watching a movie in her boudoir. He felt like a fool, a kept man all of a sudden. Not the carefree, fast-car-driving, mindless-pleasure-seeking persona he had spent years manufacturing, that she would be expecting.

By the time Sarah opened the door to her home and came in a breathless rush toward him, her arms outstretched like a toddler, he had worked himself into a proper snit. Her skin against his face was cold from the biting night air, and the fur cape was monstrously sexy, and he knew he was about to fuck it all to hell.

But some things couldn't be helped.

"So, who was the guy who just tried to... maul you... and why did you lie to me and tell me you were going out with your parents?"

She stilled and realized that he was not even returning her embrace. *Just as I've always imagined love*, she thought: *misery*.

Here she was, practically diving into this man's arms, and he was going to start an argument. Her arms fell away from him in silent reply and she started to turn back to the front hall to put the cape away, take off her sky-high pumps, and crawl into bed.

Alone.

He could take his infantile jealousy and shove it somewhere dark and private.

She wasn't more than halfway across the beautiful room when she felt him come upon her from behind and force her body around to face him, one hand gripping her upper arm, ironically, in exactly the same place Eliot had held her moments before. His other hand clenched around the paperweight.

"Sarah. I just asked you a direct question." If he was going to rip this burgeoning relationship to shreds, he might as well do it properly. "Who was the guy?"

"Fuck you."

"What?"

"You heard me." Her face was pale with rage. Her lips pressed together almost to the point of being invisible. "I hardly ever swear, so the novelty, at least, should have startled you into consciousness. But since you appear to be *unconscious*, I am not surprised you didn't recognize the words. So, for your edification, I shall repeat." She paused, then spoke, as if to a village idiot, "Fuck. You."

He was afraid he might crush the glass weight in his hand, so he loosened his hold slightly, then carefully put it back exactly where it had been placed on the spindly little French table (that he also wanted to smash coincidentally). He knew he was overreacting. This was all far too out of control for only having known the stupid woman for a week. Sarah had breached all of his defenses and he was disgusted with himself. Devon wanted her so keenly and with such an irrational, violent level of possession that he did not even recognize his feelings or, moreover, that he (not she) was responsible for them.

He attempted a coherent sentence, but the combination of his own cloud of unfamiliar emotion and the sound (and sight) of her heaving breath, along with those arctic, fierce blue eyes staring at him, challenging him, drove him into a completely irrational fury. He wasn't even mad about the guy in the limo; he was livid at *her*: Sarah was to blame for making him this way. He reached for her, almost tenderly, letting his hand slip between the cool exterior of fur and then up against the warm silk of her blouse. Her eyes flickered, softened for a second at his touch, then blinked and held fast to the look of angry determination.

He undid the fastenings at the neck of the cape, slowly, trying to control the dangerous rage that was far too near, woven into the very fabric of his desire. He removed the cape from her shoulders and laid it down on the Aubusson carpet, delicately making a soft place for the two of them. His hand was shaking with the effort required to control the tornado of feelings. How was it possible that he could adore and despise her so completely?

In silence, he lowered her and himself down onto the fur pallet, holding the back of her head tenderly as he guided her down onto the floor. He started to undo the loose fabric bow at the neck of her blouse, then, unable to fully undo the knot, he lost control and tore the fragile fabric right down the front of her torso. She looked at him with cold fury, her eyes becoming more vacant and distant with each eternal second that passed. She finally turned her head to one side, her silence letting him know that he might overpower her body, but her mind and spirit would never be overpowered.

The glow that Sarah had been feeling when she left the restaurant, her anticipatory warmth at returning to a happy, lusty, carefree Devon was a prehistoric, fossilized memory. Regardless of whatever happened tonight, this… this… whatever it had been with

Devon… was over as far as Sarah was concerned. And she never knew whether it was that thought, or the fact that her glance happened to land upon her youthful, innocent, *perfect* mother—in her white cotillion dress, her fiancée on one arm, her handsome brother on the other—that caused one treacherous tear to roll down her cheek.

She closed her eyes, thinking she could retract the evidence of her sadness, wish it away. She hated that Devon would ever know she had let him in, even a little. Sarah hated herself for dreaming that little dream. Then she hated Devon even more for making those dreams cheap and meaningless.

Devon saw himself for the hideous person he was in that moment, in her eyes, in that one tear, and made a futile effort to put the irreparable silk shirt back across her beautiful, vulnerable skin. She ignored him completely and simply rolled away from him and curled into a fetal position on her living room floor.

Sarah drew the fur cape around her like a cocoon. She kept her eyes closed, which was probably immature, but she didn't care about being mature anymore. She was the innocent party. He was the cause of her misery.

She could tell that he was sitting on the floor, leaning against the wall a few feet away from her. His breathing was labored and he was muttering self-deprecating epithets to himself.

"Sarah. I'll never be able to apologize enough for what just happened. I'm a wreck."

She curled tighter into herself and sniffed.

"And I don't expect you to forgive me—"

"Good! Because I never will!" she blurted into the fur around her chin.

He muttered another self-hating expletive.

"This was my mother's blouse—" It was such a stupid thing to say but it made her start crying all over again. "And you're the rat bastard who ruined it, and for some despicable reason, I want *you* to make me feel better."

He was on the floor behind her before she finished the sentence, pulling her into him—her back against his front—hugging her close, breathing his words into her hair and neck and ear. "Please let me make it better, Sar."

Sarah had a momentary flash of him tying her to the bed and lighting the house on fire. This was a bad, bad beginning to anything worth pursuing. But it felt so good, having him hold her like that.

She turned and faced him, looking hard into his frightened, penitent gray eyes. "What the hell came over you?"

He shut his eyes.

"Open your eyes and tell me," she ordered.

He opened his eyes and stared into hers. "I was furious…"

"I got that part…"

He took another breath. "I… I don't know what to tell you, Sarah. I spent the past few hours inhaling everything about you and wandering around your house imagining all the things I was going to do to you when you got back." He breathed again. "And then I saw that bastard—"

The fury was obviously still close to the surface, but he paused to collect himself. Sarah stiffened slightly and pulled the cape tighter around her. The oddest part was that she wasn't afraid of him, not in any real physical way. She had been the one who'd wanted to taunt him and bait him into being some sort of unreserved savage. But there was something about his eyes that terrified her, not for herself, but for him. It looked miserable in there.

They stared at each other in those tense, close inches.

"I don't think I can handle it, Devon."

No! her libido cried. *Make it work! He is forgivable! He is begging! What are you saying?! He is hotter than Hades! Get your priorities straight! Think of the makeup sex!*

He stared at her and she saw the defeat settle in his shoulders. "I totally understand." He leaned in and kissed her forehead. "No emotional mess. Those were your terms, right?"

She smiled, a small and weak lift of her lips, and nodded. "I… I just can't…"

He reached up between them and touched her cheek. "You're right. I'm totally bad news. I thought I could be… good."

She smiled a little bit more, but it was all resignation. "I liked you bad," she whispered.

"Oh, Sarah James. You sweet thing. You don't even know the half of it. I'm a rat bastard, remember?"

"Do you think you would ever hit me?"

"Never!" he answered with complete conviction, then his eyes blinked once. "But I can't answer for what I wanted to do to that prick who was trying to cop a feel when you got out of his car." He ran his hand across the fur cape where it rested along the ridge of her hip, already looking sort of nostalgic. "I should probably go."

"You don't have to." Sarah wiped her eyes and awkwardly tried to sit up.

Yesssss! Her crazy body rejoiced.

"Here, let me help you up." Devon shifted around so he was off the floor and then gave her a hand. She was still holding the cape to cover her exposed front where the blouse was ripped.

Devon raked his hair with both hands once she was standing. "Holy shit. I am so, so sorry."

Sarah looked down. "Let me go upstairs and change and maybe we can just have a drink and try to sort some of this out. Okay?"

"Okay. I'll wait in the kitchen."

"Okay." Sarah stared at him for a few seconds longer, trying desperately to repress the urge to lean into his hard chest and lose herself in him again. She turned abruptly to go upstairs to her bedroom before his body got the best of her. She caught a glimpse of herself in the gilt mirror on the hall landing outside her bedroom and almost laughed. She looked like a caricature of a washed-up lush from *Valley of the Dolls*: mascara smudged, hair tangled on one side, blouse torn… all she needed was Norma Desmond's cigarette holder and a big tumbler of scotch.

Sarah stopped short, all thoughts of scotch forgotten, when she opened the door into her bedroom. Puccini's "*O Mio Babbino Caro*" was playing softly on the sound system; the fireplace and a few candles lit the room to a romantic glow. The bed had been turned down and there was a bottle of champagne and two glasses on the side table in the bay window. It couldn't have been any more romantic if Devon had hired set dressers from Louis B. Mayer, circa 1940.

What a waste.

The room was warm from the fire and Sarah threw the cape on one of the side chairs near the window. She continued into the closet and took off the torn blouse. Her mother's blouse… why had she even told him that? Everything seemed empty all of a sudden. What did a shirt or a cape or a silver picture frame or a charm bracelet or any of it *matter* if her mother was dead? She rarely said it just like that: dead. She always euphemized the whole experience of her mother's illness and departure: she had passed away… gone… we lost her… such a tragedy… the sadness… her demise.

After Sarah took the blouse off, she let the shredded pieces of the vintage YSL silk fall across the palm of one hand. Should she even bother trying to salvage it? What an absurd, depressing reminder of a short-lived (her first!) love affair. What a cliché. The torn pieces. The remnants of her feelings. She was hating herself already. She almost laughed when she imagined repairing it with thick black wool and knitting needles, creating a sort of Frankenstein scar that would run straight up the front of the delicate chiffon. Alexander McQueen would have loved that. She made a mental note to look into incorporating some kind of scarring into the fall line of shoe designs she'd been working on.

After taking off the rest of her clothes, Sarah slipped on her favorite stretched-out gray T-shirt and black yoga pants (or whatever the right word was for baggy black pants in which one never did yoga), then went into the bathroom and scrubbed her face and brushed her teeth. She felt like it was four in the morning and was amused to see it was only shortly after midnight according to the gold clock on the mantle, yet another reminder of her mother.

And now Devon. Because that clock had marked the passage of those wonderful hours with him in her bed.

Sarah took a deep breath and walked downstairs to see if the two of them could have a rational conversation and maybe just not be so intense. Maybe they could be friends.

She smiled at the rapidity with which she was turning into a poster child for every possible romantic cliché. He's royal! He's fabulous in bed! He's insanely jealous! He's my new best friend!

Ugh.

"I made some tea," Devon said.

Sarah looked at her kitchen counter, where he'd set up a sweet little tray of cream and sugar and an actual teapot.

"Thanks. That's nice."

He kept staring at her and Sarah reached up to touch her forehead. "Do I have something on my face?"

"No. Just… so freshly scrubbed. You look ravishing. Pure as driven snow."

"Don't talk like that… please."

His eyebrows pulled together as he looked away from her pleading gaze and down at the teapot. He lifted the little top to see if it had steeped enough, then poured them each a cup. "How do you take it?"

Not well, I'm afraid, she wanted to answer, but smiled instead and said, "Lots of cream, very little sugar."

He smiled and made it the way she asked.

"Let's sit here in the kitchen. It feels appropriate for a post-mortem, don't you think?" She gestured toward the white marble countertops and the round white tulip table tucked in the corner. "All very easy to wipe down."

He smiled wider and brought the tea tray over to the small table.

"Thanks," she said, taking her cup and a grateful sip.

He took a sip of his, never taking his eyes from hers across the rim of his cup.

"So," Sarah began. "I'm afraid I'm going to resort to a kind of corporate version of myself, but I don't know how else to... talk about... to address what happened before. I just..."

She looked up and tried to appreciate him in the most objective way. He was so beautiful. Couldn't she just maybe enjoy him... *Yesssss! Yessss!* her body cheered. No. She couldn't. She knew she couldn't. Bronte was the one who was all on about no strings attached and transitional men and look where that had landed her. Knocked up.

Plus, Sarah didn't know what kind of boring sex Bronte was used to having, but there was *no way* Sarah could ever have sex again with Devon Heyworth without getting very, *very* deeply attached. Her body was already like an addict, for goodness' sake. Best to nip that part right in the bud.

He was waiting patiently for her to finish. Why couldn't he have exercised similar restraint when she'd come home from dinner? Why did he have to fly off the handle? She sighed.

"Just tell me. I can take it."

She looked back into his eyes and was relieved that the misery and grief she'd seen there before was now gone. Sarah hoped she had imagined it in the first place.

"I just can't possibly sleep with you anymore." *Noooooooooo!* "It would be too... fraught. And I like you—"

He smiled as if it were a nail in the coffin, but she smiled back wider.

"What? I do like you. But if we went on to have some torrid, sexy affair… I mean, I just don't see that working for either of us."

He didn't say anything, but he narrowed his eyes and looked like he was sorting out some kind of mathematical equation. Maybe he was developing a statistical equation to calculate the odds of ever getting her back into bed.

"I think I could see a torrid, sexy affair working for me," he said in a low, provocative whisper.

Sarah met his stare and upped the ante. "Even if I go to Milan to stay with another man next weekend?"

His face clouded immediately.

"Or when I am in Singapore with my friend Christophe?"

He looked downright stormy, then his expression suddenly lifted. "You're just trying to bait me. You were a revirgin, remember? You don't fly around sleeping with guys."

Sarah shrugged. "Look," she interrupted, "that's neither here nor there. The basic thing is that you totally freaked out and I'm just embarking on my life"—she didn't think she needed to actually say the stupid phrase *sex life*, since even Mr. Self-Absorbed seemed to finally get the hint—"and I don't want all of this drama. I have enough drama in my life. I sell drama, for goodness' sake."

Devon Heyworth was momentarily stunned to realize *he* was the one getting a lecture on being overly dramatic. He almost burst out laughing but was too dumbfounded to do much of anything. He had fucked this up so completely, there was no elegant exit strategy.

"Devon?"

He looked up again. "Sorry. Right. No more sex."

She laughed. "Yeah. In three words or less, I guess that's the deal. No more sex for us." She sighed despite herself. "Seems a shame, doesn't it?"

"Crying shame!" Devon agreed, hoping she'd have a change of heart. He could be an unemotional tosser if that's what she was after.

And then he had the sickening realization that for the first time in his life, he wasn't absolutely sure he *could* be an unemotional tosser after all. Not with Sarah James. Not in the way she was talking about. He could be a possessive, demanding, freakishly jealous tosser. No problem. But a blasé, we're-free-to-see-other-people tosser? No. Fucking. Way.

"But that's how it goes." Sarah shrugged again. "I can't afford you… the emotional price tag would be too high, don't you think?"

Devon smiled and reached out for her hand. She almost withheld it, then let him bring it to his lips for a courtly kiss. She pulled it away quickly and rubbed the spot where his lips had touched hers. *Wiping me off,* he thought miserably.

"I don't think that's a good idea," Sarah said softly.

Devon stared at Sarah and realized he had been running all the wrong programs in his mind when it came to seducing her. Because when he saw that tenderness in her eyes, the repressed longing in her heart, he no longer wanted to seduce her. He wanted to marry her.

And that was just *wrong.* He never wanted to marry anyone. *Ever.*

She caught the change in his expression. "You just realized I was right, didn't you? That we're just all wrong for each other?"

He shook his head, speechless. *Right? Wrong? Run!* his bachelor brain cried. "I… I don't know what to think anymore, Sarah. I think I'm a mess. And you're probably right. I don't think… I think…"

She smiled and patted the back of his hand. "It just shouldn't be this hard this soon. Let's just be glad we were mature enough to bow out before things got too messy. Right?"

"Right." He answered because it would have been rude to sit there like a statue, but the truth of that matter was that Devon Heyworth had never felt more removed from the shores of right and wrong in his entire life.

"Okay, whew." Sarah stood up and took the tea tray to the sink. "That wasn't so bad. You think?" She was rinsing the dishes and putting them in the stainless steel drying rack next to the sink. "It would be silly for you to go back to a hotel at two in the morning. Just sleep on the daybed in the boudoir, okay?"

"Okay." He was so far out of his depth, and he was the supposed high-ranking official in the field of seduction.

She dried off her hands, then came back to where he was sitting. "Let's shake on it, like we should have done last weekend when I left Amberley." She held her hand out to him.

He stared at it then up into her eyes. Something deep and beautiful flashed in those gray eyes, and Sarah's breasts tensed and throbbed in a split second of being in that gaze. She let her hand drop.

"Maybe too soon for a handshake," she muttered. "Sleep well, Devon."

"Thanks, Sarah. You too."

She was already scooting out of the kitchen like a terrified rabbit, taking the stairs two at a time to get as far away from Devon Heyworth as quickly as possible.

She went into her bedroom and curled up in the bed. Of course, he had been in it the entire night before, so the hint of Devon's scent filled the pillows and upholstery. She put her face down and closed her eyes. The smell of Devon made her feel safe.

How was that? she wondered sarcastically. The man had very nearly attacked her in the middle of her living room floor and the thought of him made her feel *safe*?

Who was the psycho in that equation? Duh. She was.

Well, that was already history. And if there was one thing Sarah was perfectly capable of doing, it was moving on. She had only known the guy for a week, for goodness' sake. He was Bronte's brother-in-law. It was a fling, nothing more.

She was only twenty-five-years old—soon to be twenty-six, but still—she was a babe in the woods. This was the very beginning. She was a successful, independent, attractive (Devon had said beautiful, but he was obviously playing with a partial deck), resourceful young woman. She was just embarking on her romantic life. So the first episode had been somewhat... accelerated. And doomed.

She could adjust. Maybe she should call Eliot Cranbrook and see if he still wanted to meet up for lunch—

Ugh.

That was so *not* the solution to her present circumstances.

She tried to sleep and was almost there when she heard the creak of Devon's weight on the tread of the second-to-last step. He turned away from her bedroom and she heard him settle into the boudoir, then all was silent again.

After another few hours of tossing and turning, she finally fell asleep near dawn. When she woke up Sunday morning, it was nearly noon.

And Devon was gone.

Sarah spent all afternoon Sunday and well into the evening going over all of her presentation materials for the board meeting. The financial reports for the past year, the negotiations report documenting the ongoing discussions with the new Italian leather supplier, the distribution channels in the United States, and the possibility of opening in London. She had left everything neatly piled on the kitchen counter Friday afternoon when she came up from work. Almost immediately after settling in at her kitchen table with her business documents and a large latte, she felt restored.

Sure, it was all intense and passionate and life-altering (she had to face it, she was no longer a virgin and that was that), but really, nothing had changed. She thought of her father's secretary, Wendy, and one of her favorite expressions, "You need to put on your Teflon raincoat and walk out into the shit storm." Wendy wasn't much for swearing (she called it verbal lassitude), but in certain cases, she used it to great effect.

And Devon Heyworth was a shit storm if there ever was one.

A week ago, it was all flowers and uncontrollable laughter, and a few days later, it was *The French Lieutenant's Woman*... the subplot that ended badly. Sarah smiled at the idea of Jeremy Irons or Meryl Streep ever having to beg for anything and decided that what she really needed was a powerful dose of Letitia Vorstadt Pennington Fournier. It was past supper in Paris, and her grandmother was most likely stretched out on a chaise with a large Marie Brizard and the *International Herald Tribune*.

The atonal French ring came across the phone line as Sarah waited for the call to go through.

"*Allo?*"

"*Cendrine? C'est Sarah. Je voudrais parler avec ma grand-mere. Est-elle la?*"

The sweet maid, who had lived with Letitia for as long as Sarah could remember, said something kind and doting about how much she missed Sarah and brought the phone to Letitia. Over the years, Cendrine had metamorphosed into a member of the family. Sarah frequently came upon Letitia and Cendrine sitting companionably at the kitchen table in Cap Ferrat, drinking coffee in happy silence, trading sections of the newspaper or commenting on a story in *Paris Match* or *Hello!* magazine. Letitia insisted that Cendrine always be dressed as a "proper maid" (pale blue dress with white apron in the south, black dress with white apron in Paris), but that was the extent of her responsibilities, other than bossing around the battalion of other minions who actually did all the work. "*Au revoir, ma petite. Ta grand-mere est ici.*"

Letitia took the phone from Cendrine, after pretending to chastise her for her deplorable lack of decorum when it came to phone etiquette, then greeted Sarah with a four-syllable version of the word *da-ahr-li-ing*. Her grandmother launched into a week-by-week breakdown of her upcoming winter travel plans and where it would be best for Sarah to meet up with her next.

"Fiesole would be ideal. We should be there and settled by early November, really only a few weeks from now. I think we'll stay for a bit longer this year, maybe even through Christmas. But it gets a bit too damp by the end of December, so I was thinking of St. Barts. Doesn't that sound divine? My friend Leonore has a lovely villa there and said it is just sitting empty, but I think she's angling for an invitation to France next summer and I just don't think I can bear her under the same roof for any length of time, and she tends to stay far too long, so perhaps we could stay at a plain old hotel… but that sounds so *pedestrian*, don't you think, darling? Or maybe a yacht?" Letitia paused, uncharacteristically. "Sarah?"

"Yes?"

"What are you doing, dear? Did you want to *chat* or did you want to *talk*? I am not in the mood to be chastised if that's why you're calling."

"When have I ever chastised you, Letty?"

"You're right, you haven't, but you remind me so much of your mother, even your voice, especially your voice, and I think of all those lengthy, tedious calls when she used to try to tell me what an irresponsible trollop I was. Betsy was just a little bit better than everyone. Especially me, I suppose."

Sarah remained silent.

"What is it, darling? Are you in trouble?" Letitia's voice had the underlying mettle that assured Sarah that *any* trouble could be rectified with the proper pressure applied to the proper authority, celestial or terrestrial.

"I suppose not. But I think I just watched my first love affair come and go, and it was kind of a train wreck."

"Oh, I'm so *relieved*. Come to Paris. Everyone here is either falling in or out of love. The perfect place to lick your wounds, or have someone else lick them for you—"

"Stop! You are still my grandmother!"

"Did you love him? How long were you together? Was he *délicieux*? Tell me everything. It will make you feel better to start recounting... you can eventually turn him into a wonderful story."

Sarah smiled despite her misery. Letitia *was* the perfect person to call. She might have had no idea how to relate to a sixteen-year-old runaway, but she certainly had plenty of opinions and advice when it came to raw passion. "Letty, I don't know if I can talk to you about all this—"

"I forbid you to espouse any false prudery. Your mother was so judgmental when it came to affairs of the heart—"

The involuntary swelling in her throat and bruising pressure behind her eyeballs took Sarah off guard. She was going to start crying again.

"Oh, darling. I didn't mean to speak harshly about your mother. You know she was just *too* good. So much like her father. And then she fell in love with that stick-in-the-mud. Well, your father has his redeeming qualities. I do believe he adored Elizabeth." Letitia was speaking as if to herself. "They were such an odd pair: at home, she was all vivacious authority and he just doted on her, and then in business, he ignored her... well, he ignored everyone so she never took offense. But... oh, Sarah, are you *weeping*?"

Sarah laughed and cried. "I just miss my mother and it sounds so juvenile. I'm a grown woman for goodness' sake, and this man, well, he was kind of wonderful and I thought he really was marvelous and then he became so enraged—"

"Did he hurt you, darling?!"

"No. Well, yes, my feelings of course, but he looked like he wanted to kill me—"

Sarah pictured Letitia looking out over the pale, sparkling evening light that was cast across the Seine at this time of year.

"I remember the first time your grandfather looked at me like that. I was terrified... but I must confess—because, in this above all things, Sarah, you must be honest with yourself—I was perfectly willing to go into that terrifying place as long as he was there."

Sarah tried to picture Letitia's younger self… it was impossible to imagine her being terrified of anything.

Now Sarah was sort of hiccupping and crying and laughing. "I know! I was frightened and he saw how he had scared me and he was miserable and apologized like mad and we talked it all through and agreed it was just never going to work—too much too fast and all that—and then I went upstairs where we had been… earlier in the day and the pillows smelled like him and I missed *him*, and wanted *him* to console me…" She gulped and laughed harshly at the absurdity. "I wanted *him* to console me about *him*!"

"Oh, darling. He sounds tremendous. Tell me all about him. Did you meet him in Chicago? New York? And is he fabulously rich and handsome? I'm sure he must be because I don't imagine you losing your head over anyone who isn't particularly spectacular… I used to worry that you were asexual or some such thing, but then I realized you might have inherited the *worst* of both worlds: your mother's discretion and your grandmother's passion. Oh, poor dear."

"I think you might be right in a way. I never really looked at anyone before him. But now it's like Pandora's box… I seem to be looking at *everyone*… or they seem to be looking at me. Am I making any sense?"

"Of course you are. But back to this one in particular. *Who is he?*"

It was such a direct, quintessentially Letitia way of framing the question. *Who is he?* The first answer that popped into Sarah's mind, oddly enough, was that he was an inventor. A fabulist. A fake earl.

Then she told her grandmother the annotated version of meeting Devon at a wedding in England… romantic castle and all that.

"Which castle?"

"Pardon?"

"Which castle? Cendrine and I were just looking at a wedding spread in *Hello!* over breakfast this morning… Duke of Northwood or some such thing… strapping British stock. Tall, dark, and handsome. You know the type."

"Well, that's his brother."

"His brother? So yours is the earl?"

"He is not *mine*. And he is not really an earl at all." Sarah laughed at the convoluted misunderstanding that had become Devon's public persona. "He's a bit… decadent."

"Ooooh la la! Sarah, I must meet him! He sounds positively divine. A rake! How perfect for you. Oh, he'll ruin you and you'll never get over him. It's just as it should be."

"I'm trying to be a woman of the world about this, but I don't see how my ruination could possibly be construed as a positive outcome."

"Oh dear, because it is so *dramatic*. The last thing you want is something *passable*. I know you miss your mother, and I should have been more sensitive to that over the past few years, all that coming-of-age business, but sensitivity is not my strong point, darling. I was never able to tolerate all those irrational bouts of temper that define adolescence. But irrational bouts of *amour* are most assuredly under my purview."

Sarah heard her grandmother tell Cendrine to bring the latest issue of *Hello!* and then heard Cendrine's affirmative, if not particularly respectful, reply.

"Letty, while we are being honest, when are you going to admit that Cendrine is your best friend and stop treating her like a lackey?"

"Of course Cendrine is my best friend," she whispered, "but I still write her a bank draft every week, so we both agree it's best to keep up a semblance of professionalism. For appearances. And, in any case, she just looks out of context in anything but those pristine white aprons."

Sarah laughed at that and realized that her throat-clenching sadness had passed. She had seen Cendrine on her days off numerous times, and the woman had a lovely wardrobe of clothes and was always the quintessentially stylish French lady when she strolled around Paris free from the watchful eye of Letitia Fournier.

"All right, darling, I have the magazine in front of me now. Let me find the pages with the wedding pictures." Letitia's voice mixed with the sound of rustling pages and then, "Of course I need my reading glasses, Cendrine… *please*. All right, here we are. Oh my, which one of this handsome brood is yours?"

"He's not *mine*, Letitia! I mean, especially after last night. But the one that I sort of, ugh, this is impossible. His name is Devon Heywo—"

"Oh my! Haven't you chosen the cream of the crop? There's one photo in particular where he's standing just outside the chapel doors with the bride and groom right after the ceremony and he looks particularly dreamy."

Sarah's stomach flipped when she recalled their brief interlude in the small antechamber of the church only moments before that picture must have been taken.

"I think a good bit of terror might be accommodated, Sarah. He is, as we used to say, a dish."

"You are eighty-four years old—"

"What does that have to do with anything? Just because my body is a wrinkled old husk doesn't mean that my mind—and heart— aren't still capable of recognizing virility when I see it."

Sarah sighed, mostly because her grandmother was correct. He was the cream of the crop. And he was strapping. And he was virile. And he was fabulous. And. And. And.

"I don't know if this is really the way this conversation should go," Sarah said. "I was hoping to turn lemons into lemonade and never think about him again."

Letitia laughed heartily at that. "Oh! Sarah, you won't be forgetting this one anytime soon." And then to Cendrine, "I know, isn't he fabulous? Sarah's over the moon about him, but apparently he came on a bit strong and she doesn't know how to rein him in… well, of course I told her that… just because you're French does not mean you know *everything* there is to know about men…"

"Letitia! I am sorry to interrupt your eternal bickering with Cendrine, but I am a complete novice at all of this over-the-moon business and I'm not really sure it's what I'm after right now—"

"Oh, darling! It's not up to you!" Letitia's laugh was light. "There's some terribly crass American expression about how something like this bites you in your *derriere*, and I hate to tell you, it's quite true. You can try to *avoid* it, of course, but if he became as fierce as you implied, I think he might have already fallen into your path, so to speak. Now, if you don't share his feelings, that's another matter altogether, but something about missing your mother and all of these other bits and pieces just sort of coincidentally feeling overwhelming all of a sudden… well, it might not be such a coincidence, dear. It sounds as though he may have struck a chord, as it were."

Chapter 11

AT FIRST, THE DAYS crept along at a wretched snail's pace; her mind's constant focus on Devon slowed the passage of time to a crawl. It got easier for Sarah to distance herself from her feelings as the weeks accumulated. For the following six months, she was able to avoid Devon—in person if not in her mind—very handily. She was frequently in London overseeing the construction on the new boutique but rarely strayed from the four-block radius in Mayfair that began at her room at the Connaught Hotel and ended at the construction site. Initially, she had narrowed the search for her new store location down to three properties: one was on Walton Street, a chic, upscale snake of a road, near Harrods and Sloane Square, and projected a very respectable, old-world Georgian feel; the next was just off Carnaby Street, near one of Stella McCartney's edgy boutiques, where the entire row of shops exuded hip, cool fashion; the third was on a tiny lane near Bond Street called Bruton Place, which had a mix of galleries, an upscale pub, and a falling-down former garage from the 1950s.

Sarah was looking for a situation similar to what she had in Chicago (shop below, living above), but it would have felt like too much of a carbon copy if she'd applied it to the Georgian town house on Walton Street. There was no way she could live near Carnaby Street; it was far too bustling twenty-four hours a day and she would have no rest whatsoever. She finally settled upon the Bruton Place garage property.

The location was close enough to the high-end shops of Mayfair (and Bond Street in particular) to give it the proper air of haute couture, it was relatively quiet at night, and the building itself offered an alternative, modern feel that Sarah wanted the London store to possess. The second and third floors had rough original beams and charming exposed brick walls ("More like decrepit," her father had commented dryly), so she could easily envision converting the top into a modern living space and the middle into an office and storage space, with the shop at street level.

She was finally able to wrest the freehold from the family who had been holding on to it for the past sixty years by assuring them she would not tear it down. For some reason, they were sentimentally attached to their little garage in Mayfair and had yet to meet a buyer who was willing to leave the property intact.

After she had returned from her honeymoon in late October, Bronte was also back in London to help manage the marketing and PR for the new Sarah James store. She and Max lived in an adorable mews house in Fulham that Max had bought and fixed up before they'd met. Bronte's marriage to Max Heyworth had done nothing to hamper her enthusiasm or talent for the advertising business she had built before she met him. Motherhood, on the other hand, might put a slight crimp in her plans.

When Bronte told Sarah she was expecting a baby, of course Sarah's first question had been, "What's your due date?!"

Bronte's sheepish "April first" had them both laughing at the timing and trying to come up with some good puns about fools and their folly.

Despite Bronte's initial enthusiastic flurry of questions about Devon and Sarah getting together over the wedding weekend, Sarah's firm and consistent replies that it was "only a one-time thing" finally wore Bronte's curiosity down. Sarah also suspected that Max had told Bronte to give it a rest after Devon must have told him the same thing. Sarah never mentioned Devon's unexpected visit to Chicago, and she was certain Devon wouldn't have said anything to Max about that ill-fated journey either.

When Bronte and Max asked Sarah to be the baby's godmother, even Sarah knew it would be the height of immaturity to refuse because Devon was going to be the godfather. Sarah accepted with the requisite enthusiasm (she *did* want to be the baby's godmother for goodness' sake; what could be more fun than showering a little boy or girl with all sorts of superfluous gifts… especially a girl baby… who liked shoes…), but Sarah had to admit that the actual christening ceremony, which would take place six weeks after the birth, loomed on her emotional horizon like a guillotine about to drop. Sarah tried not to let her imagination get too grim, but whenever she pictured herself standing around the baptismal font in the ancestral chapel watching Devon hold a newborn, she felt as if she had crossed into a circle of hell. The circle of seeing everything you want right there before your eyes and having it be damnably—fractionally—out of reach.

The reality was even worse than she could have imagined.

Sensing Sarah's reluctance to talk about the fling with Devon (and whatever had soured what should have led to a perfectly fun London port-of-call romance for Sarah), Bronte made sure the two were never thrown together unexpectedly. Unfortunately, there was no way to conduct a baptism without having the godfather and the godmother in the same room at the same time.

～～～

The baby, who would one day become the twentieth Duke of Northrop, arrived with the promptness his father was known for, coming into the world—at high noon exactly—on April 1. Charles Conrad William Thomas Carlisle Heyworth, Marquess such-and-such, Earl this-and-that, and Viscount hill-and-dale, was far too small to bear the burden of such an enormous name and so many courtesy titles, so from the moment his squinty, moist, baby eyes opened and gazed into his mother's adoring face, and Bronte saw replicas of Max's gray lupine eyes staring back at her, his mother simply called him Wolf.

The name was instantly adopted by everyone except the Dowager Duchess, who insisted on calling him Charles at every opportunity. The christening was scheduled for May 12. Sarah went into full panic mode around May 5.

All that kitchen-table talk about no more sex was all well and good in the abstract. It was easy enough to ignore her feelings when she didn't actually see him (or smell him or... ugh), but Sarah began to worry that she might actually dive at him across the baptismal font in order to slake her pent-up lust. *It's just physical*, she kept assuring herself rationally. Like a food allergy. She needed a temporary Devon antidote or lust inhibitor. At one point, she actually considered speaking with a doctor to see if such a drug actually existed.

And, in the midst of all this *not* seeing Devon, there was Eliot Cranbrook. The man seemed to have some sort of GPS device that casually tracked Sarah's every move. If she happened to go to Paris for the weekend, he would call on Saturday morning and ask if she happened to be in Paris. When she was back in New York for a week or two? Surprise!

She supposed the world of fashion and the luxury goods market followed a certain rhythm—trade shows, fashion weeks—so Sarah didn't give it too much thought. And, she had to confess, it was a relief to be taken out to dinner and mildly fawned over without any threat of a deeper attachment. Eliot was attentive without being dramatic. Never jealous, never prying. If they didn't see each other for a few weeks, the occasional email or text sufficed to stay in touch.

Physically, though, she was starting to have to keep him at bay.

The two of them definitely had some chemistry. Even that

initial touch at her lower back as they were leaving Charlie Trotter's in Chicago had proven that. But the frisson of excitement from Eliot was nothing compared to the roiling cauldron from Devon. She tried to convince herself that cauldrons were for witches, not sexually inexperienced shoe designers.

The weekend before the christening, Sarah decided to take the train to Paris to visit Letitia. Of course, her phone rang on Friday afternoon and Eliot wondered if she might be headed to France for the weekend. He was just finishing up a string of negotiations with a young French designer and was going to head back to Geneva, "Unless…"

"I was just thinking that you must have one of those canine chips implanted in me somewhere," Sarah laughed as she pulled her bag onto the Eurostar first-class train. (Yes, she had finally succumbed to the wheelie bag—a Louis Vuitton Damier Pégase model—but still, it had been a capitulation.)

"Excellent! I will hold on to my room at Le Meurice, unless you want to go out of town? Have you been to Normandy or Giverny?"

"Another weekend perhaps. My grandmother is just back in town"—Sarah grunted as she lifted her luggage to the overhead rack—"and I'm looking forward to seeing her. You'll finally get to meet the infamous Letitia Fournier."

"My weekend is yours. Shall I make a reservation for dinner? Does your grandmother have a particular favorite?"

"She's totally old school when it comes to restaurants, Taillevent or La Tour d'Argent, or if she's feeling particularly adventurous, she might deign to visit the upstart Alain Ducasse."

Eliot was laughing lightly and Sarah could hear the sound of papers rustling and street noises in the background.

"Where are you, anyway?"

"In the back of a limo being driven to another meeting." His voice changed then, from a casual business tone to something deeper. "I'm glad I caught up with you."

"Me too." Sarah hoped she sounded light and hoped he wouldn't choose this of all weekends to try to take their friendship to another level. She dreaded other levels. "Why don't you come to my grandmother's around seven thirty?" She gave him the address and continued, "We can have a cocktail, then head out for dinner. I'll make the reservation after I talk to Letitia."

"Sounds great"—back to casual, fun Eliot—"I'll see you then. Ciao." She heard him launch into rapid-fire Italian with one of his assistants before he had finished disconnecting his phone.

A few hours later, Sarah was happily curled up on Letitia's chaise longue in an alcove of the older woman's vast bedroom. Letitia was in her bed, looking like a caricature of a wealthy heiress in her vintage pale blue 1940s quilted-satin bed jacket.

"Letitia, I swear, who in the world has any use for bed jackets, except you?"

"Oh, Sarah darling, you and your generation of beauties are missing out on all the fun. You need to slow down! I love receiving people in my bedroom… not like I have so many callers these days, of course. But it's delightful to sit here and drink my tea, and spend the afternoon in divine comfort."

"It is fabulous… I suppose you would have to be born into it."

"As if you were not?"

"You know what I mean! My mother never would have abided all that *lying around*. Sometimes I wonder if you two were even related."

"I knew I should have chosen her nanny with more care. Your grandfather and I had a fabulous six-month trip planned and I just couldn't be bothered. I know it sounds horribly *un*maternal to your modern ears, but babies were just not part of that picture. Your mother was an angel of course, but that nanny of hers was a tyrant. She adored your mother, but she ran a tight ship. Even I was occasionally cowed."

"I doubt that," Sarah said into her teacup.

"I heard that! So tell me what you would like to do this weekend, darling."

"As a matter of fact, I have a little surprise for you."

"I hope he is tall and fabulous... and British?"

"Two out of three..."

"Fabulous and British?"

"The other two..."

"Tall and British?"

"Stop! Letitia, he's tall and fabulous. And definitely *not* British. You've got to let that one go. I have told you for months that I am not ready for all that fiery passion or possession or whatever you want to call it." Sarah waved her hand to dismiss the idea.

"You haven't listened to a word I have said, Sarah. You are not being honest with yourself. Look at you! Even when you are uttering the words, you sound like you are trying to convince a truth commission... whether you are ready or not, I don't think you can just *let it go*."

Sarah started to protest, but her grandmother held the floor. "You are too gorgeous and *fiery*, I daresay, to settle for some bland substitute. Do you mean to tell me you have been in London all these past months and you haven't seen him one time?"

"I am not having this discussion with you, Letitia. You are the only person who has not accepted that my episode of Earl Meets Girl did not have a happily ever after. Please."

"Oh! So he *is* an earl, then?!" Her excitement was palpable.

"No! That was a joke. Would you quit it already?!" But Sarah laughed despite her irritation, then mumbled, "Let's just drop it."

"Oh, don't go all *maudlin* on me. That's just emotional blackmail. I shall continue to refer to him as they do in the rags: The Earl... it has such a jaunty ring to it."

"You are impossible." Sarah rolled her eyes.

"Very well then, tell me about the American." But Letitia said it in such a way that made it perfectly clear she had no interest in the man who was obviously an also-ran to The Earl. She picked up her teacup and gazed out the window, as if to say, *Bore me with the hayseed.*

"Oh, Letitia, you are such a fabulous snob! In any case, his name is Eliot Cranbrook and he's a dishy Robert Redford type. But taller. Much taller."

That seemed to get her partial attention. "But he is *not* an earl."

"Neither is the other one!" Sarah laughed. "Trust me. You will like the American."

And when he arrived—fine clothes, perfectly tailored, a small, exquisite bouquet of spring flowers for Letitia—he had the doyenne's full attention. Eliot certainly knew how to play it.

Letitia's husband Jacques also joined them, and the quartet went to Le Grand Véfour.

The conversation, the food, the splendid wine, the centuries-old perfection of the sparkling jewel of a restaurant itself, the fading mirrored panels reflecting candlelight: everything bubbled and sang like the champagne they had with their first course.

Sarah watched as Eliot charmed her grandmother (not very difficult, since Letitia responded quite readily to his mix of genuine flattery of her person and a potent love of French food and wine, though not necessarily French people). When Eliot turned his attention to Jacques, she thought her step-grandfather might not be so easily drawn in.

She need not have worried on Eliot's behalf.

Of course, Eliot knew just the things to lure Jacques out of the crusty ill humor that he wore like an uncomfortable jacket whenever he was in Paris. On the Côte d'Azur or in Fiesole or the Caribbean, or really *anywhere* except Paris, Jacques Fournier was a cheerful, if preoccupied, artist. He sketched or painted each day, wherever they happened to be. But in Paris, he was explaining to Eliot, the weight of the blind, marching masses always depressed him.

Eliot spoke in perfect French and Sarah could tell Jacques appreciated it. "I know what you mean. The city has become all business," Eliot said. "When I am here, I am always thinking *business*. But then"—he turned to catch Sarah's eye and gave her a brief, sweet smile, then resumed talking to the older man—"I try to remember everything that is *magnifique* about the city. I call a beautiful friend, we have a beautiful meal with interesting people all around us. I can leave all that business aside."

Jacques nodded and took another sip of the spectacular Chateau Léoville-Las-Cases 1986 Bordeaux that Eliot had selected from the wine list.

"It is hard to disagree with someone who would choose such a wine," the Frenchman mused as he lifted his glass in a small toast.

Sarah had to hand it to Eliot. He had perfected the art of seduction. Not even romantic seduction. His entire life, professional and personal, was spent luring people to pleasure: taste this quintessential St. Julien; wear this perfectly cut suit; carry this hand-rubbed leather luggage. Everything he did was an invitation to…

"Don't you think, Sarah?" Her grandmother might as well have stomped on her foot under the immaculate white tablecloth for all the subtlety.

"I'm sorry. It's been a long week. I seem to be fading a bit. What were you three talking about?"

"Oh, never mind, darling," Letitia said as she patted her granddaughter's smooth hand. "Why don't we leave the men to deal with the crude matter of the bill while you and I stroll around the Palais Royal for a few moments?" Letitia leaned down and kissed Jacques on the cheek, a gesture he always enjoyed.

Sarah smiled at Eliot, who gave her a quick wink. "I certainly didn't invite Eliot to dinner and expect him to pay, Letitia."

"Of course he shall pay, dear. He's obviously a gentleman."

Sarah gave Eliot an apologetic look, then shrugged her shoulders and accompanied her Napoleonic grandmother out into the cool, spring night air.

While they were enjoying a few minutes in the splendid royal enclosure, Sarah heard her phone buzz with a text message.

"Do you mind if I see to that? It's the end of the workday in Chicago and I'd like to check in."

"Of course I mind! Here we are under a clear, dazzling night sky, the sound of the gravel crunching under our feet—it is Paris, you fool! But go ahead. I know there are important things happening in the world of young cobblers."

Sarah bent to kiss her grandmother's cool, papery cheek, the faintest hint of Guerlain's Shalimar wafting off her skin. "I love you."

"Oh, go check your Web notes or whatever you call it."

Any show of affection always made Letitia a bit awkward, and Sarah loved her even more for it.

Sarah tapped her phone and saw the text was from Bronte. Probably more last-minute info about the christening next Sunday. Earlier in the week, Bronte had pleaded with Sarah to make a weekend of it, rather than getting a car or taking the train out to Dunlear for the day on that Sunday. Sarah had finally relented, but only after making Bronte promise to put her in a room as far away from Devon as possible.

"Is it really as bad as all that, Sar?"

"Bron, I do not want to make a big deal about it, but I doubt Devon has any interest in spending time with me either. Let's just make it all about your little wolf cub and put the rest aside, okay?"

"Okay, okay. But you and Devon just seemed so—" Her sentence was cut short by her husband's obvious intervention on the other end of the phone. "Well, geez, all right. I'll drop it. When did everybody get so touchy around here? Max told me I need to leave it alone, and since I am such an *obedient* wife, I shall cease in my matchmaking efforts. I'm so grateful you will come for the whole weekend, in any case. Why don't you meet us in Fulham on Friday afternoon and we can all drive out together?" They had ironed out the rest of the plans and Sarah hadn't given it much thought (the logistics at least) since.

This text, on the other hand, which she was reading under the starry Parisian sky, was... well... upsetting.

> had 2 let u no dev bringing date nxt w/e. if u want 2 do same I totally understand. still his home so couldnt v well forbid it. what an ass. he must no that bringing bimbo 2 dunlear on Wolfs big w/e ill advised. sorry again but wanted you 2 no just in case. xx b

"Great," Sarah said under her breath.

"What is it, dear?" The two women had circled back to the entrance of the restaurant, where the men were just inside the beveled glass doors talking contentedly with the sommelier and the maître d'.

"Oh, nothing, I suppose. Seems the faux-earl has met another girl. And I will have the pleasure of making her acquaintance this weekend."

"What's that about this weekend, Sarah?" It was Eliot now, looking sated after a splendid meal in splendid company. He snaked his arm through hers and they started walking out toward the Rue de Richelieu to get a taxi back to the Île Saint-Louis, Jacques and Letitia walking slowly a few paces behind them.

"Nothing. I am going to be a godmother and the christening is next weekend in England... in Hertfordshire, actually."

They walked in a companionable silence.

Sarah tried to strategize. Maybe she should come clean and just tell Bronte that she didn't think she could bear an entire weekend watching Devon with another woman, that she simply had to come out Sunday morning. Bronte of all people would understand the devastating effect of a Heyworth male on a sex-starved female. Or maybe she just needed to bring her own buffer and fight fire with fire, as it were.

She realized the perfect solution was wrapping his arm casually around her shoulder as they walked through the eighteenth-century arcade and out to the wide avenue. She had never asked Eliot to do anything. He had always invited her places or met up with her in Milan or initiated their meetings in Paris. She wondered idly if, in the past six months, she had ever even called him, except to return one of his calls. Would it open a whole other can of worms if he thought she was finally coming around to acknowledging a deeper attraction?

"Where are you?" he whispered. The heat of his breath was unnerving so close to her hair.

"Oh. Sorry." She gave him a small smile and pulled a few inches away from him. "I'm just trying to sort out my plans for next weekend. Sorry to be so distracted." She smiled again, but it felt like an effort at concealment.

"Anything I can do? It's a shame to see you... confounded." He traced his finger along her forehead to erase the lines of concentration that must have formed there. It was a gentle, sweeping touch, and then it was gone.

He was good. He knew she was resisting him, and not in a coy or taunting way. He had been a very patient man for six months, without ever exerting the slightest pressure or even implying that she was taking way too long to acknowledge his subtle, yet palpable, attraction. Even though they had not met before that night in Chicago, he often introduced her as an "old friend of the family," thus obviating the need to define their friendship any more than that.

Not that he felt the need to elaborate his intentions, professionally or personally, to anyone at all. His parents had been in Paris a few months before, and when the four of them had gone out to dinner, it had almost been filial. She liked being part of, even peripherally, a traditional nuclear family.

"Well. There might be something you can do. You have become such a good friend... I don't even know where or how it actually happened, but—what?!"

Eliot had stopped short on the sidewalk, turned to face her, and held his fist over his heart as if he had stabbed himself. "Such is my fate? *Good friend*? Kill me now. My mother warned me... never become the good friend." But he was smiling, and Sarah was so grateful, she turned and hugged him with a fierce devotion.

He *was* her friend.

"Believe me, it would have been far more convenient for me to fall in love with you," Sarah continued in a rush, holding his upper arm tightly in her grasp, so relieved to be unburdening herself, as they resumed walking down the romantic street, the moist cobblestones glistening under the street lamps. "That night I met you in Chicago, actually, was when it all started... or ended... or I don't know. It's probably easier if I just tell you the whole thing so you can see me for the flighty widgeon I am."

They took Letitia and Jacques back to their flat, then Eliot suggested they get a drink and hatch their Machiavellian plans. The two of them went to a quiet bar in Le Marais and talked and drank until four in the morning. Sarah told Eliot about her short-lived, but seemingly unforgettable, time with Devon.

"I keep telling myself that it must just be because he was the first..." she said, then backpedaled quickly at his raised eyebrows, "you know, that I really felt strongly about."

But Eliot could tell she probably meant he was the first. Period. Lucky jerk.

"About that," Eliot tried, picking up his glass of scotch and holding it midway between the shiny black cocktail table and his lips, "does this guy know he was the first... that you felt, you know... that you loved?"

"No!" She practically sprayed the water out of her mouth.

When they'd first arrived at the bar and Eliot ordered his drink, Sarah had thought a glass of scotch sounded good theoretically—now that she was baring her soul to her solid friend Eliot and all—but after one burning sip, she had coughed with embarrassing intensity and humbly switched to ice water. "Are you crazy? I had only known the guy for a week! You think I… I don't even know what love *is*! See?! I sound like a bad song from the 1970s. It's just all wrong."

He looked at her and wondered what kind of fool would let her slip away. "All right, moving on from declarations of undying affection, then, how have things progressed since Chicago? Where does he live? When do you see him? How does he treat you?"

"See? I told you it would solidify my reputation as a total flake if I told you this sordid history. I haven't seen him or talked to him since that night in Chicago. He lives in London. He's going to be at the christening next weekend. He's the godfather. I'm the godmother." She shook her head with a self-deprecating toss. "It's totally not a big deal."

Eliot smiled at Sarah, but his eyes wandered for a split second to take in a sophisticated woman with black, straight hair who had eyed him on her way into the bar.

"Aaah. I have freed you to check out other women in my presence. This is going to be fun! By the way, I hope you know I would never allow any of this silly relationship nonsense to affect my work. I love talking to you about work and my goals for the business and—"

"Sarah. You are a gem. I would never judge you. Especially not for being honest with me. And yes, you caught me. That woman is quite something. But, even if we are just *good friends*, I won't be drooling over other women when I'm with you. You're the whole package, Sar. And if your feelings for this British seducer are still unresolved then, well, I will assist. I'm happy to run interference… or reconnaissance?" He winked and Sarah smiled.

"At this point I don't know if rekindling our feelings would be the best or the worst outcome."

"Either way, I'll be there." Eliot always made everything seem so manageable. "I'll schedule meetings in London for Thursday and Friday so we can head out of the city Friday night with your friend Bronte. Sound good?"

Sarah smiled her gratitude. "Yes. Thank you, Eliot."

"How deep do you want to play it? Are we dating? Are we sharing a bed? Is there a hotel nearby where we'll be staying?"

Sarah hadn't considered *that*. "Well, no. We'll stay at their place. There's plenty of room."

"Sarah, I'm a grown man. And a particular one at that. I don't really want to sleep on a pull-out at your friend's house. I'll pretend to be your lover—hell, I'll happily *be* your lover with no pretense whatsoever—but I will not sleep in an uncomfortable bed. With all of these people descending upon them for the weekend, they probably don't have a room to spare anyway."

Sarah smiled and took another sip of her water, her eyes sparkling with mischief.

"Why are you looking at me like that? Do they have a big house?"

Sarah nodded and continued smiling.

"Like, how big?"

"Big."

"Like how many bedrooms?"

"Like, sixty-four, give or take." She let her hair swing behind her back and looked at him. "What do you think?"

"Well. I suppose I won't be imposing anyway. Is he a jealous guy? I don't want to have a leather glove tossed in my face and be forced to walk twenty paces at dawn. My fencing is also a bit rusty."

"He is rather jealous, come to think of it. He saw you getting out of the limo that night in Chicago."

"He was at your apartment that night?!"

"Yes. Why?"

"You are a cruel beast, Sarah. I might even buy the poor man a drink."

"I don't understand men at all. *He* is the one bringing a date to his nephew's christening, for goodness' sake. I was just getting out of a car."

"Now, in the midst of all this refreshing honesty, let's not slip into deceit. You know very well that I would have come up to your bed that very night if you'd asked me. I know all that is behind us, but I'm still a man, and you are still a beautiful woman. And even from several stories above, I'm sure that fool of a man was, well, aware of my intentions. What did he do?"

"He was annoyed," she replied without elaboration.

"How annoyed?"

"Very."

"Sarah?"

"He was… well, he was in a sort of fury. And then, well, and then we talked things over and we both agreed that it was all for the best if we didn't see each other anymore. Or rather, I suggested that part, and I guess he sort of reluctantly agreed…"

"Am I going to have a leather glove thrown in my face or not?"

"Very funny. Like I said, the fact that he's bringing another woman to the baptism this weekend proves that he's *way* over me."

"Kind of like your inviting me proves that you are over him? Don't answer that. I'll bring my dueling pistols."

Chapter 12

IT HAD BEEN ALMOST seven months to the day (the night, really) that Devon had last seen Sarah. *That is not technically accurate*, he chided himself, since he had seen her every minute since then, just not in reality. He checked her website, he dreamed about her, he tried to act disinterested when he asked Max about her. He knew she had been in London and had to force himself to stay away. Her website had occasional updates about the new store scheduled for a September opening, and it was all he could do not to sneak into the building to make sure the construction work was being done properly. When he'd read an article about the owners of the old building on Bruton Place resisting her offer, he didn't think it went beyond the pale to make a few phone calls to convince them she would be an admirable buyer. He was just trying to be helpful. He didn't want to impose.

He was overcome with equal parts dread and desire at the prospect of finally seeing her in the flesh at Dunlear in three days. He had told Max last Friday at dinner that he was bringing a girl with him, hoping that would lend the whole weekend a friendly, careless tenor. Little did he know that he'd set in motion a string of events that would create a situation that was anything but friendly or careless. Unbeknownst to Devon, after he'd left Max and Bronte the previous weekend, Bronte had sworn Max to secrecy about Sarah bringing a buffer date.

"If Devon's going to try to be all what-me-worry? at the expense of *my* best friend, then he can squirm a bit," Bronte barked at her husband in the taxi home. "How dare he bring some strumpet to our first family event for Wolf?"

Max smiled softly and rubbed Bronte's forearm. "Narinda is not a strumpet. And if nothing had ever transpired between Dev and Sarah, then none of that would matter. Obviously, something happened, and maybe this is a good way for them to just move on."

"Move on? Are you blind? Neither of them can even have a conversation about the other, much less be in the same room. And all these months in London with both of them trying to be all casual every time we invite them over for supper, like, 'Uh, by the way, will fill-in-the-blank be there?' And then always happening to be busy when one or the other is already coming over? Come on. Those two have 'Unresolved Issues' written across their foreheads."

"Okay," Max replied in typical marital mode, "what should I do?"

Bronte's phone beeped with a text reply from Sarah before she could answer him.

bringing backup in form of eliot cranbrook next w/e, ok? pls
don't tell you-no-who. Dont want 2 seem tit-4-tat xos

"Perfect!" Bronte crowed. "That idiot brother of yours is going to get what's coming to him."

"I know he's an idiot, but you don't need to sound quite so pleased about his imminent torture."

"Oh, okay. But something's got to jar him out of his funk, and this is just the thing."

"And what might 'this' be?"

"One strapping American hunk named Eliot Cranbrook. He is a great old friend of Sarah's and apparently he's coming to Dunlear this weekend." Bronte practically squealed under her breath. "I think I'll put the two of them in the big yellow suite."

"You are cruel. Even Devon asked to put Narinda in a separate room."

"Look." Bronte turned to Max, all business. "If Devon is too much of a fool to step up and declare his own feelings, then it's up to the rest of us to give him a little shove in the right direction. Let's make him a little jealous. Make him see what he's missing."

"I'm not sure Devon does very well in the jealous department. Does this Cranbrook fellow own a bulletproof vest?"

Bronte smiled with a wicked gleam in her eye. "Oh, this is going to be delicious."

Max felt like a bit of a rat when he met up with Devon for lunch a few days later. Even though he hated to withhold the information about the pending arrival of Devon's supposed rival, Max was beginning to see the logic. Devon was acting like a fool.

"So are you all set with Narinda coming down to Dunlear this weekend?" Max asked casually.

Devon's head snapped up. "Yeah. Why? Did Bronte say something about it to Sarah?"

Poor, stupid git, Max thought. "She might have said something. What's up with you and Sarah anyway? Was it nothing or was it something?"

Devon stayed quiet.

Max persisted. "This weekend is supposed to be—no!—is *going to be* a happy celebration of the birth of my firstborn child, you idiot. I don't want it devolving into some weepy episode of *Downton Abbey*. Get it together, Dev."

"Thanks for the sympathy, Max."

"You know what I mean. Bronte's a bit *emotional*." Max rolled his eyes to convey that that was an understatement of gargantuan proportions. "She's got a five-week-old baby and, while she's a rock in almost every way, she was never very sturdy in the unexpected emotions department to begin with, so I am not going to tolerate any unforeseen… hiccups. Maybe you should give Sarah a call or stop by to talk to her in the next day or two, so we don't have to have any histrionics over the weekend."

"Histrionics? How multisyllabic of you. I'll give her a ring. But it's all a whole lot of nothing. We're all grown-ups."

"Are we?" Max cocked up an eyebrow, then looked out toward the busy sidewalk.

Devon's face turned stormy.

"Devon." Max put down his sandwich and slowly wiped his hands with the too-small brown paper napkin, choosing his words with purpose. "Remember that time we were meeting with the farm labor negotiators last year… when I was so keyed up about Bronte, and you punched me in the face?"

Devon smiled. "Yeah, I remember."

"I'm not going to punch you right here in this chrome and glass café, but I might take you into a nearby alley if you don't pull yourself together. One way or the other, you have to figure out what this bird is to you."

"What do you mean? She's nothing. She wants nothing to do with me." The bitterness of his denial only served to further reveal the depth of his feeling.

"Devon, it's me, Max. I am not going to pry. I don't want to know any gory or illicit details. She's my wife's best friend; you are my brother. We have to move on. Please try to reach some sort of rapprochement and we can all look back on this and smile. It was a brief encounter at my wedding for chrissake. Let it go."

Devon's hair was hanging in front of one eye and he made no move to push it out of the way.

Max continued carefully, "If, on the other hand, you have strong feelings for her, why aren't you pursuing her? I can tell you from gruesome firsthand experience, it's worth it."

"I don't mean to be evasive, Max, but I just can't have this conversation. Especially not in the middle of a busy lunch hour at Pret." Devon finally swiped the strands of stubborn hair out of his face. "I'll try to be the mature adult and call her and we can, as you say, move on."

"So pursuit is out of the question?"

"Max, I don't think she'd have me if I crawled on a bed of hot coals and begged… and if she did, then I'd just resent her for making me willing, *wanting*, to beg. It's a mess. I'll deal with it. Let's drop it. Tell me more about the wolf cub." Devon forced his tone to lighten. "Is he reciting Gibbon yet?"

The two brothers finished their sandwiches amid a genuinely amusing discussion about the sheer indignities of caring for a newborn. "I don't know how Bron can deal with all that *excrement* as if it were nothing more than a bit of crumb on the kitchen counter. She actually turned to me last night, before passing out cold, of course, and told me that she found it so amazing that Wolf's diapers didn't even smell!"

Devon burst out laughing along with his brother.

Max went on, hoping to amuse his younger brother out of his funk and enjoying any opportunity to talk about his wife and child. "Talk about *The Selfish Gene*! Can you imagine a more spectacular genetic adaptation? She honestly believes his shit doesn't stink!"

By this time, they were laughing so hard that people were starting to glance their way. They settled down a bit, then cleared the remnants of their lunch and walked back to Max's office.

"Thanks again for crossing the river to have a quick lunch with your boring brother, Dev. Sorry I couldn't get away for longer. See you Friday night at Dunlear." Max gave Devon a brief, supportive pat on his upper arm, then added, "Call her."

"I will," Devon conceded. No matter how miserable he was, he wouldn't do anything to mess up Bronte and Max's weekend. Devon pivoted back down toward Pall Mall, through Trafalgar Square, and then down toward the river. Maybe he should call her right now, walking down Craven Street. He smiled at the wordplay and put it off for a few more minutes.

He was happily distracted by the sounds and bustle of the bright spring day, one of those May days in London that made you forgive every last gray, drizzly, suicide-inducing, dark-at-four day of the past few months. The sun was almost too bright, throwing all of the new spring buds into sharp relief against the sooty limestone of a Victorian pediment or Georgian sill. Window boxes were replanted. The grass in the city parks was an intense, vivid shade that his younger sister Abby used to call "super green" when spring came to Dunlear Castle in their youth.

Now is the time to call Sarah, Devon admitted to himself. He kept his pace as he took his cell phone out of his pocket and approached the Millennium Bridge that spanned the river. He always appreciated the feeling of South Bank, his London, rising to meet him when he crossed the bridge on foot. He felt the weight and power of places like the Ministry of Defence and Buckingham Palace fall away as the southern part of the metropolis took him in. His mother's world of Mayfair and the *ton*, his brother's world of commerce and accomplishment: they were behind him. The art and music and creativity of the southern half of the city lay ahead of him. He stopped in the middle of the bridge, not immune to the irony. He dialed the number he had memorized the first time he had punched it into his phone at Heathrow last October, before his flight to Chicago. It was her U.S. phone number, but he knew she had an international phone and used the same number when she was abroad.

The line crackled then started ringing with the familiar British *beeep-beeep*. She picked up after the first ring.

"This is Sarah James."

Speechless.

He probably should have prepared a little bit more.

"Hello?" she tried again. "Anyone there?"

"Sarah. It's me—it's De—"

"I know who 'me' is," she interrupted quickly.

"Um." He looked down at the river and thought a swim, a

permanent, dark, arctic swim, sounded like a great idea right about then. She wasn't going to give him an inch.

Silence.

"Are you still there?" he asked.

"Yes."

Silence.

This had to be one of the most bizarre phone conversations he had ever had. "All right, well, I promised Max I'd call you before the weekend, to avoid any awkwardness, so that's what this call is."

Silence.

"Are you there?"

"Yes," she said, but softer this time. He heard a door close on her end of the line. "I'm at work and there are construction workers everywhere and it's distracting. I wasn't expecting..." Her voice trailed off.

"Sarah." As much as he had thought about her and *pined*, he supposed was the word for it, he had not realized the power of simply uttering her name aloud. He remembered he needed to apologize. "I don't really know where to begin, or end, or whatever, but I think Bronte and Max just want everyone to get along and make it about Wolf this weekend. I'm sorry if my inviting someone was immature or upset you. I just thought it would help to have a buffer or whatever."

What am I talking about? he wondered to himself. "Sarah?" he asked again into the void.

"I'm still here. I don't know what to say..."

A torrent of possibilities she might choose flew through his brain: *I've missed you horribly. I want to give it a go. I want you in my bed. I hate that you've invited someone when you knew I would be there.* Or even, *I don't care what you do one way or the other.* At least that last option would put an end to the limbo in which he had suffered and clung, holding on to some insane thread of hope that she might still be interested in seeing him. If he just left her alone. That made sense. Right?

Silence.

"Well," he tried again. "I don't either, Sarah." He was going to say her name every chance he got. "I still want to apologize for—"

"No!" she barked at him.

Had he really hurt her so much in such a short time that she couldn't even bear to discuss it? Or was her vehemence a perverse sign that she still had salvageable feelings for him? Or, more likely, that she was terrified he would attack her and not in a good way? He was about to speak again when she continued.

"Devon." His name sounded so good in her gentle voice. "I don't really know exactly, I mean, I think I know what happened that night, but at the time, I was so confused... in any case, you don't need to apologize anymore—"

"It was totally my fault, Sarah. Please. I won't talk about it if that's what you want, but I just don't want you thinking that I would ever behave like that again."

A short pause, then she continued, "It's not like I want to bury it or dredge it up... I just needed a little clarity. And time. And then weeks went by, and now months, and... oh, I don't know..." Now she was the one fumbling for words.

"Well, at least we are talking now. Why don't we go for a walk when we get out to Dunlear? Saturday morning?"

"I don't know, Dev—"

"Or not. Whatever you want. Probably not a good idea." And he meant it. He would probably want to devour her all over again if they were alone in the spring forest. Best to avoid the occasion of sin.

She laughed a little. "It's not like that. You don't need to be so abject about everything. Let's just try to be regular... whatever..." She trailed off again, then added, "I'm glad you called."

He breathed. He looked down at the river and thought it looked muddy and uninviting. Living might be tolerable after all.

The sun was shining. Sarah James was on the line. He might not be beyond redemption.

"Me too. It's really good to hear your voice." That might have been a bit much... that "really" was a tad emphatic. He tried to recover. "Do you want me to come solo this weekend? It's no big deal for me to change plans." *Please say yes*, he thought desperately.

"Well..." She hesitated, then said, "No need to be rude to your... friend... you might as well stick to your plan. I'll see you Friday, okay?"

He was actually smiling. "Okay."

"Thanks for calling... Devon."

"Bye, Sarah."

The line cleared and he breathed again. He tapped Max's number into his phone and hit TALK.

"Hey, Dev, what's up?" his brother answered without preamble.

"Just wanted to let you know you were right as usual. I spoke to Sarah a few minutes ago and everything is totally copacetic."

"Thanks for that, Dev. It will be a beautiful weekend. Let's do a little shooting on Saturday. We can head over to Carlton Towers and get a few birds. No reason for you and Sarah to be on top of each other if there's any awkwardness. Gotta run."

Devon laughed at the abrupt end to the conversation, then settled into willfully misconstruing the idea of he and Sarah on top of each other. He finished crossing the bridge with more optimism than he'd felt in ages and returned to his office at a brisk clip.

Narinda gave him a quick smile while she finished her phone conversation, then hung up and swiveled her chair to face him.

"So what time are we leaving on Friday, anyway?"

"Yeah, about that—"

"Listen, Dev, it's bad enough you are asking me to pose as your girlfriend—I don't know why I ever agreed—but I told you I am not going to share a room with you. It's just too ridiculous."

Devon laughed at her crystal clear understanding. She was so perfectly honest. "Kind of the opposite. I finally called Sarah James and cleared the air a bit. So you don't need to pretend at all. It should be a fun weekend regardless. I still want you to come, but your duplicity in the fake girlfriend department probably won't be part of the plan."

"Even better. Maybe there will be some other friend or foe I can lure into my clutches." She steepled her fingers and clicked her perfectly manicured nails together in a theatrical display of greed. "Your brother's already taken, I gather. Who else? Cousin? Long lost villainous heir?"

"I cannot believe you would abandon me so easily. You are such a traitor," Devon joked as he returned his attention to the project he had been working on before lunch.

Narinda gave up talking, since she knew Devon's mental energy would be elsewhere for hours to come. She watched as the incomprehensible code started scrolling up his screen. *Devon's matrix*, she thought, and swiveled back to deal with her own assignments.

In reality, Devon was working on a pet project that had nothing whatsoever to do with the architectural firm of Russell + Partners.

While he had been pacing around Sarah's apartment that unfortunate night in Chicago, all of her board reports and financial statements had been sitting on the kitchen counter, for all the world to see, more or less. He certainly didn't think it was an invasion of privacy—a little *snoopy* maybe—since it was all going to be available information for shareholders within a few days, and theoretically, he could be considering an investment, so he had taken his time going over the documents.

After his disastrous show of insane jealousy, he'd forgotten about the discrepancies he had suspected after reading over the projected sales figures several times. A few weeks later, unable to sleep and finding himself with a nasty urge to get inside Sarah's world without actually contacting her, he *did* breach the firewall of her company's website.

He could tell that Sarah was a terrific businesswoman—adept at building her brand, visually creative, financially savvy—but she was clearly an ingenue when it came to corporate security. A clever teenager could have burrowed in as far as he had in about an hour of trying some of the different security and code-cracking tricks he had picked up over the years.

Not that she was guarding state secrets or the recipes for making dirty bombs in her basement, it was just shoes after all (not that he would ever say it quite like that to *her*), but he started spending some time each evening tracking the activity on the supposedly password-protected areas of her company's site. Servers in Chicago and New York were frequently accessing varying levels of secure information on a constant basis throughout the workday, which was to be expected.

Then, after about a month, he started noticing the occasional late-night log in. Because he was painfully aware of Sarah's whereabouts—not really stalking exactly, but he always seemed to know if she was in England, for example—he knew there was no way she was the one accessing the site at three in the morning from a server in Chicago. At that point, he had to be honest with himself: tracking IP addresses was one thing; going deeper into her company files was something else entirely.

The Internet Protocol addresses were practically *public information*, he argued with himself, *like sitting across the street (maybe in an unmarked car, but still) and watching who went in and out of someone's house. Delving any further into the actual corporate documents was tantamount to sneaking around someone's bedroom and checking the contents of their dresser drawers while they were asleep in their bed.* He resisted, with difficulty, the idea of investigating the inconsistencies beyond this (already morally questionable) level.

Even so, he kept a thorough log file of all the activity on the site and stored it for future reference. Something about those three-in-the-morning site visits never seemed right.

He finished a final round of converting the data he had tracked over the past months—he'd tried regression analysis, dot plots, cryptanalysis—in a vain attempt to draw some conclusions from the seemingly meaningless compilation of data. He knew there was a pattern in there somewhere. He just needed to find it. But it looked like it was not going to present itself tonight. He logged off and shut down his computer.

Devon looked up and stretched his neck, feeling like he had returned from lunch about half an hour before. Apparently, five hours had passed. Narinda was gone for the day; the office was sparsely populated with other architects and designers who chose to work unpredictable hours or were working on deadline.

He stretched his neck in the opposite direction and double-checked the time. It was past seven o'clock. The long days of spring had begun. The sun's rays still stretched across the river from the west.

He wanted to call Sarah again.

He stuffed that thought as far down as he could and decided to meet up with a couple of friends at a pub over by the Tate Modern instead. It felt like the beginning of summer and people would be congregating in huge packs, taking in great gulps of air, and drinking large quantities of beer. Devon loved this time of year in London: the masses emerged from their respective warrens and looked to the spring sun like near-blind moles, pasty and grateful.

When Friday afternoon finally rolled around, it was only through sheer force of will that Devon had not called her again. He was preoccupied to the point of distraction.

Narinda was the perfect traveling companion: prompt, efficient, and amusing.

"Not that I am even partially adept at maneuvering a V12 Aston

Martin engine, but it might be safer if I drove," she said. "I see your body is here in the car, but your mind is clearly elsewhere."

Devon turned his attention from the crowded motorway to catch her look, then tried (again) to concentrate on the road. "I'm sorry, Narinda. I'll try to stay on task." He downshifted the powerful engine and gave up trying to squeeze between the lorry and the bridge abutment. "It might not be easy."

"Why don't you tell me more about her? I have no vested interest either way—I mean, you are a perfect piece, don't get me wrong, but the two of us were never going to work. So let's treat the next hour as a free shrink session. The doctor is in."

Devon looked at Narinda's sexy brown, almost black, eyes, slightly shaded with some smoky eye makeup, her satin skin glowing in the early evening, her long black hair hanging like a silky curtain across her shoulder, and had to momentarily remember why it was they were never going to work. She was quite something.

"Very funny," Devon said. "I don't really want to talk… well, I guess I do. But it feels like a violation of Sarah's privacy somehow. You'll meet her soon enough. She's kind of innocent and naughty all at once. She's got this thing, where she asks these really blunt questions with no artifice, and…"

For someone who supposedly doesn't want to talk, Narinda thought with a smile, *Devon certainly has plenty to say about Miss Sarah James.* He spent the next two hours talking about *not wanting* to talk about her.

The traffic had been vicious, and the trip, which should have taken an hour and a half, took nearly three. When Devon finally pulled the thundering car into the forecourt of Dunlear Castle, it was almost half past seven, and dinner was at eight.

"Do you mind if we go in through the back?" Devon asked. "It'll be quicker."

Narinda was trying to keep her jaw from dropping open at the sheer scale of the building. She worked in an architectural firm after all. She had stood on I-beams forty stories over Kowloon Harbor and in private palaces in Dubai; she had overseen the construction of bridges that spanned valleys in the Andes. The part of this that was so awe inspiring was that it was Devon's home… not just a grand, historical pile, but the place where her friend had spent most of his youth. It was incongruous and exciting.

"Narinda?"

"Yeah, sorry, Dev. It's a bit large. I don't care which entrance we go in. I'll do some sketches tomorrow for the hell of it." She craned her neck to look down a seemingly endless allée of trees toward the setting sun, then turned her attention back to Devon. "Would that be all right?"

"Of course, that would be great. Actually, maybe you could do something that I could give to Bronte and Max as a gift. I already bought the obligatory sterling porringer and rattle, so something that captures the actual day would be really nice."

"Perfect. I'll work on it tomorrow."

They had pulled into a smaller side court, near a long block of former stables that had been converted into an eight-car garage. The Aston Martin DBS engine seemed to growl defiantly one last time before Devon turned it off.

A middle-aged man in a khaki shirt and work pants came out of a mudroom and smiled broadly at Devon. "Hello, Devon!"

"Hello, Jeremy!" Devon was up and out of the car in seconds, gripping the man's hand with warmth and affection. "This is my friend Narinda Channar." Narinda had made her way around the front of the car. "Narinda this is Jeremy Paulson. He does everything around here."

"Nice to meet you, Miss Channar."

"Mr. Paulson." She shook his hand and gave him a smile.

Devon cut in. "All right, Jeremy. Enough of the niceties. The ride took an age and I'm sure Bronte is in a lather about making dinner festive and all that. Will you please show Narinda up to whichever room Bronte has chosen for her?" He handed Narinda's bag to Jeremy. "I'll grab my own things."

Turning to Narinda, Devon gave her a quick kiss on the cheek, then, in a lower voice, said, "Thanks again for the moral support."

She smiled and rubbed his upper back in an encouraging way. "It's all going to turn out well, Dev, I'm sure. You're too good a catch for her to throw you back into the water." She winked and followed Jeremy into the surprisingly plebeian mudroom of the magnificent castle.

Devon looked up toward the second floor apartments, wondering which room Sarah had been given. He suspected Bronte would have wanted her close to the ducal suite, and when he let his glance travel toward the front of the building, he froze when he saw her looking down at him.

He smiled involuntarily and gave her a little mock salute, figuring she would let the curtain fall back and turn away from the window. Instead, she stood staring at him with one hand on the glass, her palm flat against the pane, and the other hand holding the golden velvet fabric back from the window. He felt like an idiot, just standing there, his leather satchel in one hand, staring up at her, but he didn't care. She looked gorgeous.

Her head turned abruptly as if someone had called her name, then the curtain was pulled back wider to reveal a tall, despicably handsome Eliot Cranbrook. Sarah and Eliot turned away from the window and the curtain fell back into place. Devon felt like he'd been punched squarely in the gut.

He let his hand drop slowly back to his side and tried not to let a scowl of frustration show on his face, then he turned back toward the side entrance of the castle. Devon was nearly at the side door when he heard a female voice calling his name. He stepped a few paces back onto the driveway and looked up. Bronte was leaning halfout the window two to the left of where Sarah had been, and laughing. "Hurry up!" Bronte called. "I want you buffed and polished, chop-chop! Meet us in the drawing room ASAP!"

He waved to her and continued back into the house, loving the sound of Bronte's commanding American *ay-sap*, but not quite able to smile in response.

Chapter 13

SARAH HEARD THE ROAR of the Aston Martin as it shot gravel up from the driveway and rumbled into the side court of Dunlear. She had thought she could catch a glimpse of Devon without being detected, and she probably could have remained unnoticed if she hadn't been glued to the window like a little girl pining in front of a puppy pet store. The first thing she could see were his long legs stretching out from the silver car door. He was so tall and lean, looking loose and casual in a great pair of jeans (great backside in jeans, more like it) and a long-sleeved navy-blue T-shirt.

He looked a little thinner than she remembered, a little bit more tightly wound. He walked around the side of the car, opened the trunk, grabbed two pieces of luggage, and put them on the ground. She felt her stomach roll at the beautiful, strained pull of muscles across his upper back, visible through the cotton of his shirt. He flipped his hair out of his face with a familiar toss.

Then Sarah's attention went to his... companion. Did she have to look like an exotic Bollywood starlet for goodness' sake? She wasn't rail thin, but she was tall and lean: great figure, strong legs in closely fitted black pants, and a belted lavender wraparound sweater that hugged her waist perfectly. She had the good taste to finish the outfit off with a pair of Sarah's stiletto half-boots. Her black hair looked like something out of a Pasha's harem: liquid perfection. Devon gave her a peck on the cheek that, even from two stories away, Sarah could tell was more friend than fire. The woman touched Devon's back in way that made Sarah want to pitch out the window and swat her away, but he didn't seem to respond with anything but casual acceptance. Then Sarah followed the woman's silhouette as she followed Jeremy Paulson into the house.

When Sarah's gaze returned to where Devon had been standing before, with his back to her, he was looking at her right in the eye. He gave her a little salute, the perfect gesture to let her know he was glad she was looking at him. And then that smile. Oh. God.

They don't make smiles like that every day, she thought philosophically, as if such a thought were some sort of scientific discovery of Nobel Prize proportions. *He looks happy to see me.*

"What are you looking at?" Eliot's voice sliced through her little reverie like a samurai sword as he entered Sarah's room with friendly authority. Sarah turned her head to face Eliot but didn't let go of the curtain.

"Nothing." Guilty.

"What do you mean 'nothing'? You look like I just caught you with your hand in the till—"

Eliot had been walking with purpose across the expanse of the lovely yellow guestroom, then stopped short when he pulled back the curtain to see Devon's car… and then Devon. Eliot felt the tremor of—what?—fear, trepidation, and eagerness run through Sarah and reached his arm around her shoulder for moral support. "It's all going to work out. Just look at him. He's a wreck."

"I think I might be in love with that wreck," Sarah tried, in a small voice, but it came out in a kind of croak.

Eliot let the curtain fall back into place and guided Sarah away from the window. "We need to get downstairs for cocktails." He bent his arm at the elbow and offered it to her. "Are you ready for your close-up, my dear?"

"As ready as I'll ever be." She looped her arm through his and they continued speaking in low voices down the wide corridor that ran the length of the second floor. When they reached the top of the stairs, Sarah heard a sound from the other end of the hall and looked over her shoulder to see Devon striding toward them. He was still about forty feet away, but he caught her eye for a split second then turned into what must have been his bedroom. *Across the hall and three doors down from mine*, she noted with a pounding enthusiasm that she tried to repress.

A second later, Bronte came flying out of her suite. "Oh, there you two are!" She caught up with Eliot and Sarah and the three of them headed toward the drawing room.

When Bronte, Eliot, and Sarah neared the large, formal drawing room, they were met with the sounds of a swinging Ella Fitzgerald and Louis Armstrong singing a raspy, loving duet of "A Foggy Day." Bronte stood in the large doorway for a minute, holding Sarah and Eliot at bay. Max Heyworth was serenading his son, holding the baby close to his strong chest and turning the love song into a gentle bedtime story, "The sun was shining… everywhere…"

Sarah looked from Max, holding Wolf and swinging him gently in time to the swaying jazz, then back to Bronte by her side. "What is it, Bron?"

Her eyes sparkled. "I'm just having a moment, I guess. I don't think I ever believed I could feel this much… Seeing Max holding Wolf is almost painfully good."

Sarah gave her friend a comforting squeeze around her shoulders.

"Women are so predictable. A man. A baby. Bingo!" Eliot smiled as he put his arms loosely around each woman's shoulder and watched Max for a moment, before the new father caught them all staring at him and smiled like a guilty boy.

"Am I that ridiculous?" he asked, but he obviously didn't care how ridiculous he looked. Bronte crossed the room and put her arms around his waist so the baby was nestled between the two of them.

"I love you ridiculously," she whispered into his ear, then looked down at Wolf and said, "and you too."

Eliot remained in the wide entry to the spectacular, medieval room, one arm hanging carelessly across Sarah's back. She leaned into him for a moment, taking in the image of the new family. She had visited Bronte in the hospital in London, but it had felt antiseptic and the baby had seemed like a tightly wrapped science project. A month later, there in his father's arms, he looked like a magical cliché: a bundle of joy, a blessing.

She felt Devon's presence before she saw him. Her back went rigid and she shook off Eliot's arm with a brisk toss of her shoulder, then turned around to see Devon standing near the bottom of the large staircase, across the grand foyer.

Come on, she thought. *You can do this, Devon.*

Before the silence went on a moment too long, Eliot threw propriety to the four winds and nearly bellowed, "You must be Devon!" With a hearty, overly American force to his words, he closed the space between them and reached his hand out to shake.

Devon hesitated for a terrible moment and Sarah had a vision of the aforementioned leather glove flying into poor Eliot's face. Then Devon shook off whatever momentary hesitation (fear? arrogance? ego?) had crossed him and shook the man's hand. Sarah did not know whether to continue into the living room or to cross back to the foyer, so she just stood where she was.

He's going to touch you now, some voice in her head remarked in an utterly impassive tone that reminded her of—of all things—the gynecologist before he inserted the speculum. She couldn't help smiling at her totally incongruous train of thought, which meant she was smiling when Devon and Eliot crossed the few feet back to join her.

She was still tongue-tied and wavering between fear and joy. She would have to recruit Eliot more often because he was able to carry even the most awkward situations.

"Sarah James. Devon Heyworth. I'm not sure if you two have met." Eliot winked at Sarah, continued into the living room, and called out, "Stop mauling the poor baby!"

Eliot had ridden out in the car together with Max, Bronte, and Sarah and he'd hit it off with Max from the moment they met. The four of them had spent the entire trip laughing with and at Bronte about her wholly improbable new love of all things baby.

Their voices faded. Sarah simply stared at Devon. He looked so good. So. So. Good.

"Are you going to say anything?" he asked quietly.

He sounded good too. His voice was low and just for her. Was it so wrong that she wanted to devour him?

She reached up toward his cheek, tentative, but he caught her hand in his before she could reach up to his face.

"You wanted me to try to be normal, remember?" he said quietly. "And I shall try, but I cannot even attempt it if you persist in looking at me like that and—"

She had reached up with her other hand to feel the skin of his face. She couldn't help it. He pulled in his breath, his eyes closing for a second, then opening. He glanced over her shoulder and saw the other three adults were fully engaged with cooing and aahing over the cub.

"Come with me." His voice was strained. They ducked into a coat closet through a concealed door that was built into the paneled wooden wall of the area under the huge stone staircase. Devon pulled on the string that flipped on the single light bulb overhead and shut the door to the tight space.

She reached her hand up to his face again and let her light fingers feel the curve of his cheekbone, his jaw, the flickering muscle in his neck. His eyes were closed and his hands were on her waist, neither pulling her close nor pushing her away, as he leaned against the closed door for support. Her fingers trailed around his neck and she passed a sensitive spot below his ear, toward his nape. His lips parted in response. She had to kiss him.

She stretched up her body and pulled his neck closer, forcing his face to come toward hers. He groaned, almost bitterly, when her lips touched his. Then they both slipped into a tumbling flow of desire, his body pushed her back against a packed row of old coats, the faint smell of cedar and mothballs swept around them. Her hands were all over him, through his hair, down his back, around his ass, up along his solid stomach, coming to rest on his chest, as their tongues withdrew from a final, slow, parting minuet.

"Devon."

"I have waited so long to hear my name on your lips. I almost asked you to repeat it on the phone Tuesday."

"I had to work up the courage to say it even that once." Her face was scant inches from his.

"Can I come to your room tonight?"

She closed her eyes and tipped her head to an imaginary sky, seeing the red outline of the single bulb through the thin skin of her eyelids instead.

He couldn't resist her taut neck. He kissed her lightly, not wanting to leave a mark on her skin.

"You are so… tender…" she whispered.

"I'm trying…"

"I…" She gasped as one of his hands left her waist and snaked under her sweater to the smooth skin of her stomach, the underside of one breast. "Oh, Dev."

"Sarah. I'm… I don't know what to say. I can't think. I just feel. My hands are pulsing, literally, the tips of my fingers are throbbing to touch you. We don't even have to do anything—"

She laughed spontaneously at that, but he continued seriously.

"I mean it, Sar. I just feel like I want to be in a bed with you lying next to me, to feel you alongside me. I need—" His voice cracked as her finger stilled his lips.

"Stop. Of course I want you to come to my room. I was just pausing because I don't know how in the world I am going to make it through dinner without crawling into your lap and feeding you food like a sultan from my bare hands, preferably with my chest firmly pressed against you." She felt him stiffen in response to her imagined version of supper and the brief example she had just given him of her chest pressed firmly against him.

"Sarah, stop it." He shook his head to clear it. "We can do this. Why don't you go out first and—"

"Why do I have to go out first?"

"I will if you want. I just didn't think you'd want me to abandon you in the coat closet."

"You're hardly abandoning me. I think I'll go to the bathroom, which has the added benefit of plausibility. I'll meet you back in the living room." She gave him a chaste, if lingering, kiss on the cheek, then slipped around him, opened the door a crack to peek out, then opened it wider and veered quickly to the left to use the formal powder room.

Devon must have spent more minutes than he realized trying to gather his wits. He was standing there with his face pressed into old coats when the closet door opened swiftly behind him. Max's deep voice jarred him out of his attempts to steady his breathing.

"What the hell are you doing standing alone in the coat closet, you idiot?"

Devon looked out into the empty hall.

"We're all in there doing our part to adore that baby and you are having some sort of yogic breathing episode out here... I thought we agreed on no—" Max smiled when he saw a bit of lipstick on

Devon's cheek and pointed at his own cheek to let his brother know to wipe it off.

"Histrionics," Devon finished for him, rubbing his cheek and then ducking his head to step out of the closet. He pulled the door shut behind him, then fell into stride next to his brother. "You're a bastard for not telling me she was bringing Eliot, by the way."

"We all thought you needed a little wake-up call. Seeing him got you motivated, didn't it?"

"For future reference, I don't ever need that much motivation again."

"That remains to be seen." Max laughed.

"That stings."

"Remember that time when I told you I was having a hard time with Bron—after I introduced her to Mother the first time? You laughed at me and hoped that Bronte would spend the rest of her life"—Max paused to consider the exact words—"*challenging* me…" He slapped his younger brother on the back a little bit harder than absolutely necessary. "Well, I hope to enjoy a good laugh at your expense, watching Sarah *challenge* you."

Devon gave him a small smile.

They were passing near the massive front door, about to turn toward the living room, when the strong night wind and Abigail Heyworth came blowing into the large entry hall. As usual, their younger sister looked like a Gypsy tinker who had walked from Albania in the clothes on her back, pausing only briefly for water and the most basic supplies. She used the full weight of her small body to push the door closed.

Jeremy came from the back end of the hall and offered to take Abby's "…items…"

"Oh, Jeremy. You are the worst snob. Just because I don't drive an Aston Martin or wear John Lobb shoes—like some posers around here"—she stared pointedly at Devon and Max—"doesn't mean you cannot help me with my backpack and coat."

Jeremy smiled—*how could one not*, he mused—at the woodland creature before him. "Is Lady St. John in the car?"

"No."

"Very well. No need to snipe." Jeremy turned from the three siblings—all of whom he had first met in their cradles—and carried the metal-framed, oversized hikers' backpack with one firm hand at the end of a stiff arm, keeping the entire contraption slightly away from his body.

"Where is Tully, then?" Max asked.

"Not here. Who cares?" Abby was undoing the loose Indian scarf that seemed to be wrapped seventeen times around her small neck.

"I do," Max said.

"Then ask her to be *your* girlfriend because I'm finished with her. She was so *serious*, I couldn't stand it for another minute. I mean…" Abby had tossed her scarf onto one of the priceless bombé chests at the side of the hall and was looking into the gilt mirror above it to see if her wild mane of black hair could be put back into any semblance of order, then gave up and turned to her brothers. "You two are the worst! Stop looking at me like that."

"But"—it was Devon this time, softer—"you two have been together for ten years, Abby. We thought you were, you know, *together*."

"I know." Her shoulders sank a tiny bit. "So did I. But then she just got so, oh, I don't know… I mean, I'll always love her, but she's so *earnest* all the time. I care about the environment—more than the next person, that's for sure—trying to make up for all the damage you two do with your absurd cars and financing coal mines—that was a doozy, by the way, Max—but she just, I mean *please!* She is the great-granddaughter of the Duke of Bedford and she pretends she's this underprivileged farm girl, and she refuses to be honest and admit that it's much easier to be charitable and generous when you have money and resources to give away. I was just done. I couldn't stand it for another moment."

Max and Devon simply stood there and looked at this new Abigail Heyworth. She was still as Bohemian and wild as ever, but there was something sharp in her eyes.

"So, that's it. She's fine. I'm fine. We're just not *us* anymore, so stop staring at me and let me see my first nephew. Is he all wrinkly and gross?"

Devon laughed when Max nearly tripped over the edge of the carpet to defend his flawless offspring.

"By the way, Abby, we do not joke about the cub," Devon explained. "He is perfect in every way. Apparently, even his diapers smell like rose petals."

The three happy siblings entered the large living room to see the small cluster of people at the far end near the oversized stone fireplace surround. Narinda had come down and she and Sarah were playing with the baby stretched out between them on a soft blanket on the sofa. Eliot and Bronte were talking business nearby, discussing his latest difficulties managing to turn a profit in the Asian market with the attendant licensing thefts and the black market for counterfeit luxury goods that was thriving in China and Japan. He was midsentence when he noticed Max, Devon, and some wild creature coming in from the other side of the room.

"Aaah," Bronte said as she followed his gaze, "Lady Abigail Heyworth. Quite fetching, isn't she? She's looking particularly mischievous tonight. But, as my husband says, that dog doesn't hunt, so you'd best keep your eye on the lovely Narinda if you are looking for a weekend romance. I'm assuming we are all cognizant of the Devon-Sarah situation?"

"What? My *girlfriend* Sarah is interested in your brother-in-law?" He slapped his hand against his forehead in mock surprise. "How could I have missed it? She hardly looks at him."

Bronte burst out laughing as she noticed that Sarah, at that very moment, was ogling Devon with such transparent longing, lust really, that the whole idea of the angst and drama that had led up to the weekend seemed hilarious.

"Eliot. You are a peach."

"I aim to please." He bowed his head in a gesture of small obedience. "Please introduce me to your sister-in-law. I don't see *her* mooning over anyone at the moment."

"Don't say I didn't warn you," Bronte added softly, but with perfect diction.

"What's that supposed to mean?"

"Never mind." Bronte gave Eliot one last look and had the fleeting thought that if he set his mind to it, he could make a person burn like the sun. Any person.

Devon veered off to play with the baby (and to get as close to Sarah as possible without consuming her).

Max and Abby joined Bronte and Eliot.

Bronte gave her sister-in-law an affectionate, warm embrace, then said, "Abigail, this is Eliot Cranbrook. An old friend of Sarah James's… and a new friend of ours," Bronte added, taking Max's hand in hers. "Eliot, this is Abigail Heyworth. You two might enjoy one another's company—poking fun at the rest of us. Max and I are going to check on Wolf."

Abigail realized she had not really *looked* at a man in years nor *felt* the gaze of a man upon her, perhaps ever. She had always been a tomboy, following Devon and Max everywhere in her early childhood, then, when her older brothers had gone off to Eton, she found herself far more interested in sports and riding than boys. She and Tully (neé the Lady Tulliver St. John, fourth daughter of the sixth earl, et cetera, et cetera) had developed a deep attachment when they were eighteen and traveled together during their gap year. They had never really been apart since. They adored the same books; they laughed at the same jokes. They fully understood one another's bittersweet relationships toward their respective families. They loved each other's young, lithe bodies. It had been ten years of intellectual and physical mutual admiration.

But lately, Abigail couldn't deny it any longer, the relationship (oh, the irony) had become a confining adherence to its own set of prescribed behaviors. Here she was, willing to buck every social and familial expectation, and all she got in return was the feeling that she was an old, married woman at the age of twenty-eight. Even their sex life had dwindled to the occasional massage that led to the occasional orgasm. Tully was far more inspired by political activism than she was by Abigail.

They had finally had a confrontation of sorts a few nights before, when Abigail simply told Tully she was leaving.

Tully had no idea what she was talking about.

"Are you saying you don't want me to come to Dunlear for the christening? That's probably for the best. I've got a ton of work to do on the Arctic drilling petition—"

"No, Tully. I'm done. I'm just not... my heart is just not in it anymore."

"You never really cared about fighting the oil industry, in any case. David is working on the pollution along the Nepal-China border and needs help with the bureaucratic—"

"Tully. Look at me. Put the pen down. I don't care about any of that." She shook her hair out like a wet dog. "I mean, of course I care about all of that—I was the first person to give you a copy of *Silent Spring* for goodness' sake—but I can't do this"—she gestured back and forth between the two of them—"anymore. We are living in a caravan in the middle of Scotland, which is all well and good—if we still had a bit of passion, I wouldn't care if we lived in a yurt in Mongolia—but just admit it. We—you and I—have cooled."

Tully tried to deny it, but even to her own ears, it was feeble.

She finally gave in, tears streaming down her face. She was hugging Abby. "We have been together for so long. What will it be like to be apart?"

Abby felt tears on her face and didn't know if they were Tully's or her own. She laughed as she cried. "We've been together so long, I don't even know whose tears are on my face."

Tully gave a wet smile and put a small kiss on Abigail's cheek. "They are *our* tears, Abby."

The two of them spent the next several days packing up Abigail's few belongings, slipping with surprising ease into a new chapter of their relationship. Abigail felt lighter and freer as each hour passed. She caught the occasional look of fear or worry cross Tully's face, then smiled and kissed it away. "You are going to be great. You know David's sister has been dying to get her hands on you since she arrived in December. So has David, for that matter. You are going to be attacked from all sides as soon as I leave."

Tully wrinkled her nose as if she had just passed a dead animal on the side of the road. "The *last* thing I want is sex!"

Abigail laughed hard, then gave her a deadpan look and nearly shouted, "I know!"

Tully had to smile at the verbal trap. "Is it just that, Abs? Am I so drab?"

"Oh, Tull! You are so glamorous and plummy beneath those layers of sincerity and scruff, and you spend so much time worrying that you are not serious enough. Just take it all—you are *all* good."

And she *was* all those things. If she had been born in a different century, she would have been a diamond of the first water: heart-shaped face, thick blond hair that always waved in exactly the right direction no matter which way the wind blew, and blue eyes that sparkled with merriment and clouded with grief (at the least injustice). They would always care for each other; they had spent too many formative (and transformative) years together to ever separate entirely.

But… standing there in front of Eliot Cranbrook, this veritable Adonis, Abigail had her first real suspicion that there might be whole worlds of sensation that did not need to be underpinned by an earnest, demanding adherence to social revolution at every turn. She felt a hint of that burning sun that Bronte had mentioned.

She knew her looks were fiery or wild or Bohemian or whatever you wanted to call it, but that had rarely led to smoldering glances from handsome strangers. The fact that she was usually holding hands with her girlfriend might have squelched those types of advances, she admitted to herself, but still. Here was one very tall, very handsome (sort of quintessentially American-movie-star handsome) stranger, and he was giving her a good bit of smolder.

"What a pleasant surprise! A sister." He leaned in with a conspiratorial air. "I was recruited to come here, by the way, to run interference for Sarah James." He gave his head a brief nod in the direction of Sarah and Devon, who were unable to stop smiling at one another. "Just to keep you in the loop. I think my work here is done. I am like one of those people who are hired to sit in the seats at the Academy Awards when the real stars have to go present an award."

Abigail smiled a broad grin, both at his description and the shrewd, flat drawl of his American accent. Matter-of-fact. Authoritative. Naughty.

"Turns out I am usually only called in on special occasions as well," Abigail added. "Otherwise, my mother worries I might scare the horses." She gave him a wink then turned to see about this baby that everyone was so gaga over.

Eliot watched as the irreverent Lady Abigail crossed over to the couch and deposited herself unceremoniously on the floor, so she was exactly at eye level with the tiny addition to the family. He kept looking as she stared hard at the seemingly oblivious creature; the baby stilled, then held her gaze, widened his already-infamous gray eyes, and formed his mouth into a perfect *O*.

"Aren't you a little stunner?!" Abby cooed, and he blinked slowly, as if to say, *Yes. Yes, I am.* Abby started laughing and called over to Max, "You are in so much trouble. He's even worse than you are!"

Apparently, Wolf did not like being made fun of, nor did he appreciate the unexpected volume of Abigail's voice, so he transformed his face into a caricature of wretched indignity. Bronte scooped him up before a tear could even form, and Abigail could have sworn Wolf gave her a tiny wink to let her know he had this baby situation down pat.

Chapter 14

BRONTE HAD NEARLY FALLEN asleep into the plate of her main course, so Max had escorted her up to their bedroom, where Wolf was already sound asleep in the cradle next to the bed. The nanny, Carolyn Johnston, was reading a book in a chair nearby.

Max told Carolyn—the nanny who had the least to do of any nanny in the history of British nannies, as far as he was concerned—that she could turn in for the night and Bronte would call her in the morning when she needed her. Max had insisted they hire someone full-time so Bronte could rest and recover from the very real exhaustion that delivering a nine-and-a-half-pound baby wrought. But (since Bronte refused to part with Wolf, except when she was obligated to bathe herself or eat) Carolyn spent most of her time organizing Wolf's extensive wardrobe of onesies and, that done, reading. Bronte was nursing Wolf on demand and had no desire to pump her milk nor to try even the occasional bottle of formula. ("What's the point when I have all this milk right here? It will just throw off my schedule.") There was really nothing for it.

Max helped Bronte get undressed, and she was asleep before he had finished pulling the comforter up to her smooth shoulders. And she was the one who had worried about becoming obsolete when she became a wife and mother? He thought she was glorious.

He returned to the intimate family dining room and suggested the six of them head into a smaller den and watch a movie. Sarah and Devon pretended they were exhausted, nearly stretching their arms in a theatrical show of how knackered they were. Abby and Narinda, who had become fast friends over dinner, rolled their eyes at one another about Devon and Sarah, and then joined Max and Eliot in front of the small fire and the large flat-panel TV to watch a bunch of over-the-hill actors blowing each other up while foiling international assassination plots.

"Max, get me a scotch, will you?" Abby asked while her older brother was rummaging around in the small wet bar in the corner of the room.

"Neat or on the rocks?"

"Neat, of course. Sheesh."

Eliot looked at Abigail Heyworth for what felt like the hundredth time in the past two hours. He thought he might be developing a little crush on the imp. She was far too young for him—he had to be at least ten years older than she was—and she was clearly about as responsible as a delinquent high school student.

But.

There was something pure about her. She was the only one who could talk to Max in just that familiar, disrespectful, loving way when she demanded her scotch. Neat. She acted as if she wasn't the least bit interested in social conventions, yet she was totally interested in every detail of conversation once she was engaged. Over dinner, she had asked Eliot endless questions about the luxury goods market, occasionally slipping into vitriol about the injustices in many of the clothing factories in the Far East, but for the most part listening with an eager, transparent desire to learn. Then she had spoken at length and with equal intensity to Narinda about a bridge project in Chile and a large stadium proposal Narinda was working on in Dubai.

"Anyone else for a drink? Eliot?" Max offered.

"Sure, I'll have the same."

"Narinda?"

"I'd love some sparkling water if you have any there, Max."

"Sure, here you go." Max passed out the rest of the drinks, and the unlikely foursome settled in for a few hours and laughed and poked holes in the plot and predicted the obvious one-liners that followed every devastating explosion. About halfway through, Max was dozing, Abby was completely passed out, and Narinda had slipped off to bed.

Max rubbed his eyes and stood up. "I have to crash, Eliot. Do you mind? Just throw a blanket over Abby if she won't wake up when the movie's over. She's impossible to rouse."

"Thanks again for everything, Max. Sorry to be such a fifth wheel on your family weekend."

"Don't be silly. If you've helped Sarah and Devon get back on track, you're probably a more valuable asset to this family at the moment than I am. G'night."

"Thanks again. Night, Max."

Something of relative consequence may have transpired in the final half hour of the movie, but Eliot spent the entire time staring at Abigail Heyworth's gently sleeping body. She had the look of a windswept, pre-Raphaelite muse: wavy black hair tumbling everywhere, sooty black eyelashes resting against pale creamy skin. He sipped the excellent scotch and enjoyed the view.

—⁓—

Saturday dawned a splendid spring day.

The more splendid, thought Sarah, *for beginning in the secure hold of Devon Heyworth's strong arms and one of his legs cast across my hip.* She inhaled until she thought she might hyperventilate, her face burrowed into his chest, his embrace possessive even in sleep. There were distinct benefits to being with a man who slept this soundly. She was so eager to see him, all of him, she started rooting around under the sheets just for the fun of it. She lifted the edge of the blanket cover to let in a little light and started working her way down his body like a miner: touching a small scar on his leg, tracing the way his hip muscle curved over the bone and down, outlining the firm contours of his stomach. She started to doze again.

Last night, they'd made it through dinner (barely); both of them begged off coffee and after-dinner drinks, practically drumming impatient fingers on the mahogany dining room table. Thankfully, Max had suggested a movie so they could continue on their way while everyone was standing around in the hall without having to blatantly excuse themselves from the dining table to make their escape. They had very nearly sprinted up the wide stone staircase, Sarah tripping over the edge of thick hall carpet at the top landing; they grabbed at each other and tried to move in the direction of the bedroom at the same time.

"Which room?" Sarah breathed between kisses.

"I don't care. We're just across the hall from each other and a few doors down. Let's go in your room so you don't have to make the walk of shame. I'm used to it."

Her face must have shown that she didn't quite like the sound of his repeated (legendary?) late-night and/or early morning walks of shame.

He smiled. "Aaah-haaa… you *are* jealous! I meant I'm *used to it* because *you* insisted on going back to that damned hotel both nights in October, so I had not only the walk of shame, but the *drive* of shame and, the *coup de grace*, the *breakfast* of shame with Abby and Bronte and Max."

Her expression cleared and he kissed her again, then whispered, so close to her ear that she felt it like more kisses, "I want you to be jealous… to feel what it's like to want me like I want you."

"I think about you all the time, Devon." She shivered in response. "You are with me all the time. I was too much of a coward to call you."

He angled her against the wall of the hallway, gently caging her with his arms flexed taut, his hands flat against the wall on either side of her head, his body slightly away from hers. She arched toward him, her breathing labored, and he pulled slightly away. He began kissing her neck, her cheek, her ear, the line of her jaw.

"Why are we still in this corridor?" she pleaded, barely able to form the words.

"Because I might have to have you right now." His hand pushed against the crotch of her pants and he felt the concentrated heat of her body through the fabric.

She tilted her hips into his palm, gasped sharply, then moaned her exhale, her head falling toward his chest for support.

"You did not just do that!" he laughed quietly.

"I did," she whispered after a few more breaths, with a guilty, happy grin on her face. "I couldn't wait a second more, and then you touched me and, well, it's been awhile. I was… ready."

He felt like he could breathe in her words, like air. He hoped "a while" meant that she hadn't been with anyone else. He hoped—even though he tried not to—because thinking about the implication of another person touching her still brought on a wave of impossible feelings.

She half-walked and was half-carried the few yards into her room. Devon turned to quietly close and lock the door behind them. Their hands trembled like Puritans on their wedding night as they removed one another's clothes and slid into the cool, wide bed. They traveled through worlds of memory and lust, intervals of light sleep and vague caresses, ultimately falling into a deep, secure sleep of intertwined limbs and synchronized breath.

Saturday morning, Sarah gradually woke with her head resting on his stomach, looking at his… well, looking at him. The morning light in the room had lengthened somewhat, and the deep bass of his voice reverberated in her ear through his abdomen: "Did I sleep through something delicious? You are in quite the compromising position."

She turned her head to look at his face, keeping her body curled around one side of his midsection, partially covered by the sheets. She saw from the clouded look in his eyes that the sensation of her long hair accidentally falling across his pelvis had given him unexpected pleasure. She lifted her head a bit and let the layers of hair travel with more purpose across his waist, down a bit, then back up. She let her head come to rest near his neck, loving the welcome curves and strength of his body that seemed to take her in, absorb her, from every angle.

His hands were trailing up and down her bare back when both of their phones started ringing simultaneously. Hers was a shrill and insistent version of "Duke of Earl"; his, a vibrating hum.

Devon gave her the devil's smile. "Nice ringtone."

He stretched his long arm to the bedside table and grabbed both phones. He looked at her screen and passed the phone. "Bronte for you. Max for me."

"Hi, Bron, hold on a second. He's talking to Max and I can't hear you."

"Hey, Max… no, I didn't forget… when do you want to meet up?… sure I'll be down in a half hour…are we riding or walking out?… who else is coming?… really… okay… interesting… all right, I'll see you at the stables at ten."

Then Sarah said, "Okay, I can hear you now… sure, I'd love to."

Devon had resumed his aimless wanderings down her back and her body started to go limp again.

"Mmm-hmm… yes!… yes, I'm listening… okay, I'll come to your room in a half hour and we'll coo all over him."

Sarah lifted herself up to a sitting position as she turned the phone off and put it back on the bedside table, pulling a piece of sheet up to cover her chest. "What are you doing today?"

"Why are you covering your chest?"

"I don't know. It always seems sort of vulgar by the light of day. All that flesh hanging out everywhere."

"Are you crazy?" He laughed, then saw the storm approach, and silenced himself. "Don't answer that. But, come on, give a guy a break. I haven't seen you for months and you should not be covered up." He tugged gently at the sheet. "Please." He gave her his best supplicating look, flop of hair, eyes wide.

"Stop with that!" She swatted him away half-heartedly, but she couldn't help reveling in the fact that this man loved her curvy body. "I'm going to spend the day with my soon-to-be godson, the practically-perfect-in-every-way Wolf Heyworth. I think strolls and feedings are on the agenda. What about you?"

"We'll be leaving the pack to secure sustenance, then returning to the cave with ample birds for supper."

"Who else is going?"

"Abby, of course. Anything involving horseback and firearms and she's on it. Apparently your Eliot has a good seat too."

"First of all, he is not *my* Eliot. Are we going to talk about any of these lingering misunderstandings? Do we need to have The Talk? You are the one who is supposed to be older and wiser. I've never—I mean, I've never felt this way before. I don't know at all what to say or do. Do you court me? Do I get pinned?" She smiled and hoped her added levity might cover for her near-miss on the I-love-you gaffe.

"Neither have I. I have no idea what to say or do either." His sincerity was crushing her. "Of course, I've had feelings for people, and I hope you have too if you went to the trouble of bedding them—before bedding me, I mean—but I really have no interest in anyone or anything anymore except you. It sounds so trite and—"

"No, it doesn't!" she interrupted quickly, then paused and continued. "It sounds honest. And while we're being honest, I've never gone to the trouble."

"Of what? Having feelings for all those rakes? Good. The easier to leave that life of wanton revelry behind you."

"No, I mean, I've never, ugh, it's so stupid, it doesn't even matter, really, but I feel like I need to tell you for some reason, to remedy this vision you have of me as this hoyden who comes to country weddings and house parties and sleeps with the best man and I've never done that… ever… with anyone… and it seems insincere somehow to go on acting as if—"

"So I was your first best man?" Devon joked.

She shook her head slowly from right to left, then smiled. "You might be right. I guess that is basically the gist: you were my first…"—she kissed him on his neck—"…best…"—then she kissed him on his cheek—"…man…"—then she kissed him tenderly on the lips. She pulled away for a second and repeated slowly, "You were my first. Full stop."

Devon was trying to process what she was telling him: he weighed egomaniacal humiliation (he had more or less tossed her over a bedpost and driven into her like she was a serving wench when he took her virginity) against a surge of arrogant, masculine, proprietary joy (no one had *ever* touched her except him… she was *his*, totally and completely).

"Say something," she whispered.

"I don't know whether to crawl from view in shame for making your first sexual encounter the equivalent of a debauched fling or to shout from the rafters in a diabolical baritone that you are mine, all mine!"

She turned her head, maybe to hide her face, maybe to get closer to him, then buried her head deep into the crook of his shoulder and half-laughed, half-cried, then sort of hiccupped. He slowly peeled her body away from his. "Why are you crying? You waited for exactly the right person. All the rest of us wasted our time casting about and fumbling around with the wrong people, and you just… got me… right out of the gate."

He moved her gently off of him and down onto the mattress,

situating her more fully onto her back, and then he straddled her body, the sheets between them. He laced his fingers through hers and pushed them flat into the deep pillows on either side of her. Then he kissed her with such a profound tenderness, a gentle coaxing that erased any hint of embarrassment or tentative insecurity from her mind. The kiss left her warm and content, with a feline desire to curl up and nap on and off for the rest of the day, with a big book in front of a small fire.

"Luckily there's a sheet between us; otherwise I'd never make it to the stables on time." He rolled off the bed and she murmured some quip about varying definitions of luck as her eyes slid closed and she curled back into a delicate half-sleep.

A few minutes later (after hearing the intermittent sounds of a zipper and the soft sluice of fabric being pulled over skin), it was so quiet, she thought he had left the room. Sarah was already half dozing, half planning what she was going to wear for the day when she heard the gentle sound of his feet against the carpet. Then his face nestled into her hair and nape. He took a long inhale, growled low with pleasure, then turned back toward the door and left without a word.

Sarah rolled deeper into the pillows where he had slept, taking in the remnants of his warmth and scent, then forced herself to get out of bed and begin this splendid new day.

Twenty minutes later, she was fulfilling her cat fantasy, curled up at the end of Bronte's enormous bed with Wolf stretched out between them.

"It really is *ducal*, Bron!"

"Oh, cut it out."

"Seriously. Who sleeps in a room this size? It's like Grand Central Terminal."

"Stop it! I can't help it if his marauding ancestors wanted to make a splash."

"They weren't marauders, Bron."

"No one gets this much *stuff* without at least a little marauding. But enough about the internecine family lore—what the *hell* is going on with you and Devon? Max told me you guys left after dinner 'around the same time,' which is obvious Max-speak for: they were practically shagging like minks at the dining room table. So spill it. You've been so tightly wound for so many months." Bronte paused and cocked her head to get a better look at this new and improved Sarah, then smiled broadly. "It's nice to see you a bit more *relaxed*."

"Stop! You are so impossible. How can anyone get a word in?"

"I know I am the worst... after Devon, that is... he is far more..." Bronte slowed to a stop when she noticed Sarah was all of a sudden thoughtful. "What is it?"

"I think I'm falling in love with him, Bron."

"I tried to warn you, remember? I told you at the wedding he is a heartbreaker." Bronte was playing with Wolf's legs, circling them as if he were riding a miniature bicycle. "Devon's a real cipher in a lot of ways... do you know that in the nine months since we've met, I've only been to his apartment once? And even then, it was only because I finally demanded to see where he hangs his proverbial hat. He could have been living in a cardboard box in the middle of Leicester Square for all I knew. He always comes to our place for dinner and all, the perfect guest and all that. But still."

"I know what you're saying. He has that private side, but I don't think he is really a secretive person. I think it's more a result of years of habit, evading his mother, that sort of thing."

"He couldn't be more transparent with Max, I know, but I just don't want you falling into something that's all well and good on the surface, only to be held at bay, you know, on a deeper level. Does that make sense?"

"Of course it makes sense. He's perfectly open to me at every level. I promise."

"Are you blushing? How divine!" Then in a higher pitched voice, "Wolf, look at your Aunt Sarah. She has a crush on your Uncle Devon and she's getting all *missish* about it; isn't she adorable?" The infant stared at his mother with a look that only she could interpret. "I know, right? Isn't she adorable?"

Sarah started laughing at the wonderful transformation that had taken over her formerly cold-blooded, heart-of-stone, kick-ass businesswoman of a friend. "Who are you? And where is Bronte Talbott?"

"Lost." Bronte shook her head in mock dismay. "Utterly lost. She's gone the way of the dodo, I'm afraid. Last seen haunting the halls of the attic. Now, in her place, sitting here before you, you have this doting beast of a mother, fawning concubine of a wife, prying bitch of a friend—well, that last bit has stayed pretty true to form, no?—but the rest? Completely MIA. Beware of those Heyworth men. They're seductive vampires, Sarah: they gradually suck the blood from your veins and replace it with a burning desire for more bloodlettings."

The two friends laughed again; the little babe kicked his feet.

"I'm only half-joking!" Bronte added between barks of laughter.

Sarah continued to laugh softly at her friend's unexpected happiness. "Let's get some breakfast, Bron. I'm starving."

"Well, if you're going to be tight-lipped about everything in the romance department, I suppose food will have to do." Bronte swaddled Wolf into a tight ball and slipped him into the baby sling she had taken to wearing. "I look like a friggin' Navajo for Christ's sake. Who am I?" But she smiled down at her baby, then up at her friend, and Bronte had never been more certain of who she was.

By early afternoon, the three of them—Bronte, Wolf, and Sarah—were fast asleep on Bronte and Max's enormous bed.

"The best way to get him to go down for a nap is to pretend you are falling asleep," Bronte had explained to Sarah with her newfound maternal authority. So the two friends had pretended at first and then fallen fast asleep in earnest, the little cub splayed out between them, arms tossed over his head, a look of pure bliss on his face.

Max and Devon came in quietly, Max going on as usual: "Dev, you have to come look at the baby when he's asleep; it's so great."

Devon agreed but made a mental note to tell his brother in a few weeks' time that all this baby craziness needed to be curtailed at some point.

The two men pulled up short.

Speechless.

"Lucky bastard," Max said under his breath, arms crossed, staring down at the baby snuggled between the two beautiful women. "I haven't been able to get that close to her for weeks."

Wolf was nestled between Bronte and Sarah, his head turned to his mother, lips moving gently in a milky dream, and one small fist wrapped around Sarah's index finger. The three were utterly lost in a deep, gauzy sleep.

Devon just stared at Sarah's turned body as it formed a natural bend around the baby. His gut turned. "This is sublime."

"Oh, Dev, you have no idea," Max said quietly. "You need to get yourself one. Or two."

"I think just the one should do it."

Max turned to look at Devon, serious now. "Are you sure?" he said in a lower voice. "Sarah seems so young."

"Look at her Max; she's perfect. She's beautiful, she's Catherine Deneuve in *Belle du Jour*, she's a phenomenal businesswoman, and she seems to tolerate my advances with equanimity... well, at least now that she knows I am a jealous beast."

"Just be careful, Dev," he said softly, then grabbed his younger brother in a one-armed embrace and led them back out of the room. "Come on, let's let them rest. There will be plenty of time to harass them later."

Devon spent the rest of the afternoon running a few computer programs and checking on two work projects. He peeked in on the Sarah James server and saw that someone had accessed it from Chicago at three in the morning that day. He also saw two new log-ins from locations in Geneva and Milan, and added them to the still-meaningless compilation of data points that he had been amassing over the past few months.

After he'd spent the morning hunting and riding with Eliot Cranbrook, Devon knew his paranoia where Eliot was concerned was completely unfounded. Eliot was so clearly devoted to Sarah James (the friend *and* the business) that it seemed totally impossible that he would have been involved in any corporate malfeasance where she (or anyone else, for that matter) was concerned. Eliot had been speaking to Abby about how he was currently sitting on the board of a nonprofit organization that did everything they could to bring to light the financial and artistic mayhem brought about by stolen intellectual property. Within the luxury goods industry, it was rampant: clothing, handbags, shoes, you name it—the designs were being stolen, meticulously replicated or cheaply imitated.

Devon momentarily considered telling Eliot about the *attention* he had given to Sarah James's website and online (lack of) security, but the more he thought about it, the more perverted it sounded. He knew he should shut it down once and for all, but he felt like he was about to get to the bottom of the whole mess. When he did, of course he would share everything with Sarah and help her remedy her existing security vulnerabilities. Until then, he wanted to track down the perpetrator. And he was embarrassed, he supposed, and didn't really see a good moment to confess his immature prying.

There was a light tap at his bedroom door. He shut the lid of his laptop and got up to see who it was. Sarah looked a bit mussed and disoriented. "May I come in?"

"Of course." He didn't even realize that he was standing there staring at her, instead of asking her to come in. "Come in, come in. You look gorgeous, by the way."

She gave him a careless pat on his lower back as she crossed the masculine, burgundy room to a deep, brown velveteen sofa in front of the small fireplace. "Mmmm, this is exactly where I wanted to spend the rest of the day. Curled up in front of a fire."

She kicked off her suede driving shoes, pulled her legs up under her, and Devon grabbed a blanket from the large wooden chest at the end of the bed. He went over to where she was already starting to fall back to sleep and draped the warm mohair over her body.

"Mmmm, thank you." He walked back to his desk, put his computer away, and picked up a sheaf of papers he had been reading for work.

"Move over." He pushed her legs aside to make room for himself on the couch, and the two of them spent the dwindling hours of the late afternoon in a blissful silence. She rubbed her leg against his in a half-sleep of dreams and desire; he simply reveled in the nearness of her body after such a long and dismal absence. When she sat up a couple hours later, looking mussed and sexy as hell, she asked him what he was working on.

"This new polymer." He shrugged.

She smiled and rubbed her eyes. "Polymers sound sexy. What is it made of?"

He tossed the sheaf of papers on the coffee table and pulled her onto his lap. Devon began kissing her neck and whispering words like *retrofitting*, *anchorage*, and *water absorption*.

Sarah pulled back a few inches and looked inspired. "Water absorption?"

"Yeah, why?" He tried to kiss her neck again and she shoved him back a little.

"Do you want to do something for me?"

His face split into a lazy, satisfied grin. "Day and night. Night and day."

"Cut it out. I mean it, for work—"

He was trying to reach his palms up to her chest.

"Devon!" Sarah laughed, pushing herself off his lap and grabbing a piece of paper from the work documents he'd been reading. She took his pen and asked, "May I?"

He sat back and watched her. "You weren't kidding about the whole compartmentalization thing, were you?"

She was sketching a high-heeled stiletto and looked up quickly to catch his eye. "I wasn't kidding." She went back to the sketch for a couple seconds more, then showed him what she was thinking. "It's always a problem, the load-bearing capacity of such a pencil-thin heel. Also, I have a theory that steel is not the only option—it offers no give on a woman's hips and back. It has to be really strong, but I want it super-thin… it's just so much hotter, don't you think?" She peered up at him with a questioning, hopeful look.

He stared at her and felt the now-familiar pounding in his chest. *Bam. Bam. Bam.* He felt like a stranger in his own body sometimes, the way she could turn him on with a look or a quick lift of her beautiful face in his direction. It was terrifying. Exhilarating but terrifying.

"What? Why are you looking at me like that?"

He shook his head. His expression must have looked angry or confused. "I'm not—"

"Oh." She looked disheartened, then defiant. "Just dumb old shoes. I get it." She threw the drawing back onto the coffee table and let the pen drop on top of it, then folded her arms across her chest.

He pulled her back into his arms so she was reluctantly straddling him, her arms folded between them. "I have no idea what the hell you are on about," Devon said, "but I would love to help you work on the sexiest goddamned stilettos in the history of sexy stilettos."

She looked like a chastised girl, trying to avoid his gaze, then she looked up into his eyes. "You would?"

"Yes, you fool."

"Don't call me that," she said bitterly.

Devon put his finger under her chin. "What is it, love? You know I don't think you are in the least foolish. That's my job, to play the fool. I am your devoted servant. I would love to help you in your business any way I can."

She tried to look away but he held her in place. She realized he'd done that while he was making love to her last night. He didn't want her to look away. Ever.

"I… it's dumb. I just think men, or my dad, or whoever, think the whole enterprise is silly. And—" She took a shallow breath as his thumb began to touch the edge of her mouth. "I guess I just assumed you were—" Her eyes slid shut as he kissed her on her neck, then pulled at the fold of her turtleneck and kissed farther down, near her collarbone. "Oh, Devon, it just seems so unlikely that you could care for me like you do…"

He pulled back and smiled, still keeping his fingers on her neck and near her mouth. "I know exactly how you feel. I kind of lose my breath when I think of you discovering that I am totally unworthy. A sham. But apparently, we're seeing things in each other that we can't possibly see in ourselves." He raised an eyebrow and she blushed. His hands began to roam down to her chest and along her hips. His voice sounded thicker. "I see a blindingly beautiful woman." He cupped her breasts in his hands and her breath caught. "I see a body that makes me weak with longing." Sarah's eyes closed and she pressed her hips into him.

"I see a man who cares so deeply about everyone around him, but he pretends to be careless instead." She opened her eyes and looked into his dreamy gray eyes. "I see a brilliant mind that is afraid of being found out." Sarah's hands were running through his hair, massaging his scalp. He melted into her touch, his eyes softening.

He whispered, "I see a confident woman who underestimates her own power."

Sarah's body responded to his voice like it always did: melting.

She was ravenous for him and swept her lips down onto his and squeezed his head in her hands. She pulled away after a few minutes, overcome. "I love you, Devon. I just do. I'm sorry if it's too soon to say it or—"

"Oh, Sarah, you must know I love you. I can barely say the words without sounding like the biggest ass—the lover who wants to rip you to shreds—but there it is. You make me wildly happy."

"I feel the same. Just shockingly happy."

They leaned deeper into the couch, then Sarah urged his body so he was flat on his back and she began to work on his belt buckle with shaking hands. "I've been wanting to try this…"

⁓

By seven o'clock, it was almost time to start getting ready for dinner. Devon resisted waking Sarah because he was having too much fun entertaining a string of fantasies that involved Sarah napping in just the same way in palatial hotel rooms across Europe. He wanted to check into the Danieli in Venice for a few nights (and see the curve of her hip against the Grand Canal), then Villa d'Este (her hair sparkling in the reflection of Lake Como), then maybe go to Florence for a few days at the Villa La Vedetta (all that Botticellian hair framed by the domes and River Arno), and then hunker down at the Hotel du Cap, maybe forever.

He had a momentary worry that she might be booked with work engagements, then tried to push that aside: *her shoes are all made in Italy—she must have to go there occasionally*, he argued weakly. The real worry was that he did not want to be apart from her at all, a situation that was patently untenable. He figured an ongoing itinerary of glamorous travel would postpone the need to decide whether they would live at his place or hers or get a new place altogether, in London or New York or Chicago, and how soon. Even he knew he was pressing the accelerator with far too much pressure, but he was beyond reason.

Chapter 15

THE PURPORTED REASON FOR the entire weekend finally came to pass at eleven o'clock sharp on Sunday morning. The bright spring sun streamed through the beveled, lead windows of the family chapel at Dunlear Castle, shining in piercing beams that were worthy of a Renaissance annunciation picture. The trickle of water that served to welcome little Charles Heyworth into the flock glistened and sparkled as the drops caught the light. Max and Bronte both held him as the vicar said the benediction, and Sarah thought again how much they looked like some sort of holy trinity.

She was not a religious person by nature, but the entire ritual brought on a powerful surge of bittersweet emotions: the loss of her mother, the joy of Devon's hand squeezing hers as he watched the beautiful moment with her, the unspoken implication that he wanted that for them—from her—and her answering grip. After the initial baptism, the vicar continued the ceremony and the babe was passed to his godfather, for Devon to accept the responsibility he was asked to undertake.

Sarah was hard-pressed to keep her tears at bay, seeing this incredible man (tall, formal, wicked) holding this innocent creature in his arms. He smiled into the little face, then looked up and caught Sarah staring at him. His eyes twinkled with mischief as he handed her the baby, the linen of the antique christening gown wrinkling against her fingers as Devon's strong hand touched hers under the fall of the fabric.

"Ow!" Devon grumbled under his breath.

"Enough swooning. Give her the baby," Max muttered, having just kicked his younger brother in the shin, the little act of adolescent violence hidden behind the column of the baptismal font.

How is it, Devon wondered, *that everyone thinks Max is the pillar of the family?*

Devon winked at Sarah and finally released Wolf into her caring embrace. He had to keep his gaze away from hers for fear he would further embarrass himself in front of the small gathering of family and friends, by weeping or falling to his knees or something equally ludicrous.

The reception after the ceremony was a beautiful, intimate spread in the bright, sunny morning room that led out to the terrace at the southern side of the castle. Devon's mother was there, and his aunt and uncle, several cousins, and a few other close friends of Bronte and Max's, as well as Bronte's mother, who had flown in for the ceremony.

Abigail, Narinda, and Eliot had formed a little trio of rebellion, as if to announce that all this fornication and procreation and adulation was just about enough. The three of them laughed at bawdy jokes and stayed out on the terrace, taking in the midday sun for most of the party.

Devon's older sister Claire had also arrived from her home in the farthest reaches of northern Scotland. *Alone again*, Devon thought when he saw Claire's drawn expression while she hugged Bronte across the room. Her relations with her husband now appeared to be so permanently strained that no one in the family even pretended to ask after The Missing Marquess nor cared to hear the latest embarrassing scandal involving Claire's hard-partying daughter, Lydia.

Devon introduced Sarah to his mother with little ceremony. The two women had met at the rehearsal dinner and wedding in October, and Bronte had spent hours regaling Sarah with anecdotes about the formidable doyenne (did she dare say *bitch*?). Oddly enough, the rigid woman seemed to take a shine to Sarah.

"Devon, dear, wherever did you find the lovely Miss James?"

"She came prevetted"—he smiled at Sarah then back at his mother—"from Bronte."

That rankled. Of course, the Dowager Duchess of Northrop had forced herself to accept the crass American as her daughter-in-law—what choice did she have, after all?—but she was reluctant to give her anything but the most rudimentary courtesy. This lovely, feminine, blond angel, on the other hand, was quite the thing.

"I suppose certain associations must be overlooked."

Sarah nearly spewed her champagne onto the dowager duchess's stunning Chanel suit.

Devon elaborated, "My mother and Bronte are way too much alike to ever get along."

"Devon, you are cruel. How dare you compare me to that overbearing young woman?"

"Careful, Mother, she is Sarah's best friend, and I suspect Sarah does have the occasional flare of loyal indignation. If you persist in bashing her best mate, Sarah may not send you a complimentary pair of her latest stilettos. Let's move on."

Sarah watched the two as they continued a wicked game of verbal banter that often veered toward malice, but never quite got there. Devon seemed to be the only one who could manage his mother. The perfectly manicured older woman hung on his every word, if only to toss the perfect quip in reply.

"Very well. What happens in the tawdry world of commerce these days?" his mother asked Devon with impatience.

Aaaah, Sarah mused, *Devon in his role as the layabout was about to enter stage left.*

"Necessarily tedious. I show up. They pay me. It helps to fill the day. But I was thinking of going to Italy this week. With Sarah."

That champagne was destined to fly out of her mouth one way or the other.

"Excuse me," Sarah sputtered in surprise.

"I don't know," he said, looking out to the terrace as if the idea had just occurred to him, then returning his full attention to his mother. "I was thinking of Venice, maybe the Danieli? What do you think, Mother? The Danieli or the Gritti?"

"The Gritti, darling."

"Then Como for a few days. Then maybe Florence, La Vedetta?"

"Of course."

Sarah continued to watch the verbal volley that proceeded as if she were nothing more than a passing observer, then she dove in: "I hate to bring up the rather unpleasant topic of corporate responsibility, but there is no way I could do any of that this week."

The duchess rolled her eyes. "You girls today—*women*, I suppose you will correct me—are so unromantic. Look at this handsome, strapping man inviting you on a petit grand tour for heaven's sake, and you waver? It's laughable. Your priorities are completely upside down."

Sarah smiled at the woman who reminded her almost too much of her grandmother. "You must meet my grandmother. You two are cut from the same cloth. She tolerates what she calls my 'youthful foray into cobblery,' but only as long as it does not interfere with trips to Fiesole or Bequia."

"She sounds divine! I would love to meet her. Where does she live? It *cannot* be America."

Sarah ignored the nationalistic slur. "She was born in Boston and lived there and in New York for many years, but after my grandfather died, she married a fair-to-middling French artist named Jacques Fournier—"

It was now Sylvia's turn to ensure her champagne remained in her mouth. "Your grandmother is Letitia Fournier! Oh, Devon, you have landed in the honey pot, my dear. How delicious! I used to actually clip images of her from magazines in my youth. Devon's father recoiled at the idea of paying those prices for haute couture, so I used to take the images to a local seamstress in Norfolk and she made copies for me. I still have them in storage somewhere, you must come see them some time."

"Oh, how wonderful!" Sarah said. "I'd love that."

"You know I adored your father, Devon"—the dowager duchess put her hand on her son's upper arm—"but he had no patience for fashion. Early on in our marriage, he didn't see the point, but I wore him down."

Sarah stared at the quick intimacy of the mother's touch: nothing saccharine or cloying (ever), but just enough.

"Letitia has that effect on people," Sarah said. "I'd love for the two of you to meet. She's in Paris at the moment but probably heading to Florence within a week or two." Sarah turned her pointed look to Devon. "Perhaps you could visit her when you are gallivanting around Florence on your upcoming trip."

"*Our* upcoming trip, darling." He squeezed her around the waist with the arm that had been loosely draped there for most of the past hour. "You must have factories or minions or someone who needs to be prodded in northern Italy. Maybe *your Eliot* has something that requires your expertise in Milan. We can research those new stilettos you talked about. Come on, don't be such a stick in the mud."

If she hadn't known he was speaking with such careless dismissal almost entirely for his mother's benefit, she would have been furious.

"You two are devils," Sarah said. "I'm going to talk to Max and Bronte and remind myself that there are still people around here who live in the real world."

Devon smiled and let her go reluctantly after a brief kiss on the cheek.

"Marry her quickly, Devon."

His mother's voice cut through his thoughts. Her tone was not light or mocking, but probably the most deadly serious he had ever heard.

"So you like her?"

"She's the woman for you, regardless of what I think, but yes, I like her very much. And who is that handsome man fawning all over Abigail?" She gestured with her champagne glass in a tiny motion toward the terrace.

"Oh, that's Eliot Cranbrook. He's an old family friend of Sarah's and she invited him when she thought—well, it doesn't matter why she invited him."

His mother's eyebrow arched in response. "And where is Tully?" she asked.

"If you are going to wait until Sunday morning to arrive, you are going to miss the intermittent drama. They broke up."

"Well. That *is* news. Do you think it was just a phase?"

"Mother. They were together for ten years… I hardly think that can qualify as a *phase*."

"You know perfectly well what I mean, Devon. Do you think there's hope for her yet?"

"You are so antiquated, Mother. She is not a cancer survivor; she's a lesbian."

She cringed slightly. "Must you say it just like that? That word sounds so… clinical."

"What would you prefer?" Devon chortled briefly. "Perhaps 'the company of women' or her 'special friend.' Please. You are many things, Mother, but you have never been one for mincing words. As the Americans like to say, *get real*."

"Very well. You are right, I suppose. It is one of the few topics that still confounds me. I find it utterly incomprehensible. All that sameness. Where's the variety?"

"I think she and Tully were perfectly suited and complemented one another admirably. Abby is all fiery and unreliable, and Tully is all consistent and driven. They hardly lacked for variety."

"I guess it's just something I could never get my mind around. It would just be so much *easier* if she would simply fall in love with a *man*."

"Easier for whom?"

"Well, for me, of course!" She smiled the smile that she only bestowed on Devon, the warm, conspiratorial, generous smile. Then she looked up and saw Bronte approaching and resumed her brittle, shrewish affect.

Devon looked over his shoulder to see what had brought on the cooling, and asked in a low voice, "Must you be so difficult with Bronte?"

"I am never difficult, Devon. I am merely being honest. I find her gauche and ambitious."

About halfway across the room, Bronte had stopped for a moment, holding Wolf and swinging him slightly from right to left, to speak to Willa and David Osborne, another couple of close family friends invited out for the weekend to celebrate.

Devon continued quietly, "You can hardly accuse her of being ambitious when she did everything in her power to dissuade Max from pursuing her. He's madly in love with her—you might try to soften a bit."

"I am not particularly soft, Devon. With you, I seem to have made an exception, but it is only because you dote on me unreservedly. The young duchess and I shall never be friends. She refuses to *dote*, after all."

Devon had to give his mother credit for honesty, even if she was only being honest about her profound narcissism.

"Wait until you spend more time with her and the cub. You might change your opinion."

"And that nickname is outlandish," she cut back.

By then, Bronte was nearly upon them and Devon stepped to one side to include her in the conversation with his mother.

"Good morning, Duchess. Thank you so much for coming today."

"Well—" She looked as if she was about to let loose a razor-sharp quip along the lines of *what choice did I have*, but pulled up short at Devon's censorious glare. "It was my pleasure. The ceremony was lovely."

"I thought you would want to hold the baby."

At that moment, Devon felt something about Bronte that was so tender, so vulnerable, there was no way he was going to let his willful mother destroy it.

The dowager duchess started to lift her arms—champagne glass in one hand, Hermès purse hanging on the wrist of the other—to indicate that her hands were full when Devon reached across the small distance and took both glass and bag. "I'm happy to hold those, Mother."

He had already deftly slid off the bag and taken possession of the delicate crystal champagne flute before she could protest. If she demurred now, she would look blatantly cruel. Her cruelty was never blatant.

"Very well." She smiled in a small, conciliatory way.

Bronte handed the drowsy, angelic baby over with care. His antique ivory linen christening gown trailed nearly to the floor.

Sylvia Heyworth had held all of her babies in a state of surrender in those moments after delivery: exhausted, desperate, relieved. Perhaps, if she were honest, with a twinge of resentment as well, for all the pain and worry that had gone into having them. Holding a grandchild was an entirely different proposition. Here was a creature that required no particular attention, had caused her no pain upon his arrival, did not rely frantically on her for his very existence, would not extort.

Then Wolf blinked open his glassy, dilated eyes and caught hers.

She might be wrong about the extortion.

She was trapped in that glistening, infantile stare; there was nowhere to go when your own eyes were staring back at you… but deeper.

Bronte looked at Devon and smiled her new-mother smile. "See?"

Even though the dowager duchess had paid the socially prescribed attentions to Wolf over the past six weeks—the day-after visit to the hospital; peering into his bassinet while he slept on his two visits to Northrop House for tea—she had never actually held him in her arms. Nonetheless, Bronte had come to believe that Wolf was the link that would bridge the chasm between her husband and his thorny mother. Bronte had no delusions about being one of the links in *that* daisy chain, but she could do her part to help Max and Sylvia reach some sort of armistice.

Bronte slipped away with Sarah, leaving Sylvia and Devon to tend to Wolf. Max came over to ask Devon a quick question, then looked at his mother holding his son. He fought a moment of anxiety (he wanted to grab the baby from the unaffectionate arms of his own youth), then he paused and tried to let it go. She was holding him with unaccustomed care.

"Hello, Max."

"Hello, Mother."

"He's a lovely boy."

"Thank you."

"Bittersweet Symphony" was playing in the background. *Perfect*, thought Max.

After they'd returned from their honeymoon, Max had asked Bronte if there were any changes she wanted to make at Dunlear Castle, and she couldn't think of anything that would improve on perfection. Then, after a few weekend visits with the two of them hooked into their earbuds and reading, she'd asked if anyone had ever considered wiring the main rooms for sound. She'd met with the representatives from the National Trust to make sure there were no compromises to the architectural or historical integrity of the building, and then invisible wireless speakers had been installed in the drawing room, the morning room, and their bedroom. This afternoon, there was a mellow selection of contemporary acoustic music playing low in the background. Max looked at his mother and listened to the tender lyrics.

After a few moments, he asked, "Do you want me to take the baby?"

"If you wish," said Sylvia, but Max caught the possessive hesitation.

"No. You keep him. He's got your eyes, no?"

"I think he might. But babies change, of course."

Even Max could hear that her concession was an effort to reduce her own unexpected attachment, rather than a contradiction.

"Well, I need to check on something in the kitchen. Just let Bron know when you tire of holding him." He headed out of the room and watched as Sarah made her way back to Devon's side, his mother smiling up at them. There was no point in wondering why Devon had secured his mother's affection while Max had never been able to do so, nor why their respective female counterparts had elicited mirror emotions.

The rest of the afternoon sped by in a blur of family, food, and snippets of conversation. At one point around four o'clock, Eliot approached Sarah and told her matter-of-factly that he had offered to take Narinda and Abigail back to London. He knew that Sarah had hired a car and driver earlier in the week since Bronte and Max were going to be staying at Dunlear for a few days after the christening and wouldn't be riding back into town with them.

"Seeing as there are only two seats in Devon's car," Eliot elaborated, "I'm sure he wants you, rather than Narinda, to occupy the passenger seat in the Aston Martin for the return trip to London. Let me take the car and driver with Narinda and Abigail, eh, Sarah?"

Sarah had a moment of terror—here she was trying to be honest and forthright and free and encouraging Devon to do the same, but the reality was that everyone already saw them as some sort of clinging pair. In reality, it was fine (heaven, really). In theory, it was horrifying. She wanted to run into the hired car and disappear into the mass of anonymous traffic on the M4.

Devon came up from behind her, loose arm falling around her waist.

"Perfect. I was trying to figure out how to manage the switch with equanimity, and now *your Eliot* has taken care of all the details."

Sarah thought Devon might have even just winked at Eliot. She felt like a parcel being handed off from one man to the other.

"Thanks, Eliot." Sarah widened her eyes at him. "But, Devon, how soon are you heading back into the city? I have an early meeting with the architect of the new store and I need to go over some papers tonight. Maybe I should head back with Eliot and—"

"Don't be ridiculous. I'll drive you back. No problem." Devon took a sip of champagne as if that settled it.

I'm not being ridiculous, Sarah thought, resisting the urge to stomp her foot.

"I need to go, Devon. You and I can catch up later." Her voice was a touch more strident than she had intended, and Eliot beat a hasty retreat, leaving the two newly-beds to sort out the parameters of love's first blush.

Devon put a bit of pressure on Sarah's lower back and gestured for her to follow him to a quiet corner of the room, to stand in the alcove at the left of the fireplace.

"What is going on, Sarah? Why don't you want to ride back into town with me?"

"I'm perfectly happy to ride with you, but it just rankles to have you and Eliot—and your mother, for that matter—talking about me as if I'm a piece of luggage. I can take care of my own transportation quite well."

"What are you talking about? I don't want to chauffeur you around. I want to get you back to my place and attack you."

Her stomach flipped and she blushed, looking down at the beautiful parquet floor that formed a perimeter around the room.

He put her chin into the cradle of his palm and lifted her face. "What's going on?"

"Look, Devon." She tried to escape his gaze but it was impossible. As usual. She finally met him eye to eye. "We've seen the result of too much, too soon. Let's just take it easy."

He released her chin and smiled. "Fair enough. Easy does it." He stood up a bit straighter and continued in a perfectly formal voice, "Pardon me, Miss James, would you care to join me in my carriage back to the city in one hour's time or would you prefer to accompany Mr. Cranbrook now?"

She smiled and felt free again. Even though his formality was mocking and he still got what he wanted in the end, there was at least the pretense of free will woven in there somewhere. "I would be delighted to join you, Lord Heyworth," she said with prim acquiescence. Then she smiled and asked in a timid voice, "Is that your proper mode of address? Do you have a real title?"

He reached for her hand and kissed her knuckles formally, then kissed the tips of her fingers and pulled away slowly. "I think my correct title is Slave to Sarah James."

She had an involuntary surge of desire when he said it (perhaps all surges of desire were involuntary where Devon was concerned). The rational area of her brain thought that she should be enlightened and opposed to slavery, but the base, lurid, rapidly emerging part of her was quite pleased (preening even) to be the queen who reigned over Devon Heyworth. She envisioned herself lounging somewhere, partially clad, the Mediterranean sun streaming in from somewhere, a platter of fresh, exotic fruit, and Devon there to serve her.

"You are so bad," he whispered, his mouth closer to her ear than she had realized.

Her chest tightened against the silky lining of her bra and her breath hitched. "Whatever do you mean?" she asked with fake hauteur.

He pulled away a bit, then continued in that deep, sexy, lordly tone of formality, "I mean, mademoiselle, that you are quite looking forward to my enslavement and you are quite transparent about your utter lack of regret as far as my loss of liberty is concerned. I come willingly into your dominion." He ducked his head slightly as if he were being knighted. "But please be kind."

"Do we have time to run upstairs before we go back into town?" She was nearly breathless with wanting him in that moment. She didn't want to be kind either.

"Good God. You are going to be despotic. What have I unleashed?" He grabbed her hand in his and they slid out the side door at the far end of the room near where they'd been huddled together. Devon turned a quick right out of the room, instead of left toward the large formal stone staircase in the main entry, and guided Sarah into a somewhat confined set of stairs that led from the kitchen to what Sarah supposed was the servants' wing of the castle.

They got as far as the first cramped landing. Sarah had been grabbing at the back pockets of Devon's trousers, which were at eye level as he preceded her up the narrow stairs. He whipped around and took her in his arms. She laughed quickly and then his mouth took hers in a rush of nearly painful, hard kisses. She gave as good as she got, battling his tongue with her own, the strength and power of his mouth a challenge. She pushed him solidly against the wall, pinning him as he had done to her in the upstairs hall on Friday night.

Her hand reached for him; he was already hard and ready for her touch. She undid the button closure and zipper of his pants and slipped her cool hand into his warm underwear.

"Sarah, no…"

He caught the look on her face, her eyes a million miles away. Her tongue trailed slowly and methodically back and forth across her upper lip as her thumb mimicked the same motion across his tender skin.

"Sarah, please, I can't…"

Then her eyes caught his. "I thought you were my slave," she whispered in a raspy, mildly threatening, dictatorial voice she barely recognized. "Doesn't that mean you must do what I say? My bidding, as it were?" She began to stroke him in long, languorous passes. "Oh, Devon"—she breathed the words, her authority slipping—"you're so ready. What if I just knelt right here…"

Her legs started to collapse and he shoved her away, thinking he saw a flash of movement at the bottom of the stairs. He fumbled with the button of his pants as best he could, grabbed the softly laughing Sarah firmly around the waist, and dragged her roughly behind him to get her into his bed, or behind a closed door at least, as quickly as possible.

Ten minutes later, the two of them were a limp pile of half-covered limbs tossed across the down sofa in his bedroom.

"Dear God, Sarah. What's to become of me? Would that I had never mentioned my slavery."

"I thought I was a very kind master. How many masters get on their knees? I just want you when I want you, that's all." Her head was tilted back across one of the tapestry-covered pillows on the masculine brown sofa. She spoke with her eyes closed, her mouth smiling through the words. Her ivory silk blouse was untucked from her velvet pants. Said pants were unzipped and also in an acute state of disarray. "Look what I've become." She looked down the length of her disheveled body for a second, then closed her eyes again. Happy.

Devon was not looking any better: shirt unbuttoned, pants at his knees. "Yes, we are quite the picture of impropriety." He started to pull his pants up, then looked longingly at Sarah's blouse stretched across her still rising-and-falling chest. "What time do you need to be at your meeting tomorrow?"

"Don't even think about it. We are not staying here tonight." She levered herself up onto her elbows to get a better look at him. "In that regard, I *shall* reign supreme. You will not drag me down into your world of imaginary jobs that do not require attendance or dedication." She was laughing lightly, but he knew she meant every word.

"Just because I don't attend doesn't mean I'm not dedicated. Go finish packing and we'll head home as soon as you're ready," Devon said.

Probably a mistake to call it "home," as if it went without saying that she was staying with him. He had to be a bit more mindful of helping her transition away from Sarah James, Independent Woman of the World, to Sarah James, Better Half.

She gathered her luggage together and left her bag just inside the door of the bedroom she'd stayed in over the weekend. She went downstairs to say good-bye to Max and Bronte, and gave Wolf one last hug. Devon came back into the living room as Sarah was holding the baby close and cooing into the crook of his neck. It wasn't going to be easy for him to keep to any traditional timeline of dating, courtship, dinners out—this woman had completely taken him into her thrall. The sight of her holding the baby in her arms, laughing with Bronte, oblivious to his stare, was almost more than he could process.

Max came up behind him and gave him a firm shove in the middle of his back. "Get ahold of yourself, Devon. She's just a girl."

"Right. That's rich advice coming from you. I seem to recall the occasional moment or two of frantic longing in your pursuit of Bronte."

"I have no idea what you are talking about. We met. We fell in love. And we started a family. Totally uncomplicated."

"Honestly, Max, I don't know how long I can wait. I have an almost painful sense of urgency."

"You sound like you have a prostate problem, for Christ's sake. Where is my reckless brother?"

"Very funny."

Chapter 16

"OH MY, THIS IS even worse than I'd imagined."

Devon was holding the door open to his flat. The sun was setting across the Thames in crystalline splinters, reflecting in glorious, fractured bits of light against the glass walls, stainless steel surfaces, and blond wood that cut at right angles throughout his modernist apartment.

Sarah continued into the middle of the living room and sat down on a beautiful, angular though surprisingly comfortable Italian blond wood chair. "I feel like an éclair balanced on the head of pin," she pouted.

"Exactly the effect I was going for."

Devon dropped their two bags just inside the entryway and shut the door behind him, locking the deadbolt, then turning back to see Sarah in situ.

"What? The effect of a very round woman sitting self-consciously on a very square piece of furniture? I feel like a superfluous jumble compared to all this immaculate perfection."

He walked across the (immaculate, perfect) wide plank wood floors and took both of Sarah's hands in his, lifting her from the (immaculate, perfect) chair. "You are the immaculate perfection and everything else is a superfluous jumble, Sarah."

"Go on…" she started kissing his neck.

He pulled at the back of her shirt, tugging it from the waist of her pants, and she raised her arms to let him pull it up over her head.

"Don't be fooled by appearances, love." He slid her right bra strap down one shoulder in a tantalizingly slow gesture, kissing the bare part of her collarbone where the elastic had been pressed into her skin. "I want everything to pale in comparison to you."

"That sounds good... what else?" She stretched her neck and shut her eyes.

"You are a greedy minx." He kissed her again down her exposed neck.

"What is a minx, anyway?" she wondered absently.

"I have no idea," he growled as his kisses trailed down between her breasts. "A cross between a mink and a lynx?"

The reverberation of her laughter came through to his lips as he kissed her.

She put her hands on his cheeks and lifted his face so they were eye to eye. "Sorry to distract you, but I need food."

He gave her a crooked half-smile. "Do you want to eat in or out?"

"I think in," she said as she pulled her bra strap back into place and picked her shirt up from the edge of the chair where it had fallen, half touching the floor.

Devon watched as she walked, practically topless, across the Spartan room to her luggage, extended the handle of her wheelie bag, held her shirt over one shoulder, and then turned back to face him. "So, where is my room?"

"You are hilarious. *Our* bed is that way, and *our* bathroom is in there." He pointed toward the half wall that separated the living area from the sleeping area.

Here, alone with him, all this fantastic intimacy and the implications of eternal permanence were exhilarating, but the reality of, well, *reality* was niggling quietly but persistently at the very, very back of her mind. She liked having her *own* room. Of course she wanted to sleep in the same bed, but a guestroom where she could spread out her clothes and makeup and go to the bathroom... ugh.

Maybe she was more like Letitia than she cared to admit. She had a momentary vision of herself as Scarlett O'Hara, pulling at the flounces of her nightgown and calling to Rhett from her bed that he was *now* allowed to come into her bedroom. She sighed and set her bag down in the very exposed corner of Devon's bedroom.

Sarah missed doors.

She went into the bathroom to shower and change into comfortable clothes while Devon unpacked his bag, ordered dinner, and fired up his laptop in his small office at the other side of the flat.

They ate dinner at the marble kitchen counter, spicy Indian tikka masala and a couple of bottles of Kingfisher beer. After dinner, Sarah spread her work materials out onto the dining room table and spent an hour reviewing the latest cost overruns on the London shop construction. Devon wandered back and forth between his office and his bedroom, putting a load of laundry in one time, unloading the dishwasher the next.

Sarah savored seeing these little acts of domesticity. Devon Heyworth Does Dishes—the headline flashed across her mind's eye—or Devon Does Laundry. She was smiling when he passed behind her and trailed a finger along her neck.

"Stop trying to distract me," she said, ignoring him.

"I'm not trying to distract you. I just want you to remember that I'm here," he said.

Such a little boy, she thought. "How could I forget that you're here? I've had to read the same stupid cost analysis four times because my mind starts to wander, contemplating profundities like, how can he manage to look sexy while doing laundry."

"Really? I do?" He smiled the sexiest damn smile that Sarah had ever seen—just like that, *snap*, right on cue—and looked down at his low-slung striped pajama bottoms and bare chest. "In this old thing?"

"Stop fishing for compliments and let me get to the bottom of this once and for all."

He remained standing behind her back, spying the spreadsheets. "Do you want me to take a look?"

She looked up at him with new eyes. "Would you want to?" She sighed. "I'm reaching the end of my rope."

He pulled one of the metal chairs away from the table and turned it around, the back coming up between his legs, his forearms resting on top. "What's the gist?"

"I just don't know where the money is going," she admitted. "And the scheduling, even more than the finances, is making me so crazy. Why does everything take so long here? It's like, if I want a leather sofa made in New York, I just dial an 800 number and two weeks later I have it. Here?" She barked a quick laugh. "It's like, that will be nine weeks, madam, while we hand-shear the wool from the sheep that will be used for the batting, and another seven weeks while the tannery hand-dyes the skins, and then we will have the upholstery hand-sewn in our four-hundred-year-old factory on the moors outside of East Bumcrack. And *then* we will pack it into a wooden crate of the finest construction and have it hand-carried to you on the backs of our third-generation porters."

Devon laughed at the image she was creating. "It's not that bad!"

"It's worse," Sarah laughed over her words, picking up steam. "I told the carpenter last week that I wanted a half wall near the front door—to create a sort of entryway feeling—nothing much, just about four feet high and eight feet long, and I mean, that should be like a three-hour job, and the next day, I get in and he's hand-sawing oak! I was like, what's wrong with plywood and drywall? Seriously!"

Devon laughed but took the side of the carpenter. "Well"—he shrugged—"if you want it to last…"

"Oh! Stop! I want the shop to open! If it's not ready by September, I'm going to be furious." Her voice softened. "And in a serious financial mess."

"Where are we? Let me see."

He held out his hand and she slowly started handing him the sheaf of papers—the very guts of her business, the highly detailed financial reports that revealed every aspect of her company—then had a moment's hesitation. She smiled ruefully. "I think I might be more afraid of exposing myself right now than I was the night we first met." She held the documents poised in midair, then placed them meaningfully into his waiting hand.

"Sometimes it's easier to give your body," he said in a low voice. "I'll be gentle, I promise."

And then he was gone.

His body remained sitting there beside her, but she watched as his mind flew away, clicking and cycling around the different documents. At one point, he reached for the pen and yellow legal pad Sarah had been using to take notes; he didn't even look up from the financial pages, just took the pen and paper. He was completely oblivious to her mere inches away. He took the occasional note, marking down random numbers and dates.

He looked up, his eyes revealing nothing. He was a machine. "May I write on here?" Devon used the tip of his pen to point to one of the documents.

"Sure. I have other copies. Go for it."

Then, with a sure hand, he began making quick computations in the margins of various spreadsheets.

"What are you doing?" she asked at one point when he was reworking some of her long-term projections. "Those net present values are—"

"Sarah."

"What? Why do you sound so serious?"

"It's not good."

"What do you mean 'it's not good'? Thank God you are not a doctor because your bedside manner is atrocious."

He smiled, remembering she was Sarah, then his eyes went dark again. "These numbers are not consistent. They are almost a form of pretzel logic, perfectly accurate within the self-referential world they inhabit, but they are not true."

"I don't even know what you are saying."

"Who does your accounting? Are they totally reliable? Do you trust them?"

"Of course they're reliable. I use the same firm that's been doing my father's company's books for generations."

"Is there anyone within your organization that might be, you know, skimming a bit off the top? Do you ever borrow personal funds against assets—"

"Give me those documents right now." She grabbed at him and he held them back.

"Sorry. That was unnecessary."

"How dare you accuse me of stealing from my own company. It doesn't even make sense. It's all... *mine*... why would I steal from myself?"

"You'd be surprised. It happens all the time. Shareholders want their shares and owners don't always feel they're entitled to quite so much—"

"Give me the papers. Now!"

She gathered up the reports, tapped them into a neat pile, and put them into a manila folder, then put the manila folder into the trim briefcase that held her iPad and portable keyboard.

"You might also want to have your hard drive wiped on your iPad and iPhone." He got up from the table and went to the refrigerator and took out a beer. He popped the top and threw it out in the bin under the sink, then turned to face her, leaning against the kitchen counter.

She scowled at him.

"What?" he asked innocently.

"What?! You basically just raped me... or made me watch as you raped my company, and then you just mosey off to the kitchen for a refreshment and say, *what*? That's what!"

"I don't understand what you're on about. It's just numbers. Numbers don't mean anything." He shrugged again. "I was just manipulating the numbers. I wasn't manipulating *you*. And it's obvious that someone else has beaten me to it. Those numbers are compromised. They have been *raped*, if you must stick with that hideous analogy. But I'm the one who can help you *find* the perpetrator. I'm *not* the perpetrator."

She tried to still the rising tide of anger that was coming over her. He was completely unable to see the link between those numbers and the very fiber of her being. "Those numbers mean something to me, Devon."

It was as if he had been in a trance of some kind and then, in that nanosecond, snapped out of it. Her voice had cracked with emotion over the importance of those stupid numbers: the numbers that proved she was worthy of her father's respect, the numbers that attested to her value as a member of the fashion industry, the numbers that validated her.

"Oh God, Sarah. I'm so sorry." He was across the room and sitting directly in front of her in seconds. He forced her chair a quarter turn so they were facing each other, knee to knee. "I didn't mean it like that. Of course they represent everything important and meaningful."

She wiped viciously at a stupid tear that was trailing down her left cheek.

He kissed her wet lashes. "Please forgive me. I'm a robot… a machine… I'm a brute."

She swallowed and tried to explain, as much as she could explain what she barely understood herself. "We don't need to get into any Freudian claptrap, but my company is really, *really* important to me, Devon. My father has basically ignored me for the past fourteen years, since my mother died, and this business is the one way—" She coughed or choked, she wasn't sure which.

He held her hands in his, rubbing her knuckles with his thumbs, trying to massage away her worry or sadness, whatever it was. "It's okay, love. You don't need to explain yourself to me."

"I want to," she whispered, "but I just can't—" She felt the pressure of impending tears throb against the back of her eyeballs as her throat seized and silent tears slid down her cheeks.

She felt so vulnerable. So exhausted. It wasn't as if he was telling her something she hadn't been suspecting for months—she'd hired a forensic accountant months ago—but the fact that Devon could glance over the most complex reports and come to that conclusion in a matter of minutes somehow reduced all of her hard work to something foolish. Trite.

He was so lost. Devon had no idea how to navigate a proper relationship. He'd never cared about anyone the way he cared about her, and still he was an ass. He reached his hands up to her cheeks. "Sarah." He kissed her, trying to take away her sadness, her need for anyone's approval. At the height of desperate arrogance, he wanted to shake her and say, *But you don't need any of that anymore now that you have* me! He'd offer to take a swing at her father if he could negotiate that into the bargain.

She pulled away slightly, looking into his eyes. "I'm so tired all of a sudden, Dev. I know you meant well, and we can talk about it, maybe, in the morning. But for now, can we just go to bed… to sleep?"

"Of course."

He helped her up from her seat, holding her protectively against his body. He hit the main light switch that turned out all the lights in the central part of the apartment and guided her across the loft toward his enormous, spotless white bed that appeared to float over the bare, blond wood floor. Like everything else in his world, the bed appeared cool and uninviting at first glance, but once she slipped between the sheets, Sarah thought the mattress and the linens might be the most luscious she had ever felt. Devon undressed her like he would a toddler, untying the drawstring waist of her pajama pants, then sliding them off, and then carefully unbuttoning the front placket of his white Oxford shirt that she had purloined from the back of the bathroom door and put on after her shower. The Egyptian cotton sheets were like cool velvet against her bare skin. She moaned in grateful relief.

"This bed is just like you, Dev: all the outward appearance of bare-bones utility but warm and delicious and luxurious on the inside," she said.

"That mattress took months to make, just so you know, Miss-I-Want-My-Shoddy-Half-Wall-Right-Now."

"Mmmm." She hummed her pleasure and snuggled deeper under the covers. "I bet it was despicably expensive."

"It was. And seeing you in it makes it worth every penny."

She was starting to fade. "I'm sure you've seen lots of girls in it," she taunted.

"No…" He folded his arms and she rolled onto her back and looked up at him. "I've never had anyone else in this bed."

Sarah's smile was broad and grateful. "Really?" she squeaked. "I have to confess I'm glad to hear it." Then she made a mock frown. "I won't ask about your hotel bills."

He laughed and tucked her in. "I'm going to do a little work before I turn in, sleepyhead." He kissed her on the forehead. "You good?"

"Sooooo good." Sarah shut her eyes and was slowly overtaken by the exhaustion that always followed her infrequent bouts of raw emotion. Eyes still closed and half-asleep, she whispered to no one in particular, declared really, "I love Devon Heyworth." And then a small smile stole across her face and she was asleep.

Devon took a step back from the bed, afraid for a second that he might actually stumble, then righted himself and stopped. He stood there staring at her for what might have been hours. So much had passed between them in the past few days, he didn't even feel like the same person who'd stood on the Millennium Bridge, contemplating the worth (or worthlessness) that life on earth might provide.

He finally wandered back out to the living room and looked around as if for the first time, seeing his spare existence through Sarah's eyes. She was a woman who embraced color and texture and light and variety and took it all in, bent it, transformed it, created. How barren he must seem. He shook his head and refused to let his love of spartan simplicity represent more than a design aesthetic. He was delicious on the inside, after all.

He smiled at that, then turned toward his office. He spent a couple of hours running the final numbers on the structural capacity of the Chilean bridge project. He tried to resist the temptation to check on Sarah's server activity in the United States, but was unable to suppress the urge. He ran a new battery of tests based on some of the information that he had gathered that night (*at Sarah's invitation*, he reminded himself, trying to rationalize). He decided to set up a series of equations that could run for several hours through the night and that might turn up a pattern or clue of some sort by morning, now that he had access to the actual numbers that were being manipulated. He set the program running, turned off the light in the office, and crossed the length of his flat. He brushed his teeth, stripped off his clothes, and crawled into bed alongside Sarah.

She didn't wake, but her hungry body sensed his warmth and rolled closer to his, her backside nestling into his front, and she sighed and exhaled with a sleepy breath of satisfaction.

I better not screw this up, was the last fleeting thought that skittered across his mind before he fell asleep.

The next morning, Sarah woke up to the smell of coffee.

"Here you go, lovely."

She opened her eyes and Devon was standing there naked with two mugs.

"I've died and gone to heaven," she whispered.

"So have I," he replied, handing her the mug after she'd shifted into a sitting position. "So, what do you want to do today?" Devon asked.

Sarah took a sip and stared at him. "Um. I'm going to work. That's what grown-ups do."

He narrowed his eyes. "Is that right? Do grown-ups get to fool around before they go into their grown-up offices and sit at their grown-up desks?" He put his mug down on the steel bedside table and crawled onto the bed.

"You're going to spill the coffee!" Sarah squealed.

"Then you'd better put your mug down… I've got to get busy before you run off to be all grown-up…" Devon continued to prowl over her, kissing her bare shoulder and working his way down the length of her arm. She laughed and put the mug down next to his on the side table.

"Hurry then!" she said, and kissed him hard on the lips.

An hour later, they were in Devon's car heading toward Mayfair, Sarah scrolling through her emails on her cell phone while he drove.

"Maybe being a grown-up is not so bad after all," Devon said. "Sort of like playing house. I get to make coffee and pull a bird. Make toast and drive you to work." His face pinched. "Wait. That's not right. Makes me sound like a valet."

"Oooh. I love that idea!" Sarah cried, looking up from her phone. "The world's sexiest valet. Every woman's dream come true. You have to take a very keen interest in clothes!"

He shook his head. "I'll take a very keen interest in taking *off* your clothes, but that's about the best I can offer."

Sarah sighed theatrically. "Oh well. I guess I can't have everything." She happened to say it right as they pulled up in front of the construction site of her shop, where the builders were lazing about. They scurried into action when they saw her arrive.

Devon shifted the car into park but kept his hand on the gearshift. The engine rumbled aggressively in the narrow mews.

"What am I going to do? This is never going to get done."

Devon dipped his head to get a better look at the full height of the building through the windscreen. "Sarah…"

"What?" She was collecting her computer bag and her purse and looking around her seat in the car to make sure she hadn't dropped anything.

"Look. Do you want me to help? It's sort of ridiculous that I work for an architectural firm and I'm decent at maths and you just happen to be having issues with both…"

She stopped fussing with her stuff and looked at him. "Can I think about it?"

Devon looked down at her short skirt and the sheer stocking covering her thigh. He reached out his pinkie from where he was holding the gearshift and touched her there. "I just want to help." He looked up from her thigh and into her eyes. "I promise. I won't be all controlling and weird."

She looked back out at the swarm of workmen and thought about how much still had to be done if the shop was going to open for business on September 1 in time for London Fashion Week.

"Just let me think about it, okay, Dev?"

He nodded. Devon marveled, as always, at the swinging pendulum of Sarah's maturity. Sometimes she seemed so afraid and vulnerable. Other times, like this, she was wise and cautious. "Of course," he said. "Whatever you decide. Can I give you a lift home from work?"

She shut her eyes for a few seconds, then opened them. "Home?"

He looked humbled. "I knew I shouldn't have said it like that. Will you come over to my place for another sleepover date tonight? Is that better?"

She exhaled a long breath.

"That doesn't sound good at all," he said.

"Oh stop. Of course I want to sleep at your place. I just feel all discombobulated. All of my things are at the Connaught, except for what I left at your place… and I just am not the type of girl who can live out of a suitcase in the corner. I guess we should have talked about this last night over tikka masala instead of here in the idling car when I'm all stressed about getting into work."

"No worries. I'll clear out the closet in my office at home and you can put all your stuff in there. There's a small loo off that room too—"

She smiled widely. "You would clear out a closet for me?"

He shook his head. "You have no idea what I would do for you, Sarah James."

"I'm beginning to get an idea." She leaned in and kissed him. "I don't know how late I have to work tonight. I'll just stay in touch and grab a taxi."

"Just call me. I'm happy to come and get you."

"I bet you are," she teased. "Have a good day… now go to work!"

"Okay, okay."

Sarah got out of the car and watched as the Aston Martin rumbled down the narrow street then turned onto Berkeley Square.

She spent most of the day back and forth with her forensic accountant and took his recommendation that she hire a seasoned investigator to look into any possible malfeasance. After she'd had the chance to sleep on it, Sarah was actually grateful to Devon for voicing the hard truth she'd been avoiding for the past six months: that someone either inside or very close to her company was stealing from her. She decided to set aside all of her creative obligations and deal with the ugly facts until she got to the bottom of it. Despite Devon's sweet offer to help with that part of the business, she wanted to deal with it herself. It was just too personal, and she needed to figure it out.

As for the layabout construction team, she was going to put Devon on retainer and let him have the run of the place. If he was half as good at charming the workers as he was at charming the ladies, the shop would be finished by the middle of July.

When Sarah heard her stomach growl, she looked up at the wall clock to see it was nearly eight o'clock at night. Her phone trilled.

"Sarah James, sexual adventuress. Who's calling please?" she said, seeing that it was Devon.

"Your boyfriend!" He laughed.

Her stomach flipped at the matter-of-fact way he said it... like, duh, she had a boyfriend.

"So, what are you up to?" Devon continued. "Working hard or hardly working?"

She started to gather her papers together while she spoke to him. "I was working hard, but I'm ready to wrap it up for the day. Where are you?"

"Around the corner."

"You are such a stalker!"

"No, I'm not!" He paused, then laughed. "Oh, okay. I am a little bit of one where you're concerned, but not on this particular occasion. My mom invited us to join her for supper. You up for it?"

Sarah stared at her makeshift desk. The construction crew had set her up with a pair of sawhorses and a plank to work on while she was here. She often worked out of her room at the Connaught, or at Bronte's small office in Soho, but she felt like more of the construction work got done when she was physically present at the worksite, basically breathing down their necks.

She tapped a pencil against the bare wood of the tabletop. "I don't know, Dev."

"Oh, come on. She's not that bad. Just because she and Bronte don't get along."

"It makes me feel like a traitor."

"Oh, cut that out. Be down in front in five and we'll have a great glass of wine and a hunk of steak. She'll meet us at the Guinea Grill in fifteen minutes."

She hesitated again. "Oh, fine. I'll see you there."

Devon was right. The dowager duchess was not that bad. She was smart and funny, elegant and sharp. But there were a few times that her expression turned stormy, quite like Devon's actually, when the conversation veered in a direction that was not to her liking. Basically, anytime Bronte's name came up. After one particularly cruel slight, Sarah spoke up.

Sarah didn't want to be disrespectful to her boyfriend's mother (boyfriend! yay!), but she finally had to be disagreeable. "I'm sorry, Duchess, but I must defend Bronte. She is incredibly loyal and wonderfully creative. Maybe you two got off on the wrong foot."

The duchess widened her eyes and took a sip of her wine. "She's just so... what's the expression you all use these days, Devon?"

"I don't know, Mother." Devon laughed as he cut into his enormous steak and pushed his thigh closer to Sarah's. They were sitting along the banquette facing his mother, who always preferred a straight-backed chair.

"Bronte is in my face."

Sarah laughed at the turn of phrase coming out of the older woman's pursed lips.

"Well," Sarah said. "I suppose she is that. But that's what makes her so lovable."

Devon's mother raised one eyebrow. "If you insist."

"Moving on..." Devon said as he cut another piece of meat and motioned for the waiter to refill their wine glasses.

"Oh, very well." His mother shrugged her acceptance but

looked a bit like her favorite toy had just been grabbed out of her hand.

"I know what we can talk about that we all enjoy," Sarah said.

"What?" Devon asked.

"Fashion!"

He rolled his eyes.

The duchess's eyes twinkled. "Well, two out of three of us will enjoy. What did you think of the Milan shows? The colors were vile, but all that satin—"

"I know! What were they thinking? I love the citrusy yellows but that tangerine—" Sarah made a face that looked like she'd swallowed something unexpected and revolting.

"Oh, we must go together next year. Or to Paris? How divine. I would get to meet your grandmother and immerse myself in all of those delectable shows. Does she still go?"

"Occasionally, but usually the designers have her in…"

Devon watched as his mother and—he hesitated in his mind—girlfriend (there was a first time for everything) chatted on about the details and gossip of the fashion world. He looked from Sarah's long, shimmering blond hair to his mother's coiffed updo and shook his head. The two of them together would be impossible.

"Why are you shaking your head, dear?" his mother asked.

"No reason."

"He's thinking how he regrets bringing us together," Sarah said.

"Right you are, Sarah," the duchess agreed. "Well, too late now, I'm afraid. I think you're fabulous and I will have my share."

Devon rolled his eyes again, then looked at his mother. "Impossible. She's already the busiest woman in London and you know how I hate to share… I learned it from you!"

"Naughty boy. I always taught you to share but to choose very, very carefully with whom you do." She smiled at Sarah to indicate that he had chosen wisely.

Sarah loved the idea of the two of them fighting over every minute of her spare time, but she couldn't shake the feeling that they weren't really joking. They were both far too used to getting every little thing their way. She might have been raised in the lap of luxury, as it were, but between her mother's no-nonsense morality and her father's Yankee thrift—private jet Yankee thrift, but still—Sarah had always maintained a ferocious work ethic. She smiled at the turn of the conversation and they finished off the meal with a few vague promises to get together the following week for tea or lunch.

On the drive home, Devon concentrated on the car and hummed a light tune.

"What'd you do at work today?" Sarah asked.

"Oh, nothing much."

"Did you even go in?" She couldn't keep the stridency from her tone.

"Even?"

"Sorry. I'm feeling a bit tetchy, I guess. You and your mom live in some crazy dream world where the words 'getting work done' usually refer to a weekend getting plastic surgery in Switzerland."

"I worked on a few ideas for your squishy-steel stiletto idea. Does that count?"

Her stomach flipped. Maybe this was what it was like to be in love with a crazy genius. "You did?!"

"You're unbelievable. I offer to take you to Venice or Rome for a romantic getaway, and you're more turned on by a high heel."

She looked out the window to hide the smile.

He came to a stoplight and reached for her chin. "You don't have to look away. I love it."

She kissed the palm of his hand. "I love you too. I'm sorry I'm grumpy."

"I wish you'd let me help."

"I decided it's a good idea."

Finally! thought Devon. Now he'd find a way to confess he'd been nosing around for months.

"I'd love to hire you as a general contractor or whatever you want to call it, to oversee the construction... the guy who's supposed to be doing that is such a waste. Would you be willing?"

Shit! That was not the kind of help he had in mind, but he'd do whatever she needed.

She sensed his hesitation. "It's fine if you don't want to. I totally understand. You'd rather do all the financial stuff, but I really need to do that on my own. You know what I mean?"

Double shit.

"Of course I understand. I'll get on those guys tomorrow and your place will be done with plenty of time to spare."

"I feel better already," Sarah said, and sank deeper into the soft leather upholstery of the powerful car.

The next eight weeks went by in a thrilling blur. Devon and Sarah were the toast of the season. The Chelsea Flower Show. Glyndebourne. Ascot. Henley. Polo. Wimbledon.

Bronte used all of the publicity to capitalize on promotional opportunities for Sarah's store opening in London. The tabloids were ravenous: the ducal brothers, the American best friends. Sarah's head began to swim with the constant whirl of social engagements on top of all of her work responsibilities. She still kept her room at the Connaught, even though she rarely used it. Devon had begun to hint (constantly) that it was silly for her to pay exorbitant hotel fees (as if *he* cared about economy) when his large, spacious apartment was more than big enough for both of them.

"Just move in already, Sarah."

"Already? We've barely been together two months."

He was back at it one late Thursday night in July when they'd come home from an evening at the theater.

"You know what I mean. We're staying together, aren't we?"

He came up behind her in the bathroom as she finished taking off her earrings and put them in her jewelry case. She leaned back into him.

"Of course we're staying together. Eventually. But I have so much I need to get done in the next few months and you are very…" He was kissing her neck and reaching his hands under her blouse. "…distracting…" She sounded simultaneously delighted and exasperated.

"Mm-hmm…" he hummed into her skin.

"Devon!"

"Sarah!"

He was so gorgeous, staring at her expectantly like that in the mirror. He hadn't asked her to marry him, but she suspected he was only holding on by a thread. It was what she wanted, wasn't it? Who wouldn't?

"Let me just get through the store opening and then we can figure it out. Maybe we can move into my apartment over the store when it's done."

"Wherever you want…" he said into her skin when he resumed kissing her.

They slipped into bed, and as usual, the outside world slipped away.

———

Six hours later, Sarah woke up refreshed and ready to face the day.

It was four in the morning.

She tried to appreciate the comfort of Devon's warm embrace and even thought of taking advantage of him, to enjoy it further, but her mind was already racing forward to meet the day. She'd received another update from the investigator and she wanted to look at the new numbers. Corporate sabotage? Money laundering? It was all starting to seem likely.

After a few more minutes of pretending she might be able to fall back to sleep, she got out of bed, pulled on Devon's white shirt that she'd pulled off him the night before, and padded quietly back to the dining room table. The city lights were dim but cast enough of a glow that she could see her way around the apartment. She opened her computer bag and pulled out her iPad and iPhone; both were so low on battery power, they were about to crash. She grabbed the charging cable but was unable to find the wall adapter.

She headed into Devon's small office. He had cleared out the closet as promised, but he still used the immaculate desk for his after-hours work. She flipped on the light and saw his computer. She put the cable into the side of his laptop to charge her phone that way instead. When the computer screen lit up, recognizing the new device, Sarah clicked that she did not want to sync. She was about to turn back to the living room when she noticed myriad lines of data scrolling up the computer screen. She was only giving it a brief glance, not wanting to pry, but she looked more closely when she realized it was filled with information that read like a travel log from her own diary: Chicago… Chicago… Milan… Chicago… Geneva… New York… Chicago… Chicago… and she recognized the IP addresses.

She felt him standing behind her, but she couldn't bring herself to actually turn and face him. She wasn't sure she could bear the sight of him. There was something psychotic about the whole thing. "Why, Devon?"

"I was going to tell you—"

"When? Like, one day when I got around to revealing my deepest secrets to you? Like, that I was a virgin when we met? Oh, wait, I did that! Or that I am totally insecure about my father? Oh, wait—I confessed that too. You want more? Are you always going to want more, Devon? When will you have enough of me for you to reveal *you*?" By the end, she wasn't even screaming, it was more of a lacerating snipe. The bitter sarcasm in her voice was totally unfamiliar to him. She pulled the charging cable out from the side of his computer, wanting to smash his whole laptop on the floor, or better yet against the side of his head.

She turned her back to him as she passed through the narrow door, not wanting her treacherous body to respond to his slightest touch. She put all of her things from the dining table back into her briefcase. After changing into a pair of jeans and a black T-shirt, Sarah gathered a few things out of the bathroom and the closet and shoved it all unceremoniously into her luggage. The wheelie bag had been at the back of the closet since she'd started shacking up with him in May. Thank God she had kept her room at the Connaught.

"I need some space, Devon. It's not just that craziness—" She pointed toward the office. "Although that's a big part of it. I need to be on my own a bit. Please."

Devon was still in the shadows at the far end of the flat, near the door to his office, while Sarah spoke from near the front door.

"You may have cost me a small fortune, *Lord* Heyworth." For some reason the honorific seemed despicable all of a sudden; he was so far from honorable. "I have had a forensic accountant working on the books for over a year and a retired Internet fraud investigator from the FBI checking into the *perpetrator* who has been lurking around my servers for the past few months to see if the two were related. You idiot!" She pulled on her light canvas jacket and finally turned to look at him. "You were both in fucking cyberspace circling around each other. He told me to leave a few holes in my firewall to see if we could draw you out. You are quite the clever one, aren't you? Rerouting all of your late-night spying through South American open relays. And, in the midst of all this cloak-and-dagger matrix *bullshit*, I am faced with the very real possibility that one of my closest associates is stealing my designs and selling them to the thieves in China who are replicating them with cheap materials and shoddy workmanship, and shipping them so quickly that they're on a folding table on Canal Street the same week I stock them uptown on Madison Avenue." She caught her breath. "I will have to speak to my lawyers about whether or not to press charges. Probably best if you don't call me for a while. A long while! I'm so mad I don't even know the right words to convey how *fucking* mad I am right now. Are you getting that?"

At least he knows better than to answer that, Sarah thought gratefully.

She grabbed her computer bag off the dining room table and pulled at the telescoped handle of her luggage. It tilted awkwardly and almost fell over.

"And by the way," she barked, "I despise wheelie bags!"

She slammed his front door as hard as she could, feeling instantly guilty about possibly waking the innocent neighbors, then stormed down the hallway and into the elevator.

She seethed the whole way down to the lobby and out to the sidewalk, then gave a moment of pure thanks that in the midst of the barren wasteland of a neighborhood that surrounded Devon Heyworth's barren wasteland of an apartment, one sad, lonely taxi moved slowly along the wet, dark street in her direction. She flagged him down and had never been happier to say, "The Connaught, please."

How could someone so smart be so stupid? she wondered about Devon, then realized she might as well be asking the same question about herself.

She got out of the taxi when it pulled to a stop at Carlos Place, yanking her computer bag over one shoulder and then tugging the now-much-maligned wheelie bag behind her. It nearly tipped over again onto the sidewalk and she almost burst into bawling tears right at the corner of Mount Street. Luckily, the night porter dashed from the lobby and grabbed the innocent luggage.

"Thank you, Gavin." She thought she might hug him, then realized he would probably be mortified.

He widened his eyes slightly in question.

"Just… thank you," she muttered.

She trudged up the few steps to the welcoming hotel lobby, peaceful and quiet at that early hour, and tried not to think too hard about the fact that she was starting to feel more at home in this hotel than anywhere else on earth. She reached her room and thanked Gavin profusely once again for all his help (*with a piece of luggage that a toddler could have managed*, she thought with a self-deprecating sigh).

She was too peeved and wound up to get back into bed, but, after all that, it was only a quarter past five in the morning. She drew a hot bath and tried to calm down, tried to think strategically about some of the damage… to her pride and her heart.

Of course, she was not going to press charges against Devon, unless there was a law against being a complete ass. Still, even if his intentions were honorable, his entire modus operandi was suspect and disturbing. Over the past few months of trying to tease out some meaning from what had passed between them at the wedding and then in Chicago shortly thereafter, and even during these wonderful months of traipsing around glamorous London on the arm of one of the world's most eligible bachelors, Sarah had always seen herself as the younger, naïve, inexperienced party.

Now she had to contend with the fact that Devon's urbane, polished-yet-blasé, fast-car-driving persona was merely a thin veneer over a streak of immaturity a mile wide. All of that absurd posturing—or antiposturing—was ridiculous. On the one hand, he was an accomplished adult: why couldn't he just *man up* and show the world the strong, brilliant, intelligent person he was? He had it all backward, flouting convention in order to hide, rather than celebrate, his achievements.

She stepped out of the cooling bath water and tried to stall for as much time as she could, drying her hair, primping, unpacking, then finally walking the three blocks over to her office-cum-construction site at Bruton Place.

She couldn't even bring herself to check her email, still feeling Devon's stealthy, *adolescent*, spying presence snaking through the entire weave of her business operation. She telephoned the investigator, Stephen Pell, whom she had hired to research the breaches and left him a message with no specifics, but making it clear that he needed to return her call as soon as possible.

She left a similar message for Julie Cameron, her assistant in New York, then hesitated before calling Carrie Schmidt in Chicago. She let that moment stew for a while—why had she hesitated? Was it Carrie who had been stealing the computer-aided design files and leaking them to the Chinese counterfeiters? What possible motivation could she have? She had been with Sarah for years; she was paid a generous salary. Sarah made a mental note to have Pell dig a little deeper into Carrie's activities at work.

Then she didn't know whom to call. She wanted to dump everything on somebody.

Eliot Cranbrook would be a good ear on the business side; after they'd cleared up the potential-girlfriend issues, he'd become a real friend. But there was no way she could be honest with him about the extent of her emotional turmoil. As much as she had come to adore him as a friend, she was always mindful of the Sarah James of Sarah James Shoes that she wanted to present to Eliot. All of the madness about bringing him to Dunlear in May to run interference with Devon was bad enough, but at least it had worked (up until now). The possibility of Danieli-Fauchard making an offer to purchase Sarah James Shoes at some point in the future was real, and Sarah could not risk showing Eliot the full extent of her folly.

If the folly in question was not her brother-in-law, Bronte would be the next obvious info-dumpee choice. Bronte had endured her share of relationship woes, and she would tell Sarah flat-out whether or not corporate spying (albeit—one hoped—motivated by altruism) was grounds for never trusting someone with your heart.

Said heart stumbled a bit at that thought. She started to worry that she might forgive Devon anything.

Sarah sat in the single white desk chair, resting her elbows on the worktable, and looked out the wall of renovated square windows that now gleamed from floor to ceiling out over tiny Bruton Place. The raw structure of her office was starting to shape up: polished concrete floor, exposed brick walls on the east and west, and a wall of concealed built-in storage framing the frosted glass door to the stairs behind her. Devon had whipped those lazy workmen into a crew of avid craftsmen. The store was going to be beautiful.

He's not all bad! her Devon-loving half yelled in her mind.

Devon had convinced her to splurge on the glass wall of windows in order to retain the original steel frames (which had also required complete refurbishment). The glass-pane order probably accounted for the glazier's entire year's profit, but it was worth it. Sarah looked down toward the street, as if through a kaleidoscope of crisp, one-foot-by-one-foot jeweler's loops. The effect was superb. The beams of the early morning sun came through in a beautiful, fractured array. One of the young women who worked in the adjacent gallery was walking to work, chatting animatedly on her cell phone, large brown leather purse slung over one shoulder, paper coffee cup in the other hand.

It was good here.

London made Sarah feel alive and vibrant and part of the throbbing urban beat, like she did in New York, but also safe and protected—at home—like she did in Chicago. But while Manhattan was blocks and blocks of urban grid and Chicago had an urban center that gradually segued out into tree-lined neighborhoods, London somehow managed to tuck bits of country right into the weft of the metropolis. She sighed and tried to shake off the feeling that she wanted this to be her home.

She wanted this to be her home with Devon.

Her stomach fell at the involuntary direction of her thoughts.

Damn it! She'd been so busy being furious at him—at his stupid, obsessive meddling—that she had very handily avoided considering how much she loved him.

She was not meant to fall for a defective hero. *Her* hero was supposed to be flawless. Geeky, late-night, internecine Internet sabotage was definitely *not* part of the equation.

Her heart started pacing a nervous beat. She needed a distraction.

Chapter 17

Sarah called her grandmother.

Cendrine, the nonmaid maid, picked up on the second ring. They spoke in rapid French.

"You might as well stay on the line, Cendrine, to save Letitia the trouble of having to tell you everything all over again. Go wake her up and tell her I need a shoulder to cry on or to be told to quit crying, as the case may be."

Cendrine carried the cordless phone and walked back into Letitia's bedroom. Sarah smiled as she heard the two old biddies begin another day of friendly skirmishes.

After barging in on her employer, Cendrine spoke in sharp, clipped French, without ceremony. "Pick up the phone, Letitia. Your grand-daughter needs to impose upon you for maternal succor... I know, I told her that sentimental rubbish was not your area of expertise, but she seems to think you might have some sort of advice to offer."

The other line picked up with a crackle, and Sarah grinned as she envisioned her grandmother in some pink chiffon dressing gown over some highly age-*inappropriate* negligee and perfectly manicured, arthritic, bejeweled fingers holding the antique white handle of a telephone right out of a Zsa Zsa Gabor movie. Sarah used to tell her grandmother that if Marie Antoinette had ever had occasion to use a telephone, it would have looked exactly like that: gold mouthpiece and earpiece that connected with an antiquated fabric-covered cord to a delicate gold receiver above a white rotary dial.

Letitia spoke in arch, Bostonian English: "Sarah darling. It is before ten o'clock so I can only assume you are dead."

"Very funny, Letitia. I think I may be in a bit of a muddle with The Earl."

"It cannot be so! I am looking at the two of you in *Paris Match* and *Hello!* right this very minute and you are blissfully happy. It says so right here: 'The delightful couple shares a magical moment courtside.' Although, the yellow dress at Wimbledon was completely ill-advised—"

Sarah laughed through her interruption. "Letitia! This is not a fashion call! You are relentless."

"That's why you called, isn't it?"

Sarah smiled. "You're probably right. I wanted to hear your unique take on the whole situation. I do adore him." Her face heated at all the ways she had adored him… on every damned inch of his perfect body.

"Oh, darling. That's a complication. *You* are supposed to be the adored. If you adore *him*, I fear your options are necessarily limited. Try not to be too foolish when you forgive him for all of his atrocities. You might retain a shred of power if you at least wait a few days for him to beg, but he will probably know you are only stalling until you simply must dive back into his arms."

"But, Letitia, he was so *bad*."

"Did he *hurt* you, darling?"

"No, never. He's—it was nothing like that. He violated my trust. He has been spying on me—"

"Oh, how delicious! He's jealous!" Letitia sounded like a teenager. "I take it back about that shred of power. He's all yours, darling. Was he following you? Is he skulking around dark corners?!" She sounded excited. "I remember when your grandfather used to follow me around Boston—"

"No! I mean, well, maybe, in a way, if the situation were taking place back in the day, when Grandfather and you were courting—"

"Now, Sarah! You don't need to say it as though we were living alongside Paul Revere!"

"You know what I mean. Well, I suppose the details are unimportant, but he was trying to sneak around some of my business dealings to help me figure out a potential threat to my corporate—"

"What?! I thought we were talking about matters of the heart, darling. Why are you talking about business? You know I don't care about any of those petty, bourgeois details."

"He—well—it's still *me* after all!" Sarah tried defiantly. "Whether it is business or the depth of his feelings, he lied to me. Doesn't that signify?"

"Of course it *signifies*. But was it both business *and* the depth of his feelings that he lied about, Sarah?"

Sarah's silence was answer enough.

"No one wants to live in a minefield of treachery, I agree, but it sounds like you already know that he hasn't lied to you about anything of real *importance*, has he?"

"Such as?"

"Do you know how he feels about you? Unequivocally? Does he look at other women when he is with you or does he make you feel like the most beautiful woman in the room? On earth? Is he affectionate with you in front of his family and friends or only à deux? Has he introduced you to his *mother*?"

Sarah stared blindly out the wall of windows. She supposed she always knew to be careful what she wished for when she called Letitia for advice, because she would surely get it.

"Sarah?"

"Yes, I'm still here."

"Well, it is so unlike you to allow me to finish an entire sentence without interruption that I thought perhaps the line had gone dead."

"Oh, Letitia. What am I going to do? I'm a mess."

"No, you're not, darling. You are quite the perfect

granddaughter." Sarah felt a tightening in her throat at her grandmother's rare articulation of genuine affection before Letitia continued, "Do you want me to come to London?"

Sarah couldn't hold back the grateful tear that came down her cheek in a quick drip. Her grandmother had never offered to come to her. Sarah had never asked.

"Yes?" Sarah whispered, with a mix of hesitation and longing.

"Oh, darling, why didn't you just say so?" Then turning her voice away from the phone, Letitia began circling the wagons. "Cendrine! Isn't it fabulous? We are going to London. Go tell Jacques to wipe that mopey Paris grimace off his face and to pack up a few paints and brushes. I want that suite of rooms at Claridge's that we had right before we were married… oh, I don't know, probably best to take it for a month. I can't be bothered to travel for a shorter amount of time than that… oh, remember that visit, Cendrine, it was so romantic, sneaking around London with Jacques. And Elizabeth and Nelson being all *appropriate* down the corridor, and you were there, Sarah, of course." Her voice turned back toward the mouthpiece. "You must have been about four or five and your mother had you all dressed up in shiny black Mary Janes with white tights and that red wool coat with the velvet collar and that adorable oversized red grosgrain ribbon in your silky blond hair, and I—"

"Letitia!"

"Yes?"

"Thank you." The words were quiet, and Sarah had the feeling that she had never fully meant them as much as she did at that moment.

Letitia's short "You're welcome, dear" held an ocean of love.

A week later, Letitia and her small entourage arrived at Claridge's with the pomp and circumstance usually reserved for dignitaries and despots. As she always did when traveling within mainland Europe,

Letitia was happily ensconced in the comfort of her 1958 Corniche. All of the luggage ("and other bother") was sent ahead with a bustling, bossy Cendrine in the comfortable if utilitarian Mercedes van, while she and Jacques rode in the buttery leather comfort of the Rolls Royce. The Channel Tunnel was a pleasant change from her previous trips aboard the ferries from Calais, making the trip even more seamless. Luckily, Letitia's chauffeur had joined the modern age and finally acquired a cell phone. He'd called Sarah to let her know they were nearby, so she was already waiting for them in the lobby when they pulled up.

Letitia stepped out of the car as fresh as if she had just been driven from a salon across Paris to the Île Saint-Louis, rather than across countries. Her small frame was draped in a silvery gray fox fur stole (small pointed head and beady eyes intact, resting on one shoulder) over a vintage Chanel traveling suit of bouclé wool in a pale rose and gray coarse weave. And the gloves! The pale gray kid gloves. Sarah almost sighed to see a woman in her eighties have such perfect style. There was no irony, just simple, perfect class.

"Sarah, darling!"

People along the Mayfair sidewalk slowed their paces slightly, as if witnessing a sociological artifact come to life, which, Sarah supposed, her grandmother was.

Sarah thought she might crush Letitia's tiny frame with the enthusiasm of her embrace.

"There, there, Sarah dear. All will be well."

Sarah held back the tears of gratitude that threatened and gave her grandmother a shining smile instead.

"You've never been a crier, dear. That's better."

Jacques was standing near the curb, slightly behind Letitia, stretching his back and taking deep, happy breaths of the cool, moist summer air. "Aaaah, *Londres*!"

Sarah gave him a hug and welcomed him in French. "*Merci*! Thank you for coming, Jacques… I know the disruption and—"

"Ah, *non*! I am so pleased that your grandmother can still be bothered. Thank *you*." He gave Sarah a quintessentially Gallic wink of appreciation as he let one arm fall over her shoulder. He paused, holding Sarah back a step, and the two of them watched as Letitia began gathering every porter, valet, and concierge of the hotel into her thrall: directing this one toward the back of the car to retrieve her jewelry, that one to bring high tea to her room, another to make an appointment for a hair stylist to arrive in her room at eleven each morning, until it seemed that every employee of the grand establishment was hurrying off to do her bidding. The beauty of her dominion was how she managed to bend everyone to her will while somehow making them *eager* to do so. She lived in an orbit that others found so captivating, they were more than willing to scrape and bow just to be a part of it. It was enchanting there.

When they got up to the suite of rooms and Letitia was settled in a lovely, pale yellow silk-upholstered fauteuil chair, Cendrine was pouring tea, and Jacques was in his room taking a short nap, Sarah breathed a deep sigh of appreciation that they had all came to her aid.

Letitia spoke with abrupt authority into the silence: "I want to meet the mother."

"What?" Sarah blinked.

"I want to meet the mother of the earl. I presume she lives in Mayfair and I may send a calling card to her?"

"Letitia. This is not... I mean... I'm not sure that is the best way to go about it."

"Do you love this man or not, Sarah? And don't give me any impertinence about *Internets* or counterfeit *shoes*."

Sarah looked out the window. She and Devon had gone so deep, so fast. Maybe this antiquated, convoluted form of imposed grandmotherly meddling was something to consider. If the combined forces of Letitia Fournier and the Dowager Duchess of Northrop could not set things to right, nothing could.

"Yes." Her voice was barely audible.

"Congratulations." Letitia gave her granddaughter the tiniest hint of a smile and took a sip of tea. "At least we have that established. Cendrine, please bring me my stationery."

A few minutes later, Cendrine returned with an antique wooden lap desk. It was a finely hewn wood that gleamed from many decades of use. The top was inset with hand-tooled, dark green Italian leather, beautifully worn in one place where Letitia's hand always rested while she wrote. Cendrine set it down on a delicate writing table that was placed in front of French windows overlooking Davies Street.

Letitia got up from her seat, walked across the room, and sat down to her task. She lifted the lid, removed a silver fountain pen and a few sheets of pale blue stationery with her initials scrolled in an engraved navy-blue design at the top, and looked out the window in a brief moment of contemplation. Then, the scratch of the pen nib against the thick cotton grain of the paper filled the room without interruption for many minutes.

Sarah felt like a wisp of a girl, watching her future play out in the ink and purpose of her grandmother's motions across the paper. She caught the final flourish of Letitia's hand as she drew her signature across the bottom of the second page.

"May I read it?"

"Of course not! All of my correspondence is private. Including what I write to you, so you should be grateful."

"But, Letitia, what if—"

"What if *what*, Sarah?" The older woman looked at her over one shoulder, waving the sheet of paper to ensure the ink dried before she folded it and put it in the envelope. "Cendrine, please call a porter or go down to the lobby and ask for someone to deliver this." She folded it quickly, put it into the stiff envelope, and wrote "The Dowager Duchess of Northrop" across the middle of the front, then, in a smaller script at the lower left, "By Hand," then handed it to Cendrine.

Letitia turned her attention back to Sarah. "What if what? What if you are embarrassed? What if the Dowager Duchess of Northrop thinks you a fool? Or, maybe, what if you get everything you ever wanted? What then?"

Sarah's heart lurched. Her very cool grandmother was very warm indeed.

"You think because I am this old"—she gestured absently at herself from head to toe—"that I forget passion? Just one look at you and I can see how you yearn for him… and what has it been since you've seen him, a week?"

Sarah tried to hold her grandmother's gaze but faltered and blinked at the truth of her words. "Eight nights," she answered sheepishly, since Letitia seemed to be waiting for an answer to what Sarah had originally hoped was merely a rhetorical question.

"And how many hours?" Letitia asked, almost cruelly, but as Sarah started to answer, her grandmother held up a hand. "Don't answer that! I'm only making a point. Let the cunning old ladies take care of it, Sarah. You go back to work or at least go sit there and pretend you are working, and I will let you know when I hear from the duchess."

"It's already late afternoon. I only have a few more hours of work to do. Shall I return later and we can go out for dinner tonight?"

"I'm a bit *fatiguée* from the journey, dear. Let's meet for lunch tomorrow. Pick me up at one o'clock."

"Very well." Sarah stood and crossed the room, gave her grandmother a warm hug, and left.

She walked down the hotel corridor, pale yellow walls and door after door passing through her peripheral vision. Ever since she had left Devon standing in the shadows of his apartment, she had felt as though she were in some sort of half-world of surreal moments strung together. She missed him in a way that she had never missed anyone or anything. Even her mother. She felt hollowed out.

The past week at work had been chaotic and heartbreaking. After she explained that at least one of the stealth visitors to the website was a friend (she used the term loosely), Stephen Pell was able to tease out the rest of the incursions and trace them directly back to Carrie Schmidt in the Chicago office and someone within the Danieli-Fauchard organization. Sarah knew unequivocally it was not Eliot, but she had put off calling him to give him the bad news, fearing he would blame her for the wrongdoing.

She and Eliot had spoken every couple of weeks since the house party at Wolf's christening. Sarah suspected he had developed a slight *tendre* for Abby Heyworth and hoped that he wouldn't be too disappointed to learn she had no interest in men, much less strapping, American capitalists like Eliot. The information about Carrie and an unknown accomplice at Danieli-Fauchard was not something Sarah was eager to relate.

Sarah stewed for a few more days after she'd left Devon's house. She'd reached for the phone so many times to call him and was simultaneously angry and grateful that he hadn't called her. She'd told him not to call so she couldn't very well get mad at him for not calling. Ridiculous stalemate.

By the end of that week, Stephen Pell confirmed that Devon's online presence had evaporated—so at least there was that—and Pell spent the rest of the week hard at work setting a trap that would catch Carrie Schmidt in the act of corporate espionage and also reveal the identity of her accomplice. He tucked a piece of false information about some tensile steel stiletto composites into an email and let greed take its course.

Enough days had passed. Enough evidence had accrued. She had to call Eliot. Sarah returned to her office and picked up the secure phone line she'd had installed the previous week.

The absurdity of expensive spy-level security measures to protect a bunch of shoe designs would have made Sarah laugh if she wasn't so angry and, she had to admit, hurt about it. The lost sales revenue was bad enough, but Carrie Schmidt's deception was the worst part of all.

She dialed Eliot's cell number with dread.

"Hey, Sarah!" he answered. More dread: he sounded like his normal, jovial self.

"Hi, Eliot. I know this sounds ridiculous, but is your cell phone a secure line?"

"No. And it's not ridiculous. I will call you back from another line." His voice had changed completely. Humorless.

Thirty seconds later, the phone on her desk rang and she answered, "Sarah James."

"Hey, Sarah, it's Eliot." His voice was tight and impatient. "What the hell is going on over there?"

"Excuse me?"

"I've been waiting for you to call me about what's going on with someone from your company trying to sabotage—"

"Someone from *my* company? Eliot—"

"Look, I know it's not you, of course—"

"How magnanimous of you!"

"Sarah, stop."

"No, Eliot, you stop. Yes, there has been some sort of breach and I have figured out who it is on my end. I only have twenty-four employees, and the security clearance required to create this sort of *malfeasance* was necessarily limited to very few people. Can you say the same?"

"What are you talking about?"

"Are you feigning ignorance?"

"I am not feigning anything. We've seen incursions all over our corporate accounting files and design documents that have originated—"

"Eliot, please. I know. I'm horrified. But the reality is that they are working together. I've had a retired FBI investigator named

Stephen Pell on retainer for months. He has been circling in on the guilty employee here at Sarah James. We know who it is and we've created a situation that should tempt her into exposing herself. She's working with someone at Danieli-Fauchard, Eliot. Did you really think someone could penetrate your security without help from the inside? And why didn't you tell me sooner?"

"Why didn't *you* tell *me* sooner?"

"Point taken."

"Sarah, I need to talk to my security team and take a new look at this. We've been completely fixated on the idea of an outsider, and we are going to need to move very carefully to make sure we don't drive someone back into hiding. Do you trust this Stephen Pell unequivocally?"

"No question. He's part of a forensic accounting team that has worked for my father for years. Do you have someone there with whom he could be in touch?"

"Yes. My head of security is Giovanni Fortunato. I'll put them in contact with one another."

"All right, here's Pell's phone number." She scrolled through her address book and read off the number. "I'll give him a call and let him know you are going to call him. Give me ten minutes and then he's all yours. I'm sorry, Eliot. For everything."

"I'm so sorry, Sarah. I thought I might be able to get to the bottom of it and protect you from the chaos."

"What is it about me that makes everyone think I need to be protected?!" Devon. Eliot. All of them were driving her mad.

"What are you talking about? Who else is trying to protect you? And from what?"

"Nothing. Never mind."

"All right, I'll ignore that. I should have known that business and pleasure never mix. I was trying to be a gentleman in the midst of all this corporate turmoil." Sarah could hear the smile come through his voice as he continued. "It won't happen again; I will always treat you with fierce disdain in all future business dealings."

"I look forward to it." Sarah smiled back through her reply.

"All right, then. Let me get on this. And say hi to *your Devon* for me. You two cut a wide swath, Sar. I can barely get through the papers anymore without tripping over you. Let me know when you set a date."

Click.

Well, at least she had revealed *most* of the truth. If Devon had really ceased his eavesdropping, there was no reason to let Eliot know that *her* Devon had probably been muddying the waters of corporate security at Danieli-Fauchard as well.

As the days passed, Devon become more and more strung out.

How did everything get so conflated?

As soon as Sarah had gone, he'd turned back into his small home office like a zombie. He spent the rest of the day backing up all of his personal and work projects on a separate, stand-alone hard drive, then wiped his entire computer, stripping it of any evidence or reminder of his idiocy. He stared at the supposedly erased laptop and suspected it was still possible to extract a ghost of evidence, and so, in a fit of pique, Devon took a hammer to the entire expensive device. He splintered it into a satisfying pile of jagged plastic shards, then put the parts, one at a time, down the rubbish chute of his building.

Later that afternoon, he'd showered, brushed his teeth, dragged a comb through his hair, put on a pair of jeans and an old T-shirt, then went into Russell + Partners to clear out his desk.

Narinda stared at him in astonishment. "What the hell are you doing?"

"I'm quitting."

"Why?"

"Why not?"

"Because you're good at your job and need something to fill your days so you don't turn into some idiotic fop who spends his time at Henley and Ascot staying just this side of drunk and making inappropriate passes at married women of a certain age?"

Devon swiveled his chair to look right at Narinda: glowing copper skin, smooth elegant hair, obsidian black eyes that missed nothing. "You are annoying."

"Well, there's no one else around to let you know what's what, is there? Your brother is living his very organized life against a backdrop of ducal ease—as long as you don't disrupt him unduly, he'll leave you quite alone; your mother would defend you if you set the city aflame; your sister Abby thinks you are a humorous, harmless rake. And from your slouching, broody sulk, I presume that Sarah James has had the audacity to question your perfection?" She swiveled her chair back and forth, arms crossed, her eyes set on him like a cobra being charmed from a basket in the suq. "Well?"

He started to put his things back into his desk. "You're right. I was an ass; I know it. She knows it. And now what? I suffer? For how long? What's enough? I'd much rather quit showing up for my life and spend a few months in Tuscany."

"Okay. Now you *do* sound like an ass. Quit being such a coward. I have no idea what you are suffering, specifically, but in general, I'd say very little would be *more* than enough for Sarah. Could you just *attempt* to be normal?"

"You sound just like her. Obviously, I have no grasp of this normalcy about which you all speak."

"So, you just thought you'd quit your job, close up your flat, and run away."

"Am I so transparent? It seemed like a plan of sorts."

"If you can't be normal, you can at least practice patience. You never come into work this much anyway. Just keep doing nothing for a few days or weeks. Give her a little time to come around. Go invent something and pretend you have no idea what I'm talking about when I say I read about another anonymous posting on the shareware for a new metallurgical compound." She smiled, winked, and swung her chair around to answer her phone, effectively dismissing him.

He finished putting his desk back in order (which didn't require much effort since he despised any show of people's personal lives at work; no family photos or vacation postcards, thank you very much). He put the few contents back into the neat drawers and gave Narinda a squeeze on the shoulder to let her know he was leaving while she was in the midst of arguing with the engineer on the Athens project. She gave him a brief smile along with a quick, dismissive wave.

He let the receptionist know he would be reachable on his cell phone for the next few weeks if anyone needed him.

Devon walked along the south bank of the river, enjoying the midmorning summer sunshine as much as he could through his fug of disappointment and self-flagellation. He had never been a masochist, but ever since meeting Sarah James, he seemed to be in a perpetual state of self-doubt. Before he realized where his strides were taking him, he was standing in front of the mathematics department at the London School of Economics. He tapped Perry Millhaus's office phone number into his cell phone and listened to the call go through.

"This is Millhaus."

"Hey, Perry, it's Devon. I need something to distract me for… a while"—*or forever*, he thought to himself. "What have you been working on?"

"A couple of different things. I'm still thinking about the aerated steel a bit, but I've been preoccupied with a parallel equation that I came across a couple of weeks ago. Where are you?"

"I am standing in front of your building."

"Come on in."

Devon spent the next two weeks working on equations, running experiments, and being blessedly relieved of the obsessive need to think about Sarah James. He let his phone run out of juice and never recharged it. He went home to sleep and shower, then returned each day to work in Millhaus's office and adjacent lab. Occasionally, Devon checked his phone messages remotely from Millhaus's desk phone, returning only the most pressing calls from work and Max. Whenever possible, he returned messages at odd hours so as not to have to actually speak to anyone. He ignored completely his mother's frequent messages of ever-escalating urgency. Max would let her know he was alive if nothing else.

By the beginning of the third week, he felt, if not happily, at least *thankfully* removed from everyone. He had attained mathematical oblivion, his mind popping and clicking within the comfortable— engaging but emotionless—universe of numbers.

He looked a wreck.

Near midnight on a particularly warm Friday in August, he finally called it a night. He walked home in an absentminded stupor and collapsed in bed with his T-shirt and jeans still on. (He remembered to change clothes most days.) He reread a draft of the latest paper he and Perry were working on and finally turned out the lights at three o'clock Saturday morning.

Devon was woken up four hours later by the sound of his building's internal telephone intercom buzzing incessantly. He dragged himself out of bed and picked up the phone near his front door.

"Hello?"

"Mr. Heyworth?"

"Yes?"

"There is a messenger here with a letter." His doorman sounded irritated. "He has been instructed to deliver it to you in person. I have advised him that it is well within the parameters of my responsibilities to deliver a single envelope, but it seems he is unwilling to part with the item."

"Is he immaculately turned out? Graying hair slicked back, and peevish?"

"Yes, sir. Quite."

"Very well. Send him up."

A few minutes later, a sharp double knock rapped through the heavy metal fireproof front door of his flat.

Devon opened the door about a foot and stared at his mother's butler, Marsden.

"I should have known she wouldn't take kindly to being ignored."

"It's not for me to say, I suppose," Marsden said, "but she has been a bit *abrupt* these past few weeks." He handed the stiff ivory envelope to Devon through the open door. "She asked me to wait for your reply."

"Oh, all right. Come in." Devon pulled the door wide. "Do you want something to drink or is she down in the car sharpening her talons and waiting for you?"

"You know she does not cross the river unless absolutely necessary. I took a taxi."

Devon tore open the familiar creamy stationery and read the cryptic, demanding, single sentence that comprised the entire correspondence. She wanted him to come for dinner that night.

"How *abrupt* will she be if I decline?" Devon asked with a wicked grin.

Marsden looked at the ground, then back up at Devon's unshaven face and hollow eyes with supplication. "For me, if for no one else, your acceptance would be greatly appreciated."

"That bad, eh?"

"Yes. That bad."

"I accept. Please tell her I shall arrive promptly at seven." Marsden looked askance at Devon's general appearance. Devon looked down at his disheveled self, then smiled. "Not to worry, I'll clean up nicely. And thank you, Marsden."

Marsden gave a small smile and the hint of a bow, then turned and let himself out. Devon caught the door before it flew shut, watching as the man made his way toward the elevator, his mood obviously improving with each step.

Chapter 18

THAT SATURDAY NIGHT, THE gas lamps at either side of the front door flickered in the waning light of the warm summer evening. Northrop House exuded a mellow glow: the two windows on either side of the front door were brightly lit from within. Inviting. The shiny black front door gleamed at the top of four limestone steps that had been worn from years of use, beneath a modest portico that held a small wrought-iron black balcony.

Some member of the Heyworth family had lived at Number 9 Upper Brook Street in Mayfair since the home was built in 1783. It was a classic example of Georgian architecture: organized, balanced, and deceptively modest. As grand ducal mansions went, it was unassuming. Nothing like the Palladian monstrosities of Devonshire and Burlington down on Piccadilly. "And look where all that flash had got them?" the Heyworths were wont to joke. Demolished.

Just inside the right-hand front window, Sarah sat trembling.

She was trying to hold her glass of champagne steady and finally put it down on a highly polished mahogany side table. She worried momentarily that she was going to leave a ring on the priceless wood, but she was more worried that she was going to stain the carpet if she dropped it altogether. The table was the lesser of two evils, especially when the miraculous Marsden very tactfully placed a linen coaster under the delicate crystal flute while no one was looking.

The sound of Devon's Aston Martin roared down the street, then slowed to a thrumming growl as he turned the powerful car into the adjacent mews. Sarah could hear the electronic gate swing into the narrow passage and was grateful her back was to the window facing out to the street. It was bad enough anticipating Devon's arrival in the abstract, but if she had caught an actual glimpse of him driving into the alley, she might have run from the room.

All of a sudden, but certainly not for the first time in the past few weeks, this entire plan—plot, really—seemed to promise nothing but disaster. Morbid embarrassment was the appetizer, abject misery a probable dessert.

What had Sarah been thinking to let these two conniving women orchestrate her demise?

Bronte had quite literally dropped the phone on Friday morning when Sarah told her that her grandmother and the Dowager Duchess of Northrop had been stealthily devising a plan for weeks to repair the broken pieces of her botched affair with Devon.

Bronte had scrambled to pick up the cordless phone off her bedroom floor in Fulham. "Sorry, I couldn't balance the baby and the phone and my shock all at the same time. Are you nuts?"

"I sort of am, Bron. I wanted to call you, but he's your brother-in-law and Max is so—"

"She is his *mother*! You have lost your mind. She is a witch! She will do everything in her *considerable* power to thwart your every desire. She will—"

"She likes me."

"Impossible."

"She does, Bron. I told her she had to stop bad-mouthing you in front of me and she has. Other than her feelings toward you—jealousy probably—I kind of like her prickly, bitchy ways. She's honest. She kind of reminds me of yo—"

"Don't you dare! She is a cruel, heartless husk of a woman. I adore my husband—"

"She adored her husband—"

"I adore my child—"

"She adores... some of her children..."

"I can't believe this. I'm... I'm..." Bronte dropped the phone again and swore a string of seething epithets about evil women and their copulating illegitimate progeny. "Now you've gone and made me swear in front of Wolf."

"He doesn't know the difference, Bron."

"But I do. I am trying to be a better person." She sighed, at herself as much as anyone. "Let me put him down and give you my full attention. I'm apoplectic." Sarah heard Bronte call down to the nanny, Carolyn, transfer Wolf into the other woman's arms, shut the door to her bedroom, and then return to the phone. "All right, I'm sitting down. This is more traumatic than labor. You and Devon are a couple! *Hello!* magazine says so and I believe them! You were practically fornicating in the VIP tent at the polo match last weekend when I saw you together—"

"Was that you?!"

"I tried to be quick about it, but I couldn't figure out how to get to the drinks tent without passing by. All I'm saying is, I thought you'd be posting banns by now. What is it with you two? On, off, on, off, *really* on, *really* off. It's becoming tedious."

"I know. I mean, *I know!* He was an ass. Trust me, you would agree that he was an ass. But I don't want to think of him as an ass anymore, so I don't want to go into details. Just trust me. He deserved to suffer. A little. And then I was feeling all adrift, and I didn't feel like I could call you because, let's face it, he's your brother-in-law... and then my grandmother came to London to mollify me, or so I thought, and within moments of descending upon her suite of rooms at Claridge's, she had whipped off a letter to the dowager duchess and they've been fast friends ever since... coconspirators, more like..."

"Oh, Sarah. I forget that you are twenty-five—"

"Twenty-six—"

"What*ever*! You are—oh damn it!—now I'm all exercised and my milk is starting to let down. This is outrageous!"

"Bronte, please listen. It's all going to be fine… one way or the other. The main reason I'm calling is I really, *really* hope you'll come to dinner tomorrow night at Northrop House. I know you and Sylvia can barely eat at the same table, but I would really love it if you were there. For me."

"I just got her rude, demanding little note half an hour ago. Was that an invitation to dinner? I thought perhaps I was due in traffic court or that I was being *deposed*. I'm still trying to process all of this. Let me deal with one thing at a time."

Sarah smiled to herself and was quiet for a few seconds to let Bronte mull things over. "Bron—"

"Shhh! If you are going to whip everything up into a froth, just give the rest of us a moment or two to catch up, would you?" Then, "Who else is coming to dinner?"

"Abby and Eliot."

"Are they getting married too? Am I the last to know?"

"Bron, no," she laughed. "I honestly think Letitia and Sylvia are trying to help. Eliot knows my grandmother already, and Abby is in town. It sounds ridiculous, but I just cannot bring myself to call Devon… it was just too… broken… he owes me a million apologies… not that that is what this is about—I don't care about an apology, but suffice it to say I cannot make the first move—"

"What you are doing is like a *thousand* first moves—"

"I'm pathetic."

"No! Sarah, I didn't mean it like that. I just meant all this scheming is far more exhausting than simply calling him up."

"Like you just called up Max all those months after he left Chicago?"

"I guess I deserved that."

"The main thing, Bron, is that I need to meet with him on

common ground, preferably common ground that does not have a bed—"

"Or a VIP tent?"

"Touché," Sarah said with a hint of sadness. She was starting to think that Bronte *was* right and that she was about to make a colossal fool of herself, popping up from a concealed wingback chair in his mother's drawing room like a Vegas showgirl from a cake: *Surprise, Devon!*

"I'm sorry," Bronte said, sounding genuinely contrite. "You are obviously desperate—"

"Thanks."

"No, I mean, you are willing to do whatever it takes to make things work with Devon, so I won't judge. I just… I mean… I guess Max and I went through our own trials by fire to prove marital compatibility."

Sarah laughed and then quieted again. "Thanks, Bron."

"Oh, don't thank me yet. I think Devon is going to go ballistic when he realizes that a bunch of nosy Parkers have spent the better part of a month luring him into a room with you. He is maniacally private, Sarah. Don't you think he'll be pissed?"

"I was hoping he might be happy to see me." Her voice was tiny.

"Oh, Sarah, honey. I am the Worst. Friend. Ever. Okay, I get it now. Count me in. Operation Reunion, it is!" Her voice changed from genuine, if atypical, sympathy to quintessential pragmatism: "More importantly, what are you going to wear?"

Thirty-six hours later, Sarah sat (shaking) in a stunning jade-green, vintage Christian Dior silk faille cocktail dress. The ruched fabric cut a spectacular *V* down her chest, pinched her waist to a size even her stepmother would have approved of, then flared to a flattering skirt. The hem hit her legs at exactly the right spot, making her calves look like Rita Hayworth's as they slid into a deadly pair of her own black patent-leather platform pumps. The entire outfit might as well have been one of the burlap sacks that

Lucy and Ethel wore in Paris with the cardboard ice bucket hats, for all the glamorous, female power it provided in these moments before Devon's arrival.

None.

She was terrified. She heard the echo of Devon's happy, strong voice as he joked with someone in the servants' entrance that came in from where he parked his car. She listened with heightened senses as his long strides covered the distance from the back of the house, across the white-and-black marble floor of the main foyer, toward the drawing room where they all sat.

Rationally, she knew she had nothing to be afraid of: he was the one who had broken every possible social contract.

But irrationally? She was toast.

Everyone seemed to be behaving quite normally: Max was talking to Abby (advising her), Eliot was talking to the dowager duchess (charming her), Bronte was laughing with Jacques (enchanting him), and Letitia was apparently talking to Sarah herself.

Sarah closed her eyes in a moment of cowardice when she felt the wave of Devon's presence blow into the far end of the room. He was like a gale. She was glad she had dispensed with the weight of her champagne flute because she was fairly certain she would have dropped it when he caught sight of her.

"Just try to breathe, darling. You look like Veronica Lake on her best day. Gorgeous. Now just relax." Her grandmother's left hand was holding Sarah's right. Letitia was rubbing her very old, knobby thumb across the ridge of Sarah's knuckles in a comforting gesture.

Sarah tried to do as she was told. Breathing was always advantageous. She gave it a try.

She became acutely aware of the rigid, antiquated material pulling across her chest and shoulders. The stiff, decades-old silk was starchy and brittle; she thought she could actually hear it rub against her skin, the slightest whisper of crisp, papery silk against soft, burning flesh.

Devon was greeting everyone with a strangely robotic affect: he looked askance at Eliot for a split second, then grabbed his hand with genuine affection; he kissed his mother on both cheeks and whispered something brisk that made her widen her eyes and blink once (a whisper that probably would have caused a mere mortal to expire). But the dowager duchess was nothing if not adept at navigating convoluted social situations. She introduced Devon to Jacques Fournier easily, as if they were at an embassy ball, then walked Devon over to Letitia, who remained seated as Sylvia made the formal introduction and Devon bent down to kiss the back of her hand.

"It is my pleasure to meet you, Madame Fournier. I have heard many wonderful things about you."

The dowager duchess slipped away to rejoin Eliot.

"You will have to elaborate over dinner," Letitia volleyed. "I always welcome the opportunity to hear wonderful things about me."

"Then I can only hope that Mother has seated us next to each other, as we will have no lack of mutually enjoyable topics to engage us."

"Oh, isn't he charming, Sarah?" her grandmother said, her eyes still resting on Devon.

He turned from Letitia to look at Sarah, as if to say, *Well, am I charming?*

The air hung between them. Sarah was sure her pounding, erratic heartbeat was clearly visible over the décolletage of her dress. Maybe there was some way she could will herself to simply perish from heart failure now, rather than have to endure the upcoming hours of not being able to talk to Devon about anything of any real importance, while simultaneously wanting him to tear the confining clothes off her body.

Her grandmother was still holding Sarah's right hand and gave it a solid squeeze. "Sarah?"

"Yes?" She turned slowly to Letitia as if she'd just realized they were in the same room.

Everything was moving in slow motion and the entire room tilted. She heard a snippet of Bronte's laugh, saw the Dowager Duchess of Northrop's finger trail down the stem of her champagne glass—isolated, incongruous fragments floated by, and then Sarah started to feel genuinely faint. "I think I might need a glass of water."

"Allow me," Devon interjected a bit too quickly and walked a few rapid steps toward the door to ask Marsden for a glass of water (for Miss James) and a large scotch (for himself). He hesitated in the doorway when he turned back toward the room, unsure about whether to return to Sarah's general vicinity or to avoid the pain of having to stand so near her without touching her. He opted for painless—or at least *less* pain—and headed toward Abby and Max.

Sarah had no idea what she had expected: the two of them running toward one another across a meadow, arms spread wide, a Vivaldi harpsichord sonata trilling in the background? She thought she might shatter into pieces. *It's not the end of the world*, she thought idly; she just felt like she was disintegrating.

"You are fine, dear." Letitia's low, sure voice was a welcome break from the psychotic babbling in her own head.

"Thank you for the vote of confidence, but—not to be overly dramatic—I am not certain my legs will carry me to the dining room." Sarah's voice was equally subdued.

Marsden arrived with the glass of water (and another linen coaster to put beneath it if need be).

"Drink your water. You young people are so *theatrical*. Honestly. He is just a man, Sarah." Letitia returned her gaze to Devon, standing with one hand in his pocket and one hand holding a generous pour of amber liquid on the rocks. "He is just a… particularly handsome, more or less spectacularly riveting… man," Letitia said, patting Sarah's thigh and giving her a devious smile.

"Thanks a lot. Now I feel really carefree about the whole

outcome of this ill-conceived night of torture. Why didn't I just call him? Tell me again?"

Sarah couldn't help staring at him while her grandmother responded. He looked tired around the eyes, his pants were loose, his hair was a little longer than usual. If anyone had seen her critical stare, they would have thought she was trying to scan him with her x-ray vision.

"Because you have to start over... I'm sure you had some magical first moment, sparks flew, chemistry, et cetera, et cetera, but the reality is that people your age totally misunderstand the beauty and purpose of doing things in a particular *order*. Since you have managed to awaken the tender feelings of Lord Heyworth—it is delightful that he is a lord, isn't it? How wonderful to think of you being Lady Devon Heyworth; it has such a nice ring to it—"

"Stay on topic, Letitia," Sarah interrupted. "Order of events and all that."

"Oh, yes. In any case, it is as if you started at the end, with your Devon, and now you have to end at the beginning. Just act as if this is the first time you are meeting. And be a proper girl. Not some brazen hussy."

Sarah contained the water in her mouth with effort. She paused long enough to compose herself, then swallowed with a gulp. Letitia had been speaking in a low voice to begin with, but that last coda was even lower, more of a throaty Bostonian growl.

"I will do my best, Letitia. Only you could question my very interest in men one day, then accuse me of harlotry the next. Thanks for clarifying. So I should not, say, walk over and ask him to take me home now?"

Letitia turned her head quickly back to meet Sarah's gaze, then smiled wickedly. "As tempting as that might be, no, you may not walk over and ask him to take you home. First of all, you have no home here, so you would have to go to *your* hotel or to *his* home, neither of which you would ever do, of course."

"Of course." Sarah took another sip of the cool water to conceal her sheepish grin.

"Second of all, you must stop worrying. Let him lead, in this at least. Then, later, you can do what you will in the bedroom."

Water did go into the back of her nostrils that time.

Eliot came over and stood before the two women.

"Perfect," Letitia chimed. "Help me up, Eliot, and you sit here and speak to Sarah."

"Well, that's what I came over here to do, but if it makes you feel better to *orchestrate*, then I am happy to oblige. It seems to run in the family."

Letitia left the chair and walked over to Sylvia. She joined her on the couch where the two of them—dressed in black—looked like a pair of crows on a winter branch.

Devon turned his head over his shoulder for a few seconds, taking in the new seating arrangements. Sarah looked down into her lap.

"So, I know I am supposed to be one of the players on this absurd stage again, but I have to briefly thank you in person." Eliot went on to congratulate Sarah on successfully flushing out Carrie Schmidt and her Danieli-Fauchard accomplice, a junior marketing director with whom she had been romantically involved for years. The two had amassed a considerable fortune from their careful skimming, but had become greedy with the sales of the CAD files to the Chinese.

Sarah nodded absently.

"You are not hearing a word I'm saying, are you?" he asked.

"The occasional syllable penetrates." Sarah lifted her gaze from her lap and smiled wistfully at Eliot. "I know I've said it before, but it really would have been so much simpler if I had met you first. You're so easy."

"I don't think I'll analyze the double-standard, backhanded insult that resides in the midst of that veiled compliment."

She put the palm of her hand on his cheek and gave him a friendly pat-pat.

Marsden rang a miniature, handheld gong in the hall, and the dowager duchess stood up and asked everyone to come into the dining room across the foyer. Eliot escorted Sarah to the table.

Devon winced as he watched the decent man's hand guide her lower back, then threw back the rest of his scotch.

"Take it easy, Dev," Abby said as she put her arm around his waist with a squeeze of moral support.

The hostess had been merciful: the seating plan afforded Sarah a good distance from Devon. She could ignore him for the duration of a single meal and then never see him again. He was obviously disinterested, bordering on annoyed, by her presence. His face was an unrevealing shell. He was at the opposite end of the table, next to his mother, with Sarah down at the far end next to Max.

"I will just talk and you can pretend to listen," Max said.

Sarah nodded at her place without paying attention, then caught herself and turned to Max with a look of real gratitude. He gave her a quick wink and launched into a meaningless, detailed recitation about the history of prime numbers and the search for the latest, greatest prime, frequently alluding to the Sieve of Eratosthenes and other arcana.

By the time the six-course meal finally ground to a halt, Sarah thought her face might fall off. She had never expended so much effort just to remain seated and retain the appearance of interest. She was exhausted. Luckily, Bronte was equally spent. She was only four months into motherhood and nine o'clock was bedtime. Ten o'clock was practically a wild night on the town. Max stood and gave his thanks to his mother. He walked to where Bronte was sitting next to Devon, pulled out her chair with a gallant flourish, and helped his tired wife to a standing position. She smiled her good-bye to Sarah, then leaned into Max as he led her from the room.

Everyone else started to rise from the table. Jacques and Letitia bid their farewells and said many thanks again to Sylvia. Eliot had made his way around the table and was leaning over the chair next to Abby, saying something that made her laugh out loud, then she pulled her hand over her mouth and looked up at him with an impish gleam in her eye. Eliot patted her on the back and walked over to the dowager duchess, kissing the back of her hand formally and saying a few words of thanks before making his exit. Abby and Sylvia moved back into the drawing room, chatting on the way.

The sudden silence consumed her. Sarah almost knocked her chair over when she leapt to her feet after belatedly realizing she was the only person still sitting at the table, where she had been staring blankly at the empty chair next to her.

Devon was right behind her and caught the chair before it flipped completely onto the floor, then he righted it and held it firmly for her. Whether he intended for her to sit back down or to step away from the table, Sarah wasn't sure. Abby and her mother's cheerful, light voices trailed faintly from the drawing room.

"If we accomplish nothing else in life, at least we have helped foster a new chapter of happy mother-daughter relations between Sylvia and Abby." Devon's solid voice was a tonic against her ears. She closed her eyes to feel it… feel them… the actual sound waves… touching her.

Then his voice was deeper. And close.

"I have to touch you, Sarah. I can't *not* touch you."

His finger trailed like a feather along her collarbone and she filled her lungs for the first time in hours. Her knees started to buckle and she realized she was still standing, then immediately half-sat, half-fell back onto the dining room chair that had served to imprison her for the past two and a half hours.

Devon followed and sat in the chair to her left, his right hand still gripping the arched-back frame of her chair, his breathing coming hard and choppy near her neck.

Sarah kept her eyes closed, still craving the feel of his voice, the touch of his fingers, his tongue. "My grandmother specifically told me not to be a brazen hussy," she whispered, hoarse.

"That's fine. I can be brazen for both of us." His tongue trailed up the column of her neck and she groaned in a wave of relief.

"I want to marry you, Devon."

Some things just came out like that.

He gripped her head in his firm hands and turned her to face him. "Open your eyes."

Her neck felt useless and she was grateful to have him holding her head up. Her eyelids felt momentously heavy; she opened them with a concentrated effort, then smiled when his beautiful face filled her entire field of vision.

Then he spoke, the vibration of his voice strumming through her.

"I love you in the most irrational, improbable way imaginable." He shook her head with contained force on the last word, almost roughly, to ensure the words penetrated. "Can you hear me?"

"Yes. You love me." Her smile was a dream of surrender. She kissed him lightly on his lower lip. "And I love you. So there's that."

"And I want you all the time."

"All the time. Yes." She tried to kiss him again, her eyelids dropping again, her arms resting feebly in her lap, but he held her a few inches away from his face. "Please?" she added uncertainly.

He kissed her with a passion and force that electrified every nerve in her body. Her arms flew up to his neck; she gripped the muscles at his nape then pushed her trembling fingers into the thick welcome of his hair.

"Take me home," she whispered before diving back into his mouth.

"Where is home, Sarah?" he whispered after another punch-drunk kiss.

She was trying to figure out a way to crawl into his lap, into his dinner jacket, into him. "Wherever you are, Devon." She tried to kiss him again, but he had gone rigid.

"What did you just say?"

She let her Veronica Lake hair swing over one shoulder and licked her lips, trying to remember what she had said.

Yes. That was it. She remembered. "Wherever *you* are is my home, Devon," she said, each word round and distinct, like a drunk overcompensating.

He kept staring at her, memorizing her, she thought.

"Now back to the kissing, please," she said as she leaned in again and he shook her awake.

"Let's get out of here," he said, a throaty command.

"Okay," she laughed, trailing behind him as he made quick work of lacing his fingers through hers and pulling her across the foyer and into the drawing room.

Abby and Sylvia looked up from the game of gin rummy they had just started, a glass of scotch on each of the small drink tables next to the card table.

"Sarah and I are off to the Caribbean to elope. We'll see you in a few weeks or so. Thanks for dinner."

"Very well, dear," the duchess said without a hint of irony, glancing briefly over one shoulder with a slight wave—a dismissal really—then returned her attention to her hand of cards.

Abby raised her glass of scotch in a silent toast of congratulations, lifting it once to Devon and once to Sarah. "Have fun."

They were out the back door and into Devon's car before Sarah could process what Devon had just said. By the time she regained her powers of speech, she was buckled into the front seat of the Aston Martin as it snarled out of Upper Brook Street and had turned south onto Park Lane.

"Wait!"

He downshifted and turned the car into the first available street, pulling off to the side and letting the big engine idle. "What?"

"Did you just say we are going somewhere and getting married?"

"Yes. It's what you wanted, isn't it?"

"Okay. I just needed to clarify that. Kiss me, please."

Ten minutes later, the car was still idling and Sarah had somehow managed to hitch up her dress enough to straddle across Devon's lap, wedging herself between his firm chest and the steering wheel.

"Maybe we should spend a couple of nights in my room at the Connaught, for now, you know, just to seal the deal. I'm happy to get married—thrilled—even though you never really asked me, technically speaking, and a girl is supposed to care about that sort of thing, but I don't—" She smiled and started kissing him again. Another eight minutes went by. "But I don't think I can tolerate a long plane ride to some tropical paradise right now. Can't we just send bike messengers 'round to the magistrate's office for a marriage license and spend all *our* time in bed?" She wriggled farther up against his lap in an effort to keep the steering wheel from digging into her back, and Devon was finally forced to push her off and back onto her seat.

"Put your seat belt on. I will apologize in advance since I cannot be held responsible for my use of the clutch."

The gears squealed, commiserating. And then they were in front of the Connaught in less than three minutes.

Devon practically threw the keys into poor Gavin's face. The helpful doorman was momentarily paralyzed, wondering whether to congratulate Miss James or serve as bouncer. He opted for a professional expression that conveyed nothing, not that either Sarah or Devon were even aware of his presence. The doorman shook his head as he watched the young couple scramble up the stairs and into the welcoming glow of the hotel lobby.

After a few days (and nights), Sarah was able to convince Devon that—even though a girl might not stand on ceremony when it came to bended-knee marriage proposals (or their lack)—an actual wedding with a dress and family members and a photographer, and lots of champagne and music and dancing was worth something after all. Sarah called in some favors and before long, everything was in place for a New Year's Eve wedding in the Caribbean.

Devon was true to his word and the renovation of the Sarah James boutique was finished on schedule. London Fashion Week came and went in a blur, followed by the biggest orders for her spring/summer line that she'd ever received in the short history of the company.

Both of them agreed that it made sense to live on the top floor of the Bruton Place building. Sarah asked Devon to design the space, and he created a magical world that managed to balance both the spare, clean lines that he craved, punctuated with the warmth and beauty of the French antiques Sarah loved. Her only demand had been doors. And her own dressing room.

They celebrated Christmas in London. After an enormous Christmas Eve feast at Northrop House with the entire extended family, the two of them strolled home in the snapping winter wind that blew through Grosvenor Square around midnight. After the exhilaration of walking the few short blocks to their place, the two of them sat cross-legged on the floor in front of their fireplace to exchange their gifts. Devon was in his rumpled dress shirt, having tossed his tie and velvet jacket onto the sofa, and Sarah was in her rumpled green party dress, which she'd worn for old times' sake.

Sarah presented Devon with an antique set of drafting tools that she'd found at auction. He rubbed his strong hands almost reverently along the smooth wood of the case and admired how each tool was perfectly set into its own recessed area. He leaned forward and kissed her. "Thank you, darling."

Sarah never tired of those throwaway "darlings" and "loves" at the end of his sentences.

Devon reached under the sofa and pulled out a plain white cardboard box, and Sarah felt a thrill burst through her. Devon had presented her with a gorgeous emerald ring for their engagement, but oddly enough, this simple white box felt like the first real present he'd ever given her.

"I'm so excited," she said.

He looked a bit guilty. "I don't know if it's all that great. Max told me that in his experience, jewelry is always the way to go."

Sarah smiled again and leaned in to kiss him. "I love it already. Whatever it is. If you chose it, I love it."

Devon pulled her to him again and kissed her thoroughly, his hand rough at the back of her neck. "I can't wait for you to be my lawfully wedded wife."

Flushed and distracted by the unexpected intensity of the kiss, Sarah asked, "What difference does it make?"

He traced the line of her jaw with his thumb. "I don't know, but it makes me feel like you're really going to be mine… I'm a bit possessive, in case you hadn't noticed…"

"Mmmm." Sarah let her eyes drift shut while he continued to touch her. "I like the sound of that. Being yours."

She opened her eyes again and looked into his eyes, and then, with childlike longing, at the white box. "So? May I open it?"

"Yes. Sorry. Here you go."

There was no ribbon or wrapping paper, so Sarah pulled off the top slowly, trying to draw out the suspense. She saw the black-and-white pattern of the silk before she saw the entire shirt and quickly put the top back on the box, as if Pandora herself were about to escape.

"Devon?" she whispered.

"Was it a bad idea?" He ran both hands through his hair. "Damn it. It was a bad idea." He shook his head, hating himself. "I should have listened to Max—"

"Stop. Just let me look at it." Sarah opened the box all the way and set aside the top. She pulled back the white tissue paper that was folded inside and stared at her mother's vintage Yves Saint Laurent blouse. It had been sewn back together as she'd once imagined. Sort of.

Instead of her angry vision of rough, coarse black yarn making a monstrous scar against the delicate chiffon, someone had taken meticulous care to join the torn pieces together in an old-fashioned German seam. Black thread had been perfectly rendered and painstakingly sewn to make the pattern of the tear as beautiful as the blouse itself, like a tiny vein of experience running through it.

"Who did this?" Sarah looked up, her eyes shining with love and gratitude.

Devon looked ashamed. "I did it."

"You what?!" She started laughing and crying and crawled into his lap. "You sewed this with your own hand?"

He was kissing her neck and telling her how much he loved her. "Yes."

"When? How? I want to hire you!"

He smiled at her and kissed her tears. "You like it, then? It's not too weird?"

"I love it, Devon. It's so perfect. It's so you. So weird and beautiful and precise and secretive and *loving*—just the best present I've ever received in my whole entire life." She kissed him hard. "*You* are the best present."

A week later, the tropical trade winds that blew year-round between Bequia and St. Barts puffed a soft breeze through Sarah's legs, pressing the fluid silk charmeuse of her mother's wedding dress lightly against her thigh, her grandmother's veil catching on the gentle current. Her toes wriggled in the powder soft sand, all her senses alight. She turned to Devon and he tried to take her in, in that moment of sheer, unadulterated bliss, her eyes sparkling more than the diamond necklace he had just placed around her neck a few moments before, his grip on her waist firm and possessive.

The vicar was about to begin the ceremony when she whispered in her lover's ear, "I never would have imagined that I—of all people—would get married without shoes!"

About the Author

Megan Mulry writes sexy, stylish, romantic fiction. She graduated from Northwestern University and then worked in publishing, including positions at *The New Yorker* and *Boston Magazine*. After moving to London, Mulry worked in finance and attended London Business School. She has traveled extensively in Asia, India, Europe, and Africa and now lives with her husband and children in Florida. You can visit her website at www.meganmulry.com or find her procrastinating on Twitter.

A Royal Pain

Megan Mulry

A Life of royalty seems so attractive…until you're invited to live it…

Smart, ambitious, and career driven, Bronte Talbot started following British royalty in the gossip mags only to annoy her intellectual father. But her fascination has turned into a not-so-secret guilty pleasure. When she starts dating a charming British doctoral student, she teases him unmercifully about the latest scandals of his royal countrymen, only to find out—to her horror—that she's been having a fling with the nineteenth Duke of Northrop, and now he wants to make her…a duchess?

In spite of her frivolous passion for all things royal, Bronte isn't at all sure she wants the reality. Is becoming royalty every American woman's secret dream, or is it a nightmare of disapproving dowagers, paparazzi, stiff-upper-lip tea parties, and over-the-top hats?

Praise for *A Royal Pain*:

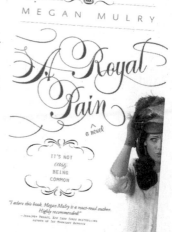

"Laugh-out-loud funny with super sexy overtones." —*Catherine Bybee,* New York Times *bestselling author of* Wife by Wednesday

"Take one sparky, sailor-mouthed American girl and one handsome English aristocrat. Put them together and watch the sparks fly. Sizzling fun!" —*Jill Mansell,* New York Times *bestselling author of* Nadia Knows Best

For more Megan Mulry books, visit:

www.sourcebooks.com

Thinking of You

by Jill Mansell

When Ginny Holland's daughter heads off to university, Ginny is left with a severe case of empty nest syndrome. To make matters worse, the first gorgeous man she's laid eyes on in years has just accused Ginny of shoplifting. So, in need of a bit of company, Ginny decides to advertise for a lodger, but what she gets is lovelorn Laurel. Yet with Laurel comes her dangerously charming brother, Perry, and the offer of a great new job, and things begin looking up…until Ginny realizes that her potential boss is all too familiar. Is it too late for Ginny to set things right after an anything but desirable first impression?

Praise for *An Offer You Can't Refuse*:

"Realistic, flawed, and endearing, [the characters] make Ms. Mansell's book shine."—*Romance Reader at Heart*

"A finely tuned romantic comedy."—*Kirkus*

For more Jill Mansell, visit:

www.sourcebooks.com